Rise

Southern Werewolves Series
Book Three

Heather MacKinnon

Rise

TABLE OF CONTENTS

Chapter 1

"We've gotta stop meeting like this."

Abraham pulled me into his office and slammed the door closed before pushing me up against it. "I just can't help myself. You're right there and I need you so bad."

My stomach tangled into a mess of knots at his words.

I needed him too. And not just my body. It was so much deeper than that. I needed Abraham on a molecular level.

He slid one denim-clad leg between my thighs and pressed. I moaned into his mouth and clutched his shoulders tighter.

This was becoming our afternoon ritual since I'd moved in about a month ago. Even though we spent every night together trying to satisfy our hunger for each other, by the time the afternoon rolled around, it didn't matter how many times I'd had him the night before. It didn't matter that I'd been sure he'd wrung every orgasm he could out of me. I needed him again.

I wrenched my mouth away from his as I struggled to pull in a deep enough breath. "I know what you mean. I've been thinking about you all day."

Abraham pressed his thigh harder between my legs and my head fell back. "You've been thinkin' about me, baby?" he asked as his lips traced patterns on my neck and chest.

"Uh huh."

He sucked on a patch of my skin and I shivered in his arms. "Were you thinking about this right here?" He plucked at my hardened nipple through my shirt.

"Uh huh," I said again. That was the best I could come up with at that moment.

His rough fingers skimmed beneath my top and circled my waist. He dragged his hands up my belly, taking my shirt with him. When he reached my heaving chest, he paused to cup both breasts in his large hands. He squeezed, massaging one and then the other. Abraham pulled my shirt over my head and slid his hands to the front of my bra. With a loud rip, the two halves split down the middle and I was exposed before him.

I gasped. "Abraham, that was a good bra." I was trying to reprimand him, but my voice shook too much for it to hold any real weight.

He buried his face between my chest, licking and sucking while his fingers pinched my nipples. "I'll buy you one for every day of the week if it means I get to rip it off you and watch your sexy tits spill out like that." His voice rumbled against my skin.

I gasped again and arched my back, pushing my chest against his face. His hands began to wander again, and soon they were unbuttoning my jeans and sliding them down my legs. My panties went next, and then I was completely naked. The only thing I had on was the necklace that held the ring he gave me.

"You're wearing way too many clothes," I breathed, my hands busy mapping out all the peaks and valleys of his body that I'd memorized a long time ago.

With a groan, Abraham pulled away from me and took a step back. There was a playful glint in his eyes and my belly flipped.

He reached for the hem of his dirty t-shirt and slowly slid it up his torso before pulling it over his head. Even though we'd been together for months, I still never got sick of seeing his body. It was powerful and thick. The kind of physique you get from hard labor, not hours at the gym.

He chucked his shirt at me and I caught it with a laugh. Next, he popped the button on his jeans and slid the zipper down slowly. I clenched my hands at my sides and swallowed. He was so damn sexy.

"Is that better?" he asked, dark blue eyes pinning me to the door.

I shook my head. "No. You're still wearing too much."

He slid his fingers beneath the waistband of his jeans and boxers and slid them down his long legs. I watched as every inch of golden skin was revealed. Soon, he was standing naked before me, so strong and handsome; he took my breath away.

He stalked forward and wrapped his arms around my waist, pulling me against his warm body. "Now, tell me again what you were thinkin' about all day."

My fingers crept up his muscled arms and circled his shoulders. "I was thinking about how sexy you are."

He dipped his head and rubbed his stubbled jaw on my neck. "Am I?" His fingers traced lines up my legs and I was shaking with anticipation.

"Yes," I hissed as one thick digit pressed inside me.

"What else were you thinkin' about?"

I dug my nails into his shoulders as he slowly pumped his big finger in and out. "Um, I was thinking about this. About you touching me."

"Hmm," he hummed against my chest. "You like when I touch you?"

He added a second finger and I gasped, my legs shaking beneath me. "I love it. I love when you touch me."

He hummed again as his fingers continued to drive me crazy. I knew I wouldn't last much longer, but I also knew Abraham wouldn't let me come like this. He liked to be deep inside me when I did. Said it made him feel more connected. He got no complaints from me.

"How about when I fuck you?" he whispered against my skin. "You like that, too?"

"Love it," I squeaked.

"Because I'm about to fuck you right now and I wanna make sure you're ready for me."

He pumped his fingers faster and my belly twisted in anticipation. I was so close. "I'm ready," I said, my voice cracking. "I'm ready now."

He pulled his fingers out, and I immediately regretted the loss. But he surged forward and hoisted me into his arms. I wrapped my legs around his waist while he lined us up. He slowly inched inside. "I love the sight of your tight little body stretched around me. Love to watch you take it all. You're so fuckin' sexy."

The feeling of him filling me along with his dirty words were driving me higher, and I knew it wouldn't be long.

He bottomed out inside me and waited a moment while we both adjusted. Without warning, he gripped my hips and slid all the way out before slamming back in, and that was enough. I clenched around him, moaning and twitching as my orgasm engulfed my senses. It felt more powerful than the last, but that was how it was. Every single time with Abraham was better than the one before.

He was still steadily thrusting into me as I came back down. He pressed his lips to my face over and over again until I tipped my head and kissed him back. Rough hands slid up and down my quivering thighs as Abraham picked up the pace.

He cupped my bottom in his hands and pulled us away from the door. His lips were still on mine as he spun us around and walked over to the leather couch pushed against one wall. Abraham lowered me to the cool cushions, his body still connected to mine.

He sat back on his heels and grabbed my hips before pumping into me faster and harder than before. "You feel so fuckin' good, baby. So wet just for me."

I nodded and raised my arms above my head to hold on to the arm of the couch. I loved it when he talked like that during sex. It never failed to boil my blood and take me higher than I thought possible.

Abraham slid an arm behind my back and pulled until I was arched with my shoulders on the couch and my butt in his lap. "Yeah. Just like that, baby," he grunted as he thrust faster than before.

"Oh my God, Abe."

"That's it, El. I wanna feel you come again."

I shook my head, but I could already feel the pressure building low in my belly. Whether I thought I could survive it or not, he was going to make me come again. It was just a matter of time.

"I want to feel you squeeze me. You're so tight when you're coming. So beautiful. I could make you come all day just to watch you squirm on my lap."

9

"Abe," I said, my voice cracking.

"I know you're close, baby. Just let go. Feel me."

He picked up one of my legs and slung it over his shoulder, reaching new depths in this position. My eyes rolled back as I gripped the leather beneath me.

"You gonna come on me again, baby?" he asked, his voice so deep I felt it rumbling through me.

I nodded frantically, unable to form sentences anymore.

"Let's come together this time," he said, his hips grinding into mine.

I nodded again, and he reached between my thighs to circle my clit. His other hand was gripping my hip so hard I was sure he'd leave bruises, but I wouldn't change anything. I loved how out of control he became. Loved the way I helped to unravel a man like Abraham. It was such a powerful feeling.

He continued to pound into me, somehow even faster and harder than before. But it wasn't until he pinched my clit between his rough fingers that I started to lose control.

"Oh my God, Abe," I moaned.

"That's it, baby. Squeeze me. I wanna feel you."

I had no choice. My body convulsed around him as another orgasm sped through me, this one even more devastating than the last. I barely heard Abraham's long guttural groan as he spilled himself inside me.

We lay like that for a long time as we both fought to catch our breath and return to Earth. Abraham crawled up my body and squeezed himself between me and the back of the couch. He wrapped his arms around my waist and pulled me even closer. His lips pressed softly all over my face and I was so sated I couldn't even kiss him back.

"I love you so much, El."

My stomach flipped. Even after all these weeks, it never failed to thrill me when he said those words. It had taken me a while to feel comfortable saying them back, but now I said them as often as he'd listen.

10

"I love you too."

He let out a deep sigh, and I snuggled closer to him. I knew he was still a little insecure about our relationship and the blame for that lay squarely on my shoulders.

He'd beaten me to the finish line with everything. He was the first to show interest, the first to say I love you, the first to talk about marriage. I'd been the reluctant one, dragging my heels when I should have been sprinting toward him.

I blamed it on my upbringing. Growing up with my parents and their loveless marriage, I didn't even know what a good relationship looked like. Convenience and climbing the social ladder was what was expected in their world. I'd grown up believing I'd never be in a serious relationship. That I'd never get married.

Now, everything was different.

There was still a lot about my future that was unknown, but the one constant was Abraham. I knew, whatever happened, he'd always be right by my side. He'd proven over and over that I could count on him and I'd learned it was okay to lean on someone else. That I didn't have to do everything on my own. That I had support.

Even a family.

Since I moved out to Asheville, I'd only grown closer to his sisters and the rest of our pack. However, my relationship with Beatrice had been the most surprising.

She was still teaching me how to fight as a wolf, but the lessons had changed drastically. She wasn't as short with me anymore. She didn't hate having to take the time for my lessons, and she acted like she actually liked being around me. I'd call that a win any day.

But even with the serial killer eliminated and the woman who threatened my relationship gone, I still had a lot to worry about.

"I was talking to Nana the other day," Abraham said.

I turned to look at him. "How's she been? I've missed her."

I hadn't seen Abraham's grandmother since the first time I met her when we'd had a family dinner here. The McCoys liked to get together once a month and have dinner, but after what happened with their cousin Calvin, no one had felt like celebrating last month and it was cancelled.

"She's good. She said she's cooking extra food for the next family dinner since she's sure we haven't been eating well without her around."

I laughed. Nana was quite the character. She was spunky and funny, but also so protective of her family. I was hoping I'd be included in that group soon enough.

"And she's been wondering about when we're gonna set a date for the ceremony."

Ah, and there it was.

The topic we'd been dancing around for a month. The newest way I was making Abraham insecure about his place beside me.

"She is, huh?" I reached up to the ring around my neck and slid it back and forth along its chain.

Abraham shifted on the couch until he was hovering over me, his face so close I could see all the different shades of blue in his beautiful eyes. "She's worried something's wrong since we haven't set a date yet."

I swallowed but held his gaze. "Are you worried about that too?"

He watched me silently for a moment before looking away. My stomach fell as I watched his jaw tense and the lines around his eyes deepen.

It didn't matter what he said next because I knew the truth. By not wanting to set a date for our mating ceremony, I was hurting him. It was completely unintentional though. I'd never purposely hurt Abraham or give him reason to doubt what we had.

I just didn't feel ready.

Realistically, we'd only known each other a few months. I used to have leftovers in my fridge older than that. It felt like we were racing ahead, and I was worried we were going too fast. That it was too soon. And we'd still never found an explanation as to how I could be Abraham's mate in the first place. We'd talked to a lot of other wolves, and no one we'd met had ever heard of a bitten wolf being the fated mate of a born wolf.

That didn't sit well with me.

I didn't bring it up to Abraham anymore though. I knew it upset him when I questioned whether we were mates or not. He always reminded me of our connection, how deeply I felt him in every inch of my body. I couldn't deny that I did, but that didn't make our situation any more believable. Didn't solve the question of how we came to be in the first place.

I could never regret saying yes to Abraham, but that didn't mean we needed to get married right away.

I cupped his jaw and turned his face until he was looking at me again. "You know I want to marry you, right?"

His eyes searched mine silently before he nodded once.

"I just don't see why we have to rush. I love you and you love me, and we're learning to live together and figure out how to do this relationship thing full time. Isn't that enough for now?"

His eyes moved between mine, seemingly searching for something. "Do you regret it?"

Abraham's voice was so soft, if I wasn't a werewolf with such sensitive hearing, I would have missed it. My heart broke in my chest as I watched the insecurities swirl in the depths of his eyes.

I reached up to hold his face between both my hands and made sure he was looking at me. "Never. Not even for one second."

He blew out a deep breath and let his head fall between my hands. I kissed his dark hair and waited for him to look at me again. When he finally did, there were fewer lines around his eyes.

"Really?" he asked.

The broken pieces of my heart clenched. "Definitely. I want to marry you, I just don't want to rush into anything. Let's give it a few more weeks. There's no hurry, right?"

He shook his head slowly. "I guess not. I don't want you to do anything you don't want to."

I squeezed his face. "Hey. I want to marry you. I promise. Just give me a little more time, okay?"

He sighed before reaching down and kissing me. "El, as long as you're mine, I can wait for everything else. Just tell me you're mine and no one else's and that'll be enough for me."

I wrapped my arms around his neck and tugged until his forehead was touching mine. "I'm always yours. I love you and nothing can change that."

His full lips spread into a grin and he kissed me again. "That I can live with."

Chapter 2

It wasn't until Abraham's phone went off a third time that we started to stir.

He kissed my bare shoulder and sighed. "I guess I should get that."

I shrugged. "You are the boss man. I've probably stolen enough of your time for one afternoon."

He rolled me over until I was facing him. "I may be the boss man, but more importantly, I'm *your* man. Being with you is always going to be my number one priority."

I laid there looking at him, studying his sincere blue eyes and wondering how I'd gotten so lucky.

Abraham was everything a woman could ask for in a man. He was sweet and thoughtful, but still protective and kind. It also didn't hurt that he was so damn good-looking he made my stomach hurt.

For some reason, this amazing man found me worthy. Elizabeth Montgomery, the woman who put her career above any and all personal relationships. The woman who was stubborn and self-sufficient to a fault. The woman who'd made him chase her every step of the way.

Some days I had to ask myself what kept him around. What was it about me that was so special? Why did I get to be the mate of such an incredible person?

Regardless of what I'd done to deserve him, he was mine. Totally and completely. I knew that with every bone in my body.

I reached out to cup his face and said the only thing I could think of to say. "I love you."

His lips stretched into a soft smile and he leaned down to kiss me. "I love you too, baby." He kissed me again, longer this time. "Do you know what it does to me when you say those words?" he asked as he pressed his lips to any available skin he could reach.

My heart was already pounding in my chest. "Probably the same thing they do to me when you say them."

He paused what he was doing and looked back up at me. "What do they do to you?"

I stared into his eyes and told him the truth. "When you say you love me, it reminds me that I'm not alone. That there's someone who cares about me. Someone who'll always be there for me. It makes me feel warm and content. Like nothing bad can really happen as long as you keep loving me. If I have you, I'll somehow make it through anything that comes my way."

He was quiet for a while after that, his eyes scanning my face over and over. Finally, he sighed and dipped his head to rest against mine. "I don't know what I ever did to deserve you, El." His voice was so deep I could feel it rumbling through his chest and into mine.

"I was thinking the same thing," I whispered.

He shook his head, his soft hair falling against my face. "Never doubt your place beside me. You're the fucking sun in my sky. You're all that matters and I'm gonna make you happy for the rest of my life."

My nose stung with tears, but I sniffed them back. I reached forward and pressed my lips against his. "You already make me so happy every day."

He leaned back and shot me a wide grin. "Then I guess I'm doin' my job."

I opened my mouth to speak when his phone went off again. "Speaking of jobs…"

He gave me one last kiss before pushing himself up and crawling off the couch. He stalked across the room completely naked and I couldn't help but watch his every move. When he reached the desk, he picked up his still-ringing phone.

"McCoy."

While he dealt with whoever that was, I peeled myself off the couch and began looking around the room for my clothes. I found my tattered bra and shot Abraham a withering look. He had the decency to look at least a little ashamed as he continued his phone conversation.

I put on the rest of my clothes, hoping no one would be in the hallway when I left.

"All right. Call me back when you figure it out." Abraham tossed his phone on the desk and turned to me. "Where are you going and why are you wearing clothes again?"

I shook my head, but my lips curled with a smile. "You know what'll happen if I stay in here naked."

He covered the distance between us in just a few long strides and wrapped his hands around my waist. His head dipped down to my neck where he inhaled deeply. "I do know. And I'm okay with it."

I laughed and pushed him away, but he didn't go far. "You have work to do."

He sighed dramatically and dragged me close again. "But I'd rather do *you*."

His lips skimmed up the side of my neck, and I knew if I didn't put a stop to this soon, we'd spend the whole afternoon in here. As much fun as that sounded, I refused to be the reason Abraham shirked his responsibilities.

"Abraham, you just had me," I breathed while my hands inched up the smooth skin of his arms.

"Hmm, exactly. So I know how fucking amazing it is."

I laughed, and with the last of my willpower, I pushed him back again. "You can have me as much as you want after you're done with work for the day."

He tsked. "But that won't be for hours."

I laughed again. He was so silly sometimes. It was such a juxtaposition to the man most other people saw. To the outside world, he was serious and commanding. Everything you'd expect in a leader. But, behind closed doors, when it was just the two of us, the other dimensions of his personality shone through. It made me love him even more.

I cupped his face in both hands and brought his lips to mine. I kissed him for a long time before pulling away and taking a step back. "That means you have hours to figure out what you're going to do with me."

One of his dark brows arched and his eyes lit up with mischief. "That's a good point, baby."

I slid out of his hold. "I'm full of those."

He laughed and slung an arm around my neck, pulling me against his chest and holding me. This was the opposite direction I'd been trying to lead us in, but I'd never complain about being in Abraham's arms. He was so big and solid, it felt like he could block out everything else in the world. Like it was just the two of us.

But then his phone rang again, and I remembered how important he and his time were. I gave him a squeeze and stepped away from him again. I could tell by the look on his face that he was considering not answering and blowing off the rest of his afternoon for me. We'd done that once, and I'd felt so guilty for taking him away from everything else that needed his attention that I swore I'd never let it happen again.

"If we have to wait, it'll be so much better when we're finally together again," I said, hoping I could convince him to let me leave. Because if he gave me one more of those bedroom looks, I'd lose any shred of self-control I had left.

He sighed and crossed his arms over his chest. "Fine. But I'm not waiting past dinner. As soon as you're done, we're going right to our room. Deal?"

A chill swept down my spine at his tone. I loved when he went all alpha on me. "Okay."

I walked to his door, but before I could open it, I looked over at him again. "I love you."

His arms fell to his sides as his whole face lit up. "I love you too, El."

With my heart full, and a pleasant ache between my legs, I slipped out of his office and crept across the hall to our room. Not only did I need to put on a new bra, I had to take a shower.

It only took one comment for me to make sure I always washed after spending an afternoon with Abraham.

On one of my first days living there, he and I had used his lunch time in his office to our advantage, much like we had today. When I'd finally torn myself away from him, I'd gone down to the kitchen to get a drink and found a few of the enforcers sitting at a table, playing cards. I greeted them all and turned to find some food when Huxley's voice cut through the quiet room.

"It smells like sex in here."

I'd frozen in place, my whole body erupting in mortifying flames. The other men at the table snickered, but I ignored them. I'd straightened my spine and grabbed a water bottle from the fridge before spinning back around to face them.

With my chin held high, I strutted past their table, but not before leaving them with an observation of my own.

"At least I'm getting some."

The men broke out in loud laughter and catcalls, but I didn't turn around. I kept my head up and my shoulders back until I made it up to our room where I melted into a puddle of embarrassment. I even ate dinner late that night, so I didn't have to see their faces again.

Ever since then, I made sure to shower the sex smell off me before doing anything else.

When I walked into our room, I found Charlie in his cat house and gave him a little scratch behind his ears. I felt bad that we had to leave him in that room all the time and vowed to figure out a better situation.

Sure, werewolves weren't very fond of cats, but if Abraham could learn to live with him, I figured everyone else in the house could too. He didn't take up much space, and he was a really good cat. If they all gave him a chance, he'd win them over easily.

"We're gonna build you some kitty ramps all around the house, boy. What d'you think about that?"

He purred loudly and bumped his head into my hand. I leaned down and kissed between his furry little ears before walking into our large bathroom.

I quickly showered and put on a new set of clothes. My old ones were wrinkled from being thrown on the floor earlier.

You wouldn't catch me complaining though.

When I finished in the bedroom, I walked back through the sitting room and into the hall where I found Abraham leaving his office.

"Hey, El. I was just coming to find you."

"What's up, baby?"

He stormed across the hallway, pressing his hips into mine and trapping me against the wall. "What have I told you about calling me baby?"

I pursed my lips and tipped my head back. "Um. I can't remember."

He growled and leaned down to nip at the sensitive skin of my neck. I gasped and pulled him closer. "I told you if you call me baby, I'm gonna fuck you again. Is that what you want?"

I dug my fingers into his shoulders and whispered in his ear, "Desperately."

His hands tightened on my hips and I had a feeling I'd be losing another bra. I tipped my head to the side to give him better access when a voice from down the hall broke the spell.

"Didn't you two already have your afternoon quickie?"

I pulled away from Abraham so fast I slammed my head against the wall behind me. He reached up and rubbed the sore spot, but his lips twitched with a smile.

"Hey, Evey," he called. So nonchalantly, like she didn't just call us out on our afternoon romp.

"Hey, Abey. I was just comin' to find Ellie."

He sighed. "She's all yours." He kissed my forehead before pulling away. "Oh, El, I wanted to remind you that you have a couple appointments this afternoon. Don't forget."

My stomach sank. I had forgotten. On purpose.

He was talking about the appointments he'd made for me with some of the pack members. Abraham thought I should start stepping into my role as alpha of the pack alongside him. This was his way of showing everyone that they should start bringing their issues to me and not just him.

Problem was, I didn't know what the hell I was doing. Or what these people would be asking me for. Or what I was supposed to tell them. Or why I had to do this in the first place.

I'd tried to explain to him that I was perfectly happy to not be an alpha. Why couldn't I be like the Queen of England's husband? Did anyone even know his name? No. He just sat in the background while the badass queen took care of everything. Why couldn't that be us?

I opened my mouth to argue for the dozenth time, but Abraham shook his head before I could even speak. "This is important, El. Please do this for me."

I sighed, my shoulders hunching. When he put it like that, how could I refuse? I'd have done anything for him, and the damn man knew it. "Fine. What time are they?"

"First one's at two. They'll meet you in the kitchen and you can decide where you want to talk."

I sighed again. "Okay."

He took a step forward and placed another kiss on my head. "You'll do great, baby. Don't worry," he whispered.

Evey slid between us and wrapped her arm around mine. "Come on. You two have had enough of each other for right now. It's my turn."

21

Chapter 3

Evey tugged me down the hallway and I struggled to keep up. For being the youngest and smallest of the McCoy quintuplets, she sure was strong.

"Where are we going?"

"My room."

"Why?"

"We have to talk about some ceremony stuff."

"Can't this wait?"

Wait for what, I wasn't sure.

Evey stopped short and turned to me with an unimpressed look. "I already had to wait for you and Abey to quit lockin' legs and swappin' gravy."

My mouth fell open. "We were not... *swapping* anything."

She raised a brow, and I had to look away. "Uh huh. Sure, you weren't." She grabbed my arm and pulled me down the hall again.

"How did you even know what we were doing?"

I thought we'd been so cautious. We were careful to not be seen together before or after our lunch-time rendezvous'. Abraham didn't care, but I wasn't comfortable broadcasting our love life to the rest of the pack. Apparently, we had anyway.

Evey scoffed. "Girl, there are no secrets in a pack."

I sighed and let her lead me into her bedroom. It was as eclectic and beautiful as ever, much like its owner.

Evey and I had always been the closest, but ever since I moved out there, we'd been practically inseparable. It helped that I didn't have a job and she worked from home. Whenever I wasn't with Abraham, I was usually with Evey.

She led me to her big fluffy bed that was covered in folders, and binders, and magazines. My belly hollowed as I took a cautious seat on the edge of the mattress.

"What's all this?" I asked.

She took a seat opposite me and pulled a black binder onto her lap. "I've been doin' some pre-plannin' and I need to get your input on some of this stuff."

My stomach clenched tighter. "Evey, is this necessary? We haven't even set a date yet."

She looked up, her blue eyes sharp. "But you are gonna mate him, aren't you?"

"Of course."

She smiled and looked back down at her binder. "Then there's no reason why we can't get to plannin'."

I sighed but didn't comment further. I knew Evey, and her love of party planning was only exceeded by her love of dressing people. When you added them together, what you got was an excited and determined werewolf. There would be no deterring her.

She flipped through a few plastic-protected pages in her binder as I looked at all the other things she had laid out. Would she really make me go through all this right now? For the first time, I was thankful I had somewhere to be in a little while.

Finally, she stopped on a page and turned the binder to face me. The image was of a woman in a beautiful wedding gown. It was voluminous with a tight, intricately-beaded top.

"What do you think of this style?" Evey asked.

I shrugged. "It's pretty."

"Of course, but can you picture yourself wearin' it at your ceremony?"

My stomach twisted. Could I picture myself wearing a dress like that? To be honest, I couldn't picture any aspect of the ceremony. Not the setup, or my dress, or the flowers, or anything.

I wasn't one of those girls who grew up fantasizing about a wedding. Never watched any of those wedding dress shows or read bridal magazines. I'd never even thought I'd get married, so when would I have envisioned any of this?

"I don't know, Evey. It's kinda big."

I picked my ring up and zipped it along the chain as she flipped the page.

"Okay, how about this one?"

This model was wearing a form-fitting gown that billowed out below her knees. It was lacy and beaded and also stunning.

I shrugged. "Wouldn't that be hard to walk in all night?"

Evey nodded again. "Okay, no ball gowns and no mermaid cuts. Got it." She shuffled through a few more pages before she turned the binder to me again. "What about this one?"

The picture she showed me was of a woman dressed in a long flowing gown with floral designs sewn into the fabric. It had an empire waist and a long train with a sash tied around the middle.

"This one's nice."

Evey's eyes lit up. "So, you like the empire waist?"

"Yeah, I guess."

Evey sighed and shut the binder before setting it aside. "All right. What's goin' on?"

"What do you mean?"

"I mean, most women would have an opinion about their ceremony dress. But you don't seem to care. Why is that?"

I looked away from her piercing blue eyes and fingered a loose thread on my shirt. "I don't know, Evey. I just never imagined I'd get married. I don't have opinions ready for this stuff because I've never really taken the time to think about it."

"But you've been engaged for a month. Wouldn't that be a good time to start thinkin' about it?"

I shrugged but didn't meet her eyes.

She reached out to grab one of my hands. "I know there's somethin' else goin' on here."

I kept my eyes on our joined hands. I didn't know what to say to her. Didn't really know what my problem was. Why wasn't I excited to plan our ceremony? Why wouldn't I set a date with Abraham? Why was I dragging my heels about getting married to the most amazing man I'd ever met?

I was an idiot.

That was the only explanation I could come up with.

Evey let out another deep breath, and I finally met her gaze.

"Are you havin' second thoughts about matin' Abey?" she asked softly.

There was so much hurt in her eyes, it made my heart clench in my chest. "No, Evey. Of course not. I love him."

Her eyes cleared the tiniest bit. "Then what's holdin' you back?"

I returned my gaze to our hands. "I guess I'm just worried."

"About what?"

I took a deep breath and met her eyes again. "Aren't we moving really fast?"

She shrugged. "Not for fated mates."

"What do you mean?"

"Do you know how long it took our parents to be mated?"

I tried to remember if Abraham had told me this but came up empty. "No, I don't think so."

"A week."

My eyes widened. "They got married a week after they got engaged?!"

She shook her head. "No. They mated a week after they met."

Somehow, my eyes widened further. "Are you freaking kidding me?"

"Nope. That's how it is. When you meet your fated mate, there's no reason to wait. They're your soul mate. The one wolf in the world that was made just for you. Why would they wait?"

I pulled my hand away from hers and got up to pace. "Because that's crazy, Evey. People don't just meet and get married in a week. Or in the course of a few months like me and Abraham. In my world, you meet, you date, you fall in love, and a few years later, you might get married."

"That isn't your world anymore, Ellie. This is."

I blew out a big breath and continued to pace. I needed to work off this excess energy. What she was saying was insane. No reasonable person would get married after a week. I felt like an idiot for even considering it after the few months I'd known Abraham.

"This might be my world now, but it's not the one I grew up in. It's not the one I've known all my life. You can't just expect me to change everything I know and believe just because I turn into a wolf every full moon. It doesn't work like that."

Evey sighed and stood up to intercept me. "Could you please sit down? You're makin' me dizzy."

I plopped onto the edge of her bed again and buried my face in my hands. "I can't do this, Evey. It's too much."

She took a seat next to me and wrapped her arm around my shoulders. "Ellie, there's no reason to stress. It's Abraham we're talkin' about. He's your fated mate. The one man who'll put your happiness above everything else. What's so scary about that?"

It was right there on the tip of my tongue. The words I'd swallowed down a hundred times in Abraham's presence. Could I confide in Evey? Would she understand?

I took a deep breath and lifted my head. "Evey, what if we're not fated?"

Her eyebrows furrowed. "What are you talkin' about?"

I got up to pace again. I couldn't help myself. "Evey, I'm a bitten werewolf. I wasn't made for Abraham. I was made a human."

She tilted her head back and forth. "Yeah, but we all know you're his fated mate anyway."

I spun to face her. "But how do we know that? What if we're wrong? What if I'm not the one for him?" Another thought swam to the surface, leaving a trail of fire and destruction in its wake. "What if he meets his real fated mate? The werewolf that was actually meant for him? What happens to me, then?" My voice was so quiet by the end that I knew she wouldn't have been able to hear me if she didn't have ultra-sensitive hearing.

"Ellie." She said my name like a good-natured but disapproving mother. "You know he's your mate. You've told me before you can feel it."

I shook my head and began to pace again. "I know what I've told you and I know what I feel, but still. You can't deny that it doesn't make any sense. There's no plausible explanation for why I'm his mate."

Evey shrugged. "Sometimes stuff just happens that way."

I shook my head again. "That's not good enough for me. I'm not going to get married to someone I've only known a few months just because I think he's my soul mate."

She was quiet for a long time while I continued to pace. I didn't look at her, though. I didn't want to see the emotions she'd have displayed on her pretty face. Didn't want to see the disappointment I knew would be there.

"So, what are you saying? Are you not gonna mate Abey?" Her voice was quiet and laced with hurt.

I released a big breath and turned to face her. "I honestly don't know, Evey. But I know I can't marry him with these doubts in my head. That wouldn't be fair to him."

27

She nodded slowly. "You're right. You can't mate him until you're sure."

I tossed my hands in the air and turned to pace again. "And how am I supposed to be sure? Is there some kind of fated mate test we can take to prove we're supposed to be together?"

"It doesn't work like that."

I growled under my breath. "I know it doesn't. Which is why I'm losing my friggen mind, Evey. I don't know what to do and I know I'm hurting him by putting off our ceremony. He's going to think I don't want him when that's the furthest thing from the truth."

"Are you more worried that you're not his mate or that he's not yours?"

I paused and turned to look at her. "Huh?"

One corner of her lips curled. "Are you worried that he's not the one for you? Or that you're not his fated mate?"

I chewed on my bottom lip while I thought about that. "Well, since I was born a human, I shouldn't have a fated mate, right? That means I always had the ability to choose who I wanted to be with."

"And?"

There was so much trepidation and hope in her voice, my heart clenched again.

"And I'd choose Abraham every time."

A big smile spread across her face.

But that left one option.

"I guess that means I'm more worried that I'm not his mate. That his real mate will come around one day, and he'll drop me for her."

She shook her head. "You know Abey would never do that."

I raised a brow at her. "If he met his real fated mate, would he have a choice?"

She held my eyes for the first few seconds, but eventually she looked away and I knew I had my answer.

"Exactly," I said softly, but the word rang through the quiet room.

"But that's not gonna happen 'cause you're his mate."

"But, how do we know that?"

She sighed loudly and stood from her bed. Her footsteps thumped across the floor before she grabbed my arm. "Let's go."

I let her drag me through her room. "Where are we going?"

"To talk to Callie."

"For what?"

"She's the smartest person I know. Maybe she'll have some information we don't."

I kept quiet as she led me down the hall to Callie's room. She knocked once, and Callie called for us to come in.

The middle McCoy sibling was sitting at her desk, curly brown hair as wild as ever. When she turned to us, her light blue eyes lit up. "Hey, Ellie! I was going to come find you, but I wasn't sure if you were done with Abey or not."

My cheeks burned, and I couldn't meet her eyes. "How does everyone know?" I whispered, mostly to myself.

"Told you there are no secrets in a pack," Evey whispered back. She turned to Callie and spoke up. "We need your help."

Callie pushed away from her desk and swiveled her chair to face us. "Of course. What's up?"

Evey shook the arm of mine she was still holding. "Ellie's scared she's not Abey's mate."

I winced at her crude summary of my debacle. That wasn't exactly the way I would have described it.

Callie frowned. "Is that true?"

My face burned hotter, and I looked down at my sneakers. "Kinda."

Evey shook my arm again, and I shot her a glare. She nodded toward Callie and I sighed.

"Okay, yes. I'm worried we're not really fated and that his real mate will show up one day."

Callie nodded slowly. "And why don't you think you're his mate? You two have all the symptoms and side-effects of being fated."

She was right. We did.

Back when I'd still been living in Raleigh and Abraham was in Asheville, our time apart had been torturous. It was hard to sleep, to eat, to even function when he wasn't around. As soon as we were together again, all that went away. When I was around him, I felt stronger and better and more whole than ever.

But that wasn't enough.

"Yeah, we do, but I'm a bitten wolf. How can I be his fated mate?"

Callie pursed her lips and tilted her head to the side. "Yeah, that doesn't make much sense, does it?"

I shook my head. "Now you see my dilemma?"

She nodded and sighed. "Yeah, I can kind of see where you're coming from. Is that why you won't set a ceremony date?"

My face heated up again. When was I going to get used to having a whole pack of werewolves up in my business?

"Yeah, kinda. That, and in my world, marrying someone you've only known a few months is something only drunk and drugged up celebrities do. Not normal people. Not sensible people. Not sane people."

Callie shook her head. "But that's not your world anymore."

I released a deep breath. "Yeah, I get that. But that's how I was raised. I can't just turn it off."

She nodded slowly and sat up straighter. "What if we could figure out how you two are fated mates? Would that make you feel better about the mating ceremony?"

I looked down at my sneakers again and thought through her words carefully. If I knew for sure, without a shadow of a doubt that I was Abraham's fated mate, would that be enough? I knew I loved him, and I knew he loved me. I also knew I'd never felt like that about anyone and I couldn't imagine my life without him. Couldn't even imagine a single day without him. Was that enough?

I met her gaze again. "Yes. If I knew we were really fated, there'd be nothing stopping me from marrying him."

Evey clapped next to me and Callie's face lit up. "Okay. Then let's focus on that. I've already done some preliminary research, but I'll do some deeper digging for you, okay?"

It felt like a weight had been lifted from my shoulders. The burden of these suspicions and questions had been a heavy one I'd been carrying around all on my own. But now I had Evey and Callie on my side. Together we could figure out what was going on and make sense of this situation between Abraham and me. I just hoped we could find an answer before I hurt Abraham any more than I already had.

Chapter 4

Evey and I were getting ready to leave Callie's room when she spoke up. "Ellie, do you have a minute? I was hoping you could look at some of these documents from our lawyer."

This wasn't the first time Callie had enlisted my help. I'd told her back when she stayed with me in Raleigh that I'd be more than happy to help whenever I could. However, this was environmental law, and I really didn't feel like I knew enough to be helpful.

"Of course I can. I'm not sure how much help I'll be, though," I warned her.

She waved my words away. "You've got to be better than the bozo we're working with."

My lips twitched with a smile. It wasn't often that Callie insulted someone. I had to wonder who this guy was to get a reaction like that out of her.

Evey sighed. "I guess I'll go get some work done while you two hippies talk about huggin' trees and savin' the planet."

Callie shook her head. "Evelyn, I've told you, I'm not a hippie."

"Then why do you drive a Prius?"

"Because it's better for the environment."

"Exactly. You might as well be huggin' trees."

"Just because I bought a Prius doesn't make me a hippie."

"I disagree."

"Well, you know what? You can just–"

"All right, ladies," I interrupted. "Let's break it up before you two break into a pillow fight."

Evey rolled her eyes. "We haven't had a pillow fight since we were ten."

"We were twelve."

"We were ten, Callista."

"No, we weren't. I remember it clearly because–"

"Ladies," I interrupted again.

They both shot me chagrinned looks.

"All right, I'll leave you two… environmental enthusiasts to it."

Callie rolled her eyes, but thankfully didn't comment until Evey was gone. "She's my sister and I love her, but that girl drives me nuts," she said once the door was closed.

I laughed. "Yeah, but you're lucky to have her. I'd have killed for a sister when I was growing up."

"Yeah, while I would have killed to be an only child."

I shook my head, my smile wide across my face. "You don't mean that."

She sighed. "You're right. I don't. I just hate when she calls me a hippie."

I laughed again. "That's why she does it."

Callie nodded slowly. "Oh, I know. That girl has thirty years of practice getting under my skin."

I took a seat in an overstuffed chair near her desk. "What did you want me to look at?"

Callie turned to her laptop again. "This new lawyer we're working with wrote up some documents to submit to the court. I'm hoping you could take a look and let me know if anything stands out to you."

"I'd be happy to, but you know I really don't know anything about environmental law. I don't know how much help I'll be."

Callie gathered up a stack of papers and handed them to me. "I promise, any help would be appreciated."

I let out a deep breath and shrugged. She knew how unequipped I was, and she wanted my help anyway. At least I'd tried to warn her.

I took the pile of papers from her and sat back in the chair. "What are these for again?"

"We're submitting these to the court in a couple days. It's for our Blue Ridge Parkway conservation project."

I nodded slowly and started to read but didn't get far. "Well, he's spelled *environmental* wrong in the first paragraph."

Callie growled, and my eyes snapped to her. I'd never heard a sound like that come out of her mouth. This lawyer must really have been getting to her.

"I knew that guy was a joke. I can't believe we've already paid him for this." She shook her head, brows furrowed and lips pursed.

I'd been on the receiving end of a Callie lecture and I was glad I wasn't that guy. I kept reading and found a few more mistakes and some sentences that could be made a lot clearer. If he was trying to convince a judge of something, having so many errors in a document was a surefire way to lose.

"Can I take this with me and look it over later? I have a few appointments coming up soon."

"Of course! That would be great! Thanks so much, Ellie. You're a lifesaver."

I didn't know about all that, but it wouldn't hurt to go through all this for her. I could probably hop on the computer and do a little research too. It wasn't like I had much else to do with my time.

Except, of course, the meetings that I was dreading.

"While you're doing that, I'll see what kind of information I can find on fated mates and bitten wolves, okay?"

"That's perfect. Thanks, Callie."

She waved a hand and turned back to her computer. "Don't mention it."

I left her room and walked back over to the wing that held our bedroom and dropped off the packet of papers. I didn't want to lose anything, and I wouldn't have time to look at them until I got through all the meetings anyway.

Had Abraham said how many there were supposed to be?

Suddenly, I wished I'd asked more questions.

I trudged down the stairs and into the kitchen, but there was no one there but Aubrey, one of the house staff. At that hour, lunch was over, and the housekeepers were cleaning up after the last meal and preparing for the next. Usually, Ms. Elsie did most of the cooking, but she was nowhere to be seen.

"Hey, Aubrey," I called as I took a seat at one of the tables to wait.

She paused what she was doing and turned around to face me slowly. "Elizabeth."

I frowned. What kind of greeting was that? Had I done something to offend her? I hardly saw her and we barely spoke, so I didn't know how that could be possible.

Before I had a chance to respond, someone walked through the sliding glass doors from the backyard. I recognized the woman, of course, but couldn't remember her name. She had pretty brown skin and curly hair that just reached her shoulders.

"Hey," I said and stood.

She gave me a little wave. "Hi. I'm here to see Abraham."

I shook my head. "No. I think you're here to see me."

She frowned. "But I made an appointment with him."

I sighed. "Yeah, and he wants me to take over."

She took a small step back. "I can just come back when he's available."

Part of me wanted to let her go. I didn't want to have the meetings in the first place, and it wouldn't have bothered me if she took her problems to Abraham instead. I really didn't know how I could help her anyway.

But then I remembered Abraham had asked me to do this for him. For some reason, he thought it was important. He really didn't ask for much, so when he did, it was even more important that I did whatever it was. Even if it was the last thing I wanted to do.

I sighed and held out a hand. "Wait. Maybe I can help. Let's go sit in the conference room and you can tell me what's going on. If nothing else, I can go to Abraham myself and make sure he addresses whatever issue you're having. Deal?"

She pursed her lips and scanned my face with her dark brown eyes. Finally, she sighed. "Okay, yeah. We can do that."

I smiled wide and waved her over. "Okay. Let's go down here and talk."

I let her walk ahead of me but paused when I remembered something. "Hey, Aubrey, if the next one comes and I'm not done, could you just ask them to wait out here for me?"

Aubrey's shoulders tensed before she turned to face me. "Is that an order?"

I jerked back like she'd hit me. What the hell was her problem?

I ground my teeth together and spoke through them. "No. That was a request because you're the only one in the kitchen. Can you do it or not?"

She shrugged a shoulder and turned back to whatever she was doing. "I guess."

I tipped my head back and stared at the ceiling for a moment, reminding myself that I was still new there. My pack mates and I were all still trying to figure out where I belonged and what role I would play.

That was the only explanation I could come up with for her attitude.

I took a deep breath. "Thanks, Aubrey."

She ignored me, and I sighed before heading down the hall to where I'd sent my first appointment.

When I walked into the conference room, the woman was clutching her bag in front of her and looking around the space like she was searching for an exit. I closed the door behind me and gave her a big smile.

"First of all, I know we've met, but I'm really bad with names. Can you remind me of yours?"

"My name's Madison, but people call me Maddy."

I took a seat at the table, waving at a chair for her. "Great. Nice to meet you again, Maddy. I'm Elizabeth, but everyone calls me Ellie out here."

She slowly took her seat. "I know who you are."

"Great. Now that we're done with introductions, tell me why you're here."

She sighed and looked down at the table. "Are you sure Abraham isn't available?"

I grit my teeth and pasted the best smile I could on my face. "I'm sure. But I'd really like to help if you'll let me."

She sighed again and met my eyes. "It's my neighbor."

I nodded slowly as I realized I should have brought some paper and something to write with. Scanning the room, I saw a small table pushed to the side with notepads and a box of pens. I held up a finger. "Give me one second."

I ran across the room, grabbed a pad and pen, and sat back down. "Okay, so your neighbor. What's his name?"

"It's Brad McDermott. He's in house ten and I'm in twelve."

I jotted down a few notes, nodding. "Okay, got it." I looked back up at her. "What's going on with him?"

She let out a deep breath and sat forward in her chair. "He's got a new car he's working on and he's out there blaring music and banging around at all hours of the night. I've been late to work three times in the last week because I overslept after being kept up all night."

37

"Okay, and what are the quiet hours around here?"

She frowned. "Quiet hours?"

I set my pen down and looked up at her. "Yeah, quiet hours. My apartment complex in Raleigh had mandatory quiet hours from ten at night to eight in the morning Monday through Friday. We all signed agreements stating we'd be quiet during those times out of respect for our neighbors."

Her eyes were wide as she shook her head. "We don't have anything like that here."

"Huh. Okay, well maybe we should start there. I can have Abraham implement some quiet hours. That way you should be able to get a full night's rest."

"You can really do that?"

I shrugged. "I don't see why not."

A wide smile spread across her face. "That would be great!"

My grin matched hers. "Consider it done. We'll get them implemented as soon as possible, and if there're any issues after that, you can come to me and I'll address them personally. Okay?"

She nodded quickly. "Yeah, that's perfect. Thanks so much, Ellie."

"My pleasure. Is there anything else you needed to talk about?"

"No. That's it. Thanks again. This was great."

She stood and so did I. I held out a hand for her to shake, but she stepped up and wrapped her arms around my shoulders instead. I returned her embrace, squeezing her tight for a moment before letting go.

"Thanks for bringing this issue to me. I'll make sure we sort it out as soon as possible," I said as I led her out of the conference room and back into the kitchen.

"Thanks for helping. Have a good day, Ellie."

I watched her walk out of the lodge with a smile on my face.

That hadn't been too bad. I actually thought I did a pretty good job solving that issue. I couldn't believe there were no quiet hours yet, and I'd be talking to Abraham about that immediately.

Aubrey was still banging around the kitchen, but I ignored her and mindlessly scrolled through my phone while I waited for the next pack member to arrive.

Thankfully, I didn't have to wait long until another werewolf came through the sliding glass door. I stood to greet him, actually remembering his name.

"Hey, Elliot."

The brown-haired man had been at the first pack barbecue I attended. He was about my height at 5'9" and had freckles all over his face.

"Hey, Elizabeth. Abraham around?"

I shook my head. "I'm taking care of his appointments today. Let's go in the conference room and you can tell me about what brought you here."

I turned without waiting for him to respond and started off down the hallway. I had a feeling he'd try to argue too, and I was hoping I could avoid that.

When I made it to the conference room, I held the door open and waited until Elliot walked through.

"Are you sure Abraham isn't available?" he asked.

I pressed my lips together and pulled them into the best smile I could manage. "I'm afraid not. But I can help, and if I can't, I'll make sure Abraham takes care of it." I took my seat and motioned for him to take one as well. "What's going on, Elliot?"

With a resigned sigh, he sat down and folded his hands on the table in front of him. "Well, I'm havin' an issue with Craig."

I wrote down the name. "Okay, and who is Craig?"

He huffed, and it looked like he was going to ask to speak to Abraham again, but instead, he answered. "He's the mechanic. We all bring him our cars here and he's supposed to give us a break."

I took a few more notes. "Has that not been the case?"

He leaned forward. "No. It hasn't. That jackass tried to charge me fifty bucks for a damn oil change!"

"That is pretty steep."

He slammed a hand on the table. "You're goddamn right it's steep. It's criminal is what it is. He said the rate went up due to product price increases, but he just changed my oil a couple months ago and only charged me twenty-five. I don't see how the price could double in just a couple months."

I shook my head. "Yeah, that doesn't sound right."

He sighed and leaned back in his chair. "So, what are you gonna do about it?"

I slowly raised my head. "Well, I'll probably start off by talking to him. See what his reasoning is and try to work out a solution with him."

He raised his brows. "And? If that doesn't work?"

I shrugged. "Then I guess we'll all be looking for a new mechanic, won't we?"

Elliot looked unimpressed, almost as if he was daring me to do something about the issue. Like he thought I couldn't. Little did he know that Elizabeth Montgomery was born to rise to a challenge like this.

I'd talk to this Craig guy and figure out what his deal was. If I could talk him into lowering his prices, great. But, if he wanted to stick to his guns, I wasn't lying when I said we'd bring our business elsewhere. Sure, it was convenient to have a mechanic on pack lands, but that didn't mean he could charge outrageous prices and we'd all just pay them. There had to be a solution, and I was determined to figure it out on my own.

Chapter 5

After I led Elliot out of the lodge, I sat waiting in the kitchen for the next appointment. When I'd been there fifteen minutes and no one had showed up, I pulled out my phone and texted Abraham.

Me: How many appointments were there?

Sexiest Man Alive: Just two for today.

I groaned and texted him back.

Me: For today? Does that mean there's more on a different day?

Sexiest Man Alive: You've got another three tomorrow.

I sighed loudly and let my head fall back. Even though the first two appointments had been relatively easy, I wasn't fooling myself into thinking they'd all be like that. And I'd only actually come up with a solution for one of their problems. The other I still had to figure out.

Me: Do you know where Craig lives?

Sexiest Man Alive: House 4. Why?

Me: I have to go talk to him.

There was a long pause as I watched the little dots dance, indicating he was typing.

Sexiest Man Alive: Give me a minute and I'll go with you.

Me: That's okay, I got this.

I waited another minute before he responded.

Sexiest Man Alive: I don't know how I feel about that, El.

I rolled my eyes and typed out a response. I knew he was overprotective, but if I was going to step into this alpha role, I had to do it on my own. Relying on Abraham would get me no respect. I needed to earn it, starting today.

Me: I'll be fine. I'll still be on pack lands.

Sexiest Man Alive: Pack lands haven't always been safe for you.

My stomach fell at the reminder. Not too long ago, there'd been a serial killer stalking me. It all started when he attacked me in the woods one night and altered the course of my life forever. He'd bitten me but was scared off before he could finish the job.

We'd later come to the conclusion that not only did the serial killer have to be a member of this pack, but that he was also likely one of the enforcers. That hadn't sat well with Abraham. He'd been devastated to learn that one of his team, the men he trusted the most, was killing women in the woods.

When we'd learned that not only was it an enforcer, but his cousin Calvin, it almost destroyed him. This was a man he grew up with, who he loved like a brother, and it turned out he was a psychopathic serial killer.

But that was all behind us now.

Calvin was dead, and the threat was gone. I knew it hadn't been that long ago, but we needed to move past it. Abraham needed to move past it. He couldn't keep me in a protective bubble the rest of my life. He couldn't shadow my every step. Abraham needed to learn that I could handle myself and that I'd be all right without his constant supervision.

Me: But they're safe now. I won't be gone long, and I'll have my phone on me the whole time.

Sexiest Man Alive: Can you come find me when you're back?

I rolled my eyes, but there was a smile twitching the corners of my lips. He was trying to rein himself in and I had to give him some credit for that.

Me: Yes, baby. I'll come find you.

Sexiest Man Alive: You know what it does to me when you call me that.

I bit my lip and glanced around the kitchen, making sure no one was around to see my cheeks turn pink. Aubrey was still there, but she was on the other side of the room and working real hard to ignore me.

Me: I believe I do.

Sexiest Man Alive: Are you trying to get fucked again before dinner, Ms. Montgomery?

My eyes darted to Aubrey again like she could hear the dirty things Abraham was texting. I crossed my legs and took a deep breath before responding.

Me: You know I'd never say no to you.

Sexiest Man Alive: You better quit now before I come down there and show you what you're doing to me.

Me: I'd love to see.

Sexiest Man Alive: El...

I laughed softly and shook my head. Sometimes it was so much fun messing with him.

Me: Okay, okay. I'll behave. I'll see you soon.

Sexiest Man Alive: Now I'm hard and I have to be on a conference call in a minute.

Another laugh spilled from my lips and I heard Aubrey huff from across the room.

Me: Sorry, baby.

Sexiest Man Alive: You're killing me.

Me: Love you.

Sexiest Man Alive: I love you too, El.

With the smile still firmly planted on my face, I stood up and tucked my phone into my pocket. As much fun as it was to flirt with Abraham, I had a mechanic to see, and I had a feeling this issue wouldn't be as easy to fix as Maddy's had been.

I left the lodge without another word to Aubrey. If she was going to be rude to me, I wouldn't go out of my way to be nice to her.

It was hot outside, the sticky July heat instantly making me wish I was back in the air-conditioned lodge. But I had a job to do, so I walked down the stairs and over to the gravel drive that led to the other pack members' houses.

I hadn't had much of a reason to come back here before. In fact, the only time I had was when Abraham gave me a tour a few weeks ago.

The pack houses were like a little village of their own, hidden by a wall of trees with only the width of the gravel drive to allow access. The homes were small, most of them only one or two bedrooms, but they looked cozy and inviting. I walked past the first few, waving to pack members as I went.

When I made it to house four, I knew I didn't have to look much farther for Craig. There was an older man with a potbelly and a long, scraggly grey beard hanging off his face. He had a bandana tied around the top of his head and was bent over the engine of a car in his driveway.

I took a fortifying breath and walked up the drive to talk to him. "Hey. Craig?"

The man lifted his head and eyed me up and down. "Yeah?"

"My name's Elizabeth–"

"I know who you are," he interrupted.

I pulled my lips into the best smile I could manage. "Okay, great. Do you have a minute?"

Craig stood up straight and pulled a dirty rag from the back pocket of his jeans. He methodically wiped his grease-stained hands as he watched me. "What do you want?"

Oh, great. He was friendly. That would make this so much easier.

I walked up the rest of his drive until I was only a few feet away. "I want to talk to you about the prices you're charging the pack. We've had some complaints that they've been raised without notice and I wanted to get your side of the story."

He shrugged a shoulder and turned his head to spit on the ground. "You ever heard of inflation?

I pressed my lips together for a moment before I tried again. "Yes, I have. But I'm not sure how inflation could explain a one-hundred percent price increase in just a few short months."

He narrowed his eyes and tucked the rag back into his pocket. "Who's the one bitchin'? Was it that asshole Elliot?"

I shook my head. "It's not important. If you're trying to rip off even one of us, it's a problem for everyone."

"Us?" He laughed derisively. "What us? You've barely been here a whole moon cycle."

I gritted my teeth and fought to keep the smile on my face. "I don't think the length of time I've been a pack member should matter here."

He took a step forward and put a hand on his hip. "Listen, little girl, I don't need to hear shit from you. It's my business and my clients, and I'll charge 'em what I want."

I took a step forward too. "Don't patronize me."

"Your fancy words don't impress me, sugar."

The slightest tremble started in my hands and I clenched them into fists. I'd gotten a lot better at containing my wolf in the past month. It helped that there weren't people in my life who purposely antagonized me anymore. But Craig was toeing the line.

"Craig, I'm going to level with you. If you can't charge reasonable prices for your services, we're going to take our business somewhere else."

He took another step forward and my shoulders tensed in warning. "Are you threatening me?"

Do not show weakness.

The voice in my head was back, and like every other time, I listened to it.

45

I tipped my chin up and straightened my spine. "I'm giving you the courtesy of informing you. You can treat your business and your clients however you like, but if you can't charge a reasonable price, the rest of the pack and I are going to find a mechanic who will."

He turned to spit again, this time closer to where I was standing. "And who the hell are you? What gives you the authority to do this?"

I stood up even straighter. "I'm the future alpha of this pack. That's what gives me the authority to do this."

He watched me silently for a moment before speaking again. "I'll take this up with Abraham," he said and moved to turn away from me.

I took a deep breath, puffing my chest out and filling my body with determination. "He'll tell you the same thing I am."

He spun back around to face me. "So, because he decided to shack up with some bitten wolf bitch, that means I just have to do whatever you say? Fuck that."

I took a step closer and lowered my voice. "I'm going to tell you one more time. Lower your prices or you're done here."

He spun around and walked back to the open hood of his car. "Whatever, lady."

It was clear I was being dismissed.

And I was pissed.

My hands shook as I spun around and stalked away from Craig's house. That hadn't gone as well as I'd expected, although I didn't know where those expectations had come from.

Peyton had warned me about this, hadn't she? That the pack wouldn't follow a bitten wolf. That I'd have no authority. That despite what Abraham said or thought, they'd never respect me as their alpha.

I stomped down the gravel drive on my way back to the lodge.

If Craig was going to be an asshole, we'd just eliminate him as the pack mechanic. We didn't need to put up with his crap or his price gouging. As soon as I got back to the lodge, Abraham and I would figure out who we could bring our vehicles to from then on.

I was still storming down the road when I felt an uncomfortable sensation. Like I was being watched. Or studied.

I slowed my steps and looked around but didn't notice anyone or anything right away. Just as I was about to turn back toward the lodge, I saw him.

Paul, Peyton's brother, was sitting on the front porch of house two, his dark eyes trained on me.

I wasn't sure why he was still a member of the pack, but Abraham refused to kick him out. His argument was that Paul shouldn't be held responsible for what his sister did, even if they were twins and really close.

And Paul had all the excuses in the world.

He claimed he knew about Peyton's feelings toward Abraham but had no idea she'd go to the lengths she did. According to him, he'd had no idea that she'd colluded with Calvin to separate Abraham and me on the night of the solstice party.

She'd cornered me in the lodge that night and filled my head with doubts and questions that had been too great to ignore. She knew it would cause a fight between Abraham and me and that was exactly what she and Calvin had been hoping for.

Once I'd left Abraham, she must have tipped Calvin off that I was leaving and that was when he caught up to me and offered a ride home to Raleigh. As desperate as I was to leave Asheville, I hadn't even questioned how he found me or why he was being so nice. I'd just taken the ride.

Later, Abraham told me that Peyton snuck into his room that night, hoping that, since she got rid of me, it would make room for her. She was sorely mistaken. Abraham had swiftly kicked her out of his room, but not before she let slip her and Calvin's little plan. That was what alerted Abraham to the danger I was in.

I suppose, in a way, it was because of her that Abraham was in time to save me. But on the other hand, it was partly her fault that I was in that situation to begin with, so I guess we were even.

After that, Abraham had excommunicated Peyton, and we'd all expected Paul to follow after her. So, when he came to Abraham and explained his situation, it surprised the hell out of all of us.

I didn't think it was a good idea to have any relative of that evil bitch still hanging around, but Abraham wouldn't be swayed. I thought part of it was due to his own guilt at not knowing it was his cousin who was murdering women in the woods. If he held Paul accountable for Peyton, that would mean he was responsible for what Calvin did too.

I thought it was all a load of crap, but I didn't push him on it. Paul hadn't done anything wrong. Yet.

Despite the fact that Abraham let Paul and his mate, Annalise, stay in the pack, he was still keeping an eye on him. He'd tasked all his enforcers with watching over him to make sure he wasn't still aligned with Peyton somehow.

If you'd asked me, it was just a matter of time before Paul betrayed us, too. Blood was thicker than water, and you'd think the man with the huge, close-knit family would know that better than anyone else. But Abraham was loyal almost to a fault, and I couldn't help but admire his big heart. That didn't mean I wasn't keeping an eye on Paul too, though.

However, it looked like he was the one keeping an eye on me at that moment.

I lifted a hand and gave him a little wave, but he didn't respond, and the look on his face didn't change. That was creepy as hell, but what could I do? Complain to Abraham that Paul was being mean to me? I'd just keep this little encounter in the back of my mind and hope I was wrong about Paul. That he was actually a good guy with a crazy sister.

I just hoped we wouldn't regret that.

Chapter 6

My brain spun as I continued to storm down the gravel drive back toward the lodge.

When we'd announced our engagement about a month ago at the first pack cook out we'd held after Abraham proposed, I'd been worried. Thankfully, it seemed like the majority of the people there had been happy for us and excited about our union. However, I'd noticed a few wolves who hadn't come up to congratulate us. And beyond that, not everyone in the pack had even been there for that barbecue.

I'd told Abraham we'd have issues with me being alpha of the pack, but he hadn't wanted to listen. Now I had irrefutable proof.

Craig's words were on repeat in my head as I slid open the glass door and stepped into the kitchen. Aubrey was still in there working, and when she saw it was me, she rolled her eyes and turned her back.

And I'd had enough.

"Aubrey, is there a problem?"

She shrugged a shoulder but didn't turn around. "I don't know what you're talking about."

I sighed and crossed the kitchen to stand behind her. "You've been giving me an attitude all day and I want to know why."

She spun around and speared me with a look. "Just because you're the alpha's mate, doesn't mean we all have to like you. Some of us can see right through your fancy outside to what's beneath."

I took a deep breath and willed my hands to stop shaking. "And what is it you think is underneath?"

Aubrey took a step closer and tipped up her chin to meet my eyes. "A bitch who'll get someone kicked out of their pack just because she doesn't like them."

I shook my head. "Are you talking about Peyton?"

She laughed once. "Are there more pack mates you've gotten excommunicated?"

This was unbelievable.

The fact that Peyton still had the power to mess with my day was ridiculous.

"Listen, Aubrey, I don't know what you think you know, but you're wrong. Peyton defied Abraham's orders on more than one occasion and was given several chances to straighten up. But she didn't. As far as I'm concerned, she got everything she deserved."

"And what gives you the right to decide that?"

I shrugged. "It's just my opinion. I didn't decide anything, Abraham did."

She laughed again. "Yeah, and he's so whipped by you he'll do anything you say."

"Is that really how you view your alpha? You don't think he has enough sense to make decisions on his own? That he's not capable of being unbiased?"

She looked me up and down. "Before you came around, I wouldn't have thought that, but everything's changed now."

I shook my head again. "Then I think you should take that up with him."

She rolled her eyes. "And risk getting kicked out because I don't like the bitch he's sleeping with? No thanks."

Wow. That was the third time I'd been called a bitch to my face that day. That might have been a record.

I straightened my spine and looked her dead in the eyes. "I'm going to be one of the alphas of this pack someday soon. You don't have to like me, but you will respect me."

She turned back around. "I don't have to do anything."

I took a deep breath. And then another. When I thought I had my temper under control, I spoke again. "Do what you want, Aubrey, but I'm not going anywhere. It would be in your best interest to learn to get along with me or things are going to be really uncomfortable around here."

She ignored me completely. Didn't answer, didn't turn around, didn't even acknowledge that she'd heard me.

Well, screw her, too.

I spun on my heel and stomped out of the kitchen, more irritated than ever. Taking the stairs two at a time, I stormed over to Abraham's office and banged on his door. When he called for me to come in, I whipped it open and slammed it behind me.

"El?"

I stood there, chest heaving and hands clenching and unclenching over and over. I hadn't felt so out of control in a while and I tried to remember my breathing exercises.

In, one.

Out, two.

In, three.

Out, four.

Abraham stood up and circled his desk. "What's going on? Are you okay?"

I took a deep breath and shook my head. "I'm fine."

He kept walking until he was only a few short feet away from me. "Then what's going on?"

The events of the afternoon boiled and bubbled up inside of me until it couldn't be contained anymore. "What's going on is I'm not wanted here. Especially not as an alpha. I knew this wouldn't work. I knew they wouldn't accept me, but you made me try anyway, and look where we are now."

He frowned and reached out to grasp my biceps. "What are you talking about? What happened?"

I let out a deep breath and looked up into his eyes that were so blue and creased with concern. He didn't deserve for me to take this out on him. It wasn't his fault there were wolves giving me trouble.

"Aubrey hates me, and Craig is a dick," I finally said.

His lips twitched with a smile, but he held it back. "Why do you think Aubrey hates you?"

"She just practically told me to my face."

He frowned. "That doesn't sound like her."

I threw my hands in the air and began pacing his office. "She said Peyton got kicked out of the pack because I didn't like her. That I'm just some bitch you're sleeping with."

His jaw tensed, and his eyes turned hard. "She called you a bitch?"

I just nodded.

He shook his head and spun around. "I'll go have a talk with her."

I rushed over as he moved to leave his office. "No, don't do that! Then she'll think I ran to tell on her."

He turned around, jaw still clenched and the impressive muscles in his arms tight and defined. "I'm not going to let her speak to you like that."

I let my head fall forward. "I can handle being called a bitch, Abraham. It's not like she hurt my feelings."

Much.

He walked over and used a rough finger to tip up my chin. "I don't care if she didn't hurt your feelings. You're my mate and the future alpha of this pack and she's going to respect that and respect you or she can leave."

I shook my head. "That's exactly what she's expecting to happen. If you don't like the alpha's mate, you get kicked out. We can't prove her right."

He studied my eyes for a long time before he sighed and looked away. "I suppose that wouldn't set a good precedence, would it?"

"No. It wouldn't. She doesn't need any more ammo."

He took a deep breath and turned to lean his back against the door. "What are we gonna do then?"

The word *we* sent a little thrill through me.

I walked into his space and wrapped my arms around his waist. "I'll just have to prove her wrong. I'll have to show the pack that I'm worthy of being their alpha, just like you did."

His hands slid to my hips, and he pulled me closer. "How are we gonna do that?"

I had to bite my lip to hold back a smile. There was that *we* word again. It felt nice. Knowing we were a team. Whatever happened to me happened to him, too. We'd get through this like we'd gotten through everything else.

I reached up and kissed his lips. "I'll figure something out, I guess."

He dipped his head and kissed me again. "So, your appointments didn't go well today?"

"Actually, they weren't that bad. At least until I had to talk to Craig." Even saying his name made the blood froth in my veins.

He kissed me again and pushed off the door. "Come sit and tell me about it." He took my hand and led me around his desk where he lifted me onto the surface and took a seat in his chair. He rolled himself close enough that he could wrap his big hands around my knees. "What happened with your first appointment?"

I suppressed a shiver as his thumbs drew circles on my legs. "Um, that was Maddy."

"Uh huh. What happened with her?"

He was still rubbing my legs, and I was having trouble concentrating. I swallowed. "Um. She was having a problem with her neighbor."

"What kind of problem?"

"He's been working in his driveway and blaring music late at night. It's been keeping her up."

"Hmm, that *is* a problem. Did you come up with a solution for her?"

I nodded and closed my eyes as his hands wandered higher. "Um. Yeah. I told her we'd implement some quiet hours."

His hands paused what they were doing, and I cracked an eye to see him looking at me strangely. "Quiet hours?"

I shrugged. "Yeah. They can be from like ten p.m. to eight a.m. while most people are sleeping. It makes sense for a community this size to have rules like that."

He sat back in his chair, a thoughtful look on his face.

"You don't agree?" I asked quietly. This was my first test as an alpha and I was nervous he'd think I did a bad job. Maybe I wasn't really cut out to lead.

He shook his head. "No, I do. That's a great idea, El. We should have had something like that in place a long time ago."

I perked up, my lips spreading into a smile. "Really?"

He sat forward again and ran his hands up my thighs to where they'd been before. "Yeah, baby. You did real good."

My smile couldn't be contained, and my cheeks were already starting to ache.

"What about the second appointment? What did Elliot want?"

"Oh, he was complaining about how much Craig wanted to charge for an oil change. For whatever reason, he doubled his prices."

Abraham frowned. "What's going on with that?"

I shook my head. "No idea. And talking to him got me nowhere."

His hands slid up and down my thighs again. "How did that go?"

I leaned back and rested my hands on the desk under me. "I asked him to explain why he'd increased his prices that much, but he said they were his clients and he'd charge them what he wants."

"And what did you say?"

I shrugged. "I told him if he couldn't charge a reasonable price that we'd find a new pack mechanic."

Abraham froze again. "You did?"

I paused too. "Um. Yeah. Was that wrong?"

He stood up and moved closer until his hips were between my legs. His head dipped down, and he pressed his lips against my neck. "No. That's exactly what you should have done."

I gasped as he nipped my skin. "Oh, okay then. Good." I brought my hands up to his thick arms and slid my fingers beneath the sleeves of his shirt.

"What else did you say?" he mumbled against my neck.

What did I say?

It was so hard to concentrate when I was being eclipsed by Abraham. He was everywhere, all over my body and under my skin. I shivered again as his hands slid beneath my shirt to circle my waist.

"Um. I told him I'm the future alpha of the pack and that he had to do what I said."

Abraham groaned and pressed his hard length between my legs. "Mmm. What else, baby?"

His hands wandered from under my shirt to beneath the waistband of my pants. He slid them around behind me and cupped my butt, dragging me closer to him.

"Um. That's about it. I think the last thing I said to him was to drop his prices, or he's done here."

Abraham's hands clenched where they held me, and I gasped again.

"What's going on?" I breathed, my fingers tracing the muscles of his broad shoulders.

He kissed down my neck and up the other side. "Hearing you talk like an alpha is so fuckin' hot."

My lips curled into a grin. "Really?"

"Mmm. I'm rock hard right now."

Heat rushed between my legs and my head fell back to give him better access.

"I don't understand." I whimpered as he nipped the skin on my chest.

He pulled back slightly until I could see his heated blue gaze. "You're so sexy when you're being all authoritative." He pulled me closer and ground his erection into me. "If I'd been with you, I probably would have fucked you right there in old Craig's driveway."

I laughed, but it fell breathy and soft from my lips. "If I'd known picking up alpha duties would turn you on like this, I'd have done it a long time ago."

He shook his head. "I get hard every time I'm in the same room as you. You don't need to do anything extra to turn me on."

My smile was smug. "That sounds like a problem. How are we gonna fix it, baby?"

He growled and pressed into me harder, making my hips buck against him. "You know when you say that word it makes me want to fuck you."

I leaned back on his desk again and shrugged a shoulder. "I don't see what's stopping you."

He growled again and pulled me upright so he could ravage my mouth. His busy hands pulled at my clothes and, soon, I was sitting on top of his desk completely naked. He ripped his lips away from mine and took a step back, his chest heaving. With his eyes locked on mine, he reached for the hem of his shirt and pulled it over his head.

For the hundredth time, I wondered how I'd gotten so lucky.

Abraham was stunning. So fit and big and powerful. He took my breath away. I watched through heavy-lidded eyes as he slowly pulled his pants and boxers down and kicked them aside.

"Spread your legs," he grunted.

I complied immediately.

He surged forward and reclaimed my lips as his hands positioned my hips and he sank his hard length into me.

Damn. How did the sex keep getting better?

I kissed him hard as he pressed into me inch by inch until he was in all the way. I felt so full, but I wanted more. We were so in sync that I didn't have to tell him I was ready, Abraham just knew. He pulled his hips back, sliding out of my slick center before thrusting forward again.

We built up a good tempo as I fought to keep up with him. Finally, I gave up and just leaned back, propping myself up on my hands and letting Abraham take over. He pumped into me furiously as I held on and felt my orgasm build inside me.

Abruptly, he pulled out and took a step back.

"Stand up and turn around."

When I did what he asked, he put a hand on the middle of my back and gently pushed until my chest was pressed against his desk with my butt in the air. His hands slid down my sides to wrap around my hips and then cup my bottom.

"You're so goddamn sexy."

I closed my eyes and lost myself in the anticipation.

He stepped closer again, and I felt his tip nudge me from behind. He lined us up, and with one great thrust, slid all the way inside me. I gasped loudly, my body clenching around him.

He pulled out and then pressed forward again, harder than before.

"Fuck, El. What are you doing to me?"

I couldn't answer, could barely see as he pounded into me from behind.

"I can't focus. I can barely do my job. Can't even hold a conversation because all I can think about is the next time I get to fuck you."

I moaned beneath him and reached up to grip the edge of the desk.

"Knowing you're in the same house as me, that I can have you up here, naked and spread across my desk like this whenever I want is enough to drive me out of my fuckin' mind."

Somehow, his thrusts got harder and deeper, and I knew I was seconds away from detonating.

"I need you so bad, baby. Need you every fucking second of every day. I'll never get enough."

"Me too," I gasped beneath him. "I need you too."

"I know what you need," he growled. "My girl needs to come. Isn't that right?"

I nodded frantically. "So bad," I said, my voice cracking.

With renewed efforts, he slammed into me, his thighs slapping against mine and filling the room with the sound.

His hands slid from my hips, one reaching up to cup my breast and the other wrapping around to circle my clit.

"Oh, Abe."

"That's right, baby. Are you ready to come?"

I nodded again.

He pulled out and rotated his hips before sliding back inside harder than ever. I could feel the coil deep in my belly tighten, threatening to snap at the slightest provocation. And then, Abraham pinched my nipple and my clit simultaneously and I exploded around him, my orgasm almost blinding me.

I moaned and whimpered, completely at a loss for words as Abraham chased his own release. Finally, he stilled, his hands pinching harder for a second before he shuddered and spilled himself inside me.

We stayed like that for a long time as we both fought to catch our breath and regain our equilibrium. Abraham recovered first, and he leaned down to kiss my spine before pulling me from the desk and into his arms.

He kissed the top of my head and sighed. "Fuck, that was good."

I giggled and pressed my lips against his bare chest. "It always is."

Would things stay like this between us? Abraham said that the bond between fated mates never fades. Did that mean we'd always be this insatiable? That I'd always feel so out of control and giddy around him?

Damn, I hoped so.

Chapter 7

It was a long time later, and we were still naked and cuddling on his office chair. I was so sated and comfortable, I was finding it hard to make myself move. I sighed deeply, and he smoothed some hair off my forehead and kissed my neck.

"What's up, baby?"

My lips twitched at his pet name. He always talked about what it did to him when I said it, but it was the same for me when that word fell from his lips. It drove me crazy.

"I'm just thinkin' about all the things I need to do when all I want is to stay here with you."

He kissed my head. "I know what you mean. I'm supposed to be meeting with some of my enforcers soon."

I sighed again. "So, we can't stay like this for the rest of the day?"

He chuckled beneath me. "If I had it my way, we'd spend every day like this."

I shook my head and giggled. I knew he wasn't lying either. Every morning, it was a struggle to tear ourselves apart. A struggle I was happy to put up with, but still a struggle.

I took a deep breath and sat up on his lap. "I guess I should find my clothes before your enforcers walk in on us like this."

He growled low and his hands clenched around me. "That would not be in their best interests."

I peeled myself off him and went looking for my clothes. Considering the fact that I'd been barely cognizant when he'd torn them off me, it took a while to locate all the missing pieces. When I was dressed, I turned to him, still naked in his office chair, watching me

I cocked a brow. "You know I don't want your enforcers to see you naked either. Who knows how many of them would prefer to see you over me?"

He laughed and shook his head. "They've seen it all before. And I'm pretty sure they're all straight."

I shrugged. "Until they get a good look at you. Then, who knows?"

He laughed again. "You really think that highly of me, baby?"

I crossed the room to stand before him. Leaning over, I put my hands on the arms of his chair and waited until he was looking at me. "You're literally the most breath-taking man I've ever seen in my life. I can't imagine anyone with a pulse not having at least a little flame for you."

He rolled his eyes and pulled me onto his lap. "You're crazy."

I wrapped my arms around his neck. "Yeah. Crazy in love with you."

It was a cheesy attempt at lightening the mood, but it had the opposite effect. His eyes got all soft and serious as he cupped my face in his rough hand. "I don't think you know what hearing those words from you does to me."

I turned my head and kissed his palm. "It's the same for me, baby."

He growled and pulled me closer on his lap. "You keep talkin' like that and I'm gonna lock that door and blow off the rest of my afternoon."

I gave him a peck on the lips and hopped up. "No, sir. We've both got things to do and they don't involve lustin' and thrustin'."

He threw his head back and laughed loudly, the sound filling the room. "Holy shit, that was a good one."

I shot him a wink. "I've been researching."

A smile was still stretched across his handsome face. "I like it."

I rolled my eyes. "You would."

"So, when do we get to lust and thrust again?" he asked, his lips twitching with a grin.

"I told you earlier, not until after dinner."

He raised a brow. "I know what you said, but clearly you're bad at sticking to your guns."

I crossed my arms over my chest. "Or maybe you're really persuasive."

He shrugged a single shoulder. "Maybe."

I shook my head and took a couple steps backward. "I need to look over some documents Callie gave me, so you need to put the bedroom eyes away."

"You're helping Callie again?"

"Yeah. She's got court coming up and wanted me to look over what her lawyer drafted."

"You seem to be helping her out a lot lately."

I shrugged and toed the carpet. "I've got nothing else goin' on."

He rose from his chair and crossed the room to pull me into his arms. "Don't worry about it, babe. You've got plenty of savings and no living expenses. You don't need to take a position somewhere unless you really want to."

I arched a brow at him. "I don't have any living expenses because you refuse to accept rent from me."

He was already shaking his head. "Of course I'm not accepting rent money from you."

I blew out a breath. "At least I still get to pay for my cell phone and credit card bills."

He pursed his lips. "Only because you won't give me access to your accounts."

I shook my head. "I'm not letting you completely support me. Just allowing me to live here for free is more than enough."

He rolled his eyes. "Allowing you to live here? Baby, I had to beg you for months to move in with me."

I patted his bare chest, his skin warm and smooth beneath my palm. "And look. Your efforts paid off. I'm right where you want me."

He dipped his head to the crook of my neck and pulled me closer. "I could think of a few places I'd rather you be right now. Like on my cock."

I shivered in his arms and had to take a few deep breaths before I could respond without my voice cracking. "Yes, well, we'll have time for that later." I slid from his grasp and took a few steps back. I needed to keep my distance if I had any hope of us getting anything done the rest of the afternoon.

He sighed and crossed his arms over his chest. "Where are you going to work on Callie's stuff?"

I shrugged and took another step back. He looked like he was going to let me leave, but he could also change his mind at any moment, and I had to create as much space between us as possible while he was distracted.

"Um, the kitchen, I guess."

Although, if Aubrey was still down there, I'd be finding a new place to work. I'd had about enough of her for one day already.

He frowned. "You could work in here."

I pursed my lips and cocked my head. "Abraham McCoy. You know damn well neither of us would get any work done if I was in here."

He shook his head. "I know. You're insatiable."

I laughed and took another step away from him. "It's not a big deal. I could work in the conference room, too."

"You need an office of your own. Maybe we could turn your old bedroom into one for you."

"Really?"

"Of course, baby. This is your home now. I want you to have everything you want here."

My heart thumped unevenly as I crossed the space between us. I couldn't not kiss him. With my arms around his neck, I reached up on my tiptoes and pressed my lips against his. When I finally pulled away again, we were both out of breath and his eyes were glassy. "What was that for?" he asked.

I kissed his chin before taking another couple steps backward. "That's for being an amazing fiancé."

He ran a hand across his mouth, his eyes bright. "You know, I kinda like the sound of that."

"Fiancé?

He nodded.

"Well, that's what you are, right?"

He shrugged. "We just don't use that word. We don't propose with rings either."

I frowned. "Then, why did you?"

"I knew it's what you'd want. I did it to make you happy."

My chest grew warm, and I covered the distance between us again to wrap my arms around his broad shoulders. Would I ever reach the bottom of my love for him? Would I ever stop being amazed by the person he was?

When I pulled away, there was a brilliant smile on his face. "Was I right? Does it make you happy?" he asked softly.

I shook my head. "You make me happy."

His smile softened as he tucked a lock of blonde hair behind my ear. "You know what I can't wait for?"

"What?"

He leaned close. "I can't wait until you call me your husband."

My stomach clenched. "Is that not a werewolf term either?"

64

He shook his head, his soft hair brushing against me. "No. We only use the word *mate*."

"Then why would you want me to call you husband?"

He pulled away and wrapped a hand around the back of my neck. "Because I want to be *your* husband."

My heart melted at his words. Would I ever stop being surprised by how sweet he was? I hoped not.

I reached up and kissed him again, but when he moved to deepen it, I pulled away with a smile. "Mr. McCoy. None of that."

His head fell forward with a sigh. "Okay, okay. I'll behave."

I laughed and turned to leave. When I made it to his door, I looked back and gave him one last perusal. He really was stunning.

"Put some clothes on before I have to fight one of your enforcers for you."

He rolled his eyes. "Not funny, El."

"Not kidding, Abraham."

He huffed out a breath and shook his head. "You better get out of here before I change my mind."

I gave him a cheeky smile and a mock salute. "Yes, sir. See you later, sir."

"You drive me crazy."

I blew him a kiss. "But you love it."

"I love *you*."

I opened his door and turned to give him another smile. "I love you too."

Closing the door behind me, I hoped he had the sense to put on some clothes. I wasn't kidding when I said I didn't know how anyone could look at the man and not want him. I sure as hell could barely control myself.

I walked over to our suite and took a quick shower. After that, I grabbed my laptop and the stack of papers Callie had given me and headed downstairs. When I made it to the kitchen, it was mercifully empty, so I took a seat and booted up my computer. As it loaded, I took another glance at the documents from her lawyer and rolled my eyes. There were more than a few mistakes in there and I was sure that meant his data wasn't sound either.

When my computer was ready, I hopped on to Google and began researching the Blue Ridge Parkway conservation efforts. Just as I'd suspected, some of his figures were off. I sighed and opened up a Word document. At that point, I might as well just re-write the whole thing myself. Despite what little knowledge I had of environmental law, I was sure I could do better with some research and effort.

The hours passed as I zipped through the internet and typed up what I found. There were some things I'd need to check with Callie, but overall, I was pretty proud of what I'd accomplished so far.

I opened up my email to send her a copy of what I'd gotten done when I took a look at my inbox. There were several unopened messages sitting at the top that looked more like neon signs than simple black letters. I took a deep breath and clicked on the first one.

Ms. Montgomery,

We are excited to offer you a coveted position in our law firm.

Blah, blah, blah.

I clicked on the one after that.

Ms. Montgomery,

It is with great honor that we welcome you to Jackson and Jackson Law Firm.

I sighed and closed that email too.

There were at least three others like it in my inbox and I hadn't read any of them either.

I didn't know what my problem was, but none of those job offers appealed to me. Maybe I was being picky. Maybe I was being difficult. But the last thing I wanted to do was join another law firm like Hildebrandt &

Moore. Don't get me wrong, I appreciated everything they did for me and I spent quite a few good years there.

But that was the old Elizabeth. The one who put her career above everything else. The one who didn't mind working sixty-hour weeks. The one who had nothing better to do than focus on her job.

That wasn't me anymore.

Now, the most important thing in my life was Abraham, with his sisters and our pack coming in as a close second and third. I had friends, and a family, and love. Things that mattered way more to me than a spot at a prestigious law firm.

Besides, I wasn't sure I even wanted to still be a lawyer.

It was all I cared about for so long, but practicing criminal law had begun to weigh on me. I didn't care about the money or the notoriety. I cared about justice and doing what was right. I couldn't always do that at my old job.

I didn't know what I wanted to do, but I knew I needed to do something. Shuffling around the lodge all day every day was getting old really fast. Despite the fun I had with Abraham every afternoon, I wanted more. I wanted to feel useful. Like I was doing something with my life.

I also wanted the independence.

Abraham wouldn't let me pay to live there, but I still needed to make money of my own. I needed to rely on myself. Just the thought of asking Abraham for money to buy something made my stomach curdle.

I knew I'd come a long way from the stubborn woman who never accepted help from anyone, but she was still in there somewhere. And it would be over her cold, dead body that she relied on a man for everything.

I just needed to figure out what it was that I wanted.

"Hey, Ellie! I've been looking all over for you."

I picked my head up to see Callie walking toward me. "Hey. I was just about to send you an email."

Her eyes widened. "What did you do?"

I gave her a tight-lipped smile. "I might have re-written the whole document from scratch."

She sighed and took a seat on the bench next to me. "I didn't ask you to do that."

I spun to face her with my hands in the air. "I know, and if you don't want to use what I wrote, I totally won't blame you. I barely know what I'm talking about, but this guy?" I picked up the papers she'd given me from her other lawyer. "Seems to know even less. All it took was one Google search to discredit half of what he has in here."

She sighed again and leaned over to prop her head up in her hand. "It was that bad, huh?"

I shrugged. "Pretty much."

She turned to place both hands on her face and took a deep breath. "We need to let him go. I'm not going to let some idiot come in and mess up all our hard work."

"That would probably be for the best. He doesn't seem very competent."

She blew out a deep breath and turned to me. "I really appreciate all your help, Ellie."

I smiled. "Anytime."

It felt good to be useful. To stretch my intellectual muscles again. Honestly, even trudging through the research had been kind of fun. I guess I missed being a lawyer more than I thought.

Chapter 8

"You know, I've been thinking about something lately and I wanted to run it past you," Callie said as she scanned through the document I'd written up.

We'd gone into the conference room to print it out and Callie had sat in the kitchen for the past fifteen minutes, reading what I wrote while I nervously watched her.

"Oh, yeah? What's that?"

She peeked a pale blue eye above the page she was reading. "I was thinking you could work with us in a more permanent capacity."

I frowned and shook my head. "Callie, I don't know anything about what you do."

She set the papers down. "You could learn though, couldn't you?"

I opened my mouth but shut it again before I could say anything.

She was right. I could learn. And to be honest, the research I'd done for that document had been kind of fun.

But that was neither here nor there.

"I'm not an environmental lawyer. I'd be just as helpful as someone straight out of school. What you guys do is too important. You don't want to work with me and have me screw it all up for you."

Callie shook her head, her curly hair swishing around her pretty face. "You may be new to the world of environmental law, but you're a phenomenal lawyer. I've heard Abey talk about your win ratio and I know you were successful practicing criminal law. There might be a learning curve, but what can it hurt?"

I sighed. "It could hurt everything you're working towards. Why don't you just find another lawyer? There's got to be someone better than the last guy you worked with."

Callie shrugged. "I could find another lawyer, but I want to work with you. I trust you and I know you're super smart. I'd be crazy not to ask you to be a part of our team."

My stomach was churning as her words flitted through my head.

Work as an environmental lawyer? I'd never imagined that. Not once had I stopped to think about a career down that path and it stumped me.

But hadn't I enjoyed working with Callie that day when she was staying in Raleigh with me? We'd visited a bunch of lakes and streams to test the water quality near fracking sites. I'd learned more that day about the threats to our planet than I had in my entire life.

Did I want to make a career out of that?

It sure sounded a lot better than criminal law. And it wasn't a secret that I'd been dragging my feet about selecting a new firm to work for. Maybe that was because it really wasn't what I wanted to do anymore. Wasn't what I was supposed to do.

Maybe my future was working with Callie. Maybe I could use my degree to actually help. To make a difference. To make a positive impact.

But I was still woefully unprepared.

"I really don't know, Callie. I feel like my lack of knowledge would be more of a liability than anything else."

She shook her head again. "I can teach you anything you need to know. The rest you can figure out through research." I was sure the doubt was still clear on my face, so Callie took a breath and reached out to cover my hand with her own. "Just promise me you'll think about it. That's all I'm asking."

I let out a deep breath and gave her a nod. "Okay. I'll think about it."

Callie pulled her hand away and clapped softly. "Yay!"

A smile tugged at my lips. "I only said I'd think about it."

She waved my words away. "Yeah, but I know you'll eventually realize what a great idea it is. And we'd get to work together! How much fun would that be?"

If I was being honest, that sounded like a hell of a lot of fun. Instead of being one of few women in a firm full of old, blustering men, I could work with my friend. My future sister. That alone made me want to just tell her yes.

But I'd think about it and talk to Abraham and we'd see. I didn't want to jump into anything without being sure. I'd hate to let Callie down, but I needed to do what was right for me.

I wanted to work somewhere I felt appreciated, where I knew my efforts were for the greater good and not just to line someone's pockets or help a criminal get away with something. I wanted to look myself in the eye at the end of the day and know I was doing something worthwhile with my time.

Callie's offer sounded better by the minute.

"Plus!" she yelled, breaking me out of my thoughts. "We just rented some new office space downtown. Abey's starting renovations on it this week and I know we can carve out space for another office for you."

"That's great, Callie! You've been working out of the lodge this whole time, right?"

She nodded with an exasperated roll of her eyes. "It's been a real pain, but we were short on funding. We finally came up with enough to put down first and last on a spot in town and we're dying to get in there."

"Who's we?"

Callie turned to face me, folding her knee onto the bench. "Well, there's me and Katie, and we recently brought on Matt, too, but don't worry, there's enough space for all of us there."

I hadn't ever worked in such a small office before. I wondered what it would be like to work at a place that intimate. And with so many women. That would be a huge change for me, and I was starting to like the idea more as the minutes ticked by.

I opened my mouth to ask her some more questions when Del strolled into the kitchen with a wide smile on her face.

71

"How's it hangin', ladies?"

Callie scoffed. "We don't have anything *hanging*, Del."

The spunky musician smirked and stepped up beside Callie. She reached out and gave one of Callie's boobs a quick poke. "That's not what it looks like from here."

Callie slapped her hand away and turned to her with furious eyes. "My boobs do not hang, Delilah."

Del rolled her eyes and took a seat on the bench behind us. "How would I know? You're always all buttoned up. I don't think I've seen your cleavage since we were teenagers. You're such a prude."

Callie straightened her modest top and glared at her sister. "Just because I don't walk around with my tits spilling out of my shirt doesn't make me a prude."

Oh, jeez.

If this was what it would have been like growing up with sisters, maybe I was lucky I was an only child.

Del opened her mouth to argue back, but I cut in.

"Okay, ladies. Let's break it up."

I felt like a referee in that house sometimes, but I secretly adored it. I loved the banter, the arguments, the sibling quarrels. It was so different from the way I grew up. Such a contrast to the way I'd spent the last several years of my life. I'd had a pretty lonely existence before I tumbled into the McCoys lives and now everything was different.

"What are you two doin' in here, anyway?"

"El was looking over a document for me that I'm supposed to submit to the courts in a couple days, and I was just trying to get her to agree to come work for me."

Del's eyes lit up. "Ellie, that's a great idea!"

I shrugged. "I'm still thinking about it."

Del waved a hand at me. "What's to think about? Can you imagine a better boss than Callie?"

I really couldn't.

"I just don't know anything about environmental law. I don't know how helpful I'll be."

Del scoffed. "You could learn, right?"

I sighed. They all had the same argument. They all believed it was just a matter of me doing a little studying and I'd be just as good as an environmental lawyer as I was a criminal one.

Maybe they were right. And I knew from experience that Callie was a patient and informative teacher. Maybe I could pick up a few textbooks and do some research. It would at least help me decide if this was the path I wanted to go down. And at the very least, it couldn't hurt, right?

I sighed again. "I don't know. I'm still thinking about it," I repeated.

The sisters exchanged a conspiratorial look, and I knew I was outnumbered and about to be ganged up on. Living with those women for the past month had taught me a lot. And one thing I knew, you didn't want to be on the other end of a McCoy shakedown. If they had their minds set on something, you'd better get out of the way or get run over.

Knowing I needed to change the subject before they started in on me, I blurted out the first thing I could think of. "Callie, did you find out anything having to do with what we were talking about earlier?"

Del scooted closer. "Ooh, what were you talkin' about?"

I bit my lip and looked at Callie. I didn't particularly want to air my dirty laundry, but I knew it was only a matter of time before she found out. There were no secrets in the McCoy family and very few in the pack. I could either tell her myself or have her hear from someone else.

With a quick look around the kitchen, I saw we were alone–a rare occurrence in the lodge. I slid closer to Del and lowered my voice, knowing that, even though it looked like we were the only ones around, that didn't mean someone couldn't overhear what we were talking about if I wasn't careful.

"Callie was looking into this whole fated mates business."

Del frowned. "What about it?"

I sighed. "She's trying to find out if there's been another instance of a bitten wolf being a born wolf's fated mate."

Del's brows were still furrowed as I watched her put the pieces together. Finally, her eyes met mine. "You don't think you're Abey's mate?"

I looked away from her, the floor between us suddenly very interesting. "I don't know, Del. It doesn't make sense, does it?"

She made a humming noise and leaned back against the table behind her. "You mean because you were bitten you shouldn't have been fated to be with Abey."

I finally met her eyes. "Exactly."

Del nodded slowly. "But you two have all the signs."

I sighed again and rubbed at my temples. It felt like there was a headache brewing. "I know we do, but that doesn't explain how it's possible that we were fated."

"She's afraid Abey's real fated mate might show up one day," Callie added.

I shot her a glare, but she just shrugged.

Del frowned again. "I guess that would bother me, too." We were all quiet for a moment, letting the words settle around us. Finally, Del spoke back up, "So, what are we doin' about it?"

I had to bite back a smile. There was that *we* word again. It felt nice knowing I wasn't alone in this. I always knew I had Abraham on my side, but seeing I had his sisters too was amazingly comforting. For the first time in my life I had a support system. A framework of friends and family that would stand beside me through anything. I'd never felt more loved and accepted in my life.

"I've been doing some research but haven't found much."

I turned to look at Callie. "Really?"

There had to be something. Someone had to have heard of this before. We couldn't be the first bitten and born wolf to be fated, right?

But what if we were?

What if this had never happened before?

My stomach clenched as the questions kept rolling through my head.

What if that meant we weren't really fated? What if that meant we'd been wrong? What if that meant I wasn't really Abraham's, and he wasn't really mine?

I felt like I was going to be sick.

"Why don't y'all ask Will?"

My eyes snapped to Del. "What?"

She shrugged. "He's old as dirt. He's probably the best resource we've got."

"Delilah," Callie chastised. "Don't talk about him that way."

Del's eyes widened slightly. "What? He is. You think it's news to him how many rings he's got around his stump?" She rolled her eyes.

Callie shook her head in exasperation. "Yes, but we don't say things like that."

Del snorted. "You might not, but I do."

The girls continued to squabble while I thought through what she'd said. Why hadn't I thought to ask Will before? He was the original werewolf, the man who first harnessed the power of the wolf. He'd been alive for thousands of years, and if there was anyone who could help us, it would be him.

"Del, that's a great idea," I said, cutting into the middle of their argument.

She turned to me, her pink-streaked hair flying. "Of course it's a good idea."

I rolled my eyes but smiled. Del really was a trip. "Does anybody know where he is?"

"He spends a lot of time in the theater room," Callie offered.

I wouldn't have pegged the original werewolf as a movie lover, but what did I know?

I closed my laptop and stood up.

"Where are you goin'?" Del asked.

I shrugged. "I might as well go talk to Will now. I'm sick of having this black cloud of indecision hanging over my head. I want to get this fated mates stuff sorted as soon as possible."

Both women nodded in approval. "Let me know what he says," Callie called after me. I gave them a little wave and made my way through the lodge and down into the basement.

It was fully furnished and had a few different rooms dedicated to leisure activities. The theater room was at the end of the hall, but voices coming from the pool room made me slow my steps.

Just as I got closer, the door swung open and Beatrice came storming out.

"Hey, Bea."

She stopped short and spun to face me. Her eyes were icy and, for a moment, it felt like we'd taken a hundred steps backward and she still hated me. Bea closed her eyes and shook her head. When she opened them again, they were slightly warmer than they had been.

"Hey, Ellie. What's going on?"

I shrugged. "Just looking for Will."

Bea's eyes frosted over again as she jerked a thumb over her shoulder. "He's in there."

I took a hesitant step forward. "Is everything okay?"

She sighed and shook her head, short, dark hair whipping around her face. "Yeah, I'm good. Just heading out. Did you want to get a session in tonight? Maybe we could spar after dinner."

Abraham's promises floated through my head and I gave her a wary smile. "I've got plans after dinner but I'm free tomorrow."

Bea sighed. "I kinda felt like fighting someone tonight."

I laughed. "I'm sure Huxley would be willing."

The corners of Bea's lips twitched. "Yeah, but then he whines like a bitch for the whole next day." She rolled her eyes. "You break a guy's leg once and you never hear the end of it."

I shook my head, biting my lips to hold back my smile. Beatrice was absolutely terrifying.

"Well, I'm not in the mood to mend any more broken limbs either, so I guess it's a good thing I can't train with you tonight."

One side of her mouth curled into a grin. "I wouldn't break your leg, Ellie. I save that shit for the guys."

"Well, I'm glad to hear that."

Bea's eyes wandered back to the door she'd just walked out of and I tried to identify the look in them. Was that wistfulness? Irritation? Or was I just imagining things?

"Anyway, I'm going for a run in the woods. I'll see you at dinner."

I watched her walk away, shoulders stiff and steps heavy. Whatever Will said or did to Beatrice, I hoped he knew what he was doing. I had real-life experience with being on her bad side and I knew it was not a fun place to be.

Chapter 9

I slipped into the billiards room and found Will at one of the tables, a stick between his fingers. As I watched, he drew the pool stick back and jabbed it forward, shooting the cue ball against a wall and into a striped one before it went rolling into a pocket.

"You're pretty good at that," I said as I crossed the distance between us.

Will looked up and smiled. "Granddaughter. How are you?"

My steps slowed as I made my way toward him. I hadn't had many interactions with Will in the month he'd been here. He always seemed to be surrounded by other pack members. I figured since I was the newest werewolf here, my questions for him were the least important. But in the few conversations I managed to have with him, he'd always called me *granddaughter,* which was strange because I usually heard him call everyone else *daughter* or *son.* Why was I different?

I finally made it to the pool table Will was playing on and leaned a hip against the edge. "I'm okay. I was wondering if I could talk to you about something, though."

Will shrugged and lined up another shot. "Of course you can. What is it?"

I took a deep breath and tried to figure out where to begin. "What do you know about fated mates?"

His eyes slowly rose from the table to meet mine, and when they did, I regretted my question. There was such a look of sadness and longing in them, it broke my heart. But then he blinked, and it was gone, and I wondered if I'd imagined it.

"I know they're a gift from the witch. I know they're rare."

"Wait a second. A gift from the witch? What does that mean?"

Will leaned back over the pool table and took a shot, eliminating another couple of balls. His eyes stayed on the green felt for so long, I wondered if I should take my question back.

Maybe Will wasn't the right person to talk about this. I mean, it was rumored that he and his heartbreak were the reasons behind fated mates. It couldn't be easy talking about the worst time of your life, even thousands of years later.

I shouldn't be here. Shouldn't be making him dredge up painful memories because I'm having commitment issues.

"You know what? Never mind. I'm sorry I bothered you," I said and spun on my heel to leave him to his game.

When I was about halfway across the room, he called out, "Wait, Elizabeth."

I stopped walking and slowly turned back toward him.

He had his pool stick resting on the ground, his hand wrapped around the top of it, looking like it was all that was keeping him upright. I knew I shouldn't have brought this up. It was unfair of me to ask him to go through it again.

"It's okay, Will. I'm sorry I asked. It was stupid of me."

He held up a hand and shook his head. "No, no. It's fine. I'll tell you anything you want to know." He jerked his head toward a stool near the table he was at and I walked over to it and took a seat. "You wanted to know about the witch, right?"

I shrugged. "You said fated mates were a gift from her? How's that?"

Will turned back to the pool table and lined up another shot as he talked. "The witch that gave me the power of the wolf kept watch over me long after our agreement. She saw what happened when Adela didn't shift."

"Adela?"

Will looked up at me briefly. "My wife."

I swallowed and nodded.

"The witch saw the devastation I wreaked in our village after my wife took her last breath. After that, she watched me still as I wove in and out of humanity over the years, hoping for death. Praying for the reprieve that the end would give me.

"That's when she decided to change the magic. To enhance it. She placed another spell on me that would ensure that when I met the woman I was fated to be with, I'd be allowed to die along with her someday."

My heart stopped in my chest. "She created fated mates so you could die one day?"

Will shrugged and took another shot. "Essentially."

"But why? Why would you want to die?"

He stood back up and leaned against his pool stick. "Imagine having to watch everyone you've ever known and everyone you ever will know die. One right after the other. The only constant is you and your inability to join them. To be free of this world. To finally rest. Now imagine doing that for millennia and I think you'll have your answer."

I was shocked speechless for a moment.

Whenever I thought about how old Will was, I imagined all the knowledge he'd accumulated over the years. The things he's seen and done and was a part of.

He'd witnessed the great pyramids of Giza climb toward the sky stone by stone. He'd watched the Roman Empire rise and fall. He's seen the industrial revolution change the world. Seen this age of technology bridge the gaps between every corner of the planet.

All of those wonderful things that came with living so long, and I never once stopped to imagine how lonely it would be.

Each time he met someone, he only had a number of decades with them before they were gone, and he had to start all over again. I couldn't imagine a life like that. One where I outlived everyone and everything around me. When life and death came and went every day, but I sat apart from it, completely untouched by time.

I cleared my throat. "So, she made it so you would someday find your fated mate and be able to live a normal life with her? And die when she did?"

Will nodded. "Essentially," he said again.

"So, what happened?"

Will's lips thinned, and he shot a look at the door. "Haven't found her yet."

Words escaped me again. After thousands of years and all the many places he'd been, he'd never found his fated mate?

"How is that possible?"

Will took a shot, the balls clacking together angrily. "I'm not sure." He shrugged. "Maybe it didn't work."

I shook my head. "But you're the reason there are fated mates, right? The magic came from you and flowed to the rest of us."

Will shrugged again. "That's what I think."

"Then how could it not work on you?"

Will sighed and stood back up to pin me with a look. "I'm not sure, Granddaughter, but I stopped looking long ago."

A tiny crack sliced through my heart. After all this time, Will deserved someone to love. Someone to grow old with. Someone to die with if that was what he wanted.

I could sense he didn't want to talk about his predicament anymore, so I changed the subject. "Have you ever heard of a bitten wolf being the fated mate of a born wolf?"

Will quirked his lips to the side and looked up at the low-hanging ceiling. "I don't believe I have."

My shoulders hunched as I sat back in the chair. If even Will hadn't ever heard of something like this happening, then what were the odds we were really fated? If the oldest person on the face of the Earth hadn't seen a situation like ours before, it was more proof that we were wrong.

I wasn't really Abraham's mate.

His real fated mate was out there somewhere, waiting for him. I was a placeholder. A stand-in.

This was the worst-case scenario.

I slid off the stool and took a shaky step toward the door. "Thanks for talking to me, Will. I'll see you around."

I'd just reached the door when Will called out to me. I turned to find him with both hands on the edge of the pool table, his knuckles white from strain. His jaw was clenched, and he was looking down, but finally, his dark eyes met mine.

"Just because Adela wasn't my mate by magic didn't make her any less mine. She was the love of my life. If you've found something worthwhile, fight for it. I know if there was a chance for me, I'd still be fighting for her."

His broken words matched the sadness in his eyes, and it was almost too much for me. My nose burned with tears, but I held them back. If anyone had a reason to cry in this situation, it was Will. The man who was still pining for a woman he lost thousands of years ago.

Was he right?

Did it not matter that we weren't fated?

I knew what I felt. Knew how much Abraham meant to me. I didn't need magic to keep me with him. Didn't need some witch's spell to solidify our relationship. Abraham was the one person in the whole world for me. I knew that from the depths of my soul. Mate magic or not, he was mine, and I was his.

That had to be enough.

I smiled. "Thanks, Will."

He shrugged. "My pleasure, Granddaughter. I'll see you tonight at dinner."

I nodded and left him there alone. As I walked back towards the stairs, I wondered why he spent so much time like that. It seemed he was always on the fringe of any group, as if he'd rather observe life than participate in it.

Was that a direct product of how long he'd been alive? Had he heard it all already? Seen it all? Was there nothing that excited him anymore? Nothing that entertained or amused him?

Will was an enigma, and the longer he hung around the lodge, the more questions he raised.

I'd just reached the end of the hall when Abraham appeared at the top of the stairs, a bright smile across his face. "I was lookin' for you."

I smiled and stood there as he descended the staircase. "Hey, baby."

He cleared the last step and wrapped an arm around my waist, dragging me into the nearest room and shutting the door behind us. My back was immediately pressed against the cool wood.

A growl rumbled through his chest and into mine. I dug my fingers into his thick hair and tugged as he kissed and nipped my skin. Finally, his lips found mine and everything else faded away.

The worry over this fated mates business.

The questions about the future of my career.

Even the sadness I felt for Will was all washed away by Abraham's presence. He had a way of doing that. Of blocking out everything but him. Everything but us.

Was that enough?

I knew he thought we were fated to be together, but what if we weren't? What if we just fit? If we just worked together. What if we were just plain old in love? Was that enough?

As he lined his hard body up with mine and his hands worshipped every inch he could reach, I knew it was.

It was plenty.

Finally, Abraham pulled his mouth away from mine. "What are you doing down here, anyway? I thought you were working with Callie?"

I struggled to catch my breath before answering him. "I already helped Callie and then I came down here to talk to Will."

Abraham took a half-step back. "What did you need to talk to Will about?"

Oh, damn.

I guess I shouldn't have admitted what I was really doing down there. Now, I either had to lie to him or admit that I was asking about fated mates. And if I did that, he'd know I was still skeptical about us and I knew that would hurt him.

So, I compromised.

"I was asking him some stuff about the wolf magic."

Abraham nodded and moved his lips back to my neck. "Oh, yeah?"

"Mmm hmm," I moaned softly as he sucked on my skin. "What are you doing down here?"

Abraham pulled back again, a smile spread across his face. "I came to find you for dinner, but then you called me the b-word and I got sidetracked."

My lips twitched with a grin. "The b-word? You mean bab–"

He covered my mouth with his big hand before I could finish. Abraham shook his head. "Don't say it. Not if you want to eat before I have you again."

I rolled my eyes but nodded to let him know I'd concede.

But where was the fun in that?

As soon as his hand was gone, my lips curled into a smirk. "I'm pretty hungry, but I'm always ready for you, baby."

He growled, but before he could wrap his arms around me again, I slipped through the door and ran up the stairs. I could feel Abraham just inches behind me and a crazed laugh spilled from my lips as I raced toward the main floor.

When I got to the top of the stairs, I flung the door open just as Abraham's hands found my hips and he jerked me back against his chest. "You ran from me?"

I was out of breath. "And you chased me."

"Because you ran."

I shook my head. "You would have kept me down there."

He pulled me closer. "You're damn right I would have."

I spun in his arms, fully prepared to have this little lovers' quarrel with him when someone turned down the hallway, headed right toward us. I smelled tobacco and knew it was Clyde even before I could make out his face in the dim lighting of the hall.

I tried to pull away from Abraham's hold, but he gripped me tighter.

"Cousin," he called to him.

Clyde lifted his head to look at us, his dark eyes darting back and forth. "Abraham. Elizabeth."

That was about the most I'd heard out of him in the past month.

Even though we'd all had some connection to Calvin, it goes without saying that no one was closer to him than his twin. That was why it was even harder for Clyde when he realized it had been his own brother who'd been killing women and dumping their bodies in the woods around the lodge.

Even worse, Clyde had been tasked with leading the investigation. He was supposed to figure out who the killer was, and it turned out, he'd been right beneath his own nose.

I couldn't image what would be worse. Finding out your brother was a serial killer, or losing him altogether. The betrayal had to be just as bad as the loss he felt.

That night in Charlotte hadn't left me, and I was sure it was the same for Clyde.

I'd almost died, and if Abraham hadn't gotten to me when he did, I probably wouldn't have made it. Calvin had caught me trying to escape the stone cottage he'd locked us in and lost his mind. He'd somehow deluded himself into believing we were fated mates and belonged together.

Apparently, the women he'd killed after he attacked me had just been substitutes for the real thing. My stomach still hurt thinking about it.

After Abraham had been forced to kill Calvin, I wasn't sure Clyde would ever forgive him. Even though his brother was a killer and a psychopath, they were still family. However, Clyde had seen the whole thing. Heard Abraham try to reason with him and watched as Calvin struggled until he snapped his own neck in Abraham's jaws.

Since that night, Clyde hadn't been the same.

He'd always been quiet and broody, but I hadn't heard him speak a full sentence in over a month. He kept to himself, only leaving his room in the lodge when he was on patrol, or for the occasional meal. It was clear he'd lost weight, and if the bags under his eyes were anything to go by, I was willing to bet he wasn't sleeping much, either.

I felt awful for him, but what could I do? Clyde hadn't been my biggest fan before all this had gone down, and I was sure nothing had changed. In fact, I was part of the reason his brother lost his damn mind in the first place. If he'd wanted to, I was sure he could have found plenty of blame to lay at my feet.

It didn't seem like he was angry, though, which was what I'd been used to from Clyde. Instead, it was almost like he'd given up. Like he no longer found any worthwhile part to his day. Nothing fazed him, nothing affected him, nothing mattered to him.

I didn't know how long he could keep that up, but I knew the whole family was worried about him. It wasn't my place, but I felt partially responsible and wished there was something I could do. Some way I could take away his pain, or at least ease it somehow.

But I knew a loss was something you had to deal with on your own. I just hoped he came out the other side of it intact.

Chapter 10

I rolled over again and tried to find a comfortable position, but it was no use. My mind was spinning, and I knew I wouldn't be getting to sleep anytime soon.

The day had been full of information and revelations, and I was having trouble keeping up. The list of things for me to worry about was endless, but there were a few items that bothered me more than the others. A few things I couldn't ignore, despite my best efforts.

At the top of the list was whatever was between Abraham and me. It was clear there was something there. Some deep profound well of love, but was that where it ended? Were we just like any other human couple who had the same chance to make things work as everybody else?

Or was there more between us?

I wanted to believe we were fated. Wanted to believe that the sickness I felt whenever I was away from him and the strength I got when he was near was all the proof we needed. But it wasn't that simple. There was still a whole list of reasons why us being fated was impossible, and I couldn't ignore them.

I wondered why Abraham was so quick to believe we were. It wasn't like he'd experienced it before and knew what it felt like. What it looked like. It wasn't like he could compare me to the last one he had. Werewolves only got one of those and he thought it was me.

I'll admit, I wanted to be his fated mate. I wanted to be the only one for him. The yin to his yang, the peanut butter to his jelly, but there were too many doubts to contend with. Still so much that was unknown and unbelievable about our love story.

To sum it up: we didn't make sense and I couldn't wrap my brain around it.

Those thoughts and more had me tossing and turning between the sheets for over an hour, and I didn't see any end in sight.

Abraham tightened his arm around my waist and pulled me closer to him. "I thought I sexed you to sleep." His voice rumbled in the quiet, dark room.

A smile tugged at my lips. "You definitely sexed me, but it doesn't seem like sleep is happening tonight."

Abraham hummed softly and propped himself up on an elbow. "What's goin' on, baby?"

I sighed and looked away. "I've just got a lot on my mind."

He used a thick, calloused finger to turn my face back toward him. "What's bothering you? Maybe I can help."

My heart beat faster in my chest as I looked up at his face in the dark room. Despite the lack of light, I could see him clearly. The strong jaw with light stubble across his tan cheeks, the blue eyes that were concerned and trained on me. He was so beautiful, it was sometimes hard to look right at him.

I studied him for a long time, not willing to admit what I'd been worried about because it would worry him too.

He was dead set on us being fated. The few times I'd brought it up had ended in arguments and I didn't want to go there again. Because, beneath the harsh words, I knew there was a lot of pain.

He was so sure of us. So unwavering. Nothing I said made any difference to him. When I mentioned a born wolf shouldn't be fated with a bitten wolf, he just told me we got lucky.

Lucky.

Like this was a slot machine in Atlantic City.

But I'd keep this to myself. I didn't have the energy to argue with him and I didn't have the heart to hurt him again.

Abraham tucked some hair behind my ear and leaned down to kiss my cheek. "Are you worried about the appointments you have comin' up tomorrow?"

Ugh. I hadn't been until he mentioned it.

I shrugged. "Maybe a little."

This alpha thing was still really new to me and I wasn't sure I was cut out for it. That I'd be able to rule the pack with Abraham.

He was such an effortless leader. He exuded this authority, this assurance. You only had to be in his presence for a few minutes to know he was someone worth following. Someone you could trust.

Did I have any of those qualities? Did my presence bring reassurance to our pack? Could anyone imagine following me like they did Abraham?

I knew I had a lot of work to do to prove myself to them, but what if I couldn't? What if I really wasn't alpha material? What if I became the leader of the pack and did more harm than good? These werewolves meant too much to me to let them down.

Abraham sighed, his breath blowing across my face. "You did so well today. Why are you worried now?"

I turned slightly so I could see him better. "Today, the problems were pretty easy. I didn't have to do much."

"El, I wouldn't have thought of the quiet hours thing. That was all you and it's a great idea."

"What would you have done?"

The corner of his lips twitched. "I would have gone and told Brad to quiet the fuck down at night and be done with it."

I giggled into his chest. "I guess it's a good thing for Brad that I was in charge of that issue."

He kissed the top of my head. "I guess it is."

I sighed and reached out to trace a pattern on the smooth skin of his chest. "You know, we never did figure out what we're gonna do about Craig and his price hikes."

"Did you have any ideas?"

I knew he probably had a solution in mind, but he wanted to hear my ideas first. Lucky for me, I'd been thinking about it all day and actually did have an answer to that particular problem.

I took a deep breath and looked up into his eyes. "I was thinking I could go and talk to Craig again tomorrow and see if he's changed his tune at all. If not, I thought we could ask Brad if he wants the position."

One of his dark brows rose. "McDermott?"

I shrugged. "We already know he works on cars. Maybe he'd want to do that for the whole pack."

Abraham was quiet for a long time while I chewed on my bottom lip.

Maybe that was a stupid idea. Maybe I really didn't know what I was doing. Maybe they were right, and I had no business being an alpha of the pack. Maybe–

"That's a great idea."

My eyes snapped to Abraham's. "Really?"

"Really, baby. I never would have thought of that."

I pulled away so I could see him clearly. "What would you have done?"

"I would have forced Craig to lower his prices."

I raised a brow. "And how would you do that? Beat him into submission?"

"Something like that."

I laughed and pushed at his chest. "You would not."

He sighed. "You're right. I wouldn't have beaten him. But I would have gone down there and forced him to charge a reasonable rate."

"You know what? You're right. I think we should go with your plan."

He shook his head. "Nope. We're doin' this your way."

"But why?" I whined.

"Because your way is a lot more fair. You're giving Craig the choice to fall in line or lose his position. He gets to make his own decision and then deal with whatever consequence comes from it."

I ducked my head and traced more patterns on his chest. "You really think it's a good idea? What if he's a dick again?"

His arm tightened around me. "Then you talk to me and I'll straighten him out."

I was already shaking my head. "I told you. You can't go around *straightening out* anyone who's mean to me. I need to stand on my own or they'll never respect me."

He sighed and dropped another kiss on my head. He was silent for a long time before he spoke again. "You're right. I don't like it, but I need to let you handle these issues on your own. The rest of the pack needs to see the strong independent woman I fell in love with. When they do, they'll follow you as easily as they follow me."

I blew out a deep breath but remained quiet. I wasn't as sure of my abilities as he was. Not at all. I was even less sure of the fact that the doubtful pack members would eventually come around.

Aubrey. Craig. Paul. None of them wanted me in that position. None of them wanted me to be alpha. Hell, they probably didn't even want me in the pack. It made me want to step back down. To tuck in behind Abraham and be the useless arm candy they thought I was. To just be *the bitch he's sleeping with* like Aubrey and Craig said.

But that wasn't me.

Elizabeth Montgomery never backs down from a challenge. Never lets someone else tell her what she can and can't do. Why would I start now?

A startling realization trickled through my head.

I'd never wanted something like I wanted to be accepted by the pack. Never had to prove my worth as a person or a leader. I was used to being doubted professionally, not personally.

Maybe that was why this was hitting me so hard. Maybe that was why I was having trouble sleeping. Maybe that was why I felt so insecure and out of sorts.

There was nothing I could do but keep pushing forward. Keep taking appointments and proving my worth. Keep standing beside Abraham as a united front. Keep breezing past the doubts and questions about the legitimacy of our relationship.

"Is there something else going on, El?"

I turned back to Abraham and found his dark blue gaze trained on me. "Huh?"

He smiled softly. "I can still see the gears turning in that pretty head of yours and I know the alpha appointments aren't the only thing bothering you. What's up?"

I sighed and looked away from him. Sometimes it was a blessing that he knew me so well, and other times, I wished I wasn't so transparent to him. Lucky for me, there were so many other things I was worried about, I didn't have to even bring up the fated mates issue.

I took a deep breath and turned to him again. "Callie offered me a position with her."

Abraham's eyes widened. "When did that happen?"

"This afternoon. She wanted me to look through some documents from her lawyer, and when I saw what a poor job he did, I just rewrote the whole thing myself. According to your sister, that means I'm qualified to work with her as an environmental lawyer." I shook my head at the absurdity of it all.

He nodded slowly. "Do you like helping Callie?"

"Yeah. It's interesting work and I like feeling like I'm doing something positive. That I'm helping in some way."

He smoothed some more hair off my forehead. "Then, why not go for it?"

I rolled my eyes. "Not you too." I took a deep breath and tucked in closer to him. "I was trained as a criminal lawyer. It's all I know. It's all I'm good at. I can't let Callie hand me the wheel when I don't even know how to drive."

"But you could learn, couldn't you?"

What was with these McCoy siblings? They all had the same response for me. They all thought it was just a matter of reading a few books and I'd be just as useful as an environmental lawyer as I was a criminal one.

"It's not that simple, Abraham."

He rolled us until I was hovering over him. "It could be, though. You're one of the smartest people I've ever met. If you put your mind to it, you could be the biggest asset Callie has. You'd be phenomenal at anything you want to do, baby. I don't know why you don't see that."

I looked away, couldn't bear to see the belief he had in me shining through his denim gaze.

Was he right though?

Could I learn what I needed to know to be helpful? Could this be a huge turning point in my professional career? Could this be the next chapter for me?

Hope built in my system, but I tamped it down. I didn't know anything yet. I didn't know if I had what it took. Didn't know if I could actually be useful to Callie's causes.

Was that even what I wanted to do with my life?

I sighed and looked back down at Abraham. "I'll tell you what I told Callie. I'll think about it."

His lips pressed into a thin line. "Thinking about it is what's keepin' you up, though."

I sighed again and hung my head. "I know."

He kissed my forehead and slid out from underneath me.

"Where are you going?" I asked.

"We're both going."

I sat up and watched as he slid on a pair of athletic shorts. "We're going somewhere?"

He nodded and tossed one of his big t-shirts at me. "Throw that on and let's go."

I did as he asked, but the questions continued to spiral through my head. "Abraham. It's past midnight. Where do you think we're going?"

He stopped in the middle of the room and turned to look at me. Damn, he was beautiful. So strong, and tan, and powerful, and big. I needed to keep my eyes above his collarbone or we weren't going anywhere.

"We're going to my favorite place to think."

His words tugged at me. A memory surfaced as I shoved my head through the shirt. "Are you talking about your lake?"

His lips pulled into a wide smile. "*Our* lake."

My answering grin wasn't far behind. "We haven't been there in a long time."

His eyes clouded, and he looked away for a moment. "I know the last time we were there was pretty traumatizing, but all that's in the past. There's no killer looking for you. No one stalking our woods anymore. It's perfectly safe and I think it'll really help you. Will you come with me?"

He held out a hand, but I was captivated by the look in his eyes. It was so hopeful, but still hesitant. How didn't he know already that I'd follow him anywhere?

I crawled out of bed and grabbed his hand. "Okay. Let's go."

Chapter 11

We ran across the lawn, the damp grass cool beneath my bare feet. Although, to be honest, we spent more time sabotaging each other than actually running. He'd tickle me, I'd pinch him in retaliation, over and over until we were both breathless with laughter.

When we reached the tree line, Abraham turned to me with a smirk and dropped his shorts. I watched the black jersey material slide down his powerful legs and pool at his feet. Swallowing harshly, my eyes trailed back up his body, stopping in all the most important places until I reached his face.

He was still sporting a lopsided grin, but now there was hunger in his eyes. "You better quit lookin' at me like that or we're not goin' anywhere."

I swallowed again. "But this was your idea."

He pressed his lips together and nodded once. "Which is why I'm still standin' over here. Come on. Let's shift before I change my mind."

I shook my head to clear it and tugged the baggy t-shirt over my head. A loud crack rang through the field and I knew Abraham was already in the midst of his shift. I followed suit and soon was standing on four legs instead of two, shaking my coat out.

"Ready?" he asked.

Instead of answering him, I darted into the woods, dodging trees and roots as I tried to create as much distance between us as I could. Abraham was impossibly fast and the only way to beat him was to get a good head start.

Some might call it cheating, but I called it a fair advantage.

"Cheater!" he yelled in my head as he chased after me.

See?

I didn't know if I was going in the right direction, but it didn't matter because, in seconds, Abraham would be on me. With my last reserves, I dug my feet into the soft forest floor and pumped my legs as fast as I could.

It didn't make a difference because his thundering footsteps were right behind me. I leapt over a small stream, but instead of landing on the other bank, I was tackled from the side and sent rolling down the hill.

Somehow, Abraham managed to take the brunt of our fall as we laughed and tumbled head over heels. When we finally came to a stop, we were both panting.

"You were going the wrong way," he said.

I laughed, which in wolf form sounded more like a coughing bark. *"You tackled me because I was going the wrong way?"*

"No. I tackled you because you were cheating."

"But you're so much faster than me. If I didn't get a head start, I'd have no shot."

He bared all his teeth in what was easily the biggest wolfy grin I'd ever seen. *"I am pretty fast, huh?"*

I laughed again and shoved him off me. *"You're impossible."*

He rolled to his feet. *"And you're a cheater, but I love you anyway."*

I shook my head. Playful Abraham was a brain scrambler. He was hard to resist on the best of days, but his silly comments and wide grin would bring any straight woman to her knees.

He jerked his head. *"The lake's in that direction."*

"Lead the way."

We started off running again, but this time, it was more of a jog than a sprint.

I'd been doing a lot more of this since I'd moved to Asheville. While I'd lived in Raleigh, it had been impossible to shift and spend time as a wolf. I limited myself to the full moon and the occasional angry outburst. Now, though, with all this land and no neighbors for miles and miles, I took full advantage.

There was something about running on four legs instead of two. Something about the pine-scented wind blowing past me and the soft thump of my paws on the ground. It made me feel connected to the world around me in a way I'd never felt before.

Running as a wolf allowed for a freedom I'd never experienced in my life. It was exhilarating and liberating, and I did it as often as I could.

While we ran, Abraham pointed out the general direction of the gem mine they'd found on his property. It was where he'd gotten the blue stone to go in my ring. Even though he'd taken me to visit the mine shortly after I moved out there, I knew I wouldn't be able to find it on my own. His property was too expansive, and I hadn't had enough time to explore yet.

We ran for a while longer and I smelled the lake before I could see it. Abraham led us to the rocky beach where he'd taken me on our first date.

It wasn't that long ago, but it felt like another lifetime. Abraham had been so sweet that day. So nervous. Back then, I hadn't known what I do today. That it was my last first date. That I was just starting out on this journey with the most amazing man I'd ever met. That I'd fall in love and plan a future with him in only a few short months from then.

It was crazy to think about how much had changed.

But with that first day at our lake, came thoughts of our last time here. We'd just wanted to get away for a little while and take some time for ourselves. What we hadn't known was the killer had murdered another woman and laid her in our path so we'd find her body on our way home. That was the last time we went there.

That was in the past though, and I needed to let it go. Needed to stop looking over my shoulder and jumping at loud noises. I needed to remember that the monster that plagued my nightmares was gone for good. That I was safe. That everything was going to be okay.

Abraham trotted over to the pile of rocks, and with a loud crack, shifted back into a human. He looked down at me and smirked. "Come on. Change back."

I looked at him incredulously. He expected me to shift into a human? A naked human? Out in the open like this? Had he lost his mind?

He laughed and walked over so he could scratch my head. I did my best to keep my eyes on his face, but damn, he was something to look at.

"Come on, baby. There's no one around for miles and I've never seen anyone even close to this lake before. No one will see you but me." His voice deepened with that last sentence and a chill raced down my spine.

I sighed and shook my head but willed myself back into a woman. When the transformation was complete, I propped a hand on my hip and shot him a look. "If someone even sneezes in a ten-mile radius, you're a dead man."

He laughed again and slung an arm around my neck, pressing a kiss to my temple. "You'll be fine, baby. I promise."

I huffed but let him lead me to the rocks we'd climbed up before. The other times I'd still been a human and needed his help to scale the rock face. Now, I looked forward to the challenge.

I stepped up to the boulders and searched for my first set of handholds. I gripped the rock and heaved myself up when Abraham wrapped his arm around my waist and pulled me down.

"What the hell, Abraham?"

He turned me around and set me down behind him. "El, I consider myself a strong man, but I know I'm not strong enough to climb up that rock behind your pretty little ass. It's best if I go first so I don't knock us both off when I can't keep my hands to myself."

I rolled my eyes but had to bite my lips to keep the smile off them. He was so absurd sometimes.

I watched Abraham climb up the rocks and did my best to emulate him. When we reached the top, I took a minute to admire the view again. No matter how many times I saw it, I knew it'd never stop taking my breath away.

Even in the dark, I could see the mountain peaks reflected in the water beneath us. A small stream cut through the boulder we stood on, trickling over the side and into the lake. It was pretty quiet, but the faint rustling of forest creatures sounded from below, just soft enough to be background noise. I sighed and wrapped my arms around my middle.

"It's so beautiful here," I said.

Abraham walked up next to me and put his hand around my hip, pulling me into him. "I know. I love it here."

"Why don't we come more often?"

He shrugged. "We can if you want."

"I think I do. You're right. This is the perfect place to clear my head."

He tugged on my hip and sat down behind me. "Come sit down, baby. Let's relax."

I let him pull me down between his legs, my back against his chest. He wrapped his arms around my shoulders and took a deep breath. We sat like that for a long time, just letting the warm breeze blow past us, quiet in our own thoughts.

Mine were centered on the perfect man behind me and his gaggle of sisters I'd come to love as my own. I wondered what he was like growing up. Was he silly with them like he was with me? Or serious like he had to be the rest of the time? Knowing how quickly he had to grow up, I figured it was probably the latter and it hurt my heart.

Finally, I broke the silence. "What were your parents like?"

He took a deep breath, his chest bumping into my bare back. "They were great."

I snuggled deeper into his embrace. "Tell me about 'em."

He took another big breath, and I wondered if this was painful for him to talk about. Maybe I shouldn't have brought it up.

"You don't have to if you don't want to," I added.

He leaned down and kissed the top of my head. "No, it's okay. I want you to know more about them." He squeezed me tighter. "They would've loved you."

My heart warmed and broke at the same time.

"My dad, Curt, was kind of strict, but also really fair. You always knew where you stood with him, you know? He always told you exactly what he expected of you and it was never more than you could handle. He was the strong, silent type. He was never the loudest one cheering you on, but he was there no matter what." He was quiet for a moment before adding, "But I think what I miss most are his Sunday breakfasts. No matter what we had going on, Dad would wake up early on Sundays and cook us all pancakes." He laughed softly. "We called him the Pancake Sensei."

I laughed too and waited a moment as the words settled around us. "He sounds like a great guy."

Abraham sighed. "He was the best."

"What about your mom? Her name was Lacy, right?"

He nodded against my head. "Aah, my mom. Where to begin?"

I could hear the sadness in his voice, and it made my heart pinch in my chest. I wrapped my arms around his and held on as tight as I could.

"I told you she loved to garden. She always had tons of fresh fruits and vegetables for us and, believe me, with five kids, she needed all the food she could get."

I could feel his smile against the side of my face.

"And she was a great cook. She even gave Nana a run for her money." He sighed, and his arms tightened around me. "She was also the sweetest woman I'd ever met. Never had a bad word to say about anyone. She was kind and so loving. Always helping whenever she could. She was the first one to show up at someone's door with soup when she heard they were sick, or load up a set of new parents with more casseroles than they knew what to do with, so they didn't have to worry about cooking."

He was quiet for so long I thought he was done, but then he spoke again.

"But I think my favorite part about them was how much they loved each other. If you'd asked my mom, she would've told you my dad hung the moon all by himself. They were so in love and, in turn, they loved us so much it felt bottomless. They were my best friends."

My nose burned with unshed tears, but I held them back. I had no right to cry in this instance. This was Abraham's family and his loss. But my heart still thumped painfully in my chest as I thought about everything he'd been through.

He took a huge breath and let it out slowly. "What about you? You never talk about your parents."

Damn. I guess I set myself up for that. I could already feel the muscles in my neck tensing. "What do you want to know?"

He paused a moment before craning his neck to look at me. "What's the matter?"

I sighed and looked away. "It's nothing. I just don't like talking about my parents."

He nodded against my head. "I know you told me they sent you away when you were young. That had to be hard."

I blew out a deep breath. "Yeah. That sucked."

He chuckled softly behind me. "What was it like living with them before that?"

I shrugged. "Lonely."

He hugged me tighter. "Because you were an only child?"

"I guess that was part of it. If I'd had a brother or sister, it probably wouldn't have been so bad when my parents blatantly ignored me."

He froze behind me. "Ignored you?"

I shrugged again. "Yeah. They were too busy with their own lives to worry about me."

"Then who took care of you?"

"Nannies."

"What about if you had a function at school? Parent teacher conference or a play or something?"

"Nannies."

His arms tensed around me. "Did you guys eat dinner together at least?"

I laughed but there was no humor in it. "That would be a no. My parents mostly drank their dinners, and I ate mine in the kitchen with the staff."

"You ate dinner with your parents' employees?"

I nodded. "It wasn't so bad. Those were the only real people in that house."

"What do you mean by that?"

I took a deep breath and tried to figure out a way to explain my shitty parents. "My mom and dad are all about appearances. It's the only reason they even had me. They'd been married for years and their friends and family were starting to ask questions about why they didn't have kids yet, so they had me. It was probably the biggest mistake of their lives."

Abraham's arms tightened before he spun me around to face him. "You are *not* a mistake."

I shrugged and looked away. "That's not how it felt."

He grasped my chin and turned my face to meet his. "El, you are the single greatest thing that has ever happened to me. I can't imagine a life without you. A world where your brilliance doesn't exist. If your parents weren't grateful for you, I'll make up for that tenfold."

The tears were back, and this time, one fell. It streaked down my face, warm and wet, before Abraham caught it with a rough finger.

"Why are you crying, baby?"

I sniffed. "Because you're so sweet. Because I'm so lucky to have you. Because I love you so much."

His eyes softened, a small smile curling his lips. He pulled me into his hard chest and held me so tight, it felt like he alone could hold all my pieces together.

I didn't realize how much my upbringing still affected me. How much I still cared about my parents and their opinion of me. How much I still wanted to matter to them.

I needed to let that go though. They were who they were and nothing I said would change them. I'd given up on that a long time ago.

Besides, with this beautiful man and his family, I didn't need the love or approval of my own. I'd found a better set than I'd been born into and I knew they'd support me no matter what. They were the antithesis of my parents and I loved them even more for it.

Chapter 12

I sat in Abraham's lap for a long time while he held me. It felt almost therapeutic. Like his arms could undo the years of neglect.

I sniffed and pulled back so I could look in his eyes. It was dark, but there was enough light from the moon for me to see their brilliant blue color. The love shining in their depths made them even more beautiful.

"Baby, I'm sorry about how your parents treated you. It wasn't fair that they let strangers raise you. It wasn't fair that they sent you away at the first sign of trouble. You didn't deserve any of that, but all of it combined is what's made you into the woman you are today. A woman I'm so in love with I can't think straight. I promise you'll never feel unwanted ever again. I'll love you enough to erase everything they've done."

The tears welled up in my eyes again as I watched his perfect mouth say such perfect words on the most perfect night of my life. I thought that had been the night he proposed, but this was better. Deeper. Realer.

It was in that instant that I decided to drop the fated mates thing for good. It didn't matter. I didn't care if we were fated to be together or not. There was no one I would rather be with. No other place I'd choose to be, besides curled up on the lap of this man. He'd become everything to me without the magic. Our bond was just as strong.

I wrapped my arms around his neck and pulled his face to mine, pressing my forehead against his. I took a deep breath and let it out slowly. "I love you."

His lips tilted on one side. "I love you too, baby."

Hearing that word on his lips after everything else he'd said tonight was like throwing gasoline on a fire. A chill coursed down my spine and I squeezed my legs together. As if sensing the shift in my mood, I could feel his erection straining to life between us.

I removed one arm from his neck and wrapped my hand around his growing length. He sucked in a sharp breath and his bright eyes met mine.

"What are you doing, El?"

I squeezed the base and slowly moved my hand up and down. "What does it look like I'm doing?"

He took a deep breath and closed his eyes. "It looks like you're trying to get fucked."

Another chill swept down my spine and I rotated my hips on his lap. "Maybe I am."

He growled low and wrapped his arms around my hips, lifting me up, positioning himself, and sliding me down onto him. He filled me while I tried to remember how to use my lungs. When he was fully inside, he leaned back on the rock beneath us and smirked.

"Fuck me, El."

I clenched around him as another tremor wracked my body. But I did as he asked and moved up and down, twirling my hips and grinding onto him. Sweat beaded on our skin as we touched, and sighed, and moaned, and loved. Soon, I froze on top of him as my climax ripped through my body. Abraham squeezed my hips and thrusted upward as he came with me.

I collapsed onto his hard chest, my body still twitching with my orgasm. His hands dug into the hair on the back of my head, one rubbing soft circles and one just holding me.

We laid there quietly for a long time, my thoughts as lazy as his fingers across my scalp. Neither one of us were in a rush to go anywhere. But then I had an idea, and I picked my head off his chest to catch his eye.

"Wanna go swimming?"

He raised a brow. "Do I want to swim with my naked fiancé under the stars? Hell, yes."

I giggled and pushed myself into a sitting position. "I think we should jump again."

He climbed to his feet and offered me a hand up. "You gonna jump on your own this time?"

I shook my head. "Nope. I wanna do it your way again."

His smile got brighter before he scooped me into his arms, and I wrapped my legs around his waist. He walked over to the edge of the boulder where the small stream trickled into the lake.

He squeezed my waist. "You ready?"

My heart was pounding, a heady mixture of adrenaline and being so close to Abraham. I nodded, my cheeks hurting with how wide my smile was.

Abraham took a few steps back then darted forward, launching us off the edge. He spun us upside down once, and I screamed while he laughed the whole way down. Finally, we sliced through the water and he let go of my waist to grab my hand.

We kicked to the surface, our heads breaking through at the same time. We gulped down air as we smiled at each other.

"What the hell was that?"

"Thought I'd spice things up."

I splashed him. "Next time, warn me when you're planning on practicing Olympic diving."

He chuckled and swam closer until he could wrap his arms around me. "Admit it was fun."

I rolled my eyes. "It was fun."

"You wanna go again?"

"Hell, yes!"

He smiled and slung me onto his back before swimming for the shore. I wrapped my arms around his neck and said, "You know, I can probably swim just as fast as you now."

He turned his head and scoffed. "No one's as fast as me."

I laughed and slapped him on the shoulder. He was so arrogant. Why did I find that so attractive?

We finally made it to the pebbled beach where we scrambled up the boulders and stood at the edge.

Abraham turned to me. "You wanna jump together again?"

I nodded. "Yeah. This time, let's see if you can flip twice."

He smiled wide and pulled me into his arms. "I bet I can do three."

He did, in fact, do three. After that, we must have jumped another dozen times, each one more fun than the last. When my skin had pruned, and I was pretty sure both ears were waterlogged, I finally threw in the towel.

I crawled onto the beach and lay back on the smooth pebbles. "That's it for me," I panted. "You can go again if you want. I'll watch you from here."

Abraham shook his head and sat down next to me, his large hand wrapping around my bare thigh. "You wanna head back?"

I looked up at the stars above us, so much brighter and plentiful than in Raleigh. In the city, it was easy to forget how magnificent the night sky could be. How calming and humbling it was.

As I stretched my neck to see as many constellations as I could, I realized this trip to the lake had done its job. My head was clear, I was thinking straight, and I knew what I wanted.

I looked over at Abraham patiently waiting for me to answer him. It was then I knew I'd cleared up two things tonight.

The first was he and I were in love. No magic could confirm or deny that. He was the only person for me, werewolf or not. I was incredibly lucky that I found him, and I'd never let him go. Ever.

The second thing I realized was I wanted to give working with Callie a shot. It excited me and scared me so much that I knew it was the right choice. Knew it was the path I was supposed to take at this point in my life.

When I got up in the morning, I'd send emails to all the firms who'd offered me a job, thanking them but passing on their offers. After that, I'd find Callista and tell her she'd got herself a new lawyer.

My heart pounded and a smile spread across my face as thoughts about my new job raced through my head.

"I'm gonna take the job with Callie."

Abraham's brows rose. "Really? El, that's great!"

I bit my lip. "You think so?"

Abraham grabbed my arm and pulled me into a sitting position. His big hands cupped my face as he looked at me. "Yes. I know so. I think this is a great next step for you. And I think you're gonna love working with Callie."

"I am, aren't I?"

He pulled me into his arms. "I'm so proud of you, baby. You're gonna be so amazing."

My heart clenched as he proclaimed his deep faith in me. I didn't know what I'd ever done to deserve it, or why he thought so highly of me, but I knew I'd work hard to prove him right. To never let him down.

He climbed to his feet and pulled me along with him. "Come on. Let's go home."

A warmth filled my chest at the word *home*. Had any place ever truly felt like home before the lodge? Had I ever really felt comfortable anywhere else?

Without another word, we shifted back into our wolves and took off through the forest. We were in no rush, so the way back took even longer, and I used that time to fill my head with the serenity of the woods at night. Of the feeling of running free through the trees. Of spending the night with Abraham.

When we made it to the lodge, we shifted back and shrugged on our minimal clothing. His arm wrapped around my waist and we walked like that back up to our room. We reached our bed and disrobed again before crawling beneath the sheets. I slept better that night than I had in a long time.

The next morning, I woke up with a list of things I needed to do. Abraham and I showered together quickly. Or as quickly as you can when your shower buddy can't keep his hands to himself and brings you to orgasm twice before you have a chance to rinse the conditioner from your hair.

I wasn't complaining. Honestly.

We walked down to breakfast hand in hand.

"You know, when I'm working with Callie, I won't be able to take lunch with you every day."

Take lunch was code for *afternoon quickie*. I didn't care how many people already knew what we got up to, I would never admit it.

Abraham squeezed my hand and pulled me close so he could whisper in my ear. "That just means I'll have to come to your office on my lunch breaks if I want to bury the weasel."

I laughed and pushed him away. "You're disgusting."

He chuckled and pulled me back into his side with an arm around my shoulders. "It also means I'll be making your office soundproof."

Now, *that* was a good idea.

"You're renovating the office?"

He rolled his eyes. "What, is Callie gonna hire someone else to do it?"

I nudged him in the ribs. "I knew your company would be doing the work, I just didn't realize the big guy himself would be there. Smartass."

He laughed again and kissed the side of my head. "This project is for my sister. There's no way I'd leave it to anyone else to do. I trust my men, but this is family. Of course I'm gonna be there throwin' up sheetrock and layin' down flooring with everyone else."

I didn't think it was possible, but my respect for him grew in that moment. I'd always known family was important to him, but this was above and beyond. I was sure Callie didn't expect him to pick up a hammer and build her an office, but that was exactly what he was going to do. And the fact that he'd be getting down and dirty with all that came with constructing a set of offices was actually kind of a turn on. I'd have to make sure I spent some time down there while he worked.

It was then I realized I didn't know what the office looked like, or even really where it was. Callie mentioned it was in downtown Asheville, but that didn't tell me much. A thrill coursed through my body as I thought about all the new beginnings I was about to have.

Ms. Elsie was filling up the eggs when we walked up with our empty plates.

"Mornin', you two."

We both mumbled our greetings as we scooped breakfast onto our plates. I noticed Aubrey near the sink doing the dishes, but I ignored her. It wasn't ideal, but I refused to be treated like that. It didn't matter if she didn't like me or my position in the pack. The facts were what they were, and it wasn't going to change because she had a problem with it.

A part of me wondered what I could do to fix it, though. I didn't want there to be animosity or discomfort whenever we were together. She worked where I lived, and we would wind up seeing each other around, anyway. I needed to figure out how to convince her I wasn't the bad guy. That I was someone she could rely on as a pack member and, one day, respect as an alpha.

I figured I'd have to start treating myself like that first if I expected anyone else to.

It was hard for me, though, stepping into a leadership position. I'd never run or led anything in my life. Never wanted to.

Now, there was no denying that being a good alpha for the pack was important to me. No hiding from the fact that I wanted them to like me and I wanted to be a positive influence in their lives.

I think having alpha appointments was a good step in the right direction. The more people I helped, the more people would feel comfortable coming to me. When they saw that I cared about their problems and wanted to help, hopefully that would make them respect me as their leader.

We finished breakfast, and I stacked my dish next to Aubrey without a word. Abraham slung an arm around my shoulders and led me toward the hallway.

"I've got a busy morning. What are you gonna be doing?"

"Well, I've got those appointments this afternoon, but in the meantime, I'm going to talk to Callie about her offer and, when I get some time, I'm going to see if Craig's changed his mind about being a dick. If not, then I'll be having a conversation with Brad."

Abraham raised a brow. "Sounds like you'll be busy, too."

I nodded once, and he pulled me closer, his lips dipping down to my neck.

"You know what it does to me when you act all bossy?"

I shivered in his arms and tilted my head so he'd have better access.

"Hmm," he hummed against my sensitive skin. "I can't wait for lunch."

I laughed and pushed at his chest. He moved a fraction of an inch, but I didn't delude myself into thinking it was because of anything I did. Abraham was a mountain of a man and only he decided if he moved or not.

"Same time?"

He nodded.

"Same place?"

He nodded again and pulled me back into his chest. "And before you ask, it'll also be the same number of torturous hours before your hot little body is wrapped around me again."

I closed my eyes and took a deep breath, reminding myself that we weren't alone, and I couldn't jump into his arms and start tearing off clothes.

He chuckled and kissed me on the lips before swatting me on the butt. "See you later, baby."

Chapter 13

I watched Abraham's impressive form disappear down the hall and up the stairs. When he was out of sight, I sighed and shook my head. He really did scramble my senses.

I turned around to find the kitchen emptying of werewolves, and soon it would just be Aubrey and me again. Not wanting to go another round with her, I figured now was as good a time as any to go talk to Craig.

I glanced at the hallway behind me.

Or, I could go find Callie. We could start talking about specifics and work out a contract for me. Even paperwork sounded better than talking to the grumpy mechanic.

I sighed and stalked through the kitchen towards the back door before I could change my mind. It was better to just get this Craig nonsense over with and move on with my day.

My footsteps crunched down the gravel path as I headed toward house four. I scanned the second house for movement, but Paul was nowhere to be seen. He was probably at work at the police station. I'd still keep an eye out for him while I was down here.

When I got to Craig's house, I found him much the same as I had last time. He had on a dirty t-shirt that stretched over his belly, and he was leaning over the engine of an older car. I took a deep breath, straightened my spine, and marched up his driveway.

"Craig," I called when I was close. I knew he'd heard my footsteps and that he was ignoring me. That didn't bode well for this conversation.

He peeked his head out from under the hood and narrowed his eyes. Turning his head, he spit on the ground and nodded at me. "What do you want?"

My hands wanted to fist at my sides, but I held them still. I didn't want him to see me react because that was exactly what he wanted.

"I'm here to see if you've changed your mind about your prices."

He spit again. "Nope. I'll charge what I wanna charge."

I ground my teeth together before trying one more time. "This is your last chance, Craig. If you don't change them, you're done as the pack mechanic."

One side of his lips twisted into an ugly grin. "Oh, yeah? And how do you think you're gonna do that?"

"I have another mechanic lined up."

His eyes widened for a moment before slitting again. "You wouldn't replace me. I've been the mechanic here almost as long as this pack's been around."

I shrugged a shoulder. "If you want to keep the position, you lower your prices. If you don't, you're out. The choice is yours."

He threw his hands in the air. "And what kind of fuckin' choices are those? Either way I get fucked."

I could smell the anger radiating off him, and I struggled to keep my cool. You'd think that after facing down a psychotic serial killer over a month ago, this wouldn't faze me, but it did. I didn't want it to, and I fought against my reaction, but it was there anyway.

Regardless of that, Craig could bluster all he wanted, but I was the one holding all the cards.

"What's it gonna be, Craig?"

He spat again, his face red with rage. "You replace me and you're gonna regret it."

"That's not an answer."

"No, I'm not changin' my goddamn prices and you can go to hell!"

I nodded once, my back still ramrod straight. "Have it your way." I spun around and walked calmly down his driveway.

Abraham was right. This was the way to handle Craig. I hadn't ordered him to do anything but be fair. He was the one who chose to be stubborn and lose his position. He couldn't really blame anyone but himself.

Not that I thought that would stop him from blaming me.

At the end of his drive, instead of turning toward the lodge, I headed deeper into the pack houses. When I reached the tenth one, I walked up and knocked on the door. A few minutes later, a tall man with a dark brown goatee and disheveled hair answered the door.

"Yeah?"

"Hi, Brad? My name's Elizabeth."

He opened his screen door and stepped out onto the small porch. "I know."

My smile got wider. "Great. Do you have a minute?"

He shrugged, but his dark eyes were wary.

"Actually, I have good news and bad news. Which do you wanna hear first?"

His brows furrowed, and he looked like he was trying to solve a complex math problem. "Um, bad?"

"The bad news is, you need the quiet the hell down at night. We're implementing quiet hours from here on out. That means you're not allowed to blast music or mess around with your car from ten at night until eight in the morning. If we get complaints, they'll start turning into fines. Got it?"

His eyes were a little wider than they were before, and his lips had fallen open. Finally, he nodded, and his Adam's apple bobbed with a swallow. "Okay, and what's the good news?"

"We need a new pack mechanic and I'm offering you the job."

His frown was back. "Pack mechanic? Isn't that Craig's job?"

"Not anymore. Craig's out and you're in."

He took a little longer this time, but finally, he nodded. I clapped my hands together. "All right, any questions?"

He took a step forward and ran a hand through his messy hair. "I don't understand. Why isn't Craig the pack mechanic anymore?"

I shrugged. "He started charging unfair prices and wouldn't change them back, so he got fired."

Brad shook his head. "So, I'm his replacement? I'm not sure how I feel about that."

Oh, jeez. Now we were having a moral dilemma?

I took a step toward him and pasted on a smile. "Listen, Brad, none of that has anything to do with you. We have an open position and I'd like you to fill it. If you don't want it, I'll ask someone else."

"I'll take it," he said, the words tumbling from his mouth one on top of the other.

I smothered a grin. "Great. Are we good here?"

Brad nodded. "Yeah, thanks. When do I start?"

"Today." I turned to leave when another thought struck me. "You are qualified for this, aren't you?" Crap. Maybe I should have checked his credentials before offering him the job.

He laughed and nodded. "Yeah. I've been a mechanic since I was a teenager. I know what I'm doin'."

Thank goodness.

I gave him a sincere smile. "Sounds great, Brad. Don't let me down."

He nodded again, and I left him on his patio, still looking a little stunned. I'd just made it back to the road when someone called my name.

"Ellie?"

I turned to find Maddy coming out of the house next to Brad's. Her smile was wide as she crossed the distance between us and wrapped her arms around me. I gladly returned her hug.

When she pulled away, there was a touch of hesitancy in her eyes. "Was Brad mad about the quiet hours?" she asked so softly I could barely hear her.

I leaned in close. "Not at all. I don't think you'll have any more problems with him."

Maddy's smile spread across her face and she pulled me into another hug. "Thanks so much, Ellie." She pulled away and took a step back. "I was just about to have a cup of tea. Can you stay for a few?"

I still needed to talk to Callie, and I'd told Bea I'd spar with her, but it was probably a good idea to get to know my pack better and this was a great opportunity.

"My roommate, Sophie, should be home soon. I don't know if you've even met yet."

"Was she at my first pack barbecue?"

Maddy nodded and threaded her arm through mine, leading me toward her house. "Yep. You'll love her."

I let her drag me inside and barely had time to look around her homey living room before she hauled me into the kitchen. She nodded for me to have a seat while she filled a kettle with water.

"What are you doin' here today? You don't come down often."

I bit my lip. I really didn't come down here very often. I needed to change that.

"I had to talk to a couple pack members about some issues."

She shot me a look over her shoulder. "Uh oh. Who's in trouble?"

My lips twitched with a smile. "No one's in trouble."

She set the kettle on the lit stove and turned to me with her arms crossed over her chest. "Uh huh. The alpha's mate comes stormin' down to the pack houses just to chat. I don't buy it."

"I did not *storm*."

She rolled her eyes. "I could hear you comin' from the lodge."

My face heated, and I broke eye contact with her. "Okay, yes. There was an issue I had to deal with, but I did, and it's done."

Her eyes lit up. "Ooh, who was it?"

It was my turn to roll my eyes. I opened my mouth to tell her to forget about it when her front door opened.

"Maddy?" a woman called.

"We're in the kitchen!"

"We?" the woman asked as she walked around the corner and scanned the room. When her green eyes landed on me, they widened. "We're hosting the alpha's mate today?"

My lips thinned, and I just barely stopped my hands from fisting. Was that all I was? Abraham's mate? That needed to change.

I stood and held out a hand. "Hi, I'm Elizabeth but everyone here calls me Ellie."

The dark-haired woman eyed my hand for a moment before she stepped closer and shook it. "Sophie. We've met before."

"Yeah, I remember. I think that was the first pack barbecue I went to, right?"

Sophie chuckled. "Yeah, and with everyone and their mom there, I'm not surprised you don't remember me."

"I remember you, I just forgot your name. I'm terrible with them."

Sophie shrugged. "It's not a big deal." She turned to Maddy and her smile grew. "Hey, Mads. What's goin' on?"

Maddy's smile was almost manic. "Ellie here was about to tell me who she came down here to yell at today."

Sophie clapped and grabbed the seat next to mine. "Was it Jimmy? I swear, I've got half a dozen complaints about him alone."

Jimmy? Did I know Jimmy?

Maddy must have noticed my blank stare because she spoke up. "He's in his thirties, long brown hair to his shoulders, scraggly beard..."

I nodded slowly. "I think I remember him now. He always eats all the deviled eggs, right?"

Maddy nodded with a smile. "That's him. Was he the one?"

I rolled my eyes. "No. And I'm not going to tell you who is."

Sophie scooted her chair closer. "We'll find out eventually. There are no secrets in a pack."

"So, I've heard," I deadpanned.

The kettle started whistling, and I was saved momentarily from any further scrutiny. They might have been right that they'd find out eventually, but it wasn't going to come from me. I knew Craig was mad enough as it was, I didn't need to go gossiping about him too.

Maddy handed us all mugs of steaming hot tea and placed some milk, sugar, and lemon on the table between us. Thankfully, we were all pretty quiet while we doctored up our drinks.

I knew that couldn't last long, though.

"Well, I at least know you talked to Brad."

"Ooh, about him being loud late at night?" Sophie asked, her hands wrapped around her mug and pressed to her chest.

I rolled my eyes. "Yes, I talked to Brad. Told him we have quiet hours now and to respect them or he'll be fined."

"Tell 'em, girl," Maddy cheered.

I bit my lips, but they curled into a smile, anyway. These ladies were fun.

"So, what's going on with you and our alpha? How come you two haven't set a ceremony date yet?"

"Sophie! You can't just ask her something like that!" Maddy chided.

Sophie shrugged. "What? Everyone's wondering the same thing I am."

118

My belly flipped deep inside me. Everyone was wondering why we hadn't set a date? Why? We just got engaged. What was wrong with these people?

I took a long sip of tea and cleared my throat. "We're not in any rush."

Both ladies raised a brow at me, and I would have laughed if my insides weren't knotting.

"Who wouldn't be in a rush to mate that man?" Sophie asked, her face making it clear how intelligent she thought I was.

I shrugged a shoulder. "I want to marry him. I *will* marry him, but I don't see what the hurry is. Who cares if I marry him next month or next year?"

They both gasped.

"Next year?" Maddy whispered.

I frowned. "Yeah. What's wrong with that?"

They were both shaking their heads, varying degrees of pity on their faces.

"That's almost worse than not mating him at all," Sophie said.

My frown deepened. "What are you talking about? A year long engagement is perfectly normal."

They turned to look at each other before facing me again. "No, it really isn't," Maddy said.

I took another long sip of my hot drink and set the mug down carefully. "As you both know, I wasn't raised as a werewolf. Where I come from, waiting a year, or even two, is perfectly reasonable."

Both sets of eyes widened simultaneously as if they'd practiced this.

"Two years?!" they both yelled at the same time.

I shrugged, but my shoulders hunched a little too. "Yeah? I'm not saying I want to wait two years, but there's nothing wrong with that."

They were both shaking their heads, and I had to wonder if the two were related they were so similar.

"Ellie, fated mates don't wait. It's almost an insult to your mate."

There was so much I could say to that, but I swallowed the words.

I didn't know if we were fated mates or not, but I wasn't about to tell them that. It wasn't something I'd even wanted to tell Callie, Evey, and Del, but they'd dragged it out of me. I would have rather stewed in my suspicions than air them.

And was I really insulting Abraham by not marrying him right away? That was the very last thing I wanted to do. I loved and respected that man so much, it hurt my heart to think I'd slighted him in some way.

I cleared my throat again. "I don't think he sees it that way. He understands that things are different for me. It has nothing to do with him and everything to do with how I was raised and what I believe."

They looked at each other again and I could see the skepticism without them having to voice it.

Was this really what the rest of the pack was thinking? No wonder no one was taking me seriously as the alpha. No wonder I was repeatedly referred to *as some bitch he's sleeping with*. I guess that was exactly how I looked to them.

But what was I supposed to do about that? Just go ahead and marry Abraham so everyone would stop gossiping about it? That didn't seem fair. Or was I being unfair to Abraham? I never wanted to hurt him in any way, and if I was, I needed to rectify that as soon as possible.

Chapter 14

I was finally able to extricate myself from Maddy's house, but only after I agreed to stop by next week. The two of them had been fun, but being the center of their attention wasn't. Their keen eyes picked up on too much and there was plenty I needed to hide.

As I passed Brad's house, I gave him a wave that he returned enthusiastically. I let the positivity of a job well done fill me as I walked back up the path toward the lodge. I resolutely ignored Craig and his house as I walked by, but couldn't help taking another peek at Paul's. He still wasn't home, or at least he wasn't outside.

When I made it to the lodge, the kitchen was mercifully empty, but I hurried out of there, anyway. Who knew when Aubrey might be back?

I hustled up the stairs and over to Callie's room where I knocked. When she called to come in, I opened the door to find her room in shambles. There were boxes stacked all over the place and papers and notebooks scattered around the floor. In the middle of the mayhem was a frazzled-looking Callie.

"Hey, Ellie. Sorry about the mess."

I carefully picked my way through the debris until I reached her. "What's going on?"

Callie sighed and placed both hands on her narrow hips. "I thought I'd get some packing done, but it seems I've just made a bigger mess." She let out a deep breath. "I can't wait until we get in the new office space. Abey said it should only be a few weeks. Two if we're lucky."

I looked around and nodded. "That's great! So, you won't have to work out of your room much longer."

"Exactly."

"Were you still looking to work with me?"

She froze and turned her wide, pale blue eyes my way. "Um, yes?"

"Then I'd love to take the position."

Callie's smile lit up her face. "Seriously?" she shrieked.

My grin was so wide I was sure it matched hers. "Seriously. I might not know what I'm doing yet, but I'm going to do a lot of research and make myself useful."

Callie threw herself into my arms and squeezed me tight. "I know you will. You're going to be awesome." She pulled back and looked in my eyes. "I'm so glad you said yes! We're going to make such a great team!"

I couldn't help but let her excitement infect me. The more I thought about it, the better this decision felt. The more sure I was that I was doing the right thing.

She finally released me and spun around to the mess she'd made in her room. "I know I have contracts somewhere in here. Give me a sec."

"Sure," I said as I walked over and took a seat near her desk. I didn't mean to, but couldn't help noticing she had a thick book on top that looked like it was about werewolves. I reached over and picked it up. "Were you doing more research on fated mates?"

Callie paused in her search for a moment to throw me a look over her shoulder. "Yeah. I was working on that before I started with the packing crap."

I pulled the book onto my lap and flipped through a few pages. The words scrambled and bled together until I couldn't make out what they said. Frustrated, I put the book back where I got it.

"Have you found anything?"

She shot me another look, this one apologetic. Standing up, she turned to face me. "No, not really." She scratched the side of her head. "Honestly, bitten wolves are pretty rare. Them being fated to a werewolf is unheard of."

I tried not to let it, but my stomach sank anyway. Taking a deep breath, I slapped the best smile I could manage on my face. "It's okay, Callie. I'm just gonna drop it I think."

Her eyes widened and she crossed the distance between us. "You're not going to mate Abey?"

I jerked back. "No! Of course I am! I'm just dropping the fated mates stuff."

Her shoulders relaxed a fraction of an inch. "Thank goodness." Then she eyed me with one brow raised. "But wait, why are you dropping it?"

I shrugged and looked away. "Because I don't think we'll find anything. I don't think it's possible that we're fated."

"Ellie, but–"

"It's okay, Callie," I cut her off. "Really. We can just be two people who are in love and are supposed to be together. That's enough for me."

She eyed me quietly for a moment. "Are you sure? This doesn't make you doubt your relationship with Abraham?"

I shook my head. "Nope. I know he's who I'm supposed to be with. We're perfect together and I couldn't imagine a single day without him. Nothing has changed that."

Callie's lips tilted into a smile. "Great. So you two will have your ceremony soon, then?"

My smile fell the tiniest bit. "Um, no."

She frowned. "I don't understand."

"Callie, we've only known each other a couple months. If we're not fated and we're just two regular people who are in love and trying to make it work together, why would we rush into something like that?"

She opened her mouth to argue but shut it instead and frowned. A moment later, she tried again, "But Abey still thinks you're fated. Are you going to tell him you don't believe that?"

My stomach sank again as my eyes drifted away from her. "Um, no?"

"Ellie."

I sighed and hung my head. "What's the point? It's just going to hurt him."

"But shouldn't you be honest? Doesn't he have a right to know you don't think you're fated?"

I threw my hands in the air and stalked away from her. "I don't know!" I took a deep breath and tried again, this time without raising my voice. It wasn't Callie I was mad at and I didn't want to take it out on her. I stopped in my tracks and turned to her again. "It doesn't matter to me if we're fated. I still love him and I'm still going to marry him. None of that's changed."

She sighed and shook her head. "How long are you going to make him wait?"

I bit my lip and shrugged. "I don't know. Until it feels right?"

She sighed and walked back over to pull my hands into hers. "I think you should be honest with him."

I shook my head. "That will just hurt him, Callie. Trust me, it's better this way. We'll get married in a few months or a year and we'll never have to talk about this fated mates stuff again. It won't matter when we're mated right?"

She studied me as I tried to fix my features into a calm façade. Finally, she blew out a deep breath. "It's your life and your relationship, Ellie. I can't tell you what to do with it. But I will say, I think you should tell him. I think you should always be a hundred percent honest. Even when it hurts the other person."

That was where we differed.

She thought honesty was the best policy when I knew sometimes it didn't work like that. Sometimes, the truth hurt worse than the little white lies.

Telling Abraham was the last thing I wanted to do. He could just stay happy and content in the knowledge that we were fated while I lived with the reality. There was no wolfy magic holding us together. We had to work just as hard as anyone else to make things last between us.

It didn't matter to me, though. I was prepared to spend the rest of my life deserving that amazing man. He was more than I ever could have asked for, and every day I was reminded of how lucky I was.

I was perfectly happy just being his mate, I didn't need to be his *soul* mate.

I shook my head and took a step away from Callie. "Anyway, let's see if we can find a contract in this mess so we can get started on making me an official employee."

Callie squealed and clapped her hands, and I knew the topic had been dropped for now. Unfortunately, I'd gotten to know the McCoys really well in the past few months, and I knew they never let anything lie for long. To make matters worse, I'd also talked to Evey and Del about this. It was only a matter of time before they brought it back up and I had to have this conversation again.

The only thing I hoped was that they kept it from Abraham. I didn't need any of this getting back to him.

I spent the next couple hours with Callie while we sorted out the particulars of my employment. Excitement zipped through my veins the entire time, and by the end of it, I was ready to get started right away.

Callie laughed when I told her that. "Well, we don't have much going on at the moment with the move and everything, but I have a few books I thought could help you in the meantime."

She turned around and began rummaging through some of the opened boxes before pulling out a stack of textbooks. She handed them over to me and dusted off her hands.

"Those should be a good place for you to get started. If you have questions about any of it, feel free to come to me."

I tucked the books under my arm and gave her a smile. "Thanks, Callie. I'll start looking these over today!"

She grinned back. "Great! Let me know how it goes!"

I left her room and headed back over to our wing of the third floor. Not having anywhere to really work, I decided to head into my old bedroom and start on the books Callie gave me. I climbed onto the bed and rolled over onto my stomach to start flipping through the texts.

That was where Abraham found me a couple hours later.

"Hey, baby. What are you doin' in there?" he asked softly as he walked across the hall.

"Oh, um, I needed a place to work in peace." I shrugged and flipped a page. I'd already gotten through half of the first book and I was on a roll.

He closed the door behind him, and the sound of the lock echoed through the quiet room. "You could have come to work in my office."

I raised my eyes from the textbook and shot him a look. "I wouldn't have gotten anything done."

He crossed the distance between us and stood next to the bed. "But it would have been a lot more fun than what I had to do the past few hours."

"What was so bad about your morning?"

"Besides the fact that you weren't naked across my desk?" he asked as he sat beside me on the bed.

I rolled my eyes. "Yes, besides that."

"I had a bunch of conference calls I had to be on."

"Construction business or alpha business?"

He smiled. "Mostly alpha today."

I nodded and smiled, my eyes wandering back to the books I'd been reading. "Are you done for now?"

A grin spread across his handsome face while the look in his eyes turned hungry. "Yep. I was just about to take lunch."

My stomach dropped at his words and I swallowed. "Hungry?" I asked, my voice squeaking at the end.

Abraham inched closer to me, his hands finding my thighs and sliding up my legs. "Starving."

I closed my eyes and tried to breathe steadily. When his fingers reached the waistband of my jeans, all thoughts of reading environmental texts flew right out the window.

"I've been thinking about what I wanted to eat for lunch all day," he continued as he shimmied my pants down my legs.

I could already feel the liquid heat pooling between my legs. "Oh, yeah? What are you in the mood for?"

He growled softly as he pulled my panties down my hips. He quietly watched me for so long, his eyes tracing over every inch of skin he'd revealed. "I'm hungry for my fiancée," he finally said, and my heart lurched to my throat.

We didn't do much talking after that as Abraham got his fill of me. I wound up underneath him again as he thrusted me into my second orgasm of the afternoon. His cries were loud in the quiet room as he found release deep inside me.

When we were finally sated, he pulled me onto his bare chest and ran his fingers through my hair. "We got so lucky, El. You ever think about that?"

I was half asleep by that point. Between the earth-shattering orgasms and the way he was rubbing my head, I was seconds from being unconscious. "Hmm?"

He squeezed me tighter and kissed the side of my head. "Luck, El. I'm so goddamn lucky I found you." He dug his face into my neck and breathed deeply. "A fated mate is a gift and you've given me the greatest one."

My eyes shot open at his words, but I stayed as still as I could. I didn't want to alert him to the change in me. Didn't need him to know the fated thing was a touchy subject.

Callie's words spun through my mind as I lay there in his arms.

Should I tell him? What would it change? What would it make better?

The answer was nothing. Him knowing I didn't think we were fated wouldn't do him any good, so why bring it up?

I did my best to relax back into his hold, but I was wide awake now. He continued to stroke my hair while thoughts raced around my head. Finally, he spoke up, "What's on your mind, El? I can almost feel it spinning."

Damn. This man saw too much.

I sighed and snuggled deeper into his hold. "Just thinking about a lot of stuff. You know I talked to Craig and Brad already?"

I deployed that distraction as soon as I could. The sooner we got off the topic of what was really going through my head, the better.

"Oh, yeah? How'd that go?"

I snorted into his chest. "Craig took it about as well as you'd expect he would. He even tossed in a *you'll regret this* parting line."

Abraham stilled beneath me. "He threatened you?" His voice was lethal, and I immediately knew I needed to diffuse the situation before Craig got another visit from an alpha.

"It wasn't really so much of a threat as it was a warning, I guess? I'm sure it wasn't meant to be personal and more like, *you'll regret hiring someone new*." At least I hoped that was what he meant.

Abraham's shoulders slowly relaxed and soon his hand was back to stroking my hair.

Crisis averted for now.

"What about Brad? What did he have to say?"

I shrugged. "He was a little wary of the position, but I told him if he didn't take it, I'd just offer it to someone else, so he changed his tune."

"So, Brad's our new mechanic?"

"Looks like it."

He reached down to kiss my head. "I'll send out notice to the rest of the pack as soon as possible. You did good, baby."

My chest warmed at his compliment. I was really trying my hardest with the alpha stuff, so it was nice to hear I was doing a good job. That I wasn't messing everything up like I'd thought I would.

I had a few more appointments coming up soon, and I just hoped I'd be as useful for those members as I'd been to the others. I hoped I'd have the answers they were looking for, or at the least I could find them if need be. This alpha business wasn't as scary as I first thought it would be. In fact, I was starting to get the hang of it.

Chapter 15

Was it possible for werewolves to get migraines? Because my head was throbbing.

"I don't understand why I can't see Abraham. He's the one I want to talk to."

I pulled the corners of my lips into the best smile I could manage. "Fran, I'd be happy to make you an appointment with Abraham, but he's booked for the next two weeks." I made that up. I had no clue what his schedule was like. "If you'll just tell me what's going on, I'll make sure it's addressed either by me or Abraham."

She eyed me speculatively from behind her pointy glasses. "Why would I talk to you? You're not the alpha."

I grit my teeth and tugged my smile up a notch. "I realize I'm not the alpha *yet*, but I will be someday."

Fran scoffed. "So, I get to be the new alpha's guinea pig? No, thanks. I'll just wait and talk to Abraham." She gathered her purse and stood.

The war between wanting to stop her and wanting to let her go was so violent, it took me a moment to react.

"Fran," I finally said, pushing my chair back as I rose to my feet. "Wait."

She paused at the door and spun around to face me. Her dark brown eyes narrowed as she waited for me to speak.

Problem was, I didn't know what to say.

She was the second pack member in a row to refuse to work with me. The first, Eric, hadn't even let me finish introducing myself before he said he wouldn't speak with anyone but the alpha. If I let Fran go too, Abraham was going to think I couldn't do the job.

I took a deep breath and clasped my hands in front of me. "Listen, Fran, your best bet is to just talk to me. The worst that can happen is I bring your issue to Abraham myself. Don't you think you have a better chance of getting what you want if I'm the one to talk to him about it?"

Her lips twisted to the side while her eyes assessed me. Finally, she said, "You'll talk to Abraham about this no matter what?"

I gave her a firm nod. "I will. Whether I'm able to help or not, he'll hear about it."

She blew out a big breath and rolled her eyes. "Fine. I can't imagine it would hurt."

I wanted to say *that's the spirit* but figured it might be too early in our relationship for me to start with the sarcasm.

We took our seats again, and I picked up my pen. "So, tell me what's going on."

Fran sighed. "It's that asshole, Jimmy."

Ah. Sophie mentioned him the other day. I wrote his name down.

"Okay, and what's happening with Jimmy?"

She slammed her hands down on the table, jolting my pen across the page and surprising the hell out of me. "He's a goddamn slob. I find his beer cans and cigarette butts all over my garden. I've told him a dozen times to keep his mess in his yard, but he never listens."

I jotted down a couple more notes. "And which houses are you two in?"

"Fourteen and sixteen."

I wrote that down too. "Okay, we'll get your yard cleaned up and have a talk with him."

She snorted, and I looked up from my notepad to her dark eyes. "*You're* going to talk to him?"

I sat up straighter. "Yes. Why?"

She rolled her eyes and chuckled. "I'm just glad I got you to promise you'll talk to Abraham about this."

I ground my teeth, my hands fisting at my sides. "I'll handle the issue with Jimmy myself. If for whatever reason I'm ineffective, Abraham will resolve your situation. I promise you that."

Fran laughed again and climbed to her feet. "Whatever you say, honey."

I cringed at her pet name. Everyone knew you only used *honey* like that when you really didn't mean it. It was probably code for something like *dumbass*.

I shook out my hands and offered one to her. "Thanks for bringing me your issue."

She shook my hand for the briefest of moments before she turned to leave. "And thank you for bringing this to Abraham as soon as you realize you're not cut out for this job."

She tossed that last remark over her shoulder, almost as an afterthought.

My hands started to shake, and I remembered my calming technique.

In, one.

Out, two.

In, three.

Out, four.

When I finally had enough control over my wolf, I left the conference room and walked back into the kitchen. Fran was just leaving through the sliding glass door and Aubrey was shooting daggers at me with her eyes from across the room.

"Afternoon, Aubrey."

She didn't answer, not that I expected her to.

I sat down at one of the tables and pulled out my phone while I waited for the next appointment. Pulling up a mind-numbing game, I thought through Fran's issue.

If she'd repeatedly asked Jimmy to clean up after himself and he still hadn't, it was clear there was no miscommunication. Fran called him an asshole, and had to agree.

So, if talking to him wasn't going to get him to act right, what would?

Then there was the problem of the mess in Fran's yard. I had a feeling, even without meeting him, that it would be a cold day in hell before Jimmy cleaned up after himself. And it wouldn't be fair to expect Fran to keep picking up after someone else. Which meant I'd need to get someone else to do it.

A tentative idea formed in my head and I pulled up my messages.

Me: Who takes care of the gardening around here?

I only had to wait a minute for a reply.

Sexiest Man Alive: Austin and George. Why?

Me: I have a job for one of them. Do you know where I can find them?

Sexiest Man Alive: They only work on Tuesdays and Thursdays, so they won't be around the lodge. You can ask Aubrey. Austin is her brother.

My eyes flicked across the room to the grumpy brunette and I cringed. I really didn't want to talk to her, but it looked like I needed to. Besides, we couldn't keep this animosity up forever. Sooner or later, something had to give.

With a sigh, I stood and walked across the kitchen. When I was a few feet away, I cleared my throat. Aubrey froze in place, her shoulders almost touching her ears.

"Hey, Aubrey. I have a question."

She resumed what she was doing and shot over her shoulder, "What do you want?"

I closed my eyes for a moment and took a deep breath. Leadership was about patience and it looked like I'd need to expend a whole lot of mine in this situation if I was going to get the information I wanted.

"I was wondering if you knew where I could find Austin today."

She froze again, but this time she slowly rotated until she was facing me. Her eyes narrowed into thin slits. "What do you want with Austin?"

"I have a job for him."

"What kind of job?"

"It's something I'd rather discuss with him."

She folded her arms across her chest. "Then I'm not going to tell you where he is."

I gritted my teeth and tried again. "I can just go ask Abraham where you live."

Her eyes widened the smallest amount. "Then do it."

I shook my head and spun around. "I will."

I stormed through the kitchen and was just about to hit the hallway when her voice reached me. "It's nothing bad, right?"

I stopped in my tracks and turned to look at her again. "Of course not. I just have a job I need done, and I figured I'd see if he wanted the extra money."

"Extra money?"

"Yeah. Obviously I'd be paying him for his time."

She unfolded her arms and took a couple steps forward. "He's probably at the house right now."

"Which house?"

She bit her lip for a moment before rolling her eyes. "Five."

"Thanks."

She shrugged and turned around.

Well, that could have gone worse.

Problem was, I was stuck in the lodge. I had another appointment and who knew how long it'd take?

I cleared my throat again and Aubrey paused what she was doing. "Do you think you could text him and ask if he'd come down here for a minute?"

"What? You're too good to go down to the pack houses?"

I bristled at her comment. "No. In fact, I've been down there twice this week. I want him to come up here because I have another appointment and I need this job taken care of immediately."

She sighed loudly and pulled a phone out of her back pocket. "I'll text him, but I can't promise anything."

A small smile crept across my face. "Thanks, Aubrey. I appreciate it."

She ignored me, but I was still smiling. At least she wasn't insulting me, right? It might take baby steps, but we'd get there.

The sliding glass door opened, and Sophie walked in. Her green eyes immediately found mine. "Hey, Ellie!"

I walked over to her and wrapped my arms around her shoulders. "Hey, Sophie! What are you doing here?"

She pulled back and held up her wristwatch. "I'm your two-thirty appointment."

The first genuine smile in hours spread across my face. "Great! Let's go in the conference room and talk."

I led her down the hallway and closed the door behind her. We both took seats, and I slid my notepad in front of me.

"What's going on?"

She blew out a deep breath and sat forward in her seat. "It's the farm manager. He's a total prick."

"What's his name?"

"Tom."

135

"Okay, so what did Tom do?"

"He's completely abusing his power as farm manager. He overworks us, makes us cut our breaks short all the time, and worst of all, he lets his stupid girlfriend get away with doing nothing."

"Who's his girlfriend?"

"Daisy," she snarled.

It was so unexpected of a sound, I looked up from my pad. "I'm guessing you're not a fan."

She sneered. "Hell, no. She's a whiny little bitch. Always complaining about how hot she is, how bright the sun is, how dirty her hands are getting. Why she signed up to work on the farm is a goddamn mystery to me because the girl's never done a day of hard labor in her life."

"So, she's not a great fit. What does Tom do regarding Daisy?"

She threw a hand in the air. "She's allowed to flit from group to group, not really doing anything at all while we all bust our asses. We're supposed to have a certain number of employees working at a time, so the labor is divided equally. With Daisy doing a whole lot of nothing, we're all having to work harder. It's not fair and I'm fed up with it."

I took a few more notes and looked up at her. "Okay. I'll talk to Tom."

She hid it pretty well, but the look of disbelief was still there on her face. "No offense, Ellie, but I'm not sure he's gonna listen to you."

I straightened my spine and shot her a smile. "He will if he wants to keep his job."

She sat forward again, her eyes lighting up. "Ooh, are you gonna fire him?"

I shrugged a shoulder. "If he can't do his job right, then yes."

Sophie clapped. "Oh my God, this is so exciting! I knew it was a good idea coming to you!"

The words filled me with the warm glow of pride. I hadn't even done anything yet, and she was already singing my praises. Now if she could just convince the rest of the pack that I could handle this job, I'd be all set.

"Was that all you have going on?" I asked.

Sophie nodded and jumped up from her seat. "Yep. You fix the Tom and bitch-ass-Daisy problem and I'll be a happy woman."

I did my best to stifle my chuckle. "I'll do my best."

We walked back out to the kitchen where she threw her arms around me. "Thanks again, Ellie. I'll see you next week, right?"

I hugged her back. "I'll be there."

I watched her leave with a small smile on my face. It felt good to feel appreciated. To not feel like I had to constantly prove myself to everyone.

A throat cleared behind me and I spun around to find Aubrey and a man standing on the other side of the kitchen. He looked so much like Aubrey, it had to be her brother, Austin.

I walked closer and held out my hand to him. "Hi, Austin. I'm Ellie. Thanks so much for coming down."

He shook my hand, but his shoulders were stiff. If his sister didn't like me, it was safe to assume he didn't either. Hopefully I could change that opinion of his.

"I have a job that I'd like you to do. Are you free this afternoon?"

He eyed me curiously for a moment before speaking. "What's the job?"

"I need someone's yard cleaned up. From what I hear, there're beer cans and cigarettes, but there could be more."

His lips thinned. "I don't work for free."

"Of course not," I jumped in. "However long it takes you, I'll double the hours and you'll see it in your next paycheck."

I wasn't sure I could do something like that, but it sounded good, so I went with it.

His eyes were still narrowed, but I could tell they were calculating now. "Which house is it?"

I opened my mouth to answer but closed it again when I realized I didn't know which house Fran's was and which was Jimmy's.

"Do you know where Jimmy lives?"

He scoffed. "Everyone knows where Jimmy lives."

"Okay, so you're cleaning up the yard next to his."

"You talkin' about Fran?"

"Yes. Exactly. You're cleaning up Fran's yard."

He watched me for another few minutes before he shrugged. "Yeah, sure. I make twenty dollars an hour, though."

"Doesn't matter. I want that yard cleaned today and I'm willing to pay you double time to do it. Are you in?"

He shrugged again. "Yeah. I'm in. I'll go get started now."

My smile beamed across my face. "Great! I'd like an update when you're done. I should be in the lodge the rest of the day."

He nodded, gave his sister a look, and left out the back door.

"He probably would have done it for half that," Aubrey said from her spot across the room.

I shrugged. "Yeah, but no one should have to clean up after a grown man. Besides, it's not really me who'll be paying him."

Aubrey frowned. "Then who is?"

My smile spread across my face again. "That would be Jimmy."

Aubrey looked confused for a second before her face cleared. It might have been my imagination, but I thought one corner of her mouth might have turned up in a grin for the briefest of seconds. But before I knew it, her stony expression was back.

I barely held back a sigh. Clearly, I had more work to do in the Aubrey department. But it felt like a step in the right direction.

Now, I just had to follow through with all the promises I'd made.

Chapter 16

After Sophie left, I realized I'd have to wait for Austin to finish the task I gave him before I could implement the rest of my plan. Seeing an opportunity for some more studying, I ran upstairs for my textbooks and hauled them back into the kitchen.

I was nose deep in my second book when someone cleared their throat behind me. I spun around to find Austin, a little sweatier and dirtier than the last time I saw him, but still smiling.

"Hey, Ellie. Yard's all done."

I looked at the clock hanging on the wall of the kitchen and frowned. "Great, Austin. What was that? About two hours?"

He shrugged and wiped the back of his hand along his forehead. "Yeah, about that. Place was a wreck."

I shook my head. How long had poor Fran been putting up with that?

I stood up and reached out a hand which Austin immediately shook. "Thanks for getting to that for me so quickly. You'll see that extra eighty dollars in your next check, okay?"

Austin shrugged, the smile still on his face. "Sounds good. Let me know if you ever need anything else." He took a step backward before stopping again. "Why don't you take down my number, so you can contact me directly?"

I smiled and pulled out my phone, programming his number into it and giving him my information. "Thanks, Austin. I'll keep you in mind."

He gave me a little wave and turned to leave the lodge. Out of the corner of my eye, I could see Aubrey on the other side of the kitchen with an indescribable look on her face.

Maybe she'd expected her brother to hate me like she did. Maybe she was surprised we'd managed to get along. And, just maybe, she'd realize she didn't need to dislike me as much as she did. That I wasn't the big, bad monster in this story.

I sighed and gathered my textbooks before walking back upstairs. When they were stowed in our room, I went back downstairs to Evey's office.

"Come in!" she called after I knocked.

I opened the door and stepped inside. She was sitting across the room at her desk, clicking a ballpoint pen. Her navy dress fit her perfectly and I would bet she had on at least three-inch heels. She always dressed up for work and it almost made me self-conscious in my jean shorts and t-shirt. Then again, I was unemployed, so I was just happy I wasn't still in my pajamas.

When she looked up, she smiled. "Hey, Ellie!"

"Hey, Evey. You have a minute?"

She tossed her pen onto the desk and leaned back in her chair. "Of course. What's up?"

I took the seat in front of her and crossed my legs. "Well, I had a couple appointments today, and I made a promise I was hoping you could help me keep."

She raised a brow. "What kinda promise?"

I folded my hands in front of me to prevent them from fidgeting. Evey managed the whole lodge. She was human resources, accounts receivable, and payroll all rolled into one. If there was anyone who could make this happen, it was Evey.

"Well, I had one of the groundskeepers do a special job for me and I promised him he'd be paid for it in his next check."

Evey picked her pen back up and slid a pad in front of her. "Who was the groundskeeper?"

"Austin."

"And how much extra is he gettin' paid?"

"Eighty dollars."

Evey froze in place and raised her head to spear me with a look. "Eighty dollars? That's quite a bonus."

I shrugged a shoulder. "It was extenuating circumstances."

Evey straightened up further and let out a deep breath. "We don't have the budget to just be givin' eighty-dollar bonuses, Ellie. I wish you'd come to me before you offered it."

I cringed but rushed to explain. "Oh, the money is coming from somewhere else. That's something else I need your help with."

She sat back, her blue eyes clouding. "Okay, now I'm confused. Why don't you start at the beginnin'?"

I launched into the story about the mess Jimmy made of Fran's yard. When I explained that Austin's bonus would be coming from a fine I was going to issue to Jimmy, her look changed from confusion to disbelief.

"You're finin' Jimmy?"

I shrugged a shoulder. "Yeah. Why?"

She chuckled and shook her head as she fired up her computer. "You've got balls, Ellie. I'll say that about you."

I sat up straighter, a frown tugging at my brows. "Why do you say that?"

She shot me a look before turning back to her computer screen. "Jimmy is an old cranky bastard. Abey's been tryin' to rein him in since he joined this pack."

I shrugged again. "Well, I figured I'd hit him where it hurts the most–his bank account."

Evey giggled. "He's not gonna like you messin' with his money, Ellie."

"Well, he shouldn't have acted like a messy child."

She laughed again, and her printer whirred to life. "Oh, I'm behind you. I just think it's not gonna go as smooth as you think it is."

My shoulders hunched the slightest bit. "Any advice?"

Evey grabbed the paper that printed out and turned to me again. "Don't back down. You go down there with a goal and don't stop 'til you get it."

I nodded slowly, letting her words seep in. "What do I do if he refuses?" I asked, my voice small.

I felt stupid asking things like that, but I had to. I was sure I could have taken this to Abraham, but I was trying to impress him. Trying to show him I could do the job. If I ran to him with every little problem, I'd be doing the opposite of that.

Evey tilted her head to the side. "Well, if he won't pay his fine, he'll be in breach of his contract."

"Contract?"

"Every wolf that lives on pack lands had to sign a contract before gettin' to occupy one of the houses. A breach could result in eviction."

I nodded again. "Okay. I think I can work with that."

She slid a piece of paper across her desk. "Here's the official document for Jimmy's fine. I'm gonna add the bonus to Austin's check right now. Was there anythin' else you needed help with?"

I grabbed the document and shot her a smile. "Nope. I'm good. Thanks, Evey." I stood up and turned to leave.

I'd just grabbed the doorknob when her voice floated across the room. "Be careful, Ellie."

I looked over my shoulder at her, ready to give a sarcastic retort when I saw her face. She was actually worried about me. I turned around and gave her my most reassuring smile. "I'll be fine, Evey. Don't worry about me."

She nodded, but her eyes were still filled with worry. "He's not gonna be happy about that fine. You should be prepared for that."

I swallowed past the lump in my throat, hoping my unease didn't show on my face. I knew Jimmy wasn't going to be happy about receiving a fine. I knew he was probably going to throw a fit and try to threaten his way out of it. But I also knew I wasn't backing down. I needed to lay down the law. Show the pack that I wasn't someone that could be messed with.

I felt like I wasn't taken as seriously because I was bitten and not born a wolf. Like people expected me to not be as strong or as fast because I hadn't always been like this.

That couldn't have been further from the truth, and my sparring partner could vouch for that.

I still trained with Bea at least five times a week and I was getting better every day. I might not have been ready to face off against one of the enforcers or anything, but I was sure I could handle some beer-drinking, cigarette-smoking blowhard.

"I'll be okay, Evey. I'll see you later. Thanks again."

I knew if I stayed there any longer, she'd try to find a way to talk me out of it. Or worse, call Abraham and let him know what was happening. He'd no doubt insist on accompanying me to the pack houses and I didn't want that. If I brought Abraham, no one would take me seriously.

The more I thought about it, the more I realized Evey was probably going to tell on me, anyway. She was notoriously mothering and overprotective. She was almost as bad as Abraham when it came to my safety.

I hustled through the lodge and out the back door before anyone could stop me. With a couple looks tossed over my shoulder to make sure no one was following, I made my way down to the pack houses.

When I reached the fourteenth one, I found the yard clean and well-maintained. Austin did a good job and I'd have to remember that.

I walked past Fran's house and over to the sixteenth which obviously belonged to Jimmy. His yard looked like it could be featured on an episode of one of those hoarder shows. There was junk lying all over the place, garbage littering every corner, and enough cigarette butts to build something with. His house was a disgusting mess, and if I was Fran, I'd have complained about having to live next to that.

I stormed up the driveway and knocked on his door, getting more irritated as time passed. When a middle-aged man with pale skin and long, greasy hair answered, I had no trouble guessing who it was.

"Jimmy?"

He frowned. "Yeah. What do you want?"

"My name's Ellie and I'm here to address an issue with you. Could you come out and talk to me?"

He pushed his screen door open and stepped outside, his dark eyes watching me warily. He crossed his arms over his flabby chest and stared me down. "What's the issue?"

I took a deep breath and tipped up my chin. "We've received a complaint about you throwing your trash on your neighbor's lawn and had to take action."

One of his busy brows rose. "What kind of action?"

I handed him the fine and waited while he slowly read it. When his eyes widened, I knew he'd reached the part about the money. He looked up at me with enough rage to almost knock me back a step.

"Is this a fuckin' joke?!" he yelled, balling the piece of paper in his meaty hand.

"Afraid not. You have a week to pay that fine before it doubles."

He took a menacing step forward. "I'm not payin' no bullshit fine."

"It's not bullshit. You couldn't contain your pigsty to your own property and that's unacceptable."

"I'm not payin' shit."

"You will if you want to remain living here."

He took another step closer, but I held my ground. "What the hell is that supposed to mean?"

"It means, when you moved here, you signed a contract agreeing to pay any fines you received from the alpha. If you don't, you're breaching the contract and can be removed."

A vein was throbbing in his forehead and I worried about his health for a moment. "You're gonna kick me out of my own goddamn house?!"

"Technically, this is a pack house. It doesn't belong to you."

He opened his mouth to speak, but nothing came out and he closed it. He did that another couple of times as his breathing picked up and his hands fisted. "Listen here, you little bitch–"

"In fact, I'm sure there was a clause in that contract about keeping the property in good shape while you're occupying it. This place is a dump. You need to clean it up or you'll be subject to more fines."

He took the final step separating us until he was hovering over me. "I'm not paying no motherfucking fines, I'm not cleaning anything, and you can get the hell off my property!"

I straightened my spine and fisted my own hands. They were shaking with the need to shift. I understood that I was in a potentially dangerous situation and my fight instincts were ready to take over at a moment's notice.

"That fine is from the alpha. Pay it or lose your house. I'll be back soon to check that you're cleaning this place up. If it's not respectable-looking within the month, you can expect more fines."

His nostrils flared, and his skin had turned a really unattractive shade of red. "I don't have to do a goddamn thing you say. You're nothing. Just some bitch that fell into the alpha's bed. You'll never lead this pack and you'll never be my alpha."

His words crept around my brain, burrowing into the darkest places and making themselves at home. He'd just voiced all my deepest fears. Announced every worry that I'd never measure up. That I'd never be taken seriously. That I'd never get them to follow me.

I shook my head to clear the thoughts. I was sure Jimmy wasn't the only one who felt that way, but that was just too damn bad.

"You have a choice: pay the fine and clean your house, or lose it. What happens now is up to you."

I spun around and walked away while Jimmy continued to sputter behind me. There was nothing more for me to say to him and staying would only escalate the situation.

As I walked back up the road leading to the lodge, I waved to Maddy who was climbing into her car, and Brad who was working on a pickup truck in his driveway. I realized that, despite everything, I was starting to make a difference. Changing things for the better. That was really all I could ask for.

As I walked by the fourth house, I noticed Craig on his front porch, watching me while I passed.

"Throwin' your weight around some more? Think that'll make 'em take you seriously?"

I stopped in my tracks and turned to see Craig with a hand on his wide waist. His face was contorted with anger and all of it was directed right at me.

"Can I help you with something, Craig?"

He descended the steps off his porch. "Just wanted to know if you were messin' with someone else's livin', or if I'm just special."

I wanted to roll my eyes, but I somehow just barely held back. "I gave you a choice, Craig, and you chose wrong."

His hands fisted at his sides as his face got redder. I sure was bringing that reaction out of a lot of men today.

"You didn't give me a fuckin' choice."

That time, I did roll my eyes. "We've already discussed this, and I have other things to do. If you're still having a problem with my decision, feel free to talk to Abraham about it."

He took a step closer, his knuckles white with how hard he was squeezing his hands closed. "You bet your ass I will."

I shrugged and left him in his driveway. He was looking for a fight and he wouldn't find it with me. My business with Craig was over as far as I was concerned, and I knew Abraham backed my decision completely. I had nothing to worry about there, but my stomach still twisted into knots.

Was I doing the right thing? Was I throwing my weight around like Craig said?

It felt necessary. Like if I didn't put my foot down, I'd never be respected. They'd continue to think I was just an accessory and not a leader. I knew I'd been putting off the actual mating ceremony, but I was treating the job like it was already mine. I knew things were rough, but I had to hope that, in the end, it would all help me gain their respect and not lose it.

Chapter 17

I placed a soft kiss on Abraham's bare chest and slid out of his hold. It was difficult extracting myself from his arms, and when I'd finally gotten myself untangled, his wandering hands grabbed my hips and pulled me back down.

"Where you goin'?" he said, his voice deep with sleep.

I leaned over and kissed his lips. "I told you, I'm observing a shift at the farm today. I need to get going."

His arm tightened around me. "Stay with me and snuggle."

My lips twitched with a smile and my heart melted. He was so adorable, and that was such a good offer, I had to stop and consider it for a minute.

I shook my head. "I'm sorry, baby. I have to do this."

He pulled me closer. "Then you better stop callin' me baby or you're not goin' anywhere."

I laughed and kissed him again before I slid out from between his arms. "I'll see you for lunch."

He cracked open an eye and watched me walk across the room. "I'm hungry already."

I laughed again and shut the bathroom door. I needed that barrier for myself as much as I did for him. Thankfully, by the time I was done in the shower, Abraham had fallen back asleep.

I watched him for a few minutes as my long, wet hair dripped on the hardwood floor.

When I was dressed in the closest thing I owned to work clothes, I wandered down to the kitchen to see if I could scrounge up some breakfast. To my surprise, Ms. Elsie was already in there at the stove.

"Ellie, what are you doin' up this early?"

I grabbed a warm biscuit off a sheet pan and took a bite. "I'm overseeing a shift at the farm today."

She nodded. "I heard they've been havin' some issues."

"You have?"

She shot me a look. "There are no secrets in a pack."

I chuckled and took another bite of my biscuit. "Yeah, I've heard."

"Can I make you some eggs before you go?"

I lifted a lid off a pot on the stove. "Nah, I'll just have some of this oatmeal and be on my way. Thanks, though."

She smiled and patted me on the arm. "You just let me know if you change your mind, hon."

I dished myself up some oatmeal and took a seat on a stool at the kitchen island. The lodge was still quiet this early in the morning and I wasn't used to the lack of movement and noise.

"It's so quiet."

Ms. Elsie chuckled. "I know. Almost too quiet, isn't it?"

I smiled. "Yeah, kinda. Never thought I'd miss all the commotion."

We were silent for a while after that as I finished my breakfast and she continued to cook. When I was done, I rinsed my bowl and threw it in the dishwasher. I opened my mouth to say goodbye when she spoke.

"I hear you've been makin' a few waves around here lately and I want you to promise me you're gonna be careful."

I frowned. "What have you heard?"

She wiped her hands on a dish towel. "Well, I know you fired Craig, and implemented quiet hours. I also know you fined Jimmy for makin' a mess and already hired a new pack mechanic."

I nodded slowly. "Oh, so you know everything."

She laughed softly before she got serious. "I just wanna make sure you're bein' careful. Not everyone is gonna take kindly to someone new tellin' 'em what to do."

"I've already run into my fair share of that in the past couple days."

She nodded again. "And I'm sure there's more where that came from. Just be careful, okay?"

I gave her my most reassuring smile. "I will, Ms. Elsie. Don't worry about me. I'll see you later."

I turned to leave and thought I heard her mumble something about her worrying about me whether I liked it or not, but I let it go. She was as bad as the rest of them. I knew what I was doing and could take care of myself.

I knew the problem was that hadn't always been the case. When I'd had to fight against Calvin, I'd been outmaneuvered and overpowered. I'd barely held on for the first few minutes of the fight before he'd gained the upper hand. After that, I was at his mercy. Hands bound behind my back, I was completely defenseless.

I'd promised myself in those dark moments that I'd never be that helpless ever again. That I'd do whatever it took to be able to hold my own. To protect myself.

That was why I still practiced with Bea. That was why I pushed myself every single session with her. I wasn't that powerless, witless new wolf I once was. I knew I still had a long way to go, but I'd also come really far.

It would take time for everyone to realize that, but in the meantime, I was sick of being doubted.

The sun was just barely peeking over the horizon as I walked down the path that led through the pack houses. When I'd asked, Abraham said the farm was past the last house and down a short path. I followed his instructions and, almost immediately, the woods opened up to a large open space full of crops.

There was a group of people nearby and I made my way towards them.

"Ellie!"

Sophie broke away from the pack and walked over to me, perky as ever, even at that ungodly hour.

"Morning, Sophie."

She gave me a quick hug and then led me to the group of people she'd been standing with. "This is Jake, Hannah, Marco, and Elliot."

I greeted each person with a handshake. When I got to Elliot, I gave him a warm smile. "Nice to see you again, Elliot."

He grinned back and pulled me closer. "Thanks for taking care of that issue for me."

"My pleasure," I said, beaming back at him.

It felt amazing to have someone tell me I'd actually helped. That'd I'd made a difference.

"All right, quit fucking around and get to work."

I spun around at the hateful tone and found a tall man with dirty blond hair and a scowl on his face. There was a younger, pretty girl hanging off his arm, and I was pretty sure I was looking at Tom and Daisy.

The rest of the workers grumbled under their breath, but dispersed anyway, heading for a shed I assumed held equipment. I turned back toward Tom and made my way over to him.

"Hi, Tom?"

He spun around and wrinkled his nose when he saw me. "Can I help you?"

"I'm Ellie, Abraham's mate. I don't think we've met," I said, holding out a hand.

He eyed me for a long minute before reaching out for a shake. "I've heard of you."

I slapped on a big smile. "Great! I'm here to observe an average day here on the farm."

His nose crinkled again. "Why would you be doing that?"

"Oh."

Shit.

I hadn't really thought up a good excuse yet. I didn't want to tell him there'd been a complaint in case it got back to Sophie. So, I fibbed a little. "Since I'm new here, I'm trying to get a feel for everything that happens on pack lands. Today, it's the farm. Next, it's the gardeners." I had zero intention of shadowing the gardeners for a day, but he didn't need to know that.

He turned his head to sneer, but I caught it anyway. "Sounds lovely," he said before stalking off.

Daisy was left standing there looking confused. She hadn't said a word the entire time, and I'd almost forgotten she was there. Her light eyes darted from me to Tom and back again.

Finally, I sighed. "Don't you think you should be getting to work?"

She jumped in place like she hadn't expected me to talk. With a nod in my direction, she scampered off after the other workers.

I followed Tom and spoke up again once I was close. "It's only five-forty-five."

His shoulders tensed. "Yes, and?"

"Well, I was told the shift didn't start until six."

He turned slowly to face me. "They know to get started early so they're well underway by the time six rolls around."

I nodded slowly. "And do they get paid for that fifteen minutes?"

His lips thinned briefly. "No, they do not."

I nodded again. "Interesting."

Without waiting for him to respond, I took off across the field to where the workers were gathered. They'd already picked up their equipment and looked like they were about to get started harvesting some eggplants. I wandered closer and watched from the sidelines.

It was clear that Sophie was the leader amongst them as everyone looked to her for guidance. With a glance across the field, I saw Tom sitting underneath a tree, looking at his phone. Obviously, they got no help from him and had learned to figure it out themselves.

As time passed, it was clear that Daisy did little if any work. She spent more time checking in with Tom than actually working. She was a weak link, and I watched as other workers repeatedly had to pick up the slack for her.

She needed to go, and to be frank, Tom needed to shape up or he'd be following his girlfriend through the door.

It was hours before Tom raised his voice from across the clearing, announcing they were allowed to take a five-minute water break.

I was shocked to my core.

I hustled to Sophie's side as she trudged over to her things and the water bottle she'd brought from home. "You all aren't allowed to take a break unless Tom says?"

She shrugged as she chugged from the bottle. "Yep. He doesn't even really allow bathroom breaks, but occasionally he'll say okay if we convince him we have to go badly enough."

What the hell?

They'd been working in the North Carolina summer heat for hours, and all that time, I'd thought they were just powering through without a break. Never once did it cross my mind that they weren't even allowed to have a drink of water in all that time.

"And water isn't provided for you?" I asked.

She smiled sadly and shrugged as Tom yelled for them to get back to work.

I spent the rest of the morning hours seething. Tom was ineffective as a leader and I'd need to replace him immediately. I'd seen at least two instances where a little more management could make production that much more efficient, and I'd only been there a few hours. It was clear there were tons of people more qualified for the job than Tom, and I was about to rectify that.

"All right, you all can take lunch now, but I want you back in twenty minutes," Tom called from beneath the shady tree I'd begun to call his office.

Finally, I'd had enough.

"Actually, you can all take an hour. Have a good lunch and we'll see you when you get back," I called over their voices.

Every single worker's eyes worked double time as they flicked from Tom to me and back again. I could hear the man in question stomping toward me and didn't need the rest of the employees to witness our conversation.

I waved my hands. "Go on. Everyone's dismissed for an hour."

They'd just started to shuffle away when Tom made it to my side. He grabbed my arm and spun me around. His face was bright red, eyes practically shooting flames. "What the hell do you think you're doing?"

I ripped my arm out of his hold and tipped up my chin. "I'm treating those employees fairly. Something you're clearly not doing."

He ground his teeth together so loudly I could hear it from where I was. "And who the fuck do you think you are? This is my farm and my team, and I'll do with them what I want!"

"Not if you want to keep working here."

His eyes widened so fast, I worried they'd pop out. "Excuse me?"

I straightened my already straight spine. "This isn't your farm or your team. You work here and if you can't do it right, you're fired."

His head tipped back, and an ugly, forceful laugh shot out of him. When he looked back down at me, his eyes were even more crazed than before. "You can't do that. You're nothing."

I pushed my shoulders back. "I'm the future alpha of this pack and what I say goes. You either agree to treat these employees fairly, or you don't work here anymore."

He took a menacing step closer, his hands shaking. "I don't give a shit what you say. You're not my fucking alpha. You mean nothing to me. You need to get your little ass back up to that lodge before you regret it."

A bolt of shock ran down my spine and I took a step closer. "Are you threatening me?"

He closed the remaining distance between us, his body wracked with tremors. "I sure as shit am. Get the fuck out of my sight or I'll make you leave."

"You're the one that needs to leave. You don't work here anymore."

His chest was rising and falling rapidly. "I'm not gonna tell you again."

I crossed my arms. "My decision is final. You're done here."

A loud crack split through the air, and seconds later, Tom was a large wolf before me. Without my permission, my body shifted, too. It must have known the danger we were in and acted accordingly. Which was lucky, because I was still struggling to catch up.

Had he really just shifted? Was he really looking to fight me?

"You little bitch. Who the fuck do you think you are?"

"I'm your alpha. And honestly, I'm getting a little sick of the bitch *insult. I'd think you all could come up with something more creative."*

He yelled loudly in my head and lunged toward me. Anticipating his attack, I jumped out of the way easily.

"Tom, I don't want to fight you. Stand down."

"I'm gonna teach you a lesson, bitch. Show you where you stand in this pack."

He leapt forward again, his teeth bared, but I danced out of his way once more. He missed by a lot and I could tell that bothered him.

I really didn't want to fight my own pack mate. But hadn't I been warned over and over that not everyone would take kindly to me rising to power? Wasn't that why I trained with Beatrice? So I could defend myself?

Tom charged again, and this time he got close enough that I struck back, sinking my teeth into his hamstring and eliciting a high-pitched bark from him. I almost laughed, but I just barely restrained myself.

"Fuck you!" he yelled, running at me again.

"I told you I don't want to fight you. Stop this now and I'll forget it happened."

He growled loudly, saliva dripping from his fangs. *"You're gonna learn your place today, bitch."*

Again with this *bitch* stuff.

He raced toward me, and this time, I dodged him, but also struck back, sinking my teeth into his back leg. He tried to kick me off, but I held on tightly. When he turned around to bite me back, I released him and darted away.

Now he was bleeding and limping and I knew he didn't have much left in him.

He lunged again, this time slower than ever. I jumped to the side and swiped a paw at his face, hitting him so hard, his head jerked back. He fell to the ground, and I watched as he struggled to catch his breath.

When he pulled himself back to his feet, he surprised me by charging once more. It was almost too sad to watch. I leapt out of his way again and spun around, wrapping my teeth around the underside of his neck. He froze in place and I made sure to keep the right amount of pressure on his artery to let him know I meant business.

"Give this up, Tom."

"Fuck you."

I clenched my jaw around his neck and tasted blood. I shook my head with his neck still between my teeth. Seeing that he still wasn't giving in, I pressed harder and finally, he caved.

"Okay, okay! I give up! Fuck, let me go!"

I pulled my teeth out of his neck and backed up until I was out of reach. Just because he said he gave up didn't make me believe he'd stay down.

"Have we settled this now?" I asked as he recovered in a heap on the ground.

He lifted his head when the thundering footsteps of a large wolf sounded from nearby. Seconds later, Abraham in wolf form was flying through the clearing, his wild eyes trained on Tom. Before I could speak, he had Tom's neck in his jaws in a death grip I wasn't sure he'd survive.

Chapter 18

"Abraham, stop!"

The large alpha werewolf just growled and shook his head, Tom's neck still in his mouth.

"Abraham. I'm fine. I won. Let him go."

"Yeah, man. Your bitch-mate already kicked my ass. Let me go," Tom whined.

Abraham's whole body froze before a sound almost like a roar rumbled out of him. *"You touched my fucking mate?! You dared to threaten what's mine?"*

"Abraham, man, listen. I can explain all this."

Abraham shook his head again, this time faster and with more strength. I could smell Tom's blood flowing freely now as he whimpered.

"Hey, are you okay?"

I turned to see Sophie, a worried look in her green eyes.

I gave her a smile and a nod, and she grinned back. "I watched the whole thing. You were fucking awesome."

My wolfy grin widened, and she chuckled. Her eyes darted back over to Abraham and Tom and her smile fell. With a nod at the men, she said, "I think you should go break that up before Abraham kills him."

I sighed and walked over to them, bumping my head into Abraham's shoulder. *"Let him go, Abraham. It's over."*

He turned far enough that he could shoot me a look. His eyes were still wild with rage and I knew this was far from over. Abraham turned back around, whipped Tom's body one way, and then tossed him the other. I watched as Tom went sailing at least twenty feet away.

Abraham was still breathing hard next to me as he took a step toward the limp wolf. At first, I thought he was going to go after him again, but then he spoke.

"You're lucky to still be breathing, Baxter. If you so much as look at my mate in a way I don't like, I'll rip your fucking throat out. I want your shit packed and you off my lands before the sun sets."

My jaw was on the floor as a shiver raced down my spine.

Abraham was terrifying.

He slowly turned around, his eyes not leaving Tom's prone body. Finally, he glanced in my direction. *"Let's go."*

Knowing exactly how unintelligent it would be to argue with him when he was like that, I shut my mouth and followed him. He stalked back through the pack houses and people literally crossed the street to get out of his way.

I'd never seen him so angry before.

It was a little scary, but also kinda sexy, and I didn't know what that said about me.

We got to the lodge just as Beatrice was coming through the back door.

"Hey, Abey. Hey, Ellie. What are you two up to?"

I heard Abraham curse in my head before there was a loud crack and he was a human again. He put his hands on his hips, his shoulders tense. "Your training sessions with Rocky here are over."

I jerked back and opened my mouth to argue when I remembered I was a wolf and couldn't talk. So, I did the next best thing and barked at him.

He shot me a look. "I'll deal with you in a minute."

I barked at him again, really not appreciating his tone.

160

He spun back around to Bea. "I'm serious. You two are done."

"Why would you say that? She's actually becoming a pretty skilled fighter. What, you don't want that for her?"

He took a menacing step toward his sister and I almost got in between them, but Bea just tipped up her chin and met his eye.

"What I don't want is her picking fights with grown goddamn men!"

Bea's eyes flicked to me and she raised a brow. "You got in a fight?"

I just tilted my head, but Abraham responded, "Yes, she got in a fucking fight. And that's because *you* trained her to fight."

Bea rolled her eyes. "I trained her to defend herself. I highly doubt she walked up and picked a fight with someone."

I snorted, and Bea shot me a small smile.

Abraham reached up and slid his fingers into his hair, pulling on the ends until it was sticking up in tufts. "I don't give a damn how it happened, it's never happening again! No more training sessions from here on out."

With that, he stormed past Bea and into the lodge. The oldest McCoy sister turned to me with a look of pity. "You know I have to do what he says, right?"

I rolled my eyes and sauntered past her. I think she got the point when she chuckled behind me.

I wasn't going to let Abraham dictate what I did and didn't do. It was a good friggen thing Beatrice had taught me to defend myself, because I'd needed to today. Abraham was just going to have to get over himself and quick.

"Elizabeth!" he hollered from inside the house, and I huffed.

I walked into the kitchen and found him on the other side, standing in the hallway, naked as the day he was born. My eyes darted around the room and I found both Ms. Elsie and Aubrey working in there.

I swore if Aubrey's eyes even flickered in his direction, I'd bite her.

"Let's go!" Abraham yelled again.

I turned wide eyes to him and wished there was a way for me to communicate how sick I was of him yelling at me. Instead, I padded through the kitchen, bumping him hard with my shoulder as I walked past. I heard him sigh, but I ignored him as I climbed the stairs to our floor.

When we got to our room, Abraham stepped in front of me to open the door. When it shut behind us, I shifted back into a woman.

"What the hell, Abraham?"

His eyes widened, and he stomped over to me. "You're asking *me* what the hell? What the hell were you thinking?!"

I propped my hands up on my hips. "I had it under control."

"It shouldn't have happened to begin with!"

"I know it shouldn't!" I yelled, trying to match the volume of his voice. "But it did, and I handled it!"

"You handled it? You were fighting someone more than twice your size! What were you thinking?" he asked again.

I threw my hands in the air. "Who cares how big he was?! I beat him! I won! What's the problem?"

He took a step closer, his jaw ticking with tension. "The problem is my mate will not fight. My mate will not ever leave the lodge again if she thinks–"

"Have you lost your friggen mind?! You're being completely unreasonable."

"I'm telling you like it is."

I closed the distance between us and stared him down as well as I could considering I was a good six inches shorter than him. "I didn't fight, I defended myself. Would you rather I just let Tom hurt me?"

His eye twitched as he watched me. Finally, he released a puff of air and turned around to pace the floor in front of me. "I don't give a shit

162

what happened or how it happened, it's never going to happen again. Do you hear me?"

"You can't just order nothing to ever happen to me again. It doesn't work like that."

He stormed back over and grasped both my arms. "Then I'll lock you in this goddamn room if that's what it takes! Nothing is going to happen to you ever again. Do you hear me?!" He shook me a little with that last question, but I was stunned speechless.

This went a lot deeper than I'd imagined.

He released me and spun around, his hand digging into his hair. His shoulders rose and fell a few more times before he took off for the hallway door.

"Where the hell are you going?"

"For a drive," he tossed over his shoulder.

"Naked?"

"I have clothes in my truck."

"So, you're just leaving? You're running away in the middle of an argument."

"I guess I'm taking a page out of your book," he said just before he slammed the door behind him.

I stood there in the middle of his sitting room, shocked silent, and beneath it all, hurt.

Abraham didn't talk to me like that. He didn't throw my past in my face and he sure as hell didn't walk out on me.

What was going on?

There was so much that went wrong today, I didn't even know where to begin. Maybe it was a good thing Abraham left. We were both yelling, and that didn't solve anything.

I looked at the door he walked through one last time and sighed. It was better that I let him go for now. He clearly needed some distance. It just stung that it seemed he needed it from me.

I shuffled into the bedroom and immediately took a hot shower. I let the water wash off all the sweat and dirt from the farm, Tom's blood that had splashed on me at some point, and every bad thing that happened that morning.

I honestly hadn't thought my day at the farm would turn out like this. I thought I'd observe, make a few suggestions to the manager, and be done with it.

However, when I saw the working conditions for those poor farmers, I knew that wouldn't be enough. Then, when I heard the way Tom spoke to and treated them, I knew he wasn't the right fit for the job.

With a personality like that, how did he get the position in the first place?

I shook my head as the hot water ran over my face and down my body.

The most shocking part of the day had to be when Tom shifted and confronted me. Never in a million years had I thought he would try to fight me. I was used to disagreeing with words, not fists. I guess I should be happy he'd chosen to fight me as a wolf and not a woman. That would have been a quick round with me the obvious loser.

I hadn't been in a fight since that night with Calvin, and despite what I told myself, it brought up memories. Dark thoughts that I did my best to stuff down and forget, but would pop up here and there, anyway.

The last time I fought a wolf, it had been for my life and I'd lost. I'd gotten distracted, and that was all it took for my opponent to gain the upper hand.

I sometimes thought about how that night could have gone if I'd won the fight. Maybe if I'd trained harder with Bea, I would have beaten him. Maybe if our lessons were two hours instead of just one, I'd have had the skills.

And if I'd won the fight against Calvin, it was likely Abraham wouldn't have had to kill him. They could have taken him into custody and sent him to werewolf prison or wherever they put their criminals.

But I hadn't won. I'd lost, and it had almost cost me my life.

In some ways, the fight with Tom was like redemption for me. Sure, he wasn't an enforcer like Calvin had been, and he probably was only trying to hurt me and not kill me, but I'd still beaten him. He hadn't even gotten one strike in before I had him in my jaws.

Honestly, it felt amazing to know I could hold my own. Even a little. That I wasn't completely helpless. That if the Calvin thing were to happen again, I'd be ready, I'd be deadly, and I'd come out on top.

Despite what Abraham thought, I had a bad feeling this wasn't the last time I'd need to defend myself. My lessons with Bea were more important than ever now.

And where had Abraham even come from? One second, I was winning my fight against Tom, and the next my fiancé had his teeth around his neck.

I knew it was logical for his first instinct to be to protect me. I was his mate, and he was the bigger, more dominant one in the relationship. I knew enough about werewolf dynamics to know that meant he'd always worry about my safety.

Why he was so angry at me was the problem I couldn't figure out. Why he'd want me to quit my lessons with Bea when they might have saved my life didn't make sense, either. He was acting irrationally, and I didn't even know how to talk to him.

When I was done in the shower, I twisted my long blonde hair into a braid before I left the bathroom in search of clothes.

That reminded me that I ruined a set out at the farm. I'd have to see if my sneakers made it or not.

Once I was dressed in a t-shirt and jean shorts, I stood in the middle of the bedroom, unsure of what I should do.

I knew Abraham wouldn't really lock me in that room, but I had a feeling he expected me to stay there. I had an even stronger feeling that if he came back and I was gone, any grip on his sanity he'd managed to restore would quickly dissolve.

With a sigh, I checked on Charlie real quick before gathering up the environmental texts and lugging them out to the sitting room. Actually, I had to return a couple of them to Callie because I'd already finished them.

The more I read, the more I was starting to understand how I could contribute to Callie's team, and the more excited I got. I couldn't wait to start my new job and kept begging Abraham to speed up the construction.

Unfortunately, although I had the time to study, I didn't have the headspace. It was all devoted to my missing fiancé.

I wondered where he was. He said he was going for a drive, but I had no idea where to. I knew he said our lake was a place he liked to go to think, but you couldn't get there by car and I didn't think he'd want to go there right then, anyway. It would remind him of me, and he was clearly trying to avoid me.

So, where would he have gone?

A bar?

A restaurant?

A movie?

There were endless possibilities, and each one made less sense than the one before.

I'd just decided to give up on the books when I heard footsteps walking down our wing. It could have been anyone, but I'd have recognized those strong, sure steps anywhere.

The hall door opened, and Abraham stepped through. He was clothed, thankfully, in a pair of mesh shorts and a muscle tank. I was trying to not get distracted by his golden biceps, but it was hard.

"Hey," he said, his voice so quiet and sad my heart lurched.

"Hey."

He took a deep breath and stepped farther into the room. "Are you still mad?"

I shrugged. "Not really. More confused."

He nodded slowly and blew out a big gust of air. "Wanna go for a ride with me?"

I could tell he was hesitant. That he wasn't sure of my answer. Given the fight we'd had, I didn't blame him. We'd never argued like that before and it was kind of scary that we did, but I think that's what happens when you love someone so much. You fight hard, but you love harder.

Despite the hurt feelings, the decision was easy. When I told him I was all-in, I'd meant every word.

I stood from my chair and reached for his hand. "Of course."

Chapter 19

We were quiet as we walked out to his truck. Once there, he opened the passenger door for me, and I climbed up and slid to the middle. When Abraham got in on the other side, I could tell he was surprised by my choice of seat, but he didn't comment. Instead, he started up his truck, threw it into gear, and wrapped his big, warm hand around my bare thigh.

We drove in silence as he navigated the steep drive and then the country roads onto the highway. He exited in downtown Asheville and I watched the eclectic city pass me by. Finally, he pulled into a spot on the street and turned his truck off.

"Where are we?"

He squeezed my leg once before pulling away and unbuckling his seatbelt. "There's something I want to show you."

I followed him out of the truck and took a look around the city block. There was a café, a bicycle repair shop, a restaurant, a couple retail stores, and what looked like residences above them all. I still had no idea where we were or why he'd brought me there.

He took my hand and led me across the street to a nondescript door with peeling paint and an old doorknob that looked like it'd seen too many winters. Abraham pulled out a key and unlocked it, ushering me inside.

When my eyes adjusted, I took in the room. It was just one big space, but it was filled with building material and equipment. There was a little table pushed against one wall and I wandered over to it. Across the surface was a blueprint of the space. I did my best to analyze it but could only really understand that the big space we were in was going to be cut into smaller sections of varying size.

"Is this our new office?"

I could feel Abraham come closer. "Yes."

I wandered further in, seeing they'd already blocked off where the rooms would be built. As I passed them by, I came upon one that was different from the rest. I walked into the space, trying to decide what made it stand out.

I took a deep breath, and that was when it hit me. The scent. It smelled exactly like Abraham. Like soap and spearmint.

I knew he'd spent time in here before, but his scent was so strong, he had to have been in there recently.

Suddenly, the puzzle pieces clicked into place and I turned to Abraham. "This is where you came when you left?"

His eyes darted away, and he ran a hand through his dark hair. "Yeah."

I crossed my arms and leaned against a wall. "Why?"

"Why did I leave?"

"No, why did you come here?"

He looked away again before he took a few steps closer. "I thought I could come here and get my mind off you, but it did the opposite."

"Why's that?"

He looked around and shrugged. "This is your new office."

My eyes searched the soon-to-be room with keen eyes. "So, you came to this construction site to get away from me and wound up sitting in my new office?"

He sighed and ran a rough hand down his face. "I wasn't trying to get away from you."

"Sure looked like it."

The words were flippant, but they sliced into my throat on their way out. It hurt that he'd left. That he felt he needed to get away from me. Now I knew how he must have felt all those times it was me doing the running and I felt even worse.

Abraham crossed the distance between us and wrapped his hands around my biceps. Last time we'd been in this situation, he'd been yelling at me. When his eyes tightened, I knew he was thinking the same thing.

"I didn't need to get away from you."

I tipped my chin up and met his blue, blue gaze. "Then why'd you leave?"

I could tell he wanted to look away again, but he held my stare. "I needed to get away from myself."

"What do you mean?"

He dropped his arms. "You called me irrational, and you were right. I wasn't making any sense. I couldn't even *think* straight." He paced away from me, his hands fisting at his sides. "I saw you two from a distance. Saw him leap at you that last time and you catch his neck in your teeth. It didn't matter that you had the upper hand. It didn't matter that you won. All I could see was the threat against my mate and I reacted."

I nodded slowly. "I understand why you attacked Tom and I don't blame you for it. What I don't understand is what happened afterward. Why were you so mad at me? Why did you forbid me from the lessons that might have saved my life today?"

Abraham paused his pacing and looked at me, the color draining from his face. "The fact that your life could have possibly been on the line today is a reality I can't accept."

I took a step toward him. "We knew not everyone would be okay with me becoming alpha. You said that yourself when you assigned Bea to teach me to fight. That was all your idea."

He blew out a big breath and dropped his head into both his hands. "I know."

I took another few steps. "Instead of being grateful that I knew how to defend myself and proud that I did so, you lost your damn mind and threatened to lock me in our room." I stopped when I was a few feet away from him and crossed my arms again. "You're gonna have to help me out, Abraham, because that just doesn't make sense."

He lifted his head from his hands and speared me with a look that almost stopped my heart. "Do you have any idea what it did to me the night Calvin took you?"

I swallowed and shook my head. Of course, I could guess it had been difficult for him to find my apartment wrecked and not know where I'd been taken. We'd talked about that night a lot, but Abraham had never mentioned his feelings about it. I'd assumed he'd rather not revisit them and left it alone.

"You were taken from me, El." His Adam's apple bobbed. "I didn't know where you were, I didn't know if you were okay, I didn't know if I'd ever find you. If I'd ever see you again." His voice got quieter the longer he talked, almost as if he was afraid to say the words too loud.

I took a step closer. I couldn't help it. Abraham was my sun and I was a helpless planet stuck in his gravitational pull. Seeing him so upset hurt me in a way I couldn't describe.

"Then, when I finally found you, when I saw you on the ground underneath Calvin, you weren't even moving, El. I had no idea if you were conscious, if you had brain damage, if you were dead, for fuck's sake." He grabbed the back of his neck roughly. "I can't do that again. You can't ask me to do that again."

I closed the distance between us and put a hand on his arm. "I'm okay, Abraham. I wasn't kidnapped. I wasn't even hurt."

He let out a deep breath and shook his head. "I lost you once and that almost ruined me." His dark eyes latched onto mine. "I know because we're fated that I can't live without you, but, El, I couldn't live if someone hurt you. If you were injured, and I wasn't there to protect you again, it would kill me."

"I wasn't injured, Abraham. I'm okay."

He watched me for a long time before he spoke again. "I know you're okay and I'm grateful you had the skills to defend yourself."

"Then, why did you tell Bea she can't train me anymore?"

He took a deep breath and let it out, his shoulders deflating until he was almost hunched. "I was afraid, El. I was so afraid today."

His words broke something inside of me. I was still upset at him and he had a lot more to explain, but I had to hold him. My arms physically needed to feel him between them.

I stepped closer and wrapped myself around him. He paused for only a moment before pulling me into his embrace. We stood there for a long time, his chin propped on my head and my face against his steady heartbeat.

Finally, he pulled away and looked down at me. "I'm sorry, El. I shouldn't have reacted that way and I shouldn't have spoken to you like that. I'm just a man who's terrified of losing the one person in the world he can't live without." He traced the back of his hand along my face before tucking some hair behind my ear. "Forgive me."

I searched his eyes, seeing the truth behind his words for myself. He was sorry, and he'd only acted out of fear. I could admit that I'd let fear rule my actions more often than I should have.

I dragged him close again. "It's okay," I said against his chest. Pulling away again to look at him, I added, "As long as you let Bea keep training me."

He tugged me back against his chest and sighed. "Okay, Rocky. I won't take you out of the ring."

I laughed against him, inhaling his scent and letting it soothe my frayed nerves. Fighting with Abraham was awful. He was the most important person in my life, and I hated when he was upset with me.

"What about Tom? Do you think it was the right decision to kick him out of the pack?" I asked.

Abraham took a deep breath, his chest rocking me backward. "I've let too much shit slide around here. I was trying so hard to not be the terrible dictator my uncle was, but I can't allow Tom to remain in the pack after what he did. There's just no other option."

I nodded against his chest and settled back into his arms. I understood where he was coming from and I wasn't going to fight him on this. To be honest, I didn't want Tom in the pack anymore, either. I just didn't like feeling like it was my fault he got kicked out. But he was a grown man, and he made his own decisions. He'd have to live with the consequences.

I pulled away one more time. "We okay?"

He leaned down to brush his lips against mine. "As long as you forgive me."

"I do," I whispered.

His body trembled slightly beneath my hands and I smiled against his mouth. His lips curled into a grin too. "What are you smiling about?"

I gave him a soft kiss. "I like the way I affect you."

He pulled me closer, his erection already pressing against my belly. "You affect me in a lot of ways, El."

His mouth trailed down my neck as I fought off a shiver.

"Like how?"

He kissed my shoulder, his lips hovering over my chest. "Like when you walk in a room and my fuckin' heart pounds." He kissed along my collarbone. "Or when you smile at me and I feel a hundred feet tall." His lips skimmed up my throat until they reached mine. "Or how when I'm deep inside you and I know I've found my place in this world. That it's wherever you are."

My heart raced at his words and I couldn't take the tension anymore. I fused my lips to his, eliciting a surprised grunt from him before he wrapped his big hands around my waist and pulled me closer.

We kissed as our hands roamed and the clothes fell off, one article at a time. Finally, he pulled away, his chest heaving. "There's no place in here clean enough for me to lay you down so I'm gonna fuck you against this wall."

I closed my eyes and let his words race through my system. They were wild and savage and tore at my insides.

He reached down to grab my thighs before he lifted me into his arms. I wrapped my legs around his hips and held on as he walked me over to the wall he'd promised. When I hit the cold surface, my back arched, pressing me closer to him.

Without warning, he slid deep into me, finding no resistance whatsoever. Our eyes were closed and our breaths were ragged as we adjusted to the position. Finally, he began to move, and I could do nothing but hold on.

He made love to me like it was the last time. It was somehow rough and tender all at once. His hips slammed into mine repeatedly, but his rough hands cupped my face like I was his most precious possession. It was enough to drive me to the edge.

"Abe," I panted.

"Yes, baby. I love you so much."

"Oh my God, I love you too. So much, Abe."

His thrusts got harder and deeper as I dug my fingernails into his shoulders, and suddenly, it was too much for me and I came hard. Abraham was right behind me, groaning against my neck and squeezing my hips as he emptied himself.

When we'd caught our breath, he slid me down his body to my feet before wrapping his arms around me. Abraham kissed the side of my head and whispered against my ear. "I'll do anything to keep you safe, El. There is no limit for me. I can't help how I react when your safety is threatened."

I pulled far enough away that I could look in his eyes. "I'll never expect you to sit on the sidelines when I'm in danger. That's not in your nature and I'd never ask you to change. But you can't hover, and you can't prevent me from living my life. I'll stay as safe as I can, and I'll train hard with Bea. Can that be enough for you?"

His eyes searched my face for a long time. I'd just accepted the fact that he couldn't handle what I'd proposed when he nodded once. "Okay. I can try."

I just barely held in a laugh, but my smile was unstoppable. At least he was honest, right?

I wrapped my arms around his neck and pulled his lips to mine. "I can work with that," I whispered.

When I finally wrenched my mouth away from his again, I realized we were standing in a construction zone in the middle of the day and there were no workers around. Then, I remembered how naked we were and panicked.

"Holy shit, Abraham. What are we doing?"

I swerved around him, searching for my clothes and desperately tugging them on.

He laughed. "What's wrong?"

I glared at him as I hopped on one leg, trying to get them both in my jean shorts. "Couldn't your men be here any minute?"

174

He smiled and shrugged. "They have the day off."

I frowned. "Why?"

He rolled his eyes. "It's Saturday, El."

Jeez. I'm unemployed for a month and already can't keep track of the days. I shook my head to clear it. "Oh, okay."

He crossed the room, a big smile on his face. "You think I'd fuck you in here if there was a chance someone could walk in?"

I tipped my chin up. "I thought there was a chance you weren't thinking straight." I just barely suppressed a cringe at my own words.

Abraham chuckled and wrapped his warm, naked body around me. "You do scramble my thoughts, Ms. Montgomery."

That made me feel a little better at least.

"If this is a top priority project, shouldn't you have men working weekends, too?"

Abraham laughed again and wrapped an arm around my neck. "Look at you. Get a dose of power and now you think you're the boss of everything."

I slapped his chest. "I do not think I'm the boss of everything."

"Okay, boss."

I hit him again, but my hand just bounced off his hard chest. He probably hadn't even felt it. "Whatever, Abraham. Just put some clothes on."

"Yes, boss."

Chapter 20

We spent more time making up that night than we did sleeping, but I wouldn't have changed it for the world. Without meaning to, I'd scared Abraham yesterday, and I'd have done anything it took to ease his fears.

I was lying on Abraham's warm chest when Charlie leapt onto the bed. He picked his way between us until he was curled up on Abraham, too. Apparently, my cat knew a good spot when he saw one.

Abraham reached out a big hand and rubbed Charlie's head. It might have been a little rougher than I'd pet my cat, but he didn't seem to mind. He arched his back and pushed into Abraham's hand.

"You're so good with him," I said softly, not wanting to break the peaceful quiet of the morning.

He grunted. "He's a good cat."

I had to bite my lip to hide my smile. When Abraham first found out I even owned a cat, he'd been less than thrilled. When I started bringing him out to Asheville with me, he tolerated him, but I could tell he didn't think of him as a pet.

Now, everything was different.

I think it started around the time Abraham built the magnificent cat tree for Charlie. I wasn't sure if the cat was appreciative or if the man was just warming to him, but I'd barely been able to pry them apart since. Wherever Abraham was, Charlie was close behind, ready for a rough head rub and a snuggle.

It was adorable, and it made me love them both even more.

"I've been thinking about letting Charlie roam the house."

Abraham turned toward me. "Yeah? You think that's a good idea?"

I sighed. "Well, you and your sisters had no trouble getting along with him. He's really a good cat, and it's not like he'd bother anyone." I was quiet for a moment while I thought it through some more, my teeth digging into my bottom lip. Finally, I nodded. "I don't want him to be trapped in this room all the time. It's not fair to him. Let's let him roam for a couple hours at a time and see how it goes."

Abraham was still watching me with heavy-lidded eyes. "You know it just turns me on when you get all bossy."

I rolled my eyes. "I'm not bossy."

He rolled over and dragged me beneath his big body. "You're *so* bossy. And it's *so* sexy," he grumbled against my neck.

Thoughts of Charlie flew from my head as Abraham showed me just how sexy he found my bossiness. When we were finally sated again, I decided that if we didn't get out of bed soon, we weren't going to. It wasn't a work day, but we had a pack barbecue that afternoon and we had to see if anyone needed help setting it all up.

I reluctantly pried myself from Abraham's arms and hopped into the shower. My fiancé would never pass up a chance to see me naked, though, so he came along too. It took me a lot longer to wash up with his hands all over me, but I managed and even had another orgasm to add to my collection that morning.

When we were dressed, I picked up Charlie, and Abraham and I walked hand in hand down the stairs. Breakfast was close to being over, so the room was mostly empty. We said hello to Ms. Elsie and grabbed some plates.

I set Charlie on the ground, but he stuck by my side as I got some breakfast and found a seat with Abraham. My poor cat didn't know what to do with himself, so he hopped up on the bench next to me and took a seat. I knew it would take some adjusting for everyone, but I really felt like this was the right thing to do.

While we ate, I got Abraham to promise to build some kitty ramps around the first floor of the lodge. That would give Charlie a place to escape if he got spooked by something. Werewolves weren't known for being quiet, and my cat was used to the silence of just one lonely owner.

Speaking of rowdy werewolves, one of the enforcers, Huxley, walked into the kitchen, trailed by Mathias. As soon as the first wolf made it to the middle of the room, he stopped dead in his tracks and lifted his nose into the air.

"Why does it smell like a fucking animal in here?" he asked.

For whatever reason, Huxley and I had an antagonistic relationship. Maybe it was because I'd never had siblings, or maybe it was because I thought he needed to be brought down a peg or two, but I never passed up an opportunity to call him out.

"You're probably smelling yourself, Huxley."

His brown eyes swung my way and to the space next to me before narrowing. "Is that a cat?"

I nodded slowly. "So, you can identify your animals. Good job, Hux."

He scowled at me and pointed a finger at Charlie. "What is a fucking cat doing in the middle of a house of werewolves? Aren't you worried someone's gonna eat him?"

He and Mathias laughed while I seethed. I rose to my feet, barely noticing Abraham running a warning hand down my arm. He thought I was about to lose my cool, but nothing could have been further from the truth.

"Huxley, I don't know what backwoods town you crawled out of, but civilized people don't eat cats."

He scoffed. "Never said I was civilized."

I shook my head, but my lips twitched with a smile. "At least you're aware that you're a Neanderthal."

He beat his fists on his chest like a gorilla and I had to laugh. He was such an idiot sometimes.

Huxley shot another look at Charlie. "I don't know how that's going to go over here."

I straightened my spine and shot him a look. "We're giving it a try. If everyone makes an effort to get along, we all should do just fine."

Huxley shook his head and nodded for Mathias to follow. The two giant men left the kitchen through the back door and I let out a sigh of relief.

"Well, that's two down, and what? Ten to go?"

Abraham wiped his mouth with a paper napkin. "Are you referring to lodge residents?"

I nodded.

"There are nine enforcers living in the lodge. You have another seven to convince." He said the words with a secret smile on his face and I thought he approved of what I was doing.

I shrugged. "No problem. I'm persuasive."

He laughed and kissed the side of my head. "I know you are."

Abraham left shortly after that, promising he'd be back down soon, but he had some business that couldn't wait. We walked back upstairs together, Charlie following us. He left for his office while I grabbed the environmental texts and hauled them back downstairs, my cat trailing me.

I was in the kitchen, reading through the last of the books Callie lent me, when Jimmy walked through the sliding glass door. I gave him a strained smile but ignored him for the most part. I was sure I wasn't even on his long list of people he liked.

So, when he cleared his throat, and I turned to see he was looking at me, I was shocked.

"Hey, Ellie."

I tried to keep the frown off my face, but I could feel my eyebrows bunching in the middle. "Hey, Jimmy."

He shoved his hands in his pockets and rocked on his heels. "You have a minute?"

"Of course. Do we need privacy?" I asked as I stood up.

He pulled a hand from his pocket and waved it. "Nah, it's not that serious. I'm here to pay my fine."

I almost stumbled forward I was so surprised. "Oh. Okay. Thanks, Jimmy."

He shrugged. "You were right, you know? I shouldn't have been messin' up Franny's yard like that. I deserved the fine."

Well, hell.

What do you say to that? *You're right, you did deserve it?*

Instead, I said, "I think Fran would probably appreciate hearing that, too."

He nodded. "I already apologized to her. She was my first stop."

"That's great, Jimmy."

He shrugged again. "Now, I'm here to apologize to you. What I said was stupid, and you didn't deserve it. I'm sorry."

You could have knocked me over with a feather.

"Th-thanks, Jimmy." I was having trouble forming the words and making complete sentences.

I'd never expected Jimmy to come around like this. To *apologize* of all things. All I'd ever heard about him was how awful and intolerant he was. But the man in front of me was admitting where he'd gone wrong and apologizing.

I may have judged him too quickly.

He scratched his bearded chin. "Anyway, I'm here to drop off a check for the fine and see if you could help me with something."

"Sure, what's up?"

"Could you hook me up with whoever cleaned Fran's yard? I'm hopin' I can hire them to do mine too."

I pulled my phone out of my pocket. "Yeah, that was Austin. Do you need his number?"

"That was the Anderson boy?

I shrugged. "Yep. I can call him if you want."

He waved me away again. "Nah, I'll just stop by his place on the way home." He dug into his pocket and pulled out a crinkled check, handing it to me.

"Thanks, Jimmy."

He shrugged and waved before walking away.

When he reached the glass door, I called out to him, "Will I see you at the pack cookout tonight?"

He turned back around, a small smile on his face. "I'll be there."

He left after that and I stood there for a long time, thinking about the kind of impact I was making in the pack. Apparently, I was doing something right.

I'd never expected Jimmy to turn it around like that. Thought for sure I'd be on his shit list for the rest of my life, but he'd surprised me. He'd owned up to his mistakes and was working toward rectifying them. I really couldn't have asked for more than that.

I sat back down with my textbooks and a smile on my face. This alpha stuff wasn't so bad, and it looked like I might be getting the hang of it.

I'd just gotten back into reading when I smelled sage and knew Bea was nearby.

"Hey, Ellie," she called, and I held back a sigh. I was going to have to talk to Abraham about setting up an office for me in the lodge or I'd never get anything done.

I looked up and gave my future sister-in-law a smile. "Hey, Bea."

She took a seat on the bench across from me, her smile wary. "So, what happened with you and Abey last night?"

I rolled my eyes. "He lost his mind and threatened to lock me in our room." I chuckled at that. I'm sure he could have *tried* to lock me in that room, but he'd have had a hell of a fight on his hands.

"That sounds like Abey."

I shook my head. "Doesn't sound like the Abraham I know."

"You weren't there with him the night you were taken. You didn't see what it did to him. I'm honestly not surprised about his reaction at all."

I sat forward and clasped my hands. "But I had it under control. Tom was lying in a panting heap on the ground with my teeth marks still in his neck."

Bea's eyes flashed with pride. "You got him by the neck?"

I tried to suppress a smile, but it spread across my face anyway. "Yeah, I did." I bit my lip for a moment before adding, "He didn't even get one hit in."

Bea laughed and reached over with her hand outstretched. I slapped it and she sat back down. "That's my friggen girl. Damn, Ellie. I wish I'd been there to see you in action."

I shrugged, but the smile wouldn't come off my face. "It was kinda fun, actually."

"Hell yeah, fighting is fun! Wait 'til you take on one of the enforcers," she said with a laugh and a slap of her knee.

"What's so great about fighting enforcers?"

She leaned back against the table behind her and sighed. "It's because they're so arrogant. They think they're the biggest, strongest, best in everything they do. Then a woman a third their size comes along, and they think it'll be an easy win." Her eyes flashed as her smile turned deadly. "The most dangerous thing they can do is underestimate me."

Beatrice was so terrifying in that moment that I actually shivered. Thank God I'd found my way to her good side.

"Yeah, but I'm not you. I didn't beat every guy in this pack already."

She shrugged. "You will. You've got great instincts and you're learning fast."

My chest warmed with pride. I knew I'd been doing better, and to hear that Beatrice, the best fighter there, thought so too was amazing.

Bea stood up and nodded toward the door. "I was going to go for a run, but now I feel like fighting. You got time to spar?"

I shrugged. Technically, I had all the time in the world since I was unemployed. I was almost done with all the books Callie lent me and knew I could spare some time to train. Besides, it was clear that my lessons with Bea were essential now and I needed to learn as much as I could as fast as I could.

I closed the book I was reading and stood up. "Yeah. Let's go."

Beatrice shot a look at Charlie who was still lying next to where I'd been sitting. "What are you going to do about your cat?"

I shrugged. "I'm trying to integrate him into the house more. Let him run free every once in a while. It won't kill him to spend an hour in the kitchen without me."

Bea didn't look convinced, but shrugged anyway. "All right. If you're sure."

Well, when she said it like that, I wasn't so positive anymore. I looked around the kitchen, finding it empty except for Aubrey. I wanted to mention Charlie to her and let her know he'd be there for a little while without me, but I didn't know how that would go over.

After my interactions with her brother, it almost seemed like she was warming to me, but I'd received nothing but the cold shoulder since. I didn't know which way was up with that girl, but I figured there was no use worrying over it. I'd just ask and see what happened.

I walked over to the other side of the kitchen and cleared my throat. "Hey, Aubrey. Can I ask you for a favor?"

She didn't bother to turn around. "That depends. Is it a favor or an order?"

I grit my teeth and clenched my hands.

Why did she always do that?

Why did she always have to be antagonistic? Why did she always have to throw the alpha thing in my face?

I took a deep breath and shook my head. "It's a favor. I'm going to be right outside with Bea for about an hour and I'm leaving Charlie in here."

She turned to me slowly. "What is a *Charlie*?"

I just barely stopped my eyes from rolling. "Charlie is my cat."

She laughed, the sound grating. "You brought a cat to a house full of werewolves."

And I'd had enough.

"Aubrey, you know damn well the cat lives here. You've known that for a while, so quit acting new. He won't bother you. I'm just asking if you'll keep half an eye on him. He probably won't even move from his spot."

She rolled her eyes so viciously I worried they'd get stuck. "Ugh, fine. Just hurry back."

My hands fisted at my sides, but I took deep breaths until I had myself under control. Aubrey was trying to get a reaction out of me and that was the last thing I'd give her. I'd keep letting her comments roll off me and keep being as civil as I could. I had to hope she couldn't keep it up forever. That eventually she'd get sick of being so rude and give me a chance. I just wouldn't hold my breath.

Chapter 21

"What'd you do to her? Piss in her cornflakes?"

I turned to Bea with wide eyes. "That's disgusting. Of course not."

She laughed and shrugged. "It's something I've heard the guys say, and I was trying it out. It is pretty disgusting, though."

I laughed too as we headed toward the grassy space we always used to spar. "Honestly, I don't really know what her deal is. Ever since I moved out here, she's been nothing but nasty to me."

"Have you asked her why?"

"I mean, not directly. It's hard to have a conversation with her at all."

"Does Abey know?"

I sighed. "Yeah, and I barely stopped him from stepping in."

Bea turned to me with a frown. "Why wouldn't you let him talk to her?"

"Because then it looks like I can't handle things myself. It'll look like I told on her. That's exactly what she's expecting."

"She's expecting you to tell Abraham on her?"

I shrugged. "She said anyone who disagrees with the alpha's mate gets kicked out of the pack like Peyton." I cringed as her name fell from my lips.

Beatrice and Peyton had been best friends for years. The two of them had made my life miserable on more than one occasion, but nothing compared to the first family dinner I'd attended. Through her brother who

185

worked at the police station, Peyton got ahold of what was supposed to be sealed records of when I'd gotten in trouble as a teenager. Peyton wasted no time divulging all that information to everyone at dinner, including Abraham's grandma, who I'd just met and was hoping to make a good impression on. Beatrice was the one who'd invited Peyton to the dinner and encouraged her to dish the dirt she'd found on me.

However, something happened to change Beatrice's mind that night.

According to her, instead of feeling happy that Peyton was making me look bad in front of everyone, she felt protective of me. She realized she'd made a big mistake by inviting Peyton and apologized to me for the first time ever. That night was the start of my friendship with the prickliest of the McCoy siblings.

Now, Bea and I had a great relationship. I might never be close to her in the way I was with Evey, but we talked frequently and sparred together five times a week. I was spending more time with Beatrice than I'd ever imagined and having a better time than I could have hoped for.

"So, she thinks you got Peyton kicked out," Beatrice said, her voice subdued.

I figured this couldn't be an easy topic for her and wished I'd kept my big mouth shut. Even though Beatrice hadn't agreed with the things Peyton did, that didn't negate years of friendship. And Beatrice might have agreed with why Peyton got excommunicated from the pack, but I was sure it still hurt to lose her friend like that.

"I guess. That's what she said, at least."

"She and Peyton grew close while they worked in the lodge together."

"I guess that explains some of it." Didn't make it any better, but if Peyton was a friend of Aubrey's, I guess it made sense that she was upset about her having to leave the pack.

We were quiet as we walked, but there was something bothering me. "Do you blame me, too?"

Bea paused to shoot me a look. "For Peyton getting kicked out?"

I nodded.

"That girl was doing everything she could to get herself in trouble. I tried to tell her, Abraham warned her, but nothing could penetrate." Bea sighed and looked away. "I always knew she had a thing for Abraham, but I never thought she'd go as far as she did. That was unforgivable. She deserved to go."

That made me feel a little better. My friendship with Beatrice was still really new and, in some ways, fragile. If she blamed me for her friend's departure from our pack, that wouldn't have boded well for our relationship.

"Listen, Ellie, I know I've said it before, but I'm sorry for everything I let Peyton do. For every time I let her get in the middle of you and Abey. For every time I let her talk to you like crap. For inviting her to that last family dinner. I'm sorry for it all. It wasn't fair to gang up on you like that." She paused for a minute before continuing. "If I'd known what kind of person Peyton really was sooner, maybe I could have prevented what happened with you and Calvin."

I just barely held back a sigh. There was someone else blaming themselves for Calvin and Peyton's actions. How many more people would lay the blame on their own shoulders for the decisions of another grown person?

I reached out and grasped Bea's arm. "There was nothing you could have done. If Calvin hadn't gotten to me that night, it would have been another one. He was on a mission to have me for himself and nothing was going to stop him. Believe me." I just barely suppressed a shiver as Calvin's words from that night sped through my head.

He'd deluded himself into thinking we were fated mates and that we were meant to be together. Concocted a story that explained how we were fated and had a plan for our future together. It still creeped me out just thinking about it.

"I'm the beta, Ellie. I'm supposed to be on top of that stuff and I wasn't."

"You're also a sister, and a cousin, and a friend, and no one expects you to be able to wear all those hats at once. Calvin fooled us all, and Peyton was more obsessed than she ever let on. Both of them were overlooked by everyone. All we can do is try to see clearer in the future. To trust our guts and do our best."

Beatrice watched me, her icy blue eyes searching my face. Finally, she smiled softly, and I realized how stunning she was. With the ever-present scowl on her face, it was easy to forget how gorgeous she really was, but there was no denying it when all her walls were down.

"Thanks, Ellie. It's good to hear you don't blame me."

I jerked back. "Blame you? Why the hell would I blame you?"

She shrugged. "It was my cousin and my best friend who orchestrated your kidnapping and almost murder."

"Well, anything sounds bad when you put it like that."

Bea's head tipped back as her loud laughter floated around the large yard and echoed back to us. When she finally sobered up, she shot me a penetrating look. "That's a relief."

I rolled my eyes and pulled her into a big hug. "I'd never blame you."

She paused for only a moment before her arms wrapped around my shoulders, too. We stood there for a minute until it felt right to pull away. It was then I realized I'd never hugged Beatrice before.

Hugging, and in fact, all displays of affection, used to make me really uncomfortable. I blamed it on a mixture of growing up an only child of two emotionless parents and never having many friends. It had taken me a while to get used to how touchy all the wolves were with me, but I'd changed a lot since then.

Apparently, I'd changed so much that I willingly pulled Beatrice McCoy into a hug. If you'd told me that two months ago, I would have suggested you get your head checked. But our relationship, like so many other things, had changed drastically.

Bea smiled at me. "Thanks, Ellie. I'm glad you're not upset with me."

"And I thought you might have blamed me for your friend getting kicked out of the pack."

She shook her head, a smile still curling her lips. "Never. Peyton got what was coming to her and it had nothing to do with you."

"So, we're good?"

She surprised the hell out of me by pulling me into another hug. "We're good," she said as she squeezed me.

This time when she pulled away, there was a different kind of smile on her face. "Now, I want you to tell me exactly how the fight went with Tom. No detail is too small. I want to know every maneuver, every bite, every scratch."

I laughed and pulled my shirt over my head. Leave it to Bea to want all the bloody details. The woman really was ferocious.

A while later, we were both panting and bleeding, but the cuts would heal soon, and we'd had a great practice. Bea and I had reenacted as much of my fight with Tom as I could remember, and she'd laughed so hard I didn't think she'd ever stop.

"He really didn't even get close, did he?" she'd chuckled, her big wolfy body rolling around the grass.

Honestly, this was a side to Beatrice I'd been seeing a lot more of lately. She wasn't always the strict, no-nonsense ice queen. She could also be warm and caring, and sometimes, really silly.

"And then he called you a bitch in front of Abey?" She'd laughed harder. *"What an idiot."*

I'd stood there watching her laugh herself out as I tried to reconcile the Beatrice I'd first met with the one on the ground, laughing so hard she couldn't get up. What a difference a couple months make.

When she'd gotten herself under control, we'd had a solid session where we both got in a lot of great hits and both had the aches and pains to prove it.

"That felt amazing," Bea panted in my head. *"But maybe we shouldn't have gone for so long, 'cause they're already setting up for the cookout."*

I turned around to see pack members arranging the picnic tables and filling the fire pit with kindling.

"Yeah. We should probably get back inside and showered and stuff."

However, now that there were so many people out there, I really didn't want to shift back. I thought I'd gotten better about the nudity thing,

189

but that was only when no one was around to see me. With that many people so close, there was no way I was going to get naked.

Bea laughed in my head. *"Don't want to shift back now, do you?"*

There was a time when I'd have lied to her. Told her I had no problem just so she wouldn't be able to get any kind of upper hand. But now I knew Beatrice better and knew she wouldn't use this against me.

"Not really," I admitted.

She nodded her big wolf head. *"Why don't you shift past the tree line and I'll bring you your clothes?"*

"What about you?"

She snorted in my head. *"They've all seen me naked enough times to not care anymore. Hell, any one of these pack members could probably draw you a picture of every one of my birthmarks."*

"Um. I'll pass."

Bea laughed in my head which sounded like barking out loud. *"I'll try not to be offended by that."*

"It's nothing personal, Bea. You just don't really do it for me."

She laughed again. *"Yeah, right, Montgomery. I know Abraham wasn't your first pick of the McCoy siblings."*

I scoffed. *"And if my first pick had been you, you probably would have actually bitten my head off."*

She chuckled and nodded. *"Yeah, probably."*

I shook my head and trotted off for the woods and what little cover it would allow me. Once I shifted back, Bea brought over my clothes and I hurried back into them. When we were dressed again, we walked back up to the lodge.

"Thank God you're back! What the hell took you so long?"

Once my eyes adjusted to the dim interior of the kitchen, I found an angry Aubrey with her arms crossed over her chest and fire in her eyes.

"Are you talking to me?" I asked.

She rolled her eyes. "Of course I'm talking to you, you idiot. I don't know where the hell your stupid cat went, and I don't have time to hunt him down."

Before I could respond, Beatrice took a big step forward and narrowed her eyes. "You don't talk to your alpha like that."

I froze in shock.

Beatrice had never called me the alpha before. Not once had she ever mentioned the fact that I'd be her new boss someday. Yet, there she was, defending me as if I already was. It made me want to hug her again.

Aubrey scoffed. "You too? What is it with all you McCoys and this stupid human? Why are you all so wrapped around her little finger?"

Bea took another step forward and Aubrey's throat bobbed. "She isn't a stupid human. She's a werewolf, just like you. Except she's your and everyone else's boss. I suggest you learn to respect her or find yourself a new pack."

Aubrey's eyes widened as she pointed a finger at Beatrice. "See! You're just like Abraham. Chucking out anyone who doesn't like friggen Elizabeth. It's ridiculous! You can't choose some brand-new wolf over your pack!"

"She is pack, Aubrey, and whether or not you like it, she's going to be your new alpha. It would be in your best interest to keep your opinions to yourself."

"This is absurd."

"And it would also be a good idea to not insult her in front of me again. I'm not as disciplined as Elizabeth or Abraham, and I might rip your fucking throat out for disrespecting your alpha."

Aubrey's eyes widened again and I'm sure there was a similar look on my face.

What the hell just happened?

I knew Beatrice was fiercely protective, but that had never extended to me before. At some point I was unaware of, I'd become someone Beatrice respected enough to defend. It seemed like not only was I on her good side now, I was also under her protection.

191

Not that I really needed it.

I took a step toward the two angry werewolves and spoke up. "It's not a big deal, Aubrey. I'm sure he's around here somewhere. Thanks for keeping an eye on him, but I'll take it from here."

Her eyes flickered from Beatrice to me and she sneered. "Whatever. Just don't ask me to watch the stupid thing again." With that, she spun around and stormed out of the kitchen.

We watched her go in silence until we heard a door open and slam shut. Finally, I turned to Beatrice. "You know you didn't have to do that."

She shrugged. "Yeah, but I wanted to. She was pissing me off."

I shook my head. "Yeah, she's really starting to piss me off too."

"Don't take any shit from her."

I turned to look at Bea. "I don't normally."

She tilted her head to the side. "So, you weren't going to let her get away with calling you an idiot?"

I looked away when it became too hard to hold her stare. "I was going to do something about it."

Bea sighed and grabbed my arm. "Aubrey is a pusher. She's the kind of person who will keep pushing and pushing until she hits a wall. Shove that wall in her face sooner rather than later and you won't have any more problems with her."

I reached up to run a hand through my wild hair. "I guess I was going for the nice-cop routine. I hoped that if she saw I wasn't someone she had to hate that she'd eventually come around."

Bea shook her head. "You could hand her a million dollars in cash, and she'd find a way to bash you. Trust me, you need to push back with her, or you'll get nowhere."

I let Beatrice's words flow through me and solidify my resolve. I needed to stop letting Aubrey get away with talking to me like she had been.

I guess my problem was I wasn't technically the alpha yet. Sure, I was taking on some of the duties, but it wasn't official. Until it was, I had a feeling I'd feel more like an imposter than anything else. If I didn't respect my position in the pack, how could I expect anyone else to?

That meant I either needed to go ahead with the mating ceremony sooner than I'd planned and become the official alpha, or just forge ahead with my pseudo-title and hope I could earn the pack's respect.

Honestly, neither option sounded appealing, and that left me back at square one.

Chapter 22

"Charlie!" I called as I wandered the halls of the lodge. "Come on, bubba. Where are you?"

I'd been searching for my cat for the past twenty minutes and I was starting to get worried.

What if something happened? What if one of the other werewolves did something to him?

Huxley had asked if I'd been worried someone would eat him and I'd thought he'd been joking, but what did I know? I'd only been a werewolf a couple months. Maybe eating cats was a legitimate thing they did.

No. Abraham would have warned me before I brought Charlie out here. I was letting my imagination run wild, and it wasn't helping anything.

I stopped in the middle of the hall and took a deep breath. That reminded me of Nana's story about the quintuplets' mom and the day she thought she lost them all. She'd finally calmed down enough to use her nose, and it led her straight to them.

I needed to do the same.

I inhaled again and knew Charlie hadn't been down this way. Retracing my steps, I made it back to the kitchen where his scent was the strongest. I followed it around the large room and out into the hallway. His scent was strong there, but had that been from earlier when he'd come down or more recently?

I ran up the stairs, Charlie's scent getting stronger the higher I climbed. Finally, I turned down our hall and found my little black and brown tabby sitting outside our bedroom door.

"Charlie," I said, exasperation lining my words. "You scared me, buddy."

I scooped him into my arms and carried him into the bedroom. As soon as he saw his cat castle, he squirmed until I let him down. When he was free, he bolted for his hidey hole and ducked inside.

Apparently, being out of this room had been a little too much for him. Or maybe it was because I left him alone. Either way, I should have brought him a place to hide down there. That had been stupid of me and I'd upset my poor cat in the meantime.

I shook my head and headed for the shower. Next time, I'd prepare better for when Charlie spent time out of the room. I wasn't giving up on integrating him into the house yet. I just needed to modify my approach.

When I was done in the shower and dressed for the cookout, I wandered over to Abraham's office and knocked. He called for me to come in, and I entered to find him hunched over the desk, frowning at his computer.

His eyes darted to me and a smile stretched across his handsome face. It made my heart thump extra hard for a few moments.

"Hey, baby."

Heat rose in my cheeks. I didn't know how he still had the power to make me blush, but he did. "Hey. You almost done?"

He sighed heavily and leaned back in his chair. I walked around the desk and took a seat on the edge next to his open laptop. His big hands instantly found my bare legs, and he squeezed.

"Yeah, I'm just about done."

I reached out to smooth the frown lines between his eyebrows. "What's wrong?"

He sighed again and turned his head to kiss my hand. "I'm worried about Conrad."

"Your uncle?"

He nodded.

"Why would you be worried about him?"

He studied me for a moment before speaking. "I'm afraid he might retaliate for what happened with Calvin."

"But that wasn't your fault!"

He shrugged. "But that's still his son."

I shook my head, but kept my mouth shut. Sure, Calvin was his son, but only when it was convenient.

From what Abraham told me, Conrad was an awful father who was never happy with anything his sons did. When Abraham and his sisters took off to form a new pack, Conrad's sons, Calvin and Clyde, joined them. Predictably, that sent Conrad into a fit and he'd disowned his own children.

Somewhere along the line, Calvin had reconciled with his father. We didn't know when that happened, only that Conrad had to have known something about what Calvin had been doing. It was on Conrad's pack lands that Calvin kept those women before killing them. There was no way Conrad didn't know what his son had been up to.

"Do you really think he'd do something?" I asked.

Abraham's deep blue eyes were wary. "I don't know, El, but I have a bad feeling about it." His hands slid up my legs to my hips where he pulled me closer. "I need to do whatever it takes to protect you."

I wrapped my hands around his. "You will protect me. You always do."

He let out a deep breath and his shoulders hunched. "I think I need to call in a few favors with some other packs. Get some alliances going, so if Conrad moves against us, we won't be completely outnumbered."

"What about the packs that came to the solstice party?"

He nodded. "That's who I'll start with, but I'll have to get in touch with other packs, too. Who knows if Conrad is making alliances of his own, building his enforcers to even larger numbers? I need to have as many North Carolina packs on our side when something happens."

I swallowed. "You said *when*, not *if*."

His hands squeezed me as his eyes searched mine. "I told you, I've got a bad feeling about this." He was quiet for a moment before he spoke again. "Besides, I'd rather fortify our numbers here and have nothing happen than to be caught under-manned."

"That makes sense." I chewed on my bottom lip. "How are you going to get other packs on our side?"

He sighed and leaned back again, dragging his hands down my legs and making me lose track of our conversation.

"I'm not sure yet. I'll start with our friends first, though, and maybe talk to some of their friends. Go wherever I can get an introduction."

"Go?"

He winced and looked away. "I think it would be best if I met with all these packs in person."

I swallowed again and willed my heart to stop clenching in my chest. "How long do you think you'll have to be gone?"

He met my eyes again. "It probably won't be for long and it probably won't be for a while. Let's not worry about it."

I didn't want Abraham to leave. We used to have to spend tons of time apart, but now I couldn't imagine it. I'd been practically glued to his hip since I moved in with him and I didn't know what I'd do with myself if he had to leave for a few days.

I shook my head and slid off his desk. I'd worry about that problem when it arose. In the meantime, we had a pack barbecue to host and people were probably already arriving.

"You're right. Let's not worry about it. Let's just go down to the cookout and spend some time with our pack."

He stood up and wrapped his arms around my waist before pressing his lips against mine. He kissed me for a long time as I slowly lost my senses and drowned in him. When he pulled away, my vision was hazy, but I could see he was smiling at me.

"I love you," he said, his words so quiet and sincere my heart squeezed almost painfully.

He'd said the words hundreds of times, but they never failed to rock me to my core. I had the love of one of the most amazing people I'd ever known. How many others got that lucky?

I reached up to cup his perfect face. "I love you too."

His eyes got really soft as he smiled. He grabbed the hand from his face and kissed it before twining his fingers with mine. "Let's go get some deviled eggs before Jimmy gets here."

I laughed and let him lead me down to the first floor. "I asked, and he's definitely coming, so that's a legitimate concern."

He stopped walking and pulled me up next to him. "You talked to Jimmy? When? Where?"

When I'd told Abraham about my interaction with Jimmy when I'd given him his fine, I'd purposely kept the details sparse. I knew the more Abraham knew, the more he'd want to go down there and wring Jimmy's neck. I also knew I needed to handle the situation on my own and not let Abraham butt in.

But I didn't like being dishonest, so I'd given Abraham a general summary of what happened and left it at that. He didn't need to know the specific names Jimmy called me. All he needed to know was that he wasn't happy, and he was a jerk about it. Something that seemed to be pretty common with the men in this pack lately.

"This afternoon. He came in to pay his fine."

His eyes widened. "He came to pay his fine already?"

I shrugged. "Yeah. He dropped off a check that I gave to Evey."

He reached up to scratch his stubbled chin. "Well, shit. I never expected him to come around so easily." He turned to look at me, the corners of his lips twitching with a smile. "I knew it would only be a matter of time before you had this whole pack eating out of the palm of your hand."

I scoffed. "They're hardly eating out of my hand, Abraham. In fact, one tried to fight me yesterday."

His whole face fell, anger twisting his features. "I remember."

Damn. There I went with my big mouth again.

"But, yeah, Jimmy came by to pay his fine and apologize to me. He said he talked to Fran too and said sorry to her as well. He also asked about hiring someone to clean his yard for him."

Abraham nodded slowly. "His property is a goddamn wreck."

"Well, that was something else I said to him while I was down there. I told him he had a month to clean his yard or there'd be more fines."

His eyes widened again. "You did?"

I shrugged. "Was that wrong?"

He laughed and pulled me into his arms. "No, it's not wrong. I'm just surprised. It seems like you're always one step ahead of me," he murmured in my ear.

I shivered in his hold. "That's because your mate is a smart, capable woman."

He nodded against my face, his stubbled jaw tickling my sensitive skin. "Hmm. Smart, and capable, and strong, and so fuckin' sexy I can't think straight."

I laughed, but it was breathy and needy. Abraham had this way of turning the mundane into something extraordinary. We were just talking about fining pack members, and now I was in his arms, ready for him to pull me into an unused room and make us even later for the barbecue.

The barbecue.

Right.

I gave him a swift kiss and then reluctantly pulled myself from his arms. He gave some resistance, but eventually caved, and I took a few steps back to separate us further.

"We have a pack dinner to get to," I said, still a little out of breath.

His eyes were heated with promises of what I had to look forward to later. I shivered again.

"That's the only reason you're still dressed," he said, his voice deep and rumbling across the space between us.

Clearly, a few feet wasn't enough of a separation because I was about to launch myself back into his arms.

I cleared my throat and shook my head. "Let's go, McCoy. Save your bedroom eyes for the bedroom."

I turned away from him to head toward the back of the lodge while he laughed loudly behind me. He caught up as I made it to the kitchen.

As expected, it was in chaos, but also seemed to be under control. I checked in with Ms. Elsie to see if she needed anything before heading out back.

To my surprise, it looked like almost every pack member was already there. There hadn't been this many people at any of these cookouts since my first one. And that one was only popular because rumor spread that I'd survived an attack by the serial killer that had been haunting their woods for months.

I turned to Abraham who slung his arm over my shoulders. "It looks like everyone's here."

He grunted. "They better be."

I turned in his arms. "What do you mean?" He looked away from me to study the lake in the distance and my stomach turned. "What did you do?"

He sighed and pulled me closer. "I just called a mandatory meeting before the pack barbecue."

I glared up at him. "And what kind of mandatory meeting are we having and why wasn't I told about it before now?"

He took a deep breath and let it out slowly. "El, something has to be said. I know you want to handle this all on your own, but what happened with Tom was unacceptable." I opened my mouth to argue, but he continued, "And before you try to fight me on this, know that if he'd attacked any other member of this pack, I'd be doing the same thing."

I raised the most incredulous brow I could, and he had the decency to look away again.

"Okay, so maybe I wouldn't have called a mandatory meeting about just any pack member, but I would have addressed it."

I sighed and turned away. Clearly, I wouldn't get through to him and he'd have this meeting no matter what I said. I just hoped he'd be able to rein it in enough to not completely discredit me.

I felt like I'd been doing a pretty good job of finding a solid foothold in the pack. If Abraham came along and negated all that, I was going to be really irritated.

The kitchen staff began bringing out tray after tray of food as Abraham grasped my arm.

"I promise I won't do anything to jeopardize the respect you've gained with this pack so far. But, El, you can't expect me to not address this. It would make me look weak if I didn't."

I did my best to see it from his perspective, and unfortunately, he had a point. If he just let this slide, it would make him look bad. Like he didn't care that I'd been attacked by another pack member.

So, I'd go along with this pack meeting and let Abraham say what he needed to say, but when he was done, it'd be my turn.

Chapter 23

"Can I have everyone's attention?"

I tried to slink away from Abraham's side, but he held on tight. The last of the kitchen staff had just made their way outside and, apparently, it was time to start the pack meeting.

We were still on the raised back patio with the entire pack on the grass below us.

"It seems like we've had a miscommunication between us somewhere, and I want to rectify that today." He paused while he looked at every wolf and tightened his arm around me.

"Elizabeth is my mate. It doesn't matter that we haven't had an official ceremony yet. She is my mate, and that means she is your alpha. I've heard of far too many instances of her being disrespected and defied and that all stops here. She has as much authority in this pack as I do, and what she says goes. If you can't respect her, you can't stay here. The same goes for me. You respect me, or you get out of my pack. That's the way it is because that's the way it's always been."

His words rang through the clearing and I watched the different pack members take in his proclamation. It seemed like most of them agreed, but there were a few that didn't look happy at all.

"As for yesterday," he continued, and I turned to look at him again. "Violence against your alpha is an excommunicable offense. However, violence against my mate is a death sentence."

If I'd thought the clearing was quiet before, it was nothing compared to now.

"Elizabeth has my full protection and I will not hesitate to defend her in any way. You've all been warned."

No one spoke, no one moved. I wasn't even sure if they were still breathing. Everyone looked shocked silent and still as his words settled around us.

I looked up at Abraham and saw him staring down his pack as if daring them to make a move against me right now so he could prove he meant business.

I needed to speak up.

Stepping out of Abraham's hold, I cleared my throat. "I'd like to say something too."

"El?" Abraham whispered, but I ignored him.

I took a step closer to the railing and wrapped my fingers around the wood. "I know change is difficult." I chuckled softly. "I've had more of it in the past few months than I've had my entire life. Turns out, I'm a pretty stubborn person, and so I fought against all those changes."

Abraham chuckled behind me, but I ignored him again.

"The things I fought against the hardest wound up being the greatest changes of all." My eyes drifted to Abraham, and I gave him a soft smile. "But I'm not a change you need to fight against. I know I'm new here, but I'm learning. Every day, I'm trying my hardest to be the very best alpha I can be for you. If you give me a chance, I promise you won't regret it."

I looked around the clearing again, trying to decide if there were more happy faces than angry. Realizing it didn't matter, I pressed on, "All that I ask is for some time for me to become an alpha worthy of a great pack like this."

I finished my speech and did my best to meet the eye of every pack member standing there. Their facial expressions varied so much from person to person, I couldn't get a good feel for how my words were being received. That was until Jimmy started clapping.

It started out slow and as just one person, but it grew and swelled, and soon it sounded like a hundred people were applauding.

My smile stretched my cheeks while my heart thumped extra fast. Abraham slid an arm around my waist and kissed the side of my head. "You're a great alpha already."

His words settled deep within me. I turned to say something, I'm not even sure what, but when I saw the loving look on his face, I had to kiss him. Not caring that the whole pack was watching, I grabbed Abraham's face and pressed my lips against his.

Soon the clapping was rhythmic, and the catcalls were too loud to ignore. I finally pulled away from him and stared into his eyes.

His lips curled into a smile. "What was that for?"

I shrugged. "For loving me."

He pulled me close again. "I really do. So much."

He held me while the noise died down and the pack members dispersed. To my surprise, almost everyone stayed past the end of the meeting.

I finally pulled out of Abraham's arms only to entwine my fingers with his. "Let's get some food while we still can."

When we'd filled our plates, we wandered down to the picnic tables and found an empty one. I knew it wouldn't be long until his sisters found us and took the remaining seats.

"Oh my God, Ellie, I loved your speech!" Evey's voice preceded her. When she finally made it to the table, she plopped her plate next to mine and slid onto the bench. "I mean really, you sounded amazing. So alpha-like."

I rolled my eyes. "It's not a big deal, Evey."

Callie, Del, and Beatrice filed in the other side of the table.

"Actually, I think it was a really big deal," Callie spoke up.

I always thought of her as the least dramatic of the sisters. The one I could count on to not exaggerate or exacerbate a situation. So, if she thought it was a big deal, maybe it was.

"What's so special about my speech?" I asked as I popped a deviled egg in my mouth.

"Ellie, you were a total boss up there. Hell, I was about to drop to a knee," Bea said before stuffing half a dinner roll in her mouth.

I rolled my eyes again. "You were not."

She nodded, her icy blue eyes wide. "Honestly, I can't imagine that speech not affecting the whole pack. You did good."

I tried not to let it show, but Beatrice's compliment meant a lot to me. It was a bumpy road that led us to this place in our friendship. There'd been times I never thought we'd get there. And never in a million years did I imagine Beatrice giving me compliments or defending me to others like she'd done with Aubrey today. Things had really changed between us and I loved it.

"You really did good, baby. Trust us," Abraham said softly in my ear.

Maybe they were right. Maybe I actually had done a good job. Honestly, it was the most half-assed speech I'd ever given. Usually, I'd prepare for months for something like an opening or closing statement. Today, I'd only decided to speak once Abraham insisted on addressing the issues I'd been having.

That gave me no time to prepare, so I winged it. I dug deep and spoke from my heart. I didn't want to lead the pack out of fear, I wanted it to be out of mutual respect. I just hoped that was attainable.

I'd just eaten the last possible bite of food I could hold when Sophie walked up to our table.

"Hey, Ellie. You got a minute?"

I barely suppressed a groan. It wasn't her fault I'd stuffed myself too full on Ms. Elsie's pecan pie and could barely move.

Instead, I gave her a grim smile and heaved myself off the bench. I heard Abraham snickering from beside me and jabbed an elbow into his ribs. Honestly, my elbow lost that fight hands down.

I followed Sophie away from the crowd until we had a bit of privacy. "Is everything all right?" I asked.

She had a look on her face I couldn't place, and it was starting to bother me.

She sighed and shoved her hands in the pockets of her jeans. "Well, yes and no."

205

"Tell me what's going on."

Her shoulders fell with a deep exhale. "Well, we're all glad Tom and Daisy are gone, but we're having trouble replacing them."

My stomach fell as the problem swam to the surface.

I was an idiot.

I fired the farm manager and didn't bother to replace him. I'd gotten so caught up with my fight with Tom and my subsequent fight with Abraham that it completely slipped my mind.

I took a deep breath. "Okay, so you need a new employee, but Daisy wasn't doing much to begin with, so it's probably not that different from before, right?"

She nodded. "Yeah, we're getting by without her. It's really Tom's job that we're having trouble with. The team needs direction or we're pretty useless."

I wracked my brain for a solution to this problem. I needed a farm worker, and I needed a farm manager. Part of me wanted to run back and ask Abraham for his opinion, but I knew I needed to work this out for myself.

And then it came to me.

"What about you?"

Sophie raised a dark brow. "What about me?"

"Why don't you take the farm manager position?"

Her eyes widened. "Why would I do that?"

I shrugged. "You clearly care about the team if you're coming to me with this, and it was obvious you know what you're doing out there. Plus, I could tell the other workers already look up to you. It would be easy for you to slide into his role."

She didn't look convinced. "Are you sure about that, Ellie?"

The more I thought about it, the more sure I was.

"Absolutely. As of now, you're the new farm manager."

Her eyes got wide again as she slowly shook her head. "That is not what I was expecting."

I shrugged again. "I'm sorry. I don't know what to do about you being down an employee. Well, two if you count yourself."

She waved a hand. "We'll figure it out."

My smile was wide as I looked at her. I could see she was already thinking like a manager. Already planning what her next move would be and how she'd make things better. My belief in this solution was only growing.

"So, we're good here?" I asked.

Sophie smiled. "Yeah, we're good. I'll tell all the workers about the change in my title."

"If you need any help with anything, come to me, okay? I'm here to help."

Sophie's smile grew before she tugged me into her arms. "Thanks so much, Ellie. You have no idea what you've done for us."

I hugged her back as I let her words sink into my head.

I really was making a difference.

I really was making the right choices.

I really was an alpha.

Sophie bounded off to go talk to her co-workers while I made my way back to the McCoys. My eyes wandered around the space and I was greeted by more friendly smiles than ever. But when my eyes landed on a pair of men, my instincts automatically twitched to life.

On the outskirts of the party stood Craig and Paul, his mate, Annalise, close by. I didn't know if the two men knew each other well or not, but I had a bad feeling about this. I tried to remind myself that they'd lived in the same pack together for years and there was nothing strange about them talking, but something told me it was more than that. Something told me to watch out for the both of them because, if they were working together, there could be trouble.

I kept those thoughts to myself as I reclaimed my seat next to Abraham. The siblings were talking and laughing, and I was enjoying watching them, not necessarily a part of the conversation.

"Ellie, did Abey really threaten to lock you in your room?"

That question was from Del, of course. The biggest pot-stirrer of them all. If there was something uncomfortable that you'd rather not talk about, leave it to Delilah to bring it up.

"Um. He might have said something like that."

I shot a glare at Bea, knowing she must have been the one who told Del and now everyone knew.

"Abey! You can't lock her in a room!" Evey said, her little hands fisted on the table in front of her.

Abraham sighed. "I wasn't really going to lock her in a room."

"You sure as shit weren't," Del piped up. "You saw what she did to old Tom the other day? This one's a hellcat. I'd love to see you try to lock her in a room."

I bit my lip and looked down at my lap to keep from laughing. Abraham nudged me and leaned close. "You think this is funny?"

I shook my head quickly. "Nope."

He dipped his head closer and whispered, "Liar."

That was all it took.

My head fell backward as I laughed so hard, the sound echoed around the clearing. When I'd finally regained some control, I turned my teary eyes toward Abraham. He had this look on his face that he sometimes got. It made my insides twist and my heart pound.

"I don't think you're a hellcat," he said.

I had to bite my lip to hold back another round of laughter. "You haven't tried to lock me in a room yet."

His lips curved into a lopsided smile. "I'll have to remember that."

A while later, we were all around the fire listening to Del perform. Abraham's arm was wrapped tight around me as he rocked us to the beat.

Between the heat of the fire and the warmth from the man behind me, I almost fell asleep.

Finally, Del set aside her guitar and several pack members rose to their feet. Abraham leaned down to speak in my ear, "We should probably say goodbye to everyone."

He pulled me from my seat and led me over to a small group of departing werewolves. We gave everyone hugs and promised to see them soon.

As the crowd thinned, I noticed Jimmy and Fran making their way toward us. I hadn't seen them much during the barbecue, but it was clear they'd been seeing a lot of each other. Jimmy was leaning close to Fran, his head dipped to speak in her ear while she giggled.

Huh. I hadn't seen that coming.

When they reached us, Fran stepped up to me and wrapped her arms around my shoulders. I was shocked frozen for a moment before I returned her hug.

"Ellie, I wanted to thank you for everything you've done. My yard looks great and I've never been happier."

I didn't miss the way her eyes drifted to Jimmy when she said that last line.

"Yeah, and thanks for talking to the Anderson kid for me," Jimmy added. "He's comin' by to clean up my place sometime next week."

I'd gone ahead and sent Austin a text about Jimmy's yard after we talked. I guessed he'd already gotten in touch with him.

"That's great, Jimmy!"

He shrugged. "Yeah, well, I wouldn't have gotten my act together if it wasn't for you." His eyes slid to Fran, and I knew he'd meant that in more ways than one.

"It was nothing," I said.

He reached out and pulled me into a hug next and I just barely got my arms around his big frame. When he pulled away, he grabbed Fran's hand, and they took off for the pack houses.

Abraham wrapped an arm around my neck and pulled me close. "I see you're not just an amazing alpha, but also a matchmaker."

I turned to look at him. "Wouldn't that be amazing? If I just went around hooking up the pack with their future mates?"

He laughed and kissed the side of my head. "One thing at a time, El."

Chapter 24

"Quit fidgeting, El."

I tugged at the sleeve of my blouse once more. I couldn't help myself. Today was the first day at my new job and I was nervous as hell.

The two weeks it had taken for construction had initially seemed to trudge by, but the last few days had blown past me. One minute I was leisurely preparing for my new role, and the next I was racing to do more research and order more books online.

I was a mess.

"I'm sorry. I'm just nervous."

Abraham walked up behind me and wrapped his arms around my waist. I leaned back against his broad chest and stared at our reflections in the bathroom mirror.

"You look beautiful and you're gonna kill it today. There's no reason to be nervous."

My worried eyes met his. "What if I can't do this job? What if I suck at it? What if I make Callie regret hiring me?"

He squeezed me and shook his head. "None of that is gonna happen. You're smart, and capable, and resourceful, and nothing is too difficult for you. You're gonna nail this like you do everything else."

I sighed and felt more tension leave my body. "I wish I had that kind of faith in myself."

"If you could see yourself through my eyes, you'd already know how amazing you are. How you can literally do anything. I've seen you handle change after change without breaking a sweat. Think about how much you've accomplished in the last few months and you'll know you can do this too."

I watched his blue eyes and read the sincerity in them. He really believed I could do anything. Maybe I could believe him too.

I took a deep breath and closed my eyes. I needed to reach deep for the woman that rose to the top of her last firm. The woman who did what it took to do the job no matter what it was. I knew she was still in there and I knew she'd never let me down in the past. I needed to trust her.

When I opened my eyes again, Abraham's deep blue gaze was still focused on me. He leaned down and pressed a soft kiss on my cheek. "Better?"

I sighed. "You always make everything better."

He smiled and squeezed me again. "Come on. Let's get some breakfast and get on the road."

Abraham was driving me to work. He'd said he wanted to show me the renovations himself. I hadn't seen the office since the day he'd taken me there, and it was just a shell then. He'd insisted on keeping it from me until it was done, and now, he wanted to be there when I saw it.

The kitchen was a hive of activity as we dodged other pack members on our way to the food. Knowing I was too nervous to keep much down, I only grabbed a bowl of oatmeal and a banana. Abraham gave me a disapproving look, but thankfully, didn't comment.

We ate in relative silence while I mentally went over everything I'd learned in the past few weeks to prepare for my first day. I'd been working with Callie and she'd been showing me the more personal side to environmental law. I'd learned about the people it affected and not just the law and legal jargon. It made me even more anxious to get started and make a difference.

When Abraham finished his breakfast and my oatmeal was cold, we handed our dishes off to Aubrey and made our way outside. I only had my briefcase with my laptop inside, but Callie had assured me that was all I'd need. Even so, I felt under-prepared.

Abraham grabbed my hand and entwined his fingers with mine. "I can hear you worrying from over here."

I sighed. "I'm just hoping I'm prepared for today. Callie said I didn't need much, but how could that be the case? It's a brand-new office. Won't I need like pens and staplers and stuff?"

He squeezed my hand as he led me to his big black pickup truck. "The office is fully stocked with all of that stuff. All you need to bring is your computer and your fine self."

I rolled my eyes, but my lips stretched into a grin.

We climbed into his truck and he fired up the engine. I couldn't see Callie's silver Prius, so I assumed she'd already left for the office. Nervous butterflies raced in my stomach as we drove down the driveway and headed toward the highway.

"El, you need to take it easy. You sound like you're having a heart attack."

"You know I've only ever had one job before."

He turned to me with a frown. "Yeah? Not even as a kid or anything?"

I shook my head. "My parents supported me. I didn't need to work. After I got sent to boarding school, all I focused on were my grades. College was the same thing and by the time I got to grad school, I didn't have time for another job. Hildebrandt & Moore was the firm I interned with and then they eventually hired me. I've never worked anywhere else."

He nodded slowly as he navigated the light morning traffic. "Huh. So, this is kind of a big deal for you, then?"

I blew out a deep breath. "A huge deal."

He reached out and picked up my hand. My palm was probably a little sweaty from nerves, but he didn't seem to mind. "It's okay to be excited and nervous, but I want you to go in there knowing you're gonna be amazing. Know that they're lucky to have you. Know that you could go anywhere with your skill set and work ethic, but you chose to work for Callie. She and everyone else should be grateful they got you."

My lips twitched with another smile. If you asked Abraham, he'd probably tell you I invented the wheel, too. His unwavering belief in me was quickly becoming my very foundation. It was so easy to build on the compliments and praise he heaped on me.

"Thanks, baby," I said.

His hand squeezed mine. "Don't forget, I did make your office soundproof."

I laughed. "Then I guess I'll be seeing you for lunch?"

He grunted. "You bet your sweet ass you will."

My smile was bright as the butterflies died down inside me.

I knew then that everything would be okay. Even if I wasn't great at this job at first, I would learn and adapt and become the best I could be. It was what I'd done with the alpha position and it was what I'd do with this one. Like Abraham said, I was great at my last job. There was no reason I couldn't be great at this one too.

He wound his way through the city streets until he reached the office and found a parking spot on the street. When the truck was off, he squeezed my hand again. "You ready to go in?"

I took a deep breath and nodded. "Yeah, I'm ready."

He kissed the back of my hand and released me as we both climbed from his truck. He rounded the front and picked up my hand again before leading me across the street and to the office. The door had been repainted a really pretty mint green, and they'd installed a new, modern door handle.

I gripped my briefcase in one hand as Abraham opened the door and ushered me inside. My jaw fell open as I tried to take in all the changes.

The floor was a beautiful shiny hardwood that looked like it had just been waxed. There was a small sitting area off to the side with tons of potted plants, and a long hall down the middle of the space. The walls were painted a crisp white and there was art hanging intermittently.

I headed down the hall, taking in the other closed door and wondering what was behind them. That could wait, though, because I needed to see my office first.

Abraham had been hinting that he did something special in there, but he wouldn't say what. No amount of cajoling on my part could get a single word out of the man. He'd insisted I had to wait until my first day to see it.

When I reached the office I remembered being mine, I grabbed the doorknob as Abraham spoke up behind me.

"Listen, El, if you don't like what we did with your office, it'll be no trouble to change it. I thought you might like this, but if you don't, that's totally okay."

I turned to look at him. "What did you do?"

He shrugged, his cheeks darkening. "I just gave the designer some information about you and, together, this is what we came up with. But, like I said, we can change it to whatever you want."

Now I was even more curious. Why was Abraham so nervous? What was behind this door?

I turned back to my office and twisted the knob. When the door opened, I stood frozen in the hallway, my eyes widening as they tried to take in everything all at once.

The walls were still a plain white and the floors hardwood, but that was where the ordinary ended.

There were colorful tapestries hanging from every wall, and bright, textured chairs sitting in front of my large desk. A desk that was painted in gold glitter and shining from across the room.

I stepped inside as my eyes zipped around the room, finding more things to look at.

There was a large shelving system that was shaped like a great oak with each branch holding a set of books. Beside it was a floor lamp that looked like a golden palm tree. The rug beneath the desk was a white shag, and even the filing cabinets had been painted a shiny brass color.

I stood there, trying to absorb the room when Abraham stepped up beside me.

"So," he said, rocking on his heels. "What do you think?"

I turned wide eyes toward him, unable to find the right words. Or any words, really. The office had completely robbed me of my faculties.

Abraham sighed. "It's too much, isn't it?" He sighed and ran a hand down his face. "I thought I could make this office remind you of your place back in Raleigh. You had so much individuality and personality in that apartment, and I wanted to bring a little piece of that here for you." He sighed again. "Maybe I should have asked you first."

I shook my head and reached out a shaky hand to grab his arm. "Abraham, I love it."

He whipped his head toward me, a smile tugging at his lips. "Really? Are you sure? Because we can change anything you want."

I shook my head, tears gathering in my eyes.

He'd done all this for me. He'd remembered the kind of wild colors and design I'd had in my old apartment and tried to replicate it for me here. I'd never been more grateful to have him in my life.

I turned and launched myself into his arms and he caught me with a laugh. Reaching up, I pressed kiss after kiss all over his handsome face. He laughed harder while he tried to catch my lips with his own. Finally, I relented, and I stopped long enough to kiss him with all the gratitude I felt so deeply inside me.

When I was out of breath, I pulled away and smiled up at him. "Honestly, it's perfect. It's everything I'd want in an office." I grabbed his hand and clutched it to my chest. "Thank you so much, Abraham. You didn't have to do all this for me."

His eyes got soft. "Of course I did. I love you."

My stupid eyes filled with tears again, but I blinked them back. "I love you too."

A knock on my open door broke the moment between us. I turned to find a tall man with black hair and bright green eyes standing in the doorway.

"Are you Ellie?"

I stepped away from Abraham and toward the man. "Yes. You must be Matt."

Callie told me they'd taken on a new scientist to help with some of their field research and this had to be him. He was good looking in a sort of generic way, with his crisp suit and his perfectly styled hair.

He nodded and stepped into my office with his hand outstretched. "That's me. Matt Miller. So nice to finally meet you, Ellie."

I shook his hand for what felt like just a second or two longer than necessary. When I had my hand back, I turned to Abraham. "This is my fiancé, Abraham."

Matt's green eyes slid from me to the large man beside me. He smiled wide and held out his hand again. "Nice to meet you, man."

Abraham shook Matt's hand, but I could see his shoulders were tight with tension.

What was that about? Did he know Matt already?

My new co-worker clapped his hands and looked around my office. "You've got a... colorful office here."

I smiled and turned to Abraham. "He designed it for me."

Matt's smile widened. "Maybe not the direction I would have gone in, but if you're happy."

"She is," Abraham cut in.

I whipped my head in his direction. What was his problem?

"Anyway, my office is right next to yours. Feel free to stop by anytime."

Abraham stiffened beside me, but I ignored him.

"Thanks, Matt. It was great meeting you."

He smiled and waved as he backed out of my office. "Maybe we can get lunch together later."

Abraham growled this time, and I turned wide eyes his way.

"She's busy for lunch." With that, he slammed my office door, effectively ending any conversation with poor Matt.

I poked him in the shoulder and propped my hands on my hips. "What the hell was that?"

His jaw was ticking with how hard he was clenching it. "I don't like him."

"You just met him."

"So did you and you're already defending him."

"I'm not defending him. I'm trying to figure out what crawled up your ass and how we can get it out."

"I'm not in the mood for jokes, El."

"Well, neither am I. I just met my first new coworker, and you were rude to him. How do you think that looks for me?"

He shrugged. "Don't care. I don't like him."

I threw my head back and groaned. "What is there not to like? He said like two words."

Abraham took a step closer until he was hovering over me. "He said a lot more with his eyes than he said with his mouth." He reached out and grabbed my waist, squeezing almost painfully. "He couldn't stop staring at you and I don't like other men staring at my mate."

I rolled my eyes as my stomach flipped deep inside me. Despite how unreasonable he was being, there was something so sexy about a possessive man. Or at least a possessive Abraham. Yeah, that was probably it.

I put my hands on his biceps and tried not to notice how strong and warm he was. "He was just being friendly, Abraham. There's nothing to worry about."

"He wanted to have lunch with you."

I slid my hands up to circle the back of his neck. "That's what co-workers do, baby. They have lunch together."

He growled softly and pulled me closer. "You're only allowed to have lunch with me."

My breath caught in my chest and I fought to speak calmly. "He wasn't talking about the kind of lunches you and I have."

He grumbled again and dipped his head to my neck. "That's not what it looked like."

I sighed and shook my head, running my fingers through Abraham's dark hair. "There's no one else I want to have lunch with."

He grunted. "Good."

I rolled my eyes again but couldn't help the grin on my face. Abraham was acting a little jealous, and although I'd never feed it, it was nice for him to have a little taste of what I went through with Peyton when she was still around.

She'd always been flirting with Abraham and hanging off him any chance she got. It drove me nuts and Abraham hadn't even been able to see it at first. He'd finally caught on to her double-layered motives and did his best to keep her at a distance, but she was still a member of his pack. Or at least she used to be.

I hoped working with Matt wouldn't be a problem for Abraham. There was no competition for him, and it wasn't even like Matt had made an advance. It seemed to me like he was making a big deal out of nothing, but I'd have to make sure not to stoke the fires of that particular flame. I'd hate to see what an angry, jealous Abraham was capable of.

Chapter 25

"I don't want to go."

I laughed and kissed his lips again. "But you have a site you need to be at this morning."

He pouted, and it was so adorable, I had to kiss him again.

His big hands were wrapped around my waist and he pulled me closer to his hard body. "I'm used to you bein' home with me. I'm gonna have to miss you all day now."

My heart clenched in my chest. "I'm gonna miss you too."

I really hadn't spent more than a few hours away from Abraham since I'd moved into the lodge, and thinking about a whole eight of them without him seemed daunting.

"But you'll be back for lunch, right?" I asked, my hands sliding up and down his thick arms.

He sighed and dropped his head to mine. "I'm going to try my hardest, but this site is far away, and I might not be able to get here in time."

Now it was my turn to pout. "So, we won't get to christen my new office today?"

His heartbeat picked up its pace, and I tried to hide my smile. "If we don't, I'll make sure we christen it twice tomorrow."

My belly flipped at his promise and eight hours seemed longer than ever. Finally, I sighed and gave him one last kiss before stepping back. "If you don't go soon, you'll never go."

He shrugged. "Okay. I'll just hang out with you all day."

I shook my head, but a smile was tugging at my lips. "No, sir. We both have work to do and if you were in here all day, none of it would get done." I cupped his scruffy face in my hands and looked into his eyes. "You can text and call me whenever you want, and I'll see you when you pick me up later."

He sighed and turned to press a kiss to each of my palms. "Okay, baby. I'll let you get to work."

He sounded so sad and my heart twisted in my chest. "I love you," I reminded him.

His blue eyes lightened as he smiled at me. He was so beautiful in that instant, it was hard to look directly at him. "I love you too, baby. I hope you have the best first day ever."

I kissed him again. I just couldn't help myself. "Come on. I'll walk you out."

I wrapped my hand around his and dragged him from my office. The hallway was empty as we walked down it and I wondered where everyone else was. When we got to the front door, I reached up and gave him another kiss. This one so sweet and lingering it took all my willpower to end it.

When I pulled back, there were probably stars in my eyes, but when I looked up at Abraham, his expression was still and tense. I wondered what was wrong until a voice spoke up.

"We're getting ready to start, Ellie, if you're done here."

I turned to find Matt watching us closely from the other side of the waiting room. My cheeks burned with embarrassment, but I tried to shake it off.

I turned back to Abraham who was glaring at Matt. I cleared my throat, and he looked back down at me.

"I'll see you soon, okay? Love you."

His eyes softened the slightest bit. "Love you too, El." With that, he leaned down and captured my lips with his. He quickly deepened the kiss, and soon my heart was thundering in my chest and my hands were shaking where they held his shoulders. Everything flew from my mind as I lost myself in Abraham.

When he finally pulled away, I swayed toward him before I caught myself and straightened back up.

With a satisfied smile on his face, he shot one more look over my shoulder before pinning me with his gorgeous smile. "Have a good day, baby."

He was almost through the door when my senses returned to me.

"You have a good day, too!" I said, my voice still breathy from that kiss.

He shot me a wink and closed the door behind him. I took a deep breath to steady my racing heart and pasted on the best smile I could before I turned back toward Matt.

"Sorry about that. I'm ready now."

Matt smiled, but it didn't seem to reach his eyes. He jerked his head toward the hall behind him. "Come on. They're in the conference room."

We walked silently down the hall while I tried to get my racing libido under control. I knew none of the humans would be able to tell, but unfortunately, not much escaped a werewolf and Callie would totally pick up on it.

"So, how long have you two been together?"

I shot him a curious look out of the corner of my eye. We'd met less than an hour ago and his first question for me was about my relationship? I would think things like my prior job experience would be more pertinent, but I guess he didn't.

And honestly, that was a question I'd been dreading answering.

Sure, while I was on pack lands, the length of our relationship didn't raise any eyebrows, but we were in the real world now. Things were completely different, and my skin itched as I tried to think up a suitable answer.

Finally, I just decided to tell him the truth. So what if he judged me? I barely knew him, and his opinion shouldn't have mattered. That was what I told myself, at least.

"Um, only a few months, actually."

I could see Matt turn to me with an incredulous look out of the corner of my eye.

"You've been engaged a few months?"

I cleared my throat and shook my head. "No, we've only been together a few months."

He was quiet for a while and I regretted telling him the truth. What would a white lie have really cost me in that instance? I should have just told him it'd been years instead and avoided this all together. But I really didn't like lying, and keeping up with a fake story seemed like more trouble than it was worth.

Finally, he spoke up. "Wow, you two moved fast, huh?"

I shot him a strained smile. "When you know, you know, I guess."

Matt hummed in the back of his throat. "So, you two met and got engaged in just a few months. Wow, I wish I met someone that I knew I wanted to be with for the rest of my life so quickly."

My smile felt more forced than ever as I shrugged. "His family is known for moving fast." That was the closest I could get to explaining werewolf relationships.

"What about you? You're okay with moving this quickly?"

A million questions flew through my brain in that instant.

Why was he so curious?

Why did it matter to him?

Why did he care?

I cleared my throat. "Well, we're not getting married right away or anything. We'll probably wait at least a year for that." Why I was explaining myself to someone I just met, I didn't know, but I felt like I had to.

"That's good, I suppose."

Finally, I'd had enough of being on the other end of his microscope.

"But they're our lives and we'll live them how we want. We might get married next year, or we might get married next month. It doesn't really matter to me because I love him, and I know I want to be with him."

"Even though it's only been a couple months, huh? Man, he's a lucky guy."

I opened my mouth to respond, but we'd made it to the conference room, and I didn't need anyone else knowing what we'd been talking about. I wouldn't forget this conversation, though, and swore I wouldn't let Matt make me doubt my decision again. I'd just met him, and I didn't owe him anything, least of all an explanation about my relationship with Abraham.

"Ellie, Matt, come on in and we'll get started," Callie called from the other end of the room.

I took a seat as far away from Matt as I could at the table in the middle of the room. The only other people present were Callie and another woman I assumed was Katie. She had light blonde hair that was almost white and big blue eyes. She looked almost like an angel, but the look on her face made me think she was anything but.

When we were all seated, Callie clapped her hands together and looked around the room at all of us. "First, I'd like to welcome you all to The Asheville Initiative. I'm so glad to have you here today in our new office. I hope you're satisfied with your spaces, and if there're any issues, feel free to come to me with them. In the meantime, I wanted to dive right in now that we have a proper place to work. Since we've got a couple new faces, let's go around the room and introduce ourselves. We can start with you, Matt."

The dark-haired man sat up straighter and shot Callie a wide smile. "I'm Matt Miller, and I'm an environmental scientist. I've worked for a number of large companies but wanted a change and decided to seek out a private organization. I found this place, and the rest is history."

He looked around the room, his smile wide, almost as if he was expecting a round of applause. I just barely held back an eye roll as I turned to the woman on his left and waited for her to speak.

"I'm Katie Phalen, and I'm an environmental scientist as well, but I do most of my work outside of the lab. I met Callie a couple years ago and we've been working hard to do our part to change what we can ever since. I'm excited that we got some new office space and I'm looking forward to working with you all."

Everyone in the room turned to me and I guessed it was my turn to speak. I cleared my throat and pasted on a smile. "I'm Ellie Montgomery, and I'm a lawyer. I've only worked in criminal law until recently, but I've been studying environmental policies and hope to make myself as useful as possible. There might be a slight learning curve, but I'm here to work with you all and make the greatest contribution I can."

Callie's smile was wide as she watched me from across the room and I couldn't help returning her grin.

"As you all know, I'm Callie McCoy, and I've assembled you all as my team. I'm looking forward to helping to make a lot of great changes in our state and preserving our environment while making sure it's safe for the current inhabitants and future generations. I know we're all pretty new here, but I think we'll work just fine together."

She flipped open the folder in front of her and passed around some sheets of paper to everyone. "This is a list of everything we'll be working on in the coming weeks. As you all know, we just submitted our case to a judge regarding the Blue Ridge Parkway conservation efforts. While that's pending, I thought we could get started on the plastic bag issue in this city. We're putting together a proposal for Asheville to ban single-use bags from all stores in the city by this time next year. After that, I thought we could all focus our attention on the No Bees, No Food movement."

There were soft groans from both Katie and Matt.

Callie's lips thinned. "I know we are all tired from that uphill battle, but we can't stop now. I'm working on a program that will offer free bee-friendly flower seeds to locals. I know it's only a small step, but hopefully that paired with some education can make a difference and inspire other cities to do the same."

She looked around the room at our nodding heads and her smile turned satisfactory. "Does anyone have any questions?"

Oh, I had about a million, but I wasn't about to bring them up in front of everybody. They didn't all need to know how unprepared I was for this job. I took a deep breath and shook my head. I could do this. It would take some time to get my feet under me, but I knew I could do it.

Hell, if I could survive the shift and a serial killing psychopath, a career change should have been easy.

Callie clapped again. "If no one has anything to add, let's all get to work."

There was another round of head nods as chairs screeched across the hardwood floor and everyone go to their feet.

"Hey, Ellie. Do you have a minute?" Callie called.

I made my way to the front of the room, noticing that Katie was already leaving, but Matt had hung back for whatever reason.

"I thought I could give you a quick tour and then we can talk about what we need you to work on first."

"I can give her the tour," Matt spoke up from behind me.

Callie's brows furrowed slightly, but she shrugged. "Okay, that works. Matt can show you around and when you're done, come find me and I'll get you caught up."

I nodded and gave her a smile. "Sounds good, Callie. I'm happy to be here and excited to get started."

Her smile widened. "It's going to be great, you'll see."

I wished I had the kind of confidence in myself that she seemed to have in me, but I figured that would come with time. Every chance I got to do something good would be another thing I could feel proud of. Every time I helped them make a small difference in the courtroom would be another reason to work even harder next time.

I still had some doubts, but I was determined to be the best lawyer she'd ever worked with.

I turned to find Matt standing a little closer than I'd expected and gave him a smile too, although it was a bit less genuine than the one I'd given Callie.

"You ready?" he asked.

I shrugged. "Lead the way."

He placed his hand on the small of my back and led me out into the hall. "I'm sure you've already seen the waiting room, so we can skip that." He continued to talk, pointing out where his and Katie and Callie's offices were, as well as the break room and the bathrooms.

It was all pretty standard, although much smaller than my last office. When we got to the end of the hallway, he pushed open a glass door and led me into a fully stocked lab. My wide eyes tried to take in all the different machinery and equipment while Matt droned on behind me.

"This is where I'll spend most of my time, so if you're looking for me, this is probably a safe bet."

I shot him a small smile while he continued to explain what each instrument did. I wasn't sure why he felt the need to explain it all since I wouldn't be spending any time in there, but I let him talk anyway. It seemed he enjoyed the sound of his own voice, and who was I to get in the way of that?

Finally, he spun back toward me and asked, "Do you have any questions about anything?"

I shrugged. "I don't think so. Thanks for the tour, Matt."

He smiled, his green eyes bright. "Anytime, Ellie. My door is always open for you."

I shot him a smile and left the lab to find Callie, Matt's words still ringing in my head. Maybe Abraham was right, and Matt was looking to be more than just a co-worker. Too bad he was barking up the wrong tree.

Chapter 26

I made my way to the office Matt pointed out as Callie's and knocked on her door.

"Come in, Ellie!"

I opened the door and walked in with a frown on my face. "How'd you know it was me?"

She smiled as I closed the door behind me. "I could smell you." My face heated, and Callie laughed. "No, don't take that the wrong way. I'm just so used to your scent, it's easy for me to pick it up. It's not a bad thing."

I felt the tension seep from my shoulders as I took a seat in front of her desk. When was I going to get the hang of this werewolf stuff?

"How'd your tour go?"

I shrugged. "Good, I guess."

She raised a brow and eyed me. "Is everything okay?"

I pasted a smile on my face and gave her a nod. "Everything's great. What did you want to talk to me about?"

She didn't look completely convinced, but let it go. "First, I want to know what you thought about your new office." Her eyes were bright and her smile wide as she waited for me to respond.

"I love it."

She sat back with a satisfied smirk on her face. "I told Abey you would. That man worries too much."

"Yeah, he was nervous about showing it to me which is ridiculous. He knows me better than anyone else has in my entire life. Of course he knew exactly what I'd want in an office."

That thought brought me up short.

Callie was talking, but my own words were ringing through my head.

Abraham really did know me better than anyone else ever had. He knew my faults and my good qualities as well as everything in between. There was no doubt in my mind that I'd never be able to find someone else like him.

So, why was I pushing the wedding back? If I knew he was the one, why wait?

"Ellie?"

I shook my head and looked up at Callie. "Yeah? Sorry, what were you saying?"

She frowned and folded her hands in front of her. "Are you okay?"

I sighed and relaxed into the chair. "Sorry. I just have a lot on my mind. What were you talking about?"

She eyed me like she wanted to ask more questions, but thankfully, dropped it. "I was just saying I have some literature for you about plastic bag waste and the repercussions it has on our environment. I thought you could spend some time reading up on the issue before we ask you to write something for the court."

She handed me a thick manila folder that I took from her.

"Yeah, of course. That sounds great!"

Callie smiled. "How do you like the rest of the team?"

My smile faltered just the tiniest bit. "Well, Katie seems nice enough, but I haven't really talked to her yet, and Matt is... exuberant."

Callie laughed softly. "I think he thinks he's got something to prove here."

"Yeah, I could see that."

She sighed and shuffled a pile of papers on her desk. "He's still new, so I don't know how he's going to work out, but everyone deserves a fair chance, right?"

How could I disagree with that when Callie was taking a huge chance on me?

"Yeah, I think they do."

She smiled again and glanced at her watch. "Do you have any questions? I have a conference call in a few minutes."

I shook my head and stood. "No, I'm good. I'll go get started on this right now."

"Sounds good. Feel free to reach out to me with any questions you have."

I promised I would and left her office.

When I got back to my own, I took a minute to admire everything Abraham had done again. There were still more details that I was just now noticing, and it all filled my heart with so much love for him.

My stomach rumbled uncomfortably, and I placed my hand over it. I was probably a little hungry since I'd had such a small breakfast. Luckily, I'd stuffed a few granola bars in my purse to bring to work.

I munched on a cereal bar while I went over what Callie gave me. The more I read, the more strongly I felt about the cause. It made me feel bad that I'd never even thought of any of this before.

I finished the granola bar and threw the wrapper in the glittery trash can beneath my desk. Unfortunately, it didn't seem to have done the trick. My stomach was still bothering me, and I wondered if it was the distance from Abraham that was the culprit. It had been so long since I'd spent any real time away from him, it was easy to forget how sick it made me.

I'd promised myself I didn't care if we were fated or not, but wasn't this more proof that we really were? Normal couples didn't feel that kind of discomfort when separated. That was pure wolfy magic, and it was clearly at work today.

I did my best to ignore my rolling stomach while I perused the rest of the documents in the folder. When I was done, I hooked up my laptop and did some research of my own. I was so wrapped up in my work that I hadn't even realized it was lunchtime until my phone rang from inside my bag.

When I pulled it out, I saw that the *Sexiest Man Alive* was calling and a smile spread across my face.

"Hey, baby."

He grunted. "Don't do that right now."

I frowned and sat up straighter. "What's the matter?"

He sighed. "I won't be able to make it for lunch today and I'm irritated."

I laughed softly. "Well, I'm not too happy about that either, but I'll see you as soon as I get home."

"Not soon enough."

I laughed again. "You're silly."

"And you're mine and I want you now."

I squeezed my legs together as the nerve endings in my whole body lit up. How did he do that? Make me feel such strong emotions from so far away?

"Let's look on the bright side."

"There is no bright side."

My smile widened. He was so impossible sometimes. "Imagine how good the sex will be after we have to wait all day for it."

He grunted again. "That's a small consolation."

"What if I promise to make it worth it?"

He paused for a long moment. "I'm listening."

I bit my lip to hold back my laugh. "Well, I'm not giving away any details, but just know I'll be taking care of *you* tonight."

He groaned softly into the phone. "You're killing me."

I couldn't hold back my laugh this time. "I love you. I'll see you as soon as we get home."

"I'm counting down the minutes."

My heart squeezed in my chest and I closed my eyes for a moment. I'd never had anyone make me feel so much before. Someone who cut me to the core with just a few words.

"I am too."

After a few more *I love yous,* we finally hung up, and I checked the time on my laptop. It was after noon and I figured I'd better get some real food in me before my stomach revolted even more than it already was.

There was a knock on my door, and I decided to try out the werewolf identification trick. I lifted my nose in the air and took a deep breath. I smelled roses and a smile spread across my face.

"Come in, Callie!"

She walked in with a smile on her face. "I see you sniffed me out."

My grin was wide as she made her way toward my desk. "Sure did. What's up?"

She took a seat in one of the colorful chairs in front of my desk. "Abey just texted me saying he couldn't stop by for lunch and asked me to take you somewhere."

I rolled my eyes. "It's like he thinks I can't feed myself. I did just fine without him for twenty-eight years."

She shrugged. "He just loves you, Ellie. He's a werewolf, an alpha werewolf at that. He's always going to worry about you."

I sighed. I knew she was right, and truthfully, it didn't bother me like it used to. I knew his actions came from a place of love and he wasn't trying to be overbearing. He just sucked at the delivery sometimes.

I shut my laptop and grabbed my purse. "Did you have somewhere in mind?"

She opened her mouth to speak when there was another knock on my door. I took a deep breath and got a big whiff of strong cologne and knew it was Matt.

"Come in," I called.

He opened the door and stuck his head through, a grin already on his face. He opened his mouth to speak, but when his eyes found Callie, his smile slipped. "Hey, Ellie. I was just stopping by to see if you were interested in getting lunch with me."

Suddenly, Abraham's message to Callie made more sense. He wasn't so much worried about me eating alone as he was worried about me having lunch with Matt. My blood simmered slowly in my veins as the thoughts swirled through my head.

I didn't need Abraham orchestrating a lunch date for me because I wouldn't have gone out with Matt, anyway. I was in a relationship with a man I loved like crazy. One who I knew was possessive and already had an intense dislike for my coworker. I wouldn't have disrespected him by having lunch with another man behind his back, but now I was irritated. Instead of talking to me, he'd gone behind my back to fix the situation to his liking.

Well, tough nuggets.

"I was actually going to get lunch with Callie, but you're welcome to come along."

There. Abraham could suck on that.

Matt's smile fell slightly again, but he nodded. "Sure, sounds good. I was thinking about heading over to this little deli about a block away. That sound good?"

I looked to Callie who shrugged. A sandwich actually sounded pretty amazing, and hopefully it would be enough to calm my stomach. I shouldered my purse and gave him a smile. "Sounds great. Let's go."

We found Katie on our way out and invited her along too, and the four of us headed out for lunch.

This wasn't something I'd done before. I'd never gone out to lunch with coworkers or really spent any time with a colleague outside of the office. I got invited a few times when I first started at my last firm, but after I turned them down so often, they finally stopped asking.

I realized then that I'd been isolating myself my whole life. I didn't know if it was out of fear or what, but I'd pushed people away for as long as I could remember. Abraham was the first person who'd pushed back. Who hadn't let me get away with the crap I was used to pulling. He saw right through my defenses and found a way around them.

It made me miss him even more.

We'd just sat down with our sandwiches at a little table when I pulled out my phone.

Me: Next time, don't send Callie to babysit me. I wouldn't have gone to lunch with Matt anyway.

Seconds later, there was a response from him.

Sexiest Man Alive: I just didn't want you to have to eat lunch alone.

Me: Don't lie.

The little dots bounced on my phone's screen while everyone around me talked and ate.

Sexiest Man Alive: Okay, maybe I was intervening a little. I don't like him.

I sighed and glanced at the man in question. He might have been a little interested in me, but that didn't make him a bad guy. I think Abraham was judging him too harshly too soon.

Me: I know you don't, but he's my colleague and I need to work with him, so you need to cool it.

Sexiest Man Alive: I'll do my best.

I shook my head, but a smile was tugging at my lips. You couldn't blame the guy for being honest.

Sexiest Man Alive: Where did you and Callie go for lunch?

Me: Actually, we all went out to this deli down the street.

The lines danced for a long time again and I set my phone aside to pick up my sandwich. I took a big bite of the turkey and cheese, but it didn't taste right. Not wanting to embarrass myself, I chewed and swallowed before pushing my plate away. It seemed that the symptoms from being separated from Abraham were as strong as ever.

Whenever we'd been apart in the past, it had always been hard for me to eat. Even my favorite foods tasted wrong. Every day I had to spend without him was harder than the last, but it had never come on this fast before. Usually, it was at least a day or two before I felt that bad, not a few hours.

Maybe it was worse because we'd been spending so much time together. Maybe before I'd built up some immunity to the side effects that I didn't have anymore. Whatever the case was, my sandwich tasted awful and there was no way I'd be able to choke it down. I figured I'd wrap it and save it for later.

My phone buzzed, and I picked it up.

Sexiest Man Alive: As long as you're not alone with him.

I rolled my eyes again as my fingers furiously tapped out my response.

Me: I know how you feel about him, and I wouldn't have done that to you. Give me a little more credit, please.

I set my phone down with a huff which attracted Callie's attention.

"Everything okay, Ellie?"

I sighed. "Yeah. Your brother is just being a little overbearing."

She smiled and shrugged. "He has a tendency to do that."

I shrugged at her as we shared a look of mutual commiseration. Somehow, I kept forgetting that she's had to put up with a lifetime of an overprotective Abraham.

"Wait. That man you were with this morning is Callie's brother?"

I turned to Matt. "Yep. We're practically related." I shot Callie a wink and her smile widened.

"Well, that changes things," Matt muttered. I knew he hadn't meant for me to hear that, but he didn't know that I was a werewolf with excellent hearing.

235

I shot a look at Callie who was frowning at Matt. She'd clearly heard him too and was as confused as I was.

I didn't know what Matt's deal was, but the more time I spent with him, the less I wanted to. He seemed nice enough, but there was something just a little off about him. Something that rubbed me the wrong way.

I couldn't put my finger on it, and I wondered if it was Abraham's opinion that was helping to form my own. He'd instantly disliked him without even giving the guy a chance. Was I doing the same? Or was Abraham right to not trust him? I figured it wouldn't hurt to keep an eye on him and keep my distance until I figured out if Abraham was right or just being overprotective.

Chapter 27

"Abraham, I really need to go," I said between kisses.

He groaned and dropped his forehead to mine. "I don't like you working out of the house."

I sighed and closed my eyes. We'd had this conversation a few times already, and it seemed like we couldn't stop cycling back to it.

I reached up and cupped his face, waiting until he was looking at me. "You know I didn't like just sitting around the lodge all day. I like to work, I like to feel useful, and I like to make my own money. Please don't try to take that away from me."

He sighed heavily and covered my hands with his big, rough ones. "I would never take that away from you, baby. I just miss you when you're gone."

I knew what he meant because I'd missed him like crazy, too. How we'd gone months living hours apart was a mystery. But being independent and having a career were things that were really important to me.

"I'll miss you too, Abraham, but I'll see you for lunch today, right?"

He growled softly and dipped his head until his lips were hovering over mine. "Yes, and I believe I promised you we'd christen your office twice today."

I shivered against him and his lips curled into a smile. I reached up and kissed his perfect mouth. "Yes, you did, and I know you're a man who keeps his word."

He pulled me closer. "You're damn right I do."

I chuckled and kissed him once more before taking a step back. I opened my mouth to speak when there was a loud knock on the door.

"You two need to stop threading the needle in there before we're late!"

My face heated, and I ducked into Abraham's chest. "No," I whined. "Not Callie too."

Abraham's chest was rumbling with laughter beneath my face and I couldn't help but smile too. It seemed his whole family was out of their minds.

He pulled away and met my eyes. "You don't want to keep Callie waiting. She might seem like the most mild-mannered of my sisters, but that just means her crazy is hidden deeper than the others'."

"I heard that!" she yelled from the hallway.

A loud laugh shot out of my mouth and I shook my head. Honestly, every last McCoy was nuts. And I loved all of them.

I reached up and kissed Abraham one more time. "I love you. I'll see you this afternoon."

He sighed and nodded. "I'll be there."

With more difficulty than I expected, I pulled myself out of Abraham's arms and left our room. Callie was waiting in the hallway for me, a look of mild exasperation on her face.

"Finally," she said before grabbing my arm and dragging me down the hallway.

"Sorry, Callie."

She sighed and shook her head, her mess of curly hair flying everywhere. "Don't be. It's not your fault. Fated mates are all like this."

I swallowed down the words that were on the tip of my tongue. Despite not being able to find any information about bitten and born wolves being fated, it seemed like she still believed we were. I wasn't about to correct her. Especially after how bad my separation from Abraham had felt yesterday.

We made it down to the first floor and out to Callie's Prius. When we were loaded into the car, she took off right away. To be honest, I didn't think her car had that kind of pickup, but Callie was speeding down the road toward the highway in no time.

"Are we really late?" I asked, feeling bad for keeping her.

Technically, I could have taken my own car, but it seemed pointless. We were going *to* the same place *from* the same place at the same time. Why would we take two separate vehicles?

Callie sighed and shook her head. "No, we're not late. I just like getting there before everyone else."

Sometimes it was easy to forget that soft-spoken Callie was the boss of this organization. That she had responsibilities and duties that I knew nothing about. It made me feel even guiltier for making her wait.

"I'm sorry," I said again.

She shot me a look and a wry smile. "It's okay. Honestly, it's great seeing the two of you so in love. It gives me hope for my own future."

Speaking of her future, since I'd moved out to Asheville, I'd noticed quite a few awkward encounters between her and Wyatt. Evey hadn't had any information regarding them and I figured it was time to go to the source.

"Maybe it'll be your turn next."

She snorted as she changed lanes and exited the highway. "Doubtful."

I watched her profile as she navigated the city streets. "Oh, I don't know about that. There are plenty of eligible bachelors that live right in the lodge."

She shook her head. "Not interested."

I could tell she didn't want to have this conversation, but I wasn't ready to drop it.

"What about Wyatt? He's a really great guy, and he's single. Ever thought about going out on a date with him?"

Her knuckles were turning white with how hard she was gripping the steering wheel and I was thankful we weren't barreling down the highway at high speeds anymore.

"That would be a solid no."

I twisted in my seat so I could see her better. "Well, why not? You're both available and there seems to be some tension between you two. Why not give it a chance?"

It might have been my imagination, but I thought I heard the steering wheel groan beneath her tight grip. "Not interested," she said again.

"I think he might be."

I didn't actually know if that was true or not, but I'd caught him looking at her a few times in a way that made me think there might be more to their awkwardness.

She shot me a look out of the corner of her eye. "Believe me, he isn't."

"How do you know?"

She shrugged a shoulder. "I just do."

"But, Callie–"

"Ellie, I love you, but I really don't want to talk about this right now. Can we please drop it?"

I studied her for a while as we sat at a red light. I knew she knew I was looking at her, but she refused to meet my eye. My gut told me there was more to this Callie and Wyatt thing, but it didn't look like I'd be getting anything out of her today.

I sighed and reached out to pat her arm. "Sure, Callie. I'm sorry I brought it up."

She let out a deep breath and shrugged. "It's okay. I've just got a lot more on my mind than some meat head enforcer."

I frowned at the side of her face, but she wouldn't meet my gaze again. Sure, Wyatt was built like all the enforcers were, but I wouldn't have called him a meat head. In fact, he was one of the most decent men

I'd ever met. Why she had such a low opinion of him I wasn't sure, but I figured I had plenty of time to figure it out.

Callie found a parking spot on the street and had the car off and was out the door before I'd even unbuckled my seatbelt. Clearly, I'd struck a nerve, and I was feeling pretty awful about it.

I got out of the car to apologize again when I first smelled it. I covered my nose with my hand. "What the hell is that?"

Callie shrugged, but her eyes were sharp as they darted around the street. "It smells like something is dead."

That was exactly what it was. I hadn't been able to place it before because I'd never smelled anything like it. Now that she mentioned it, the scent was distinctly rotten, and it made my stomach roll.

"Where is it coming from?"

Callie shrugged again before taking off down the sidewalk. I jogged to keep up with her fast pace as she sped toward the office. The scent kept getting stronger, and it felt like I'd lose my measly breakfast.

Finally, we got to the front door of The Asheville Initiative and found where the smell was coming from.

Pinned to the front door was what used to be a tabby cat. A very familiar-looking tabby cat with black and brown markings and a distinctly broken neck.

Instantly, my rolling stomach heaved, and I knew I'd be sick. I ran to the alleyway between our building and the next and threw up everything I'd eaten that morning.

Callie followed me to the alley and stood next to me while I tried to get myself under control. Her soothing hand on my back helped, but nothing could erase that image from my head.

"Callie, please tell me that wasn't Charlie," I said as soon as I could form words past my retching.

She was quiet for so long, I turned to her. There was a tight look on her face and her shoulders were stiff. "I'm not sure, Ellie. I don't think it smells like him, but it looks just like your cat."

I leaned over and gagged again. Unfortunately, there was nothing left in my system, so I dry heaved until I could get myself back under control. I heard a couple soft beeps and then Callie was speaking.

"Abey, I think you need to come down here."

I straightened up and held my hand out for her phone. She gave it over willingly and the first thing I heard was Abraham's frantic voice.

"Callie! What the hell is going on?! Is El okay?"

I took a deep breath and swallowed the bile that wanted to make its way back up my throat. "I'm fine, Abraham, but I think something happened to Charlie."

"Charlie?!" he yelled. "I just saw him a little while ago."

I closed my eyes and willed my heart to keep beating in my chest for just a little longer. "Can you please go check on him right now?"

I heard his heavy footsteps pounding through the phone line and crossed every finger and toe I had.

It couldn't have been Charlie out there. I'd just seen him that morning. How could something have happened to him so soon? And why? He was just a harmless cat. Who would have hurt him like that?

I heard a door slam before Abraham called out, "Charlie! Where are you, buddy?"

I held my breath while I waited for him to confirm that Charlie was there. That he was all right. That he was in one piece and not nailed to the front door of our office.

My stomach heaved again, and I swallowed the saliva in my mouth, hoping I could keep it together for another couple of seconds.

Finally, Abraham let out a deep breath that gusted through the phone line. "He's here. He's okay."

I slumped against the dirty brick wall behind me as tears welled in my eyes.

It wasn't Charlie.

My cat was okay.

My cat was safe.

It wasn't him.

I let out a shaky breath and turned to Callie. Relief was painted across her face, and I knew she'd been worried about Charlie too.

"El, what the hell is going on down there?!" Abraham yelled into the phone and I remembered we hadn't explained anything to him.

I took a deep breath. "When we got to the office, there was a dead cat that looked just like Charlie nailed to the front door."

"What?!" he bellowed.

I pulled the device away from my face as my ear rang.

"Put Callie on the phone!"

I handed the phone to his sister and slumped against the wall again. My stomach was still churning, but I thought I was past the worst of it. Now that I had myself back under control, I needed to get a better look at what had been left for us.

When Callie saw me making my way back toward the street, she followed as she filled Abraham in on everything that happened. Which didn't take very long, because we knew next to nothing about what was going on.

The smell grew stronger the closer I got to the door, and I had to pull the collar of my shirt up over my nose to tolerate it. My stomach was still queasy, and I knew it wouldn't take much for me to start throwing up again.

The poor cat's head was at an awkward angle, its little limbs dangling lifelessly from where it was nailed to the door. Whoever did this had taken what looked more like a railroad spike than a nail and hammered it right through the cat's chest. There was blood streaked down the newly painted mint green door and pooled on the ground.

Above the dead cat was a message written in blood that I hadn't noticed before.

Go back where you came from.

What kind of message was that? And who was it directed at?

243

I scanned the words over and over, but they still made little sense.

Who would kill a cat to send a message like this?

Who could be this cruel?

My nose burned with tears as I thought about what that poor cat must have gone through before it died. My only hope was it wasn't aware of much and it had been over quickly.

I swallowed again as I tried to control my reaction to what I was seeing.

"Okay. We'll wait right here for you," Callie said behind me.

I turned to see the worried expression still on her face.

"What going on, Callie? Who did this?"

Her eyes darted between both of mine as she bit her lip. She glanced over at the door and winced before looking at me again. "I don't know, Ellie, but I don't think it's anything good."

We both turned back to look at the door as the strong smell of cologne met my nose and fought against the stink of death. We both turned at the same time to see Matt walking down the street towards us.

"Damn it," Callie muttered under her breath. "All we need is for a human to get involved with this."

I turned to her. "You think a werewolf did this?"

She shrugged. "I'm not sure, but I don't think we can rule that out."

My mind struggled to come up with an explanation for what happened. Something to explain what was going on.

"Maybe this message isn't for any of us. Maybe this was for whoever rented this space before us."

Callie shook her head softly. "That last tenant here was a florist. I highly doubt they made an enemy like this selling flowers."

I bit my lip and looked back at the door. "So, it's definitely for us."

244

Callie sighed from behind me. "If I had to make a guess, I'd say the message isn't for *us*, it's for *you*."

Chapter 28

"Hey, ladies! Are we working outside today?" Matt asked as he joined us on the sidewalk.

Our faces must have expressed how unimpressed we were with his lame attempt at a joke because his expression slowly changed to one of confusion.

"What's going on?" he asked.

We were standing in front of the door, blocking the sight of the dead cat. I hoped Callie had a plan because I was coming up blank.

"Um, sorry, Matt. We're not working in the office this morning," Callie said.

Matt frowned. "How come? What's going on?" he asked again.

Callie looked at me with wide, pale blue eyes, but I just shrugged. My mind was reeling from the site of the dead animal, worry over my own cat, and my stomach was still churning, threatening to cause more problems.

"Um. A pipe burst."

Matt's frown deepened. "I thought this whole place just got renovated. You're telling me something went wrong already?"

Callie shrugged, her smile tense. "Yeah. They'll be hearing from me today, that's for sure."

Matt sighed and shook his head. "So, what's the plan?"

Callie glanced at me again, but I was even less help than I'd been last time. "Um. You know what? Why don't we all meet at the coffee shop down the street? Hopefully, we'll have this issue sorted soon and we can get back in the office by this afternoon."

Matt didn't look convinced but nodded anyway. "Okay, yeah. Sure." His eyes darted to mine. "You coming with?"

I opened my mouth to speak, but really didn't have anything to say. Thankfully, Callie jumped in. "I need her to wait with me."

Matt glanced back at Callie. "For what?"

"Oh. Um," Callie said, and I could almost hear the gears in her head turning from where I stood next to her.

"My dad was a plumber. She wants me to talk to them when they get here," I finally spat out. It wasn't one of my finer lies, but with the shock I'd had, I was just lucky I was making complete sentences.

Matt's eyes were shrewd as he assessed the both of us, but finally he shrugged and took a step back. "Okay. I guess I'll go get us a table."

"That would be great!" Callie said a bit too loud. She cleared her throat. "Could you get in touch with Katie and have her meet you there? No sense in her coming down here just to get sent away."

I liked the way Callie thought. Holding Matt off had been hard enough. We didn't need Katie asking her own set of questions. We'd barely survived Matt's.

He shrugged and pulled out his phone. "Yeah, no problem. I'll give her a call now."

"Thanks, Matt. The plumbers should be here soon and then we'll be right over," Callie said.

He put his phone to his ear and shot us a thumbs up before turning around and heading down the street. As soon as he was out of earshot, I released a big breath and turned to Callie. "That was close."

Her lips twisted into a grim smile. "Yeah, but at least he's out of the way now. We don't need to have any of the humans getting involved with this."

Something she said before Matt showed up was still reverberating through my head and I knew I needed to bring it up, although I had a feeling I didn't really want her answer.

"Callie, why do you think this message was for me?"

She turned to me with a raised brow. "You think it's a coincidence that cat looks just like yours?"

I opened my mouth to answer her when there was the loud screech of tires against asphalt and the slam of a door.

"El?!" Abraham boomed.

We both turned to find my fiancé barreling towards us. He didn't stop until he had his arms wrapped around my shoulders and his nose in my hair.

"I was so worried, baby." He pulled me back and looked me up and down. "Are you okay?"

"I'm fine, Abraham. Nothing happened to us."

He turned to Callie and assessed her for damages too. When it seemed he was satisfied, he pulled me back into his hard chest and let out a deep breath. We stood there like that for a long moment while the frantic beat of his heart slowly decreased. Finally, he sighed and stepped away from me.

"Okay, tell me everything."

Callie launched into the story of how our morning began. It didn't take her long because not much had happened, but Abraham's brows furrowed more with every word she spoke. When his eyes darted behind us, his lips thinned, and his shoulders tensed.

He walked up to the desecrated front door and took his time examining it. His shoulders dropped with another heavy sigh as he pulled his phone from his pocket.

"I need you down here as soon as possible with a new door for The Asheville Initiative." He paused for a moment while the man on the other end questioned him. "Yes, I know it was brand new, but it needs to be replaced and I need it done now." He nodded a few times and then pocketed his phone again. He turned to Callie. "I should have a new door up here within an hour."

"What about this mess?" Callie asked. "I can't have my employees walk past a pool of blood on their way into the office."

Abraham nodded and pulled out his phone again. "Wes, grab Aubrey and a bunch of cleaning supplies and bring them downtown to Callie's new office. Tell her she'll get paid double time for this." He answered a few more questions with single syllables until he ended the call and shoved his phone in his pocket again.

"Neither one of you have gone inside, have you?" We both shook our heads, and he nodded. "Stay here."

He went to stalk past me, but I grabbed his arm. "Wait. Where are you going?"

He looked down at me, his expression still hard. "I'm going to check the office to make sure there's nothing else inside."

He tried to walk away again, but I held on. "Don't you think you should wait for Wes?"

He shook his head. "No. I want to take care of this now."

"But, Abraham, what if there's someone in there?"

His expression hardened. "Then that would just make my morning."

What did I say? The McCoys were insane.

I dug my heels in and gripped his arm tighter. "Abraham, I don't like this. Please, just wait for Wes so I know you'll have backup in case anything happens in there."

He looked down at me, his expression softening the slightest bit. He leaned down and kissed my forehead.

"I'll be fine, baby. Just give me a minute and I'll be right back out."

I tried to hold on to him, but I was no match for his strength. He gently disentangled himself from my grip and unlocked the front door before slipping through it.

I waited outside, my hands fisted at my sides and my heart clenching in my chest. I couldn't shake the fear that someone might be in there waiting to strike. Or several someones. I knew Abraham could fend off one or two men, but a whole group?

I held my breath until I heard his footsteps heading back toward the door. Seconds later, he slipped outside, and I rushed to wrap my arms around him.

He held me close and chuckled. "Were you really worried about me, baby?"

I pulled back to glare up at him. "Of course I was! What if there'd been a gang in there waiting for you?"

He shrugged. "I could take 'em."

I rolled my eyes and let out a big breath. My heart was still thumping hard in my chest and I had to remind it that Abraham was fine. He was whole and right in front of me.

Abraham looked at the both of us and then back at the door before his eyes turned hard. "Why don't you two wait inside while I take care of this?"

"What are you going to do?" I asked.

"I'm going to grab a bag and get rid of the cat before Aubrey and Wes get here. She already has a mess to clean up. She shouldn't have to deal with a dead animal too."

I looked at Callie who shrugged. We walked to the door, making sure to keep our distance from the poor dead animal. When we were inside, Callie told me to wait in the front lobby while she did an inspection of her own. She came back with a look of relief on her face.

"It doesn't seem like anything was tampered with and it doesn't smell like anyone else was in here. I think whoever did this only made it to the front door."

I raised my nose in the air and gave a sniff of my own. She was right. I could only smell the scents of the other employees and Abraham. I constantly forgot about my enhanced senses and how much information I could get from them. It was so easy to forget when I'd spent the first twenty-eight years of my life as a human with normal senses.

We waited in silence while we listened to Abraham on the other side of the front door. Thankfully, the smell was a lot weaker inside because I wasn't sure how much more my stomach could take.

And now I had time to think about it, I was ashamed I'd reacted that way. What was wrong with me? Callie hadn't had a problem with the stench, so why did I? Why had it affected me so strongly?

Those thoughts were put on the back burner when Abraham opened the front door and stuck his head through. "They're here."

We both hopped up from our seats and walked back out front to greet Wes and Aubrey. The former had the same tense expression Abraham was wearing, and the latter just looked irritated. To my surprise, Beatrice had also come along, too, and she looked just as angry as the two men.

"I should have known you'd have something to do with this," Aubrey muttered under her breath as she sorted through the cleaning supplies they'd brought.

This wasn't the day to piss me off, apparently.

While the other four were busy talking, I stomped up to Aubrey and got close enough so only she could hear me.

"Now is not the time for your bitchiness, Aubrey. You were brought here to do a job, so just do it and shut your mouth, or I'll shut it for you."

I wasn't used to making threats. My whole life, I'd fought with my words and my intellect, and not my fists. However, all that changed when Beatrice started training me. Now I knew I could hold my own, and I'd have had no problem proving that to Aubrey.

Living in a werewolf pack, I'd come to realize they were much more physical than the average human. It wasn't uncommon for an argument to end in a scuffle out back with claws and fangs. When I'd first moved in, I'd found the violence unsavory, but I guess I'd gotten used to it. So, used to it, I was making threats of my own.

Aubrey's eyes widened slightly, and I caught a small whiff of fear before she rolled her eyes and scoffed. "Whatever, Elizabeth. Just let me do my job."

"That's all I'm asking."

She rolled her eyes again but refrained from commenting. Which was smart considering the morning I'd had. My stomach was still queasy, but I felt sure I could go at least a few rounds with her if I had to.

Abraham broke away from the group and headed toward me. "We need to talk."

My stomach dropped, and I knew whatever he had to say wasn't going to be something I wanted to hear. Instead of arguing, I quietly followed him into the building and down to my office. When the door was closed behind us, he turned to me with his hands on his hips.

"You're done working here."

It felt like my eyes were going to fall out of my head they were so wide. "What?" I screeched.

His lips thinned, and he shook his head. "Clearly this was an attack against you. I'm not putting you at risk. You're staying on pack lands from now on."

I took a step closer to him, my hands fisted at my sides. "The hell I am."

He sighed. "El, be reasonable."

"No! You be reasonable, Abraham! I'm not letting you hole me up in your lodge. I'm keeping this job and I don't care what you say."

His eyes assessed me for a quiet, tense moment. "I could have Callie fire you."

I folded my arms across my chest. "She wouldn't do that."

He watched me again as his chest rose and fell faster and faster. Finally, he threw his hands in the air. "El, what the hell do you want me to do here? You're clearly in danger and instead of co-operating, you're being difficult as usual."

I narrowed my eyes at him. "Difficult as usual?"

He sighed and shook his head. "I didn't mean it that way."

"Well, you're being overbearing and unreasonable as usual."

He took a deep breath and crossed the space between us, but I backed up before he could reach me. His eyes flashed with hurt, but I hardly cared. He was trying to clip my wings and I wouldn't let him. "El, please, be reasonable. You know what happened the last time there was someone after you."

252

"How do we even know they're after me?! Maybe that message was for Callie! Did you even consider that?"

He swung an arm around and pointed at the closed door. "The cat looks just like yours! How could you think that's anything other than a message for you?"

I gripped my sides and ground my teeth. "I don't care. I'm not quitting."

He let out a deep breath and ran a hand through his hair. With a look in my direction, he began pacing the floor. "I'm not willing to let you be in any kind of dangerous situation, El. You need to understand that."

"How is this a dangerous situation? I'm not a cat! They didn't kill a person and leave them on our front door."

He stopped his pacing and turned to face me. "You're not even making any sense!"

I took a deep breath and looked down at the floor. Neither of us was making much sense, and it seemed the higher the tensions rose, the more we were saying things we didn't mean. I let my arms fall to my sides and looked back up at him.

"This job means a lot to me and I'm not willing to quit."

He sighed and looked at something over my shoulder. "Fine. Then I'm assigning you a bodyguard."

"I don't need a bodyguard."

His eyes met mine again. "Damn it, El! I will not compromise on your safety. You either accept a guard or you keep your ass in the lodge. Pick one."

I ground my teeth so hard my jaw ached. I didn't like his high-handed attitude. I didn't like being told what to do. I didn't like being treated like a child.

All of this was true, but as I looked at my fiancé, I could see what this morning had done to him. There were deep lines creased in his forehead and around his eyes and I knew they came from worry for me. I also knew that all he wanted to do was protect me and this was the only way he knew how.

It seemed like I needed to work with him. He'd compromised by offering the option of a guard instead of making me leave my position and now it was my turn to do the same.

"Fine. You can send Wyatt to work with me until we figure out what's going on."

Abraham sighed deeply and crossed the room to pull me into his arms. There, I could hear the frantic beat of his heart and my own clenched in my chest.

He was worried about me and I really couldn't blame him. It was becoming more obvious by the minute that the dead cat and the bloody message had been meant for me. Now the question was, who'd sent it?

Chapter 29

"You really don't need to wait with me."

Abraham shook his head and crossed his legs so his ankle was resting on his other knee. He'd squished his big frame into one of the colorful chairs in front of my desk and I'd have laughed if the morning hadn't been such a disaster.

"Nope. I'm staying until Wyatt gets here."

I sighed and took a seat behind my desk. "Then suit yourself because I'm going to get some work done."

"Go right ahead."

I shot him a look, but all he did was smile at me. I shook my head and turned on my computer, ready to do some more research on the plastic bag issue we were working on. I'd only been at it a few minutes when Abraham spoke up.

"You know, you're pretty sexy when you're concentrating."

I shook my head again, but my lips twitched with a smile. Figuring it was better to not instigate him, I dipped my head and continued reading the article I'd just pulled up. I'd only gotten through a few paragraphs when he spoke again.

"You didn't dress like this at your last job, right?"

I took a look at the khaki pants and collared shirt I had on and frowned. "Well, no, not really. I dressed a little fancier at my last job."

"Why?"

I sighed and looked up from my computer. "It's what was expected."

He nodded. "So, why not dress like that here?"

I shrugged and looked back at my screen. "Callie said it would be a more laid-back atmosphere."

"I think you look sexy."

I shook my head again, but this time couldn't fight the smile. "You always think I look sexy."

"Because you are."

I rolled my eyes and shot him a look. "Are you going to let me get any work done?"

He smiled wide and my heart thumped extra hard for a couple beats. "I can think of something better to do than work."

Instantly, heat pooled between my legs, but I tried to fight it. We'd already gotten a late start because of the dead cat debacle. I really needed to get some research done so I could work with Callie on this later.

But Abraham was so damn hard to resist. He was so sexy, and sweet, and funny, and silly that I couldn't help myself.

I crossed my legs under the desk and shot him a look. "Wyatt is gonna be here any minute."

His smile widened as he held up his phone. "He's helping his mom with something and won't be here for another thirty minutes at least."

I leaned back in my chair and raised a brow at him. "And you think thirty minutes is enough time?"

His smile turned feral as he rose from the little chair. "I bet I can make you come twice in that time."

Heat rushed to my face as my heart thundered in my chest. "You sound pretty sure of yourself."

He stalked across the room and I suddenly knew what it felt like to be the prey of a large animal.

"Oh, I am."

He reached my desk and walked around it until he was standing next to me. Taking my hand, he gently pulled me from my chair and took a seat in it. His hands wrapped around my hips as he maneuvered me onto my desktop. My laptop and notes were shoved aside unceremoniously as he made room for me.

"What makes you so sure?" I asked, my voice breathy.

He smiled up at me as he raised my shirt over my head and tossed it aside. "I've been studying you, El. Every time I get my hands on this sexy little body, I learn more. I know what gets you hot, I know what drives you crazy, and I know how to make you come so hard you scream."

I shivered under his hands as he unfastened my bra and tossed it toward my shirt. His big hands reached up to cup my breasts and my head fell backward.

"Abe, someone could walk in here," I breathed as he pinched and pulled my nipples.

He shook his head and leaned forward to suck one into his mouth. When he pulled back again, he shot me a smile. "I locked the door when I came through."

Damn. He had all the answers, didn't he?

While his mouth worked on my nipples, his hands unfastened my pants and shimmied them down my legs. When he pulled away again, his eyes were so clear and sincere, I couldn't look away.

"I need you, El. I need to feel you. To have you wrapped around me and know you're okay."

I wasn't going to deny him anyway, but hearing that made the decision even easier.

I reached out and ran my fingers through his thick, dark hair. "I'm fine. I'm right here."

His eyes closed while my fingers massaged his scalp. When they opened again, there was a glint in them that made my belly clench.

He grasped my shoulders and pushed me backward until I was lying across my desk. Soon, my panties were gone, and I was naked before him. I should have felt self-conscious, but that was impossible when a man like Abraham McCoy was looking at me the way he was right then.

"The first time you come today is gonna be on my tongue."

I shivered again and squeezed my legs together. He wasn't having that, though, and gently pried my knees apart. This was another position you'd think I'd have felt vulnerable in, but I didn't. I felt sexy, and powerful, and so needy, it felt like I'd explode if he didn't touch me soon.

He slid his hands from my ankles to my thighs where he gently spread them farther apart. My chest was rising and falling so quickly as I lay there waiting to see what he'd do next. A long groan left his mouth and his hands tightened on my thighs.

"You're so fuckin' sexy. I could come just looking at you."

I gasped softly as he ran a single finger down my slit. "Abe, please."

He slid that thick finger inside me, and my back arched off the desk.

"You know you only call me Abe when I'm fucking you?"

I was panting and having trouble concentrating. "Huh?"

He chuckled and blew a soft stream of air at my heated center. "No one's ever called me Abe before." His finger was pumping in and out of me so slow it was torture, but the most beautiful kind. "I've always been Abey or Abraham. You're the only one who calls me Abe, and it's only when I've got you naked. Why do you think that is?"

My head was rolling around on my neck as I struggled to keep up with the conversation. I could already feel my climax building and knew it wouldn't be long before he tore from me the first of the two orgasms he's promised.

"I-I-I don't know. It just slips out," I breathed.

He pulled his finger from me and I felt so empty. Thankfully, I didn't have to wait long for his touch again. His warm, wet tongue traced a line up my thigh to my core and back down the other side. He did this a few times before finally licking where I needed him the most.

My back arched again, and I dug my fingers into his hair.

"I like it a lot," he said between licks.

What were we even talking about?

His tongue plunged into me quickly, and I gasped. He pulled out just as fast and I was left shaking and needy as ever.

"I like hearing you scream it when I make you come."

"Oh, my God, Abe," I panted, yanking on his hair to bring him back to my heated flesh.

He chuckled and another shiver ran up my spine.

"Okay, baby. I'll give you what you want."

A second later, his whole mouth was on me and everything else faded away. All I could do was hold on to his thick hair as he licked and sucked me to an orgasm I knew would rock me to my core.

Faster than I thought possible, my belly clenched, and my toes curled as my climax raced forward. I could barely catch my breath as intense waves of pleasure washed over me. Finally, he sucked my clit into his mouth, and I lost all control.

My back arched while my legs stiffened, and my hands gripped his hair tighter than ever. I screamed as my orgasm ripped through my body, bringing with it the kind of sensations only Abraham had ever been able to pull from me.

He lapped at me softly as I came back down, reality slowly returning to me. For a quick second, I was intensely grateful he'd made my office soundproof. But with how loud he'd just made me scream, it might not have even mattered.

Abraham pulled away and my hands slipped from his hair. He stood up, a smug smile on his face as he unbuttoned his jeans. "Was that good, baby?"

I sighed as another aftershock ran through my limbs. "You made me scream," I panted.

He laughed softly and dragged my hips toward the edge of the desk. "I'm about to make you scream again."

Without warning, he plunged inside me, filling me so completely, all I could do was moan. When I regained some of my senses, I wrapped my legs around his waist and did my best to meet his thrusts with my own.

His hands came down on either side of my body on the desk as he plowed into me.

"You feel so good," he grunted as his hips met mine over and over.

I gasped again as he somehow reached even deeper inside of me. "So do you, Abe. You feel so good."

His hands grasped my hips, his grip almost too tight. "I love you so fucking much."

"I love you too."

He growled low and deep. "I'm never gonna let anything happen to you." His hands squeezed me tighter. "You're mine, and I'm gonna protect you from anyone who thinks they can take you from me."

Another orgasm was on my horizon and it was so powerful, it was already making me shake. The ability to talk was so far beyond me at this point. All I could do was grip the edge of the desk above my head and revel in the feel of him driving me higher.

Without warning, my orgasm hit, and I screamed his name as I lost myself to the pleasure. His hands squeezed me tighter as he roared with his own release.

When he'd emptied himself, he slid me off the desk and into his arms before lowering us to the floor. Our bodies were slick with sweat as we fought to catch our breath and come back down to earth.

He reached up and ran his thick fingers through my hair. I closed my eyes. His heartbeat thumped against mine, syncing up and beating as one.

I loved this time. These stolen moments after we made love. I felt so close to him. Like we were just two halves of the same whole and we were finally reunited. There was absolutely no place I'd rather be than on the floor of my new office in my fiancé's arms.

He leaned down and pressed a kiss against my forehead. "I was so scared today," he said so softly I almost missed it.

I pulled far enough away that I could see his face. His eyes were clouded with worry and the lines around them were deep.

I reached up and cupped his face. "I'm okay, baby. Nothing's gonna happen to me."

He sighed and kissed my hand. "I'm afraid that's not true. I have a really bad feeling about this, El."

I sighed and pulled him closer, hoping I could infuse some of my calm into him. "I can defend myself, Abraham. I'm not the defenseless human I was before. I'm a strong, capable werewolf, just like you."

He sighed heavily, his breath blowing strands of my hair. "I'll never stop worrying about you, El, because I'll never stop loving you. Those two things go hand in hand."

My lips curled into a smile while my heart skipped a beat. "I love you too, baby. I promise I'll be safe."

He kissed my head again for a long time. "Please take care of yourself and please don't fight against having Wyatt with you. When you're on pack lands, you don't need to keep him around, but as soon as you leave, I need him to be with you. I can't let anything happen to you."

I pursed my lips but nodded. I didn't love the idea of having a babysitter again, but if it would put his mind at ease, if it could erase even just a few lines from his forehead, then I'd do it.

"Okay. I won't fight it. At least until we figure out who's behind this and what they want."

He let out a deep breath and squeezed me tighter. "I think I know who this was."

I pulled away so I could look into his eyes again. "Who?"

He looked away, his jaw ticking with how hard he was clenching it. "Conrad."

My heart dropped to the base of my stomach while the ramifications sped through my mind. Abraham's uncle was behind this?

"Why would he come after me? I didn't do anything to him."

Abraham shook his head, his eyes so sad it made my heart ache. "He's trying to use you to get to me. I'm who he's really after."

I frowned while I thought through all that. "But what about the message? What could that mean?"

Abraham shrugged beneath me. "I guess he's trying to get you to leave me."

I snorted and shook my head. "He'll have to try a lot harder than that."

Abraham's arms tightened around me. "Don't even joke about that."

I rolled my eyes, but a smile was tugging at my lips. Pulling away, I made sure to catch his eyes before speaking again. "Abraham, nothing could make me leave you. Absolutely nothing."

He watched me for a long time, his eyes darting between both of mine. I expected the worry lines in his forehead to lessen, but they didn't. "Even if it was safer for you? Even if it meant you could live your life without all this bullshit?"

I shook my head. How could he be so blind? How could he not know how crazy in love with him I was? How could he think anything could tear me away from him?

I cupped his face between both my hands. "Nothing could ever make me want to spend even a single day without you. It doesn't matter what Conrad throws at us because I'll be by your side through it all. I love you and I need to be with you. Nothing can change that. Understand?"

I needed to make sure he did. Needed to get that look off his face permanently. He was it for me in every way possible and I wouldn't let him believe otherwise.

He watched me for a long time and I simply stared back at him. I hoped my eyes showed him all the love I felt. I hoped he'd see in my face my determination to stick with him through anything. Elizabeth Montgomery didn't hide when things got hard, she just got harder.

Finally, he sighed and pressed a long kiss to my forehead. "Okay, baby. We'll do this together."

Chapter 30

We were still naked and lying on the floor when there was a knock on my office door. I jolted upright and turned wide eyes toward Abraham.

"Shit! That's probably Wyatt!"

I scrambled to my feet and located my clothes, yanking them on as quickly as I could. I turned back to see Abraham was still lying on the floor, naked, and just watching me.

"Get dressed, McCoy," I hissed as I hopped on one foot while putting my shoes back on.

He laughed but finally rose to his feet. If I wasn't so worried about Wyatt being on the other side of my door, I'd have taken the time to admire his masculine beauty. But that would have to wait until later because my bodyguard was probably wondering what the hell was taking me so long to answer the door.

I watched Abraham slowly shrug on his clothes and cursed him for taking his sweet time. When he was finally dressed, I swung the door open and found Wyatt there with his arm raised to knock again.

"Hi, Wyatt. Sorry about that. We were... um... busy," I finished lamely.

He raised his nose in the air and gave a sniff before shooting Abraham a look. "Yeah, I can smell how busy you two were," he said, a smile curling his lips.

My face heated to atomic levels while I looked anywhere but directly at my pack mate. Despite the room smelling like sex, I invited him in, and he strolled inside.

"Alpha," he greeted Abraham. "What's going on?"

Abraham walked over and shook his hand before rehashing everything that happened this morning. Wyatt's face hardened the longer Abraham talked, and I was thankful I wasn't on the other end of that look.

"Were there any scents left behind?" Wyatt asked.

Scents? Why hadn't I thought of that?

Abraham nodded. "It smelled like a werewolf but none that I'm familiar with."

"So, there was just one of them?"

Abraham shrugged. "Only one of them touched the cat or the door."

Wyatt nodded and shot a glance at me before looking at Abraham again. "What are your theories?"

Now Abraham's face turned to stone. "Conrad."

Wyatt sighed and shook his head. "I was afraid of that."

"So was I."

"What are we going to do about it?"

"You know his pack far outnumbers ours, but with some help, I think we could take him. I have plans to meet with some other packs soon."

My stomach fell to the bottom of my feet. "Soon?" I cut in. "I thought you said you wouldn't be leaving for a while."

Abraham turned to me with a sigh. "In light of what happened today, I think it would be best if I got this over with sooner rather than later."

I studied his face, reading the determination there clearly. I knew there was nothing I could say that would change his mind. And what would my argument be? Don't go finding the pack allies for this fight you foresee because I'll miss you?

"When?" I asked softly.

Abraham crossed the room and grasped my arms. Ducking his head, he met my eyes. "I'll probably leave Monday."

I swallowed, my throat suddenly dry. "That's only a few days away."

He nodded, his mouth a thin, grim line. "I know, baby. I don't want to go, but I need to."

I looked away and nodded. "I know." I took a deep breath and met his eyes again. "How long will you be gone?"

His eyes searched mine before he answered. "I'll try to be back by Friday."

That was a blow I hadn't expected. How was I going to go that long without him?

I nodded slowly. "Okay."

He squeezed my arms and turned back to Wyatt. The two men talked out some more details, but my mind was spinning with thoughts of my own.

I know I used to spend that much time away from Abraham before I moved here, but now it was inconceivable. I needed him like I needed the air in my lungs. He'd become essential to me on every level. I missed him already.

"El?"

I looked up to find both men staring at me. I shook my head and pasted a smile on my face, but even I could tell how frail it was. "Sorry. What's up?"

"I'm heading out now."

My stomach twisted and my heart fell. I knew I'd see him later, but any distance from him hurt right then. I wanted to spend every available minute with him until he left.

I hurried over and wrapped my arms around his waist. Abraham sighed and pulled me in closer.

"Wyatt, could you give us a minute?"

The other man agreed, and his heavy footsteps crossed the office, heading toward the door. I kept my face buried in Abraham's chest and my arms tightly wrapped around him.

I heard the office door swing open and instantly smelled the overpowering scent of men's cologne.

"Um, hi. I'm here to see Ellie."

I ripped myself out of Abraham's arms and turned to face the door. Matt was standing there, eyeing Wyatt suspiciously and holding two paper cups.

"Hey, Matt. What's up?"

His eyes darted from Wyatt to Abraham and back again. "Am I interrupting something?"

"Yes," Abraham said.

"No," I countered at the same time.

I shot a look at my fiancé, who only had eyes for Matt. But they were hard, unflinching, irritated eyes.

I rushed over to the door and shoved Wyatt out of the way. "What's up, Matt?" I asked again.

His eyes were still wary when they finally met mine. "Well, since you never showed up at the coffee shop, I thought I'd bring you something back."

"Oh. Um. Yeah, the burst pipe didn't affect my office, so I figured I'd get some work done."

Matt frowned. "Where did the pipe burst?"

"The bathroom."

"The break room."

One of those answers was from me and one was from Abraham and it did nothing to clear up this situation.

I laughed, but it was a little on the shrill side. "It was a pipe that led from the bathroom to the break room and they said they needed to replace the whole thing." I winced at my lame excuse and could tell Matt was still suspicious.

"And they've fixed it already?"

I shrugged. "It helps to have friends in high places."

I didn't know if that made sense and I hoped Matt didn't push me on it. I didn't actually know a single plumber, and if he dug deep enough, he'd figure that out.

Matt's shrewd eyes continued to watch me, and I did my best to look confident in the lies I'd just told. Finally, he shrugged. "Well, good thing it didn't affect the lab."

I could feel that my smile was too wide but there was nothing I could do about it. "Yeah, your lab is all good thankfully."

He shot a look down the hall. "Was there a lot of damage to the other rooms?"

"Oh, uh, not really. Just some water we had to clean up, but it's all good now." I needed to get rid of him before I ran out of lies. "What did you come here for again?"

Matt shook his head and held out one of the paper cups in his hands. "I don't know how you take your coffee yet, but I figured no one could turn down cream and sugar."

I took his offering and gave him a weak smile. "Thanks for thinking of me, Matt."

His smile was wide and genuine. "Of course, Ellie."

Abraham cleared his throat behind me, and I knew I needed to wrap this up. "Anyway, thanks for stopping by. I'll see you at lunch."

His eyes widened. "You're going to lunch with me?"

"No," Abraham growled from behind me, but I ignored him.

"I figured we'd all get lunch together again," I said, hand on the edge of my door, waiting to close it as soon as possible.

The light in Matt's eyes dimmed the slightest bit. "Oh. Yeah, that sounds good." He sighed and shot a look at the other two men once more before meeting my gaze again. "Well, I'll see you then."

"Great. Bye Matt," I said and shut the door behind him.

I stood there facing away, knowing the second I turned around I'd be staring down an angry werewolf.

"I want you to keep an eye on him," Abraham growled.

I spun to find him looking at Wyatt, who also wore a grim expression.

"No one needs to keep an eye on anyone," I said.

They both ignored me.

"Is he always that... friendly?" Wyatt asked.

Abraham grunted. "Yes."

Wyatt nodded. "He smelled desperate."

How did they know this stuff? Was there a handbook I could get that would explain what different emotions smelled like or something?

I stomped toward them and got right in the middle. "I don't need Wyatt watching over Matt. We're worried about Conrad's pack, not some human who decided to bring me a coffee."

Abraham's jaw ticked. "That's the second time he's invited you out to lunch."

"He didn't invite me, and even if he did, so what? We're coworkers. That's what you're supposed to do."

He shook his head and looked over me to Wyatt. "Keep an eye on him."

I huffed. "You're being ridiculous."

Abraham's eyes met mine again and their blue depths were electric. "He wants what's mine."

I rolled my eyes. "You don't know that."

He shook his head. "El, I love you, but you're oblivious to the effect you have on men. That one," he pointed at my closed door, "is after more than being your friend. Trust me."

I sighed. "What does it matter, Abraham? Don't you trust me?"

His eyes widened, and he rocked backward on his heels. "Of course I do."

"Then why don't you trust me to take care of him? I'm not leading him on. I'm not giving him the wrong idea. Eventually, he'll just drop it."

Abraham's eyes searched mine for a long time. Finally, he let out a deep breath and nodded. "Okay, El. I'll let you handle this. But I want you to tell me if he tries anything."

I rolled my eyes again. "If he tries anything, I'll break his hand. Happy?"

His lips twitched, and his eyes lightened with humor. "Moderately."

I shook my head. The man was impossible.

He reached out to pull me into his arms, and I went willingly. No matter how irritated I was at his high-handed alpha nonsense, there was still nowhere I'd rather have been.

Wyatt cleared his throat. "I'll just go wait in the hallway."

We both ignored him as Abraham gently rocked me side to side. When the door closed, he sighed and pulled away to catch my eye. "I'm sorry."

"I know you are. I just wish you trusted me more."

"It's not you I don't trust."

"But you're not trusting me to handle the situation."

He sighed and looked away. "There's just something about seeing another man look at you like that. It makes me crazy, El. Like I could snap his neck with my bare hands for just laying his eyes on you."

I shook my head and reached up to cup his face. "There's no reason to feel like that. I'm yours."

His eyes softened. "That's the only reason he's still alive."

I chuckled and reached up to give him a kiss when I heard loud voices coming from the hallway. I shot Abraham a questioning look before disentangling myself and hurrying over to the door.

When I opened it, I found a red-faced Callie staring down an unconcerned-looking Wyatt.

"What's going on?" I asked.

Callie turned her fiery eyes toward me before they glanced toward Abraham. "What the hell is he doing here?"

I frowned at my friend, but she still had her eyes pinned to her brother.

"He's here to watch over El," Abraham explained.

Her lips curled into a sneer. "Why wasn't I informed of this?"

I shot a look at Abraham who seemed just as confused as I was. "I didn't know I needed to run it by you."

"This is my office, and everything needs to be run by me."

Abraham held up both hands. "Okay, Callie. I assigned Wyatt to guard El until we figure out what's going on."

Her eyes glanced in Wyatt's direction, then mine, and finally back to Abraham's. "Assign someone else."

What the hell?

I looked back at Abraham who looked even more confused than last time. "Excuse me?"

She took a menacing step forward. "I said assign someone else. I don't want him here."

"Callie, you're being ridiculous."

"I am *not*," she said, and I almost expected her to stomp her foot. "This is my company, and I get to say who comes in here and I say he can't. I want him out of here right now."

Where was all the animosity coming from? I couldn't imagine what Wyatt could have done to make the normally mild-mannered and soft-spoken Callie react that way.

"Callie, El needs a guard."

"Then assign someone else."

"There is no one else."

She crossed her arms over her chest and stared him down. I'd have hated to be Abraham since her withering look was intimidating me and it wasn't even pointed my way.

"You're telling me out of all your enforcers, he's the only one who can do this job?"

Abraham shrugged. "He's the only one I trust with her safety. This is for El, Callie."

Her angry eyes darted from Abraham to me and I really wished he'd left me out of it. I wasn't thrilled with having a babysitter, either, and if it was going to upset Callie so much, I'd rather have dropped the whole thing.

"I'll stay out of your way," Wyatt finally spoke up.

All of us turned to him but his eyes were trained on Callie.

"Not good enough," she said.

He pushed off the wall and stood to his full, impressive height. "There's someone out there that's willing to snap a cat's neck and nail them to your door, and it seems like their sights are set on Elizabeth. You're going to let whatever's between us get in the way of protecting her?"

Callie's face turned redder the longer we stood there, and I was genuinely worried for her. It couldn't be healthy for her face to turn that color. Finally, the most menacing sound I'd ever heard come from the middle McCoy sister rumbled out of her chest and she threw her hands in the air.

"Fine. But I don't want to see you. You stay in this office and the hell away from me."

With that, she spun around and stormed down the hall to her office. We were all silent and still until we heard her door slam violently.

Abraham and I both turned to Wyatt who was still looking toward where Callie had disappeared. The expression on his face was impossible to read and I wondered how he felt about all this. Or what happened between them to make her so angry.

Finally, Abraham spoke up. "I don't know what you did to piss her off like that, but I suggest you fix it."

Wyatt tore his gaze away from the empty hallway and turned to Abraham. "I'll do my best."

I really didn't envy Wyatt in that moment. It took a lot to get Callie to that place and I doubted it would be an easy road working his way back into her good graces. Whatever he'd done was going to take some serious work to undo. I hoped he was ready.

Chapter 31

I stood in front of the large mirror in Evey's room and admired her work. I was wearing a tight white dress that wrapped around curves I didn't even know I had. My hair was curled and draped around my shoulders and my makeup was smoky with a bright red lip.

"I did good, didn't I?"

I turned to find the youngest McCoy sibling with a smug smile spread across her pretty face.

It was Saturday night and Del had a show downtown. I used to complain when Evey insisted on dressing and making me up like I was her personal life-sized Barbie doll, but I didn't anymore. Honestly, leaving the decisions up to her took the pressure off me and she enjoyed it so much, who was I to take that away from her?

"You did good, Evey. I look great."

She scoffed. "Of course you do. Now, I have three-inch heels and six-inch heels. What'll it be?"

Looked like I wasn't giving her complete control after all.

"I'll take flats."

"Flats?!" she yelled like I'd just suggested she cut her arm off and use it as a baseball bat.

"Yes, flats."

"You can't wear flats with that dress!"

"Watch me."

"Ellie, be reasonable."

I turned away from the mirror to face my future sister-in-law. I loved her, but sometimes her love for fashion overruled her common sense.

"Evey, I'm gonna be standing in a concert venue all night and I don't wanna do that in heels." She looked like she was going to keep arguing, which forced me to throw in a threat. "I'll go change into jeans and sneakers instead."

Her eyes narrowed, and I knew she was trying to think of a way to convince me to wear her ridiculous heels. Finally, she sighed and tossed the offending footwear aside. "Fine! But I'm pickin' 'em out."

I smiled and shrugged. "Sure."

She turned for her closet, grumbling the whole way about ungrateful women who know nothing about fashion. I chuckled and turned back to the mirror. Unfortunately, the humor was short-lived.

Now that I wasn't fighting with Evey, my mind raced back to the one thing I hadn't been able to get off my mind all week.

Abraham was leaving in two days. And he was going to be gone for at least five. Maybe more.

I gulped and watched my made-up face fall into the same expression I'd been sporting since he'd given me the news. My eyes were sad and lifeless, my lips turned down at the corners, and there were new lines marring my forehead.

I'd continued to feel sick all week every time I'd gone to work, and my stomach curled just thinking about how bad I was going to feel with him gone for so long. But that wasn't the only reason I didn't want him to leave.

Abraham had become an essential part of my life. A limb I never knew I needed but now couldn't live without. What was I going to do with myself without him for so long?

"You thinkin' about Abey?" Evey asked from behind me.

I spun around to face her, doing my best to paste a smile on my face. "Huh?"

She pursed her lips and raised a brow at me. "You can't fool me, Ellie. You've been like this all week. You think we haven't noticed?"

I blew out a deep breath and, with it, my shoulders slumped, and the smile slipped from my face. If I wasn't fooling anybody, why waste the energy pretending I was okay?

"Yeah, I'm thinking about him."

She crossed the space between us and linked her arm through mine. "He won't be gone that long."

I nodded. "I know. I just don't want him to be gone at all."

Half her mouth ticked up into a smile. "You'll have all of us. I promise to not leave your side for a single minute."

I gave her a weak smile. "Thanks, Evey."

She sighed. "I know it won't make you miss him any less."

I shook my head. She was right, it wouldn't. Knowing I wouldn't be alone was nice, but nothing compared to having my fiancé home where he belonged.

"You two used to spend days apart all the time," Evey reminded me.

I nodded. "Yeah, but that was before."

"Before what?"

I shrugged. "Before I knew I loved him. Before the whole mess with Calvin. Before we got engaged. Things were so different back then and I'd somehow convinced myself I was fine without him. I wasn't really, but that delusion did a lot to help me get through the time we spent apart."

I sighed and looked down at my bare feet. "Now, I know how much I need him. I know how important he is to me. I know who I am when I'm with him and who I am without him and I don't want to be that woman again."

Evey blew out a breath and tightened her arm around mine. "He won't be gone for long, Ellie. And this is an important trip. He's doin' this for you."

I sighed again. "I know he is. That just makes it worse."

She reached out to rub my arm as we stood there silently. I knew she could tell how upset I was, and it was obvious there wasn't anything that was going to make this better.

I took a deep breath and shook my head. We needed allies if we were going to be able to defend ourselves against the Charlotte pack. I needed to suck it up and put on my big girl panties.

Thankfully, I'd been able to hide how upset I was from Abraham for the most part. He could tell something was wrong, but I just played it off like it was work that was bothering me. It didn't feel good to lie to him, but I knew it was necessary. If he realized how upset his impending trip was making me, he'd cancel it and we couldn't afford that. There was a conflict on our horizon, and we needed all the help we could get.

I pulled my arm from Evey's and pasted on the brightest smile I could manage. "Let's stop talking about it. It's only five days. I'll survive."

She eyed me for a moment before shrugging. "I know you will. You're stronger than you think."

I hoped she was right.

There was a knock on her door right before it was thrown open and Callie and Beatrice spilled into the room. Both women were in tight dresses and high heels, looking like they belonged on the runway.

"You guys ready?" Callie asked.

Things had been tense between us since Wyatt was assigned as my bodyguard. She hardly talked to me and I'd barely seen her. I knew she was trying to keep her distance from Wyatt, but it felt like she was keeping it from me instead. I was glad we were all going out together tonight. I'd missed her.

"I just need to find Ellie some shoes and we're ready to go," Evey said before she scurried into her massive walk-in closet.

Callie walked up to me and wrapped her arm around my shoulders. "You look beautiful, Ellie."

I smiled at my friend. "So, do you, Callie."

She sighed and pulled me closer. "I'm sorry I've been distant all week."

I gave her a small smile. "It's okay, I get it." But then I thought more about it and decided to be honest. "Actually, I don't really get it."

She sighed again and averted her eyes. "It's kind of a long story."

I slid my arm around her waist and squeezed. "I'd love to hear it someday."

She looked back up at me and smiled, her pale blue eyes clear. "Okay. I promise I'll fill you in."

I squeezed her again and her smile widened.

"Are we ready to go, ladies?"

We both turned to find Abraham standing in the doorway, looking so damn handsome he took my breath away. He had on dark blue jeans, his typical work boots, and a plaid short-sleeved shirt. Damn, I was a lucky woman.

My eyes met his, and he smiled so wide I almost couldn't look directly at him. He crossed the room, his eyes locked on mine and I pulled away from Callie. When he was close enough to reach me, he wrapped his arms around my waist and tugged me against his chest.

"You look so damn beautiful," he said, his nose pressed against my neck.

"Funny, I was thinking the same thing about you."

He pulled back and shot me an unimpressed look. "Men aren't beautiful, babe."

I shrugged. "Well, you are."

"I think I prefer *devastatingly handsome*."

My head fell back with a loud laugh and I felt the earlier tension melt from my body. "Okay, devastatingly handsome. I can get behind that."

He leaned closer and whispered in my ear. "And I'll be getting behind you later."

"Ugh, we can hear you!" Beatrice whined from across the room.

I giggled and pressed a kiss on his lips before pulling out of his arms. If I didn't put some distance between us, I knew his sisters would be in for more bedroom talk.

Evey rushed over to me with a pair of nude flats and shoved them into my arms. "That's the best I can do with your absurd demands."

I rolled my eyes at Abraham. "Apparently not wanting to kill my feet in high heels all night is a ridiculous request."

He shook his head, a smile spreading across his face. "What's wrong with you, El? Why would you do that to her?"

I chuckled as Evey narrowed her eyes at the both of us. "I've already had enough of you two."

I looked at Abraham and we both laughed. Evey sighed and turned to grab her purse. "If you two are done bein' annoyin', can we go?"

We were still chuckling as Evey stormed out of the room followed by the rest of the sisters. I reached down to slide the shoes on my feet and sighed in satisfaction. I was so glad I'd stood up to Evey and demanded reasonable footwear. Which wasn't always an easy thing to do. The smallest and youngest of the McCoy quintuplets was also often the most tenacious.

Abraham wrapped an arm around my waist, leading me out of Evey's room and down to the first floor. The girls were already piled into the back of Abraham's truck and he helped me into the passenger side before taking his seat behind the wheel.

"Where is this place, anyway?"

Abraham navigated the steep gravel drive before heading toward the highway.

"It's at the same venue as last time."

A heaviness settled between us in the truck. Last time we'd been to one of Del's shows, I'd almost shifted in front of everyone. Peyton had been there, hanging all over Abraham and purposely riling me up. My blood boiled just thinking about it.

Abraham reached over and squeezed my thigh. "Things will be different this time," he said softly.

Thankfully, the other women were in the back seat chatting amongst themselves, so I didn't think they heard him. I didn't need them knowing I was still upset about that night.

Once I'd caught Peyton all over him for the second time, I'd left the venue to get some air, but Calvin found me and offered me a ride home. I barely suppressed a shiver just thinking about how many times I'd been alone with him. How many times he could have hurt me or worse.

After Abraham figured out I'd left and gone back to the lodge, he'd sped home to confront me. He'd asked me repeatedly not to just take off, that it wasn't safe for me, and I'd been too upset to care. When he got to the lodge, we'd had a huge fight and gone to bed separately. Thankfully, I'd come to my senses a few hours later and apologized, but that night was still fresh in my memory.

I remained quiet while Abraham drove us toward the venue and the thoughts continued to swirl around my head. What I needed to do was let the past go. There was nothing I could do to change it and I shouldn't have let it darken my present. I had precious few hours left with Abraham and I wanted to spend them without a black cloud hanging over my head.

Just like last time, Abraham stopped his truck at the front doors and helped us all out. He gave me a kiss and promised to find me as soon as he parked.

Evey must have sensed there was something wrong because she linked her arm with mine and led me inside.

"What's goin' on in that pretty head of yours?" she asked as we followed Callie and Beatrice.

I sighed and shrugged. "Just letting some ghosts haunt me."

She shook my arm until I had to look at her. "You talkin' about the last time we were here?" I shrugged again, and her smile turned grim. "I know that was a bad night for you, but this is a new day. Don't let what happened back then keep affectin' you now."

She was saying what I already knew, but somehow, hearing it from someone else helped. I gave myself a little shake and pulled my lips into a smile.

We were there to support Del. Her music career was doing better than ever, and this show was proof of that. When last time she'd been the opening act, tonight she was the headliner. I was so proud of her I could have burst. I needed to remember why we were there and let go of what happened last time.

We grabbed drinks at the bar and turned to find places to stand that were close enough to the stage that Del would be able to see us. She claimed she always had a better show when we were in the crowd, and we would all have done anything to support her.

I was just wondering when Abraham would get inside when two thick arms wrapped around me from behind and I was tugged into a hard chest. The scent of spearmint and soap engulfed my senses and I knew my man had found me.

"Hey, baby. You get me a drink too?" I held up the beer in my other hand and he kissed my cheek. "That's why I love you."

I turned to him with a raised brow. "Is that the only reason?"

He took a big swallow of beer, his eyes trained on me. When he tipped the bottle back down, he leaned closer to whisper in my ear. "It's just one of many, baby. One of hundreds. You want me to list 'em?"

I smirked and shrugged a shoulder. "Why don't you tell me one or two?"

He smiled against the side of my neck and breathed me in deeply. "Okay, well there's how fucking sexy you look in this dress."

I bit my lip and nodded. "Okay, go on."

His arms tightened around my waist. "Then there's the way your big brown eyes light up when I walk in a room," he whispered against my skin.

A shiver ran down my spine and I squeezed the glass in my hand. "What else?" I asked, my voice breathy.

"Then there's–"

"Hello, Abey."

I froze in place, my heart thundering a mile a minute. Slowly, as one, we turned to the sound of the high-pitched voice that was way too close for comfort.

Standing just a few feet away was none other than Peyton, with a smug smile on her face.

A million thoughts swam in my mind, but the only one I voiced was, "You've got to be fucking kidding me."

Chapter 32

"Have you guys missed me?"

My stomach flipped deep inside me and I felt like I was going to be sick. "Not in the least."

Peyton narrowed her eyes at me before turning back to Abraham. "Hey, Abey. How've you been?"

His shoulders were tensed, and his jaw was tight. "What are you doing here, Peyton?"

She shrugged. "I'm here to see Del perform."

"She doesn't need your support. You shouldn't be here."

Fire flashed in her black eyes. "It's a free country and these aren't McCoy lands. I can be here if I want."

Abraham shook his head and wrapped an arm around my waist. "Fine. But stay the hell away from us."

He turned us around but her high-pitched voice rang out again. "I didn't know he was going to hurt her!"

We slowly spun back around to face her.

"What?" Abraham asked, his voice quiet and deadly.

Peyton took a step closer and my hands were already shaking with the need to shift and tear her throat out.

"Calvin. I didn't know he was going to hurt her. He said he was in love with her."

Abraham's laugh was full of derision. "She's my mate, Peyton. And you tried to take her away from me."

She took another step forward, her dark eyes narrowed in anger. "She's not your *mate*," she hissed. "She's not like us. She's not worthy of standing beside you as your mate. You have to see that."

Abraham took a step closer to her, his body tightly coiled and ready to strike. "What I see is a woman who doesn't know when to give up. You've been excommunicated, and that means I don't want to see your face and I don't want to hear your voice. Nothing you say means a damn thing to me. Walk the fuck away, Peyton."

Her eyes were just barely slits now as her whole body trembled. I looked around at the humans that were crushed around us and knew it would be a disaster if she shifted. My eye caught Beatrice's and Callie's, and from their faces, I could tell they were just as pleased to see Peyton as we were.

"You know what, Abey? Fuck you. I tried for years to make you see me as more than just your sister's friend and I'm done. You've got a whole shit storm heading your way and I'm just going to sit back and laugh while it destroys everything you've worked for."

She spun around, but Abraham reached out and grabbed her arm before she could get far. "Explain yourself."

She tipped her head back with a humorless laugh and shook him off. "I don't have to tell you shit."

Beatrice and Callie had made it to where we were standing, and the former spoke up. "What are you doing, Peyton?"

Peyton turned her fiery black eyes toward Beatrice and the shaking in her limbs got worse. "What are *you* doing? I thought you hated her just as much as I did, and now look at you. Best buds with the human that fucked everything up."

Beatrice shook her head. "She's not the enemy, Peyton, and I had no reason to dislike her. She's a great wolf and I'm happy to call her my friend."

"You're just as bad as him. Just as wrapped up in this piece of shit human. Can't you see what she's doing to our pack? Can't you see she's ruined *everything*?"

Beatrice shook her head slowly. "It's not your pack anymore."

Peyton's pale face turned an ugly shade of red as her body shook more forcefully. "And where were you when I was getting excommunicated? What did a decade of friendship mean when I needed you the most?"

Beatrice was still shaking her head, her face the saddest I'd ever seen it. "You brought this on yourself. I told you to leave it alone. To leave Ellie alone and you wouldn't listen. You got yourself excommunicated and you need to grow up and accept the consequences for your actions."

Peyton's head fell back with another laugh that held no joy in it whatsoever. "Accept the consequences of my actions? Here's some acceptance for you: pretty soon you won't have a pack. Pretty soon I'll watch as everything gets taken from you like it was taken from me." She turned to Abraham, and I watched the longing slither across her features. As much as she hated him, she was still in love with him and it made my stomach turn. "I came here today to give you one more chance. To see if you'd come to your senses."

Abraham shook his head. "If you think I'm letting you back in my pack, you're wrong. You lost the privilege of being a part of us when you betrayed one of us."

"Betrayed who?!" she screeched.

Abraham nodded toward me and Peyton's eyes widened.

"*Her*?! I betrayed *her*?! Who the fuck cares about some pathetic human who couldn't even die when she was supposed to? I never accepted her as a member of my pack."

"Well, unfortunately for you, the decision of who is or isn't a pack member isn't up to you. El is my mate, and the future alpha, and you almost got her killed. There's no way I'd let you back in."

Peyton's face was almost the same color as the crimson dress she had on. "Alpha? You're going to make this human the *alpha* of one of the most prestigious packs in North Carolina?"

Abraham shrugged. "She already is."

Peyton laughed again, the sound even more vile than before. Her eyes landed on me and I stood up straighter. I wouldn't let her think she could intimidate me for even a second. This woman had clearly lost her mind, but I'd never back down from her.

"You've ruined everything, and soon, I'm going to take it all back from you."

"What does that mean?" I asked.

She shrugged and looked away. "Just that you don't cross me and get away with it. If I can't be a part of the McCoy pack, then I'll make sure there *is* no McCoy pack."

Beatrice and Abraham stepped forward simultaneously, growls rumbling from both of them.

"Is that a threat?" Abraham asked between gritted teeth.

Peyton shrugged again. "More like a warning. You really don't deserve one, but I guess I still have a soft spot for you." In the next instant, her demeanor changed completely. Instead of a woman feigning nonchalance, she was spitting mad again, the craziness she kept so well hidden splayed across her pinched face. "War is coming to your doorstep. You can try to prepare for it, but you can't stop it. I'm going to watch as everything you love is ripped away from you. Then, maybe we'll be even."

"Peyton get the fuck out of here," Beatrice growled, her body crouched and poised to attack.

Peyton reeled all that crazy back in, and her face transformed again into an almost bored expression. "Don't say you weren't warned. See you all soon."

With that, she spun around and was lost in the surrounding crowd.

For a long time, we just stood there, our eyes doing all the talking because I figured, like me, everyone else was too shocked to actually speak.

A loud roar went up around the room and we turned toward the stage.

"How're y'all doin' tonight?!" Del called from the center of the stage. She had on a flowy pale pink dress and her signature cowboy boots on her feet. She lifted the guitar hung around her neck and strummed the first chords of what I recognized as one of her original songs.

Abraham wrapped his arms around the four of us. "We all need to seriously discuss everything Peyton just said, but for now, we need to shelve it and support Del. As soon as her show is over, we're all getting out of here and reconvening at the lodge. Got it?"

We all nodded, varying degrees of apprehension and anger dancing across our faces. As one, we turned toward the stage and did our best to participate in Del's show. We clapped at the appropriate times and swayed to the music, but I could tell none of our hearts were in it.

I honestly didn't know how I'd get through her whole set after what just happened with Peyton, but before I knew it, Del was thanking the audience and exiting the stage. Abraham grasped my arm and leaned down to whisper in my ear.

"We need to collect Delilah and get out of here."

I nodded and let him lead me and his sisters toward the back of the stage. It took some convincing from an intimidating Abraham, but finally we were granted access by security. Abraham dragged us down hall after hall, presumably following her scent until we came to a closed door and he knocked loudly.

When Del opened it, my stomach sank. Her face was so bright, she was almost glowing with happiness, but as she took in the rest of us, her expression slowly fell.

"What's goin' on?" she asked.

Abraham nodded toward her room. "You need to pack up and we need to go. Now."

She glanced at each of our faces once more before nodding. "Okay. Let me get my things."

She raced around the room, packing up her instrument and gathering anything else she brought with her, and within minutes, Abraham was leading all of us toward the back door of the venue.

Once we were out in the fresh air, I took a deep breath with the hope it would settle my nerves. I knew it was Peyton we were talking about, but her threats sounded real. And I had a bad feeling we hadn't seen the last of her.

"What's goin' on, guys?" Del asked as she struggled to keep up with Abraham's long legs.

"Peyton," he grunted.

Del slowed down, but Abraham grabbed her arm and dragged her behind him.

"Wait, what about Peyton?"

"She was here at your show," Beatrice supplied, the anger brimming in her voice, too.

"Okay, so what? Tell her to fuck off."

I would have laughed if my head wasn't still swirling with Peyton's threats.

"We'll tell you more when we get to the lodge. We need to brief the enforcers," Abraham said as we reached his truck and he opened the doors for all of us.

Now that we had an extra person, I had to slide into the middle of the front bench seat, but I didn't mind. Despite my best efforts to not let Peyton's words bother me, I was worried, and being this close to Abraham alleviated a lot of that anxiety.

We drove the twenty minutes back to the lodge in mostly silence. I didn't know about everyone else, but I was playing her words over and over in my head, looking for anything we could use. Anything that might hint at what she was up to.

We made it back to the lodge in record time and filed out of his truck as quickly as we could.

"Beatrice, round up the enforcers. Evey, Callie, and Del, meet us in the conference room in ten. El, you come with me."

We all broke apart at Abraham's command. I slid my hand into his and let him lead me into the lodge. He stormed up the stairs and into our room without another word. When the door was closed behind us, he spun around and pulled me into his arms. He squeezed so tight it was a little hard to breathe, but I wasn't complaining.

"Are you okay?" he asked into my hair.

I chuckled once. "Of course. Why wouldn't I be?"

287

He pulled back so he could look in my face. "I know how you feel about her."

I shrugged. "She doesn't mean anything to me anymore. I have everything I want, and she has nothing. I think that's an appropriate outcome after what she did."

Abraham sighed and pulled me back into his chest. "I think I need to leave tonight."

I wrenched myself out of his arms, my heart thundering in my chest. "What?" I breathed.

His face was grim, mouth a thin, determined line. "The sooner the better."

"But, why?"

He sighed and looked over my head before meeting my eyes again. "You heard her. Trouble is coming our way and we need to prepare for it. The sooner I go, the sooner I can bring back reinforcements." He leaned down and cupped my face between his big, rough hands. "I'll do anything to keep you safe. Anything. That means finding the help we need to defend ourselves. That means being ready when Conrad moves against us."

I took a step back. "You think Conrad is behind this?"

I nodded slowly. "I think Conrad is behind all of this."

My mind raced while the pieces slipped into their places and the picture was revealed to me. "You think Peyton's working with Conrad."

It was more of a statement than a question, but he nodded anyway.

"It makes sense that she would turn to him after she was excommunicated. No other pack would have taken her and I'm sure she found a kindred spirit in my uncle. Both of them want revenge against me. Why not team up?"

He was right. I could feel in my bones that he was right, but I still didn't want to believe it.

"Maybe Peyton was just talking out of her ass. Maybe her threats don't mean anything."

Despite the situation we found ourselves in, Abraham's lips twitched with a grin. "Talking out of her ass?"

I shrugged. "Just something I've picked up from Del. I think it's appropriate here, don't you?"

His lips were still twitching like he was fighting a smile. "I need to keep you away from that sister. She's a bad influence."

I rolled my eyes. "She could be though, couldn't she?"

The smile fell from his face. "Could Peyton be talking out of her ass?" He shrugged. "Sure, but I think we both know she isn't."

I sighed, my shoulders slumping as I let the realization sink in that he was right. Peyton was really up to something and we had a huge problem on our hands.

I spun away from Abraham and paced the length of his sitting room. "This is bad, Abraham."

He sighed. "I know."

"Do you realize how much she knows about this pack? About these lands? She knows this lodge inside and out and now she's working with someone who's out to hurt us. There's no telling what kind of information she's given Conrad."

He sighed again. "I know, baby."

I continued to pace while my mind raced with all the possibilities. Having Peyton as an enemy was going to prove to be a bigger pain in the ass than I'd thought. As my legs pumped furiously across the room, I realized something else.

I came to a stop in the middle of the room and turned to face him. "You need to leave as soon as possible."

His face was grim when he nodded. "I know."

My nose burned with tears, but I held them back. Instead, I crossed the distance between us and wrapped my arms around his waist. I would miss him so much, but this was more important. It didn't matter how I felt about it, Abraham needed to find us some help and he needed to get back here as soon as possible. We could only hope that help got here in time.

Chapter 33

"I've been made aware of some new intel that I need to share with you."

We were all squished into the conference room, eyes riveted on Abraham. Every enforcer and every McCoy was present, the latter of which wearing grim expressions. We already knew what Abraham was there to discuss.

"It is my understanding that the Charlotte pack is preparing to move against us."

Murmurs erupted from every corner of the room. Abraham waited while the initial shock wore off and everyone quieted back down.

Finally, he nodded and spoke again. "I'm leaving tonight to meet with as many packs as possible to reinforce our numbers. I will return with enough enforcers from our allies to stand against Conrad and his pack." He looked around the room, meeting every pair of eyes there. "While I'm gone, Elizabeth and Beatrice will be in charge. You are to defer to one of them as you would me."

I swallowed harshly as that news sank in. He hadn't mentioned he'd be leaving me in charge. I suppose it made sense, but I felt woefully unprepared for the job. I shot a glance at Beatrice who didn't look surprised at all. Hopefully, the enforcers would turn to her for help because I had no idea what I was doing.

"I want patrols doubled running around the clock. No one gets within a hundred miles of these lands without one of us knowing about it. I know that will stretch our resources to the max, but I'll be sending back help as soon as I find it, so our numbers should swell soon. Speaking of our numbers, it's about to get pretty cramped in here."

Someone snorted, but most of the men stayed silent.

"Anyone who has a single room, I'll expect you to triple up immediately. If you don't want to be rooming with someone you don't know, I suggest you invite some of your fellow enforcers in now. Things are going to be tight around here, but this is all necessary."

Abraham grasped the back of a chair and dipped his head. His shoulders were drawn with tension and I yearned to reach out to him. To comfort him. To take some of his burden. To help in any way I could.

But I knew it wasn't the right time, so I fisted my hands in my lap and waited for him to speak again.

"As you all know, the Charlotte pack outnumbers us about three-to-one. We don't know exactly how many of them are enforcers, but we can assume about a third of them are. I don't have to tell you that's a fight we would be hard-pressed to win."

He looked around the room again and I took a minute to do the same. The familiar faces of my pack came into focus and my chest swelled with pride. Instead of fear, all I saw was determination. Instead of submission, I saw the desire to fight harder.

In that instant, I knew we'd come out on top. That there was nothing the Charlotte pack could do that would break us. These werewolves had fought from the beginning to find a foothold and they weren't about to let it go now. I'd never been more proud to be a member of the Asheville pack.

I sat up straighter and gave Abraham a small nod. He shot me a tiny smile before the grim determination was back on his face.

"With the help of our friends, we'll come out on top. We'll push the Charlotte pack back and defend our homes. If there's any way to avoid the conflict, I'll do it, but I want us to all prepare for the worst-case scenario. War is coming to our doorstep and we need to be prepared."

A cheer went up somewhere in the back of the room and the rest of the wolves joined in. I felt that warmth in my chest blossom as I hollered along with them.

We had a treacherous road ahead of us, but we'd come out on top. There was no other option.

Abraham stood up straight and crossed his arms over his chest. "Are there any questions?"

The room was quiet for a prolonged moment and Abraham nodded. "You all know what is expected from you while I'm away. Make me proud."

There were murmurs of agreement as the enforcers filed out of the conference room. When they were gone, that left just me and the McCoy siblings. Abraham shut the door behind the last enforcer and walked over to have a seat at the head of the table.

He took a deep breath and let it out slowly, his shoulders falling a fraction of an inch. "Evey, you're in charge of accepting the visiting enforcers I send this way."

I looked to the youngest McCoy who nodded, her expression grave.

He turned to Beatrice. "Bea, you're in charge of the enforcers. I want you to double the amount of drills we're running and make sure every enforcer makes it to at least two a day. We need to be sharp and strong for the coming fight."

"No problem," she said as she cracked her knuckles and leaned back in her chair. If I didn't know any better, I'd say she almost looked excited at the news. I didn't know if it was because she'd get to ride the enforcers harder or if she was spoiling for a fight with the Charlotte pack, but it was pretty terrifying.

"Del and Callie, in between practices and work, I want you to help out Aubrey and Ms. Elsie. There'll be a lot more wolves to feed and clean up after and they're going to need the extra hands."

When both women nodded in agreement, he turned to me. His eyes softened the slightest bit and my heart thumped an extra beat just for him.

"El, you're going to be in charge of making sure the pack runs smoothly. All the wolves are going to be coming to you with their issues and you'll have to find solutions for them without me." He took a deep breath and ran a rough hand down his face. "I never intended to leave you with such a responsibility this early on, but it's unavoidable." A small smile tugged at his mouth. "However, considering how you've been handling yourself without my help, I know you'll do just fine. Probably better than I could do."

I shook my head. "I doubt that."

He sighed. "You underestimate yourself. I've seen you rise to this position with the grace and poise of a natural leader. You'll do fine. I wouldn't worry too much about pack issues, anyway. When the rest of the wolves hear about the coming conflict, I suspect most of them will set aside their petty problems for the time being. You'll mostly be a figurehead. Someone for them to look to. I need you to be strong and present a calm front for them. If they see you're not worried about the coming confrontation, they'll be less likely to worry too. Okay?"

I took a deep breath and nodded. "I'll do my best."

His smile was wide and bright, and my heart pounded again. "That's my girl."

He looked around the table at every woman present before tapping the table twice. "Any of you have questions?" When we all shook our heads, he stood from his seat and held a hand out to me. "Then I'm going to spend some time with my mate before I have to get on the road."

My stomach sank at the reminder, but I rose from my seat and took his hand. It was warm and calloused and so big it engulfed mine. He led me out of the conference room and up the stairs to our wing. He didn't stop until he'd made it to our bed.

He kicked off his boots and crawled onto our king-sized mattress. I did the same and when I was close enough, he pulled me into his arms, tugging until I was spread across his chest.

My heart beat in time with his while we lay silently in each other's arms. My head was racing with everything that happened today as my heart broke inside my chest. This was the last time I'd have his arms around me for nearly a week and I wanted to cry just thinking about it.

We'd only been lying there a few minutes before the bed dipped beneath the small weight of my cat. Charlie walked right past me to curl up into a ball on the other side of Abraham's chest. He chuckled and reached around to scratch his head.

"It wouldn't be a real cuddle without him, would it?" he asked.

I shook my head as I willed the tears from my eyes. I needed to be strong. It was essential that Abraham visit these packs and find us some help. It didn't matter that I already missed him so much it was hard to breathe. It didn't matter that I didn't know how I was going to make it through this week without him. I needed to stuff my feelings in a box and seal them up tight.

He let out a deep breath, the movement jostling me on his chest. "I'm going to miss you so much," he said softly into the darkness.

I sniffed back the tears. "I'm going to miss you too, baby."

He hummed softly as he stroked his big hand through my hair. "It feels like it's been so long since we've been apart. I've forgotten how I lived without you."

My nose burned with tears, but I did my best to stifle them. "I feel the same way," I whispered.

"I'm doing this for us, baby. I'm doing this so you have a safe place to live. So our pack can be safe. So we can live our lives without this threat. You understand that, right?"

I nodded against his chest, knowing that if I opened my mouth, the only thing that would come out would be sobs.

"I wish I didn't have to go, though. There's not much that could tear me away from you, El. The only thing making this decision easy is the need to protect you. That's the only desire in me that's stronger than the one to be with you."

This time I couldn't stop a tear from escaping my lids and rolling down my face. Abraham must have smelled it because he paused and pulled away again.

"You're crying?"

I sniffed and nodded. "I'm sorry. I can't help it. I'm going to miss you so much."

He watched me for another couple of seconds before pulling me against his chest and holding me tighter than before.

"I'll call you all day every day. As often as I can. You're going to get sick of talking to me," he promised.

My chuckle was watery. "Not possible."

"And I'll video chat with you every single night," he said. "I bet I can even make you come through the phone again."

I gasped. "Abraham."

He chuckled as his hands slid from my hair to the tops of my thighs. His fingers slid beneath the hem of my dress and I shivered in his arms.

"Let me love you one more time before I have to go. Let me leave you with a little piece of myself. Give me something I can take with me."

His big hands were cupping my bottom as he pulled my dress even higher.

"Yes," I breathed.

It didn't matter what was going on or what we had to face, Abraham's hands on my skin never failed to light up my senses.

He slid my dress up and over my head, leaving me in nothing but a small pair of white panties and a white lace bra. His hands quickly removed the rest of my clothes and I was left lying naked on top of him.

My own hands were roaming his body as well, unbuttoning his shirt and pulling it off his shoulders. Soon he was as naked as I was.

We were still at first. Quiet. I didn't know what he was thinking, but I was trying to carve into my memory the way his body felt against mine. The way we fit together like two halves of one whole. How my skin erupted in flames anywhere it touched his.

Abraham's hands skimmed up my neck to cup my jaw. "I love you, El. With every single piece of me, I love you. I know this next week is gonna be hard, but we're gonna get through it like we get through everything else. I promise."

I nodded slowly before leaning toward him, my lips seeking his. When we found each other in the dark, all thought of talk quickly fled our minds.

Abraham slowly and meticulously made love to me as I tried to memorize every inch of his body. I did my best to hold back my tears, but a few escaped as he brought me to my second orgasm. He kissed them off my face, his fingers threading through my hair and tipping my head back for better access. When he reached his own climax, he stilled inside me, his body tightening in pleasure before he sighed heavily and pulled me into his arms.

We lay like that for a long time, our naked and slick bodies still twitching with the aftershocks of our pleasure. In all the times we'd been together, I didn't think we'd ever quite made love like that before. It filled me with so much joy that was weighed down by so much heartache.

His fingers were stroking my scalp as I slowly drifted off to sleep. A little while later, Abraham woke me with a kiss on my lips.

"I'm getting ready to leave, baby. Come say goodbye to me."

I sat up in the bed and rubbed my eyes. When I looked out the window, I could see the moon had risen further in the sky and realized I'd lost precious time with Abraham.

I slid off the bed and threw on the first set of clothes I could find. He watched me with half a smile on his face and his suitcase at his feet. I couldn't even look at the offending luggage.

When my hair was thrown into a messy bun and I was as presentable as I was going to get, I took Abraham's hand and let him lead me down to the ground floor. We made it to the door near the lot and he stopped us before turning to me.

"I'm only going to Boone tonight, so I should be there in under two hours. I'll call you as soon as I arrive."

I nodded and pasted on the best smile I could manage. "Say hi to Grady for me."

Abraham's smile was as weak as mine. "I will." He sighed and dropped the handle of his suitcase before pulling me into his arms. "I love you, baby," he whispered into my hair.

The tears were burning in the backs of my eyes, but I closed them and hoped they'd hold. "I love you too."

He pulled far enough away that he could capture my lips with his own. He kissed me so long I forgot what I was upset about. But then he let me go and picked up his suitcase.

"I'll talk to you soon," he said before walking through the door and taking my heart with him.

Chapter 34

I watched his truck drive away through the small window on the door. When I couldn't see him anymore, I sighed and turned around. Every step felt harder than the last. Not knowing what to do with myself, I wandered into the kitchen, hoping there'd be some food left over from dinner.

We were supposed to go out after Del's show, but with Peyton showing up and the meeting Abraham had to call, we'd all forgotten about it. When I got to the kitchen, I found Ms. Elsie in there and her warm smile was almost my undoing.

"Hey there, Ellie. What are you up to?"

I shrugged and slid onto a stool at the island across from her. "Just thought I'd see if there were any leftovers from dinner."

Ms. Elsie chuckled. "Leftovers in this house? Not likely, but I can whip you up a sandwich or somethin'."

I waved a hand and slid off the stool. "No, don't bother. I'll just go to bed."

The elderly woman frowned, her expression so stern I paused. "Go to bed on an empty stomach? Not while I'm around. Plop your little butt back in that seat and let me make you somethin' to eat."

The tears swam to my eyes again, but I sniffed them back and climbed back on the stool. Since when did I become this weepy woman who almost cries over a sandwich?

"Okay, Ms. Elsie. I appreciate it."

She nodded once and spun around to the fridge. "I've got turkey, ham, chicken, and bologna."

"Sounds good."

I almost laughed remembering the first time Abraham made me a sandwich in that kitchen. He'd offered me a variety of different lunch meats too, and I surprised him by accepting all of them at once.

Ms. Elsie was no exception.

"You want 'em all?"

I shrugged. "The more the merrier."

She smiled and shook her head. "Now that's what I'm talkin' about. One everything sandwich comin' right up!"

She chatted while she worked, thankfully not needing much input from me. Which was good because every corner of the house reminded me of Abraham. From the sandwich meat to the stool I was sitting on, it all brought me back to him. I wondered for the hundredth time how I was going to get through a whole week with him gone.

"I know you're already missin' that man of yours."

I jerked my head up toward Ms. Elsie who just smiled at me knowingly.

"You'd be hard-pressed to not miss a fine specimen like that," she said with a wink. Just like that, the tears were turned into giggles as I listened to Ms. Elsie go on about my fiancé. "Hell, if I had a man like Abraham warmin' my bed you'd have to pry me from it."

She slid a plate in front of me with a bag of chips and a bottle of water. I was still laughing as I picked up one half of the sandwich.

"I can barely control myself around him," I admitted as I tore off a bite of the overloaded sandwich. It was then I realized how hungry I really was.

Ms. Elsie just nodded with a knowing look in her eyes. "And why should you? Y'all should be thumpin' thighs every chance you get."

Thankfully, I'd already swallowed the bite in my mouth, or it would have been sprayed all over the older woman in front of me. I calmed myself down enough to take a gulp of water, but I just barely kept it down, too.

"Where do you guys come up with this stuff?"

She winked and wiped a rag across the counter between us. "Google is your friend, girl. Never forget that."

I laughed again as I tore into the second half of my sandwich. She'd handed me barbecue chips which were normally my favorite, but as soon as I opened the bag, my stomach churned. I quickly sealed them back up and pushed them away.

Ms. Elsie frowned. "Somethin' wrong, hon?"

I swallowed another bite of sandwich and nodded toward the bag. "I think those have gone bad."

Her frown deepened. "That's strange. I just bought 'em the other day."

I shrugged and stuffed the last bite of sandwich in my mouth. "It's no big deal. This sandwich was enough. Thanks again, it really hit the spot."

Her smile was warm, and her brown eyes lit up. "That's what I like to hear."

She grabbed my plate before I could protest and began washing it while I finished my bottle of water. When she was done, she turned around to look at me as she dried her hands on a dish rag.

"That man of yours will be home before you know it, Ellie."

I sighed and looked down at the marble counter. "I just keep thinking that maybe I should have gone with him. Maybe I can be more help that way."

Ms. Elsie shook her head and hung the rag on the stove. "You listen to me, girl, this pack needs you. I know some of 'em have been givin' you a hard time, but this is when it counts. When things get hard, they need someone to turn to and that someone is you now. The best thing you can do is be here for your pack. Abraham will be home soon and you two will be together again. In the meantime, you need to put your duties before your heart and do what's best for your pack."

I let her words swirl around my head. I hadn't really thought of it like that before. That the pack needed me more than I needed Abraham. It filled me with a renewed purpose. With a desire to be there for my pack in any way I could.

Abraham mentioned that with all the turmoil coming our way, they'd need to turn to me, but I hadn't believed him. I'd thought for sure they'd find out I was the only alpha left and just wait until Abraham got home, but maybe I was wrong. Maybe I could be of some use. Maybe I could help ease their minds and prepare the pack for the confrontation coming our way.

I looked up and met Ms. Elsie's wise eyes and knew she was right. My place was here. My role was to lead the pack. I needed to stow my sorrow and pack away my longing because I had a job to do.

I slid off the stool and walked around the kitchen island. When I was close enough, I wrapped my arms around Ms. Elsie and squeezed her tight. She froze for the briefest second before hugging me back even harder.

She kissed the top of my head and pushed me back until she could look in my face. "You're doin' a good thing here, Ellie. It's no time to stop that. You need to be stronger than ever now."

I nodded slowly. "I know. You're right. I'll get my act together, I promise."

Ms. Elsie pursed her lips. "You can still miss him, hon, but you need to keep livin' in the meantime. You got folks countin' on you now."

I nodded again. "I know. I'll figure it out."

She squeezed one of my cheeks. "I know you will. Now, go get some sleep."

I gave her one last squeeze and left the kitchen. Once in our room, though, the old sadness crept in as I looked around at all the empty space. It was strange being in here without him. And I knew sleeping in that big bed was going to be almost impossible. With a sigh, I picked up Charlie, hoping he'd be enough company that I'd get some sleep. I had a feeling it wouldn't matter much, though.

Just as I reached the big king-sized bed, I heard the hall door open and several sets of feet pad across the sitting room before there was a knock. I lifted my nose in the air, but the scents I was getting were layered one on top of the other and I couldn't make sense of it.

I walked over to the door and opened it to find all four McCoy sisters standing there with pillows and blankets in their hands.

I frowned. "What are you guys doing here?"

Evey shoved past me and the rest of the women filed through. "We're havin' a sleepover."

My frown deepened. "A sleepover?"

"Yeah. We knew you'd have a tough time tonight, so we thought we'd all join you," Del said as she walked across the room to the bed.

I raised a brow and shut the door behind them. "And who says I want company?"

Del and Evey laughed while Bea and Callie just smiled. "You're family now," Evey said. "You don't get a choice."

My heart was so full, it felt like it would burst. When my nose started burning with tears for the hundredth time that day, I willed myself to calm down. There was no reason to cry over a sleepover.

I walked over to the bed where all four sisters were making themselves comfortable.

"You sure we'll all fit?" I asked, eyeing the mattress.

Evey shrugged. "We'll just have to snuggle. If it's too tight of a fit, we can just make Bea sleep at the foot of the bed."

"Hey! How come I have to sleep down there? You're the smallest, it should be you."

"Well, this was my idea in the first place, so I get to decide the sleeping arrangements."

"That's a lie. We all came up with this idea together!"

"No. I brought it up."

"You just think you did. You always think–"

"Ladies!" I interrupted before things got more heated and I needed to send them to opposite sides of the room.

Both women turned to me with sheepish smiles that I couldn't help but laugh at. I swear, those four took any opportunity to argue.

I crawled onto the bed and found a spot in the middle. "So, what do we have planned?"

Callie picked up the laptop she'd brought with a smile. "We brought movies, and once we know what you want to snack on, Evey can run down to grab it."

"How come I have to go get the snacks?"

"Because, like you said, this was your idea."

"That doesn't mean I'm your errand boy!"

"Ladies!" I said again but couldn't get the smile off my face. "I just ate, so I don't need a snack. Let's just see what movies you brought."

They settled down again as Callie scrolled through her digital library. "Are you in the mood for comedy? Romance? Horror?"

Romance was the absolute last thing I wanted to watch. I was trying to forget how much I missed Abraham, and the tears were still close to the surface.

"You know what? Since we're all sleeping in here together, let's watch a scary movie."

"Yes," Del hissed with a fist pump.

Callie rolled her eyes and selected a relatively new paranormal thriller. She set the laptop up on some pillows at our feet while we all crawled beneath the blankets.

An hour later, we had the sheets pulled up to our faces and our hands interlocked as we tried to make it to the end of the movie.

"I'm gonna have nightmares," Evey whispered.

"You just better not wake me up with them," Bea warned from my other side.

"Would it kill you to console me, Beatrice?"

"No, but would it kill you to keep your night terrors to yourself?"

"Ladies!" I whisper-yelled as the main character unwittingly walked right into danger.

The rest of the movie passed uneventfully, and soon we were all scared and thankful for the bedmates. A yawn fell from my lips and Callie set the laptop on the nightstand.

"It's late. We should try to get some sleep. Abey should be sending some enforcers our way tomorrow so we'll all have a long day."

Almost as if he'd heard his name, my phone rang and *Sexiest Man Alive* scrolled across the top of the screen. Beatrice laughed at the display and handed it to me.

"Hey, baby," I said as I climbed from the bed.

"El," he breathed, and a shiver raced down my spine.

How did he do that? How did he affect me like this with just a single word?

"Did you make it to Boone?" I asked as I slipped into the sitting room. I knew the other women could still hear my conversation if they wanted to, but this felt like I had some privacy at least.

He sighed through the phone line. "Yeah, I'm here. Grady's already agreed to loan us five enforcers."

"That's great!"

"Yeah, it is. I don't expect all the packs to be as generous, but Grady's had problems with Conrad before. I think he's hoping we knock him down a couple pegs."

"Yeah, Conrad seems to make friends everywhere he goes."

Abraham chuckled, and the deep husky sound sent another shiver down my spine.

"What are you doin', baby?"

I smiled against the phone. "I'm having a sleepover."

"With who?" he asked, his voice stern.

I laughed. It might have been fun to mess with him a little bit, but I was too tired to drag it out. "Down, boy. It's just your sisters."

"My sisters?"

I nodded even though I knew he couldn't see me. "They all decided to sleep in the room with me tonight, so I wouldn't miss you so bad."

He grunted softly. "Is it working?"

I sighed. "It's helped get my mind off you being gone, but nothing will make me stop missing you."

He let out a deep breath that rushed through the phone line. "I miss you too, El. It feels like I left a limb behind in Asheville."

The tears swam to the surface again, and I blinked them back. "Then hurry back to me."

He sighed again. "I will, baby. I promise."

"I love you."

"I love you more, El. Try to get some sleep and I'll talk to you in the morning."

I hung up the phone feeling both better and worse. It was like just hearing the sound of his voice made my longing that much more real. I went to bed that night, stuffed between the McCoy sisters, wishing the next few days would pass as quickly as possible.

We all woke up around the same time the next day, and it was actually kind of nice. I hadn't had a proper sleepover in decades, and I'd forgotten what it was like to wake up to a bed full of my friends.

"Are y'all ready for today?" Del murmured from one end of the mattress.

Beatrice stretched her arms above her head and nodded. "Can't wait."

"That's just 'cause you get to beat on the enforcers extra hard now," Evey muttered.

Bea shrugged. "Yeah, but it's for a good reason at least."

I shook my head with a smile. "Maybe I'll join you for a couple sessions."

"Yeah, if you can get away from the lodge."

I turned to the oldest McCoy sister and frowned. "What do you mean?"

"Haven't you checked Abey's schedule yet?"

My frown deepened. "I don't even know how to do that."

She shrugged. "I'll show you after breakfast. He's got about a dozen appointments today and I'll bet they're all about the same thing."

"The coming conflict?" I guessed.

Bea nodded. "Yep. Get ready to field the same questions over and over again."

My stomach dropped as I realized how unprepared I was for this job. "You'll help me prepare? At least for the first one."

"Of course, Ellie. We're all here to help you."

I settled back down on the mass of pillows and sighed. Last night I'd been jabbed in the ribs by rogue elbows more times than I could count, but at least I'd gotten some decent sleep. And thoughts of Abraham had taken a backseat for a few hours. Now, I just needed to get through the day and hope I had the answers my pack was looking for.

Chapter 35

"I heard there's ten packs that have declared war on us and I wanna know what you're doing about it!"

It had been like that all day. Each and every pack member was there to ask the same question, except with each one, the story got more ridiculous.

"There aren't ten packs who've declared war on us, Maggie."

"Well, that's not what Monica said."

"Well, Monica is full of shit."

Maggie gasped and clutched her shirt over her chest. "Monica is my *sister*."

I sighed and let my head fall forward.

This day was turning out to be a disaster.

I felt sicker and sicker as the hours passed, and I'd had to deal with pack member after pack member demanding to know what was being done about the coming threat. I didn't have much in the way of answers for them, but I did my best to placate.

I took a deep breath and lifted my head so I could look in Maggie's dark brown eyes. "We've received word that the Charlotte pack is preparing to move against us."

She gasped again. "So, we *are* at war!"

I shook my head. "We *aren't* at war. This is one pack with a grudge against our alpha, but we're handling it."

She scoffed. "It's because of that Calvin, isn't it? I always knew that boy was no good."

What could I say? She wasn't wrong.

"Yes, we believe it's because of what happened with Calvin about a month ago. But like I said, Abraham is handling it."

"And how is he doing that?"

I wanted to sigh again, but just barely held it in. "He's out meeting with other North Carolina packs right now. He's sending back extra enforcers to beef up our forces. We're doing everything we can to make sure this threat is eliminated."

"So, we're going to attack the Charlotte pack?!"

I shook my head and this time just barely held back an eye roll. "No. We are not going to attack the Charlotte pack. We are going to continue to live our lives the way we always have, but we're also preparing for the worst-case scenario. None of this affects your day-to-day life. Keep getting up in the morning, keep going to work, and keep cooking dinner at night. Abraham and I are working to make sure we can preserve our way of life here."

"And if we can't? What if the Charlotte pack wins?"

I swallowed harshly and did my best to hold her gaze. I knew I was being tested. My resolve was on the line and my leadership was in question.

"The Charlotte pack will *not* win. We'll make sure of that."

Maggie looked just the least bit mollified, but when she opened her mouth again, I cut her off.

"Thanks for dropping by, Maggie, but I've got a ton more people to see. If you have any more concerns, feel free to stop by."

She gripped her purse by the strap and stood from her chair. "When is Abraham getting back?"

A small lightning bolt of pain jolted through my heart because that was the question playing over and over through my head all day.

I pulled my lips into a smile. "He should be back by the end of the week."

"What if something happens while he's gone?"

"We've got Beatrice and all our other enforcers, plus everyone Abraham sends our way. Five new enforcers showed up just this morning." I wrapped an arm around Maggie's shoulders and led her toward the door. "Trust me, Maggie, we have everything under control and there's no reason for you to worry. We'll keep everyone in this pack safe and that's a promise."

She eyed me critically for a moment and I did my best to hold her gaze. I'd meant every word I'd said. I knew Abraham and every enforcer in the lodge would lay down their lives to protect his pack and I included myself in that. I'd come to love those people as if they were my family. I'd have done anything to protect them, anything to keep them safe and happy. I just hoped it didn't come to that.

I finally got Maggie through the door and closed it behind her. Slumping against the cool wood, I let my head fall back and my shoulders slump.

I was feeling sicker than I'd ever felt and I knew it was only going to get worse. I'd been able to choke down the smallest amount of food that morning and decided to skip lunch all together. That might have explained why I was feeling lightheaded, but didn't really account for the way my stomach churned with nausea.

I figured I should grab something to eat in between appointments, even if it was only a granola bar.

When I made it to the kitchen, it was blessedly, and surprisingly empty. I hustled across the room and grabbed a cereal bar before anyone could stop me. I'd just ripped open the wrapper and taken the first bite when someone called my name.

I spun around slowly to find Austin standing on the other side of the kitchen with a serious look on his face. I swallowed the dry oats in my mouth and gave him a smile.

"Hey, Austin. What's going on?"

He shrugged. "I think I'm your next appointment."

Holding in the sigh that wanted to release from my body, I hiked my smile up a notch and nodded toward the hall.

"Sure. Let's go to the conference room."

I was able to sneak a couple more bites of my granola bar as we made our way down the hall. When we got to the conference room, I gestured for him to take a seat while I took my own. I raised the bar to my mouth again when he started speaking.

"I wanna help."

I paused with the granola inches from my lips before lowering it slowly. "Help with what?"

He looked down at the hands he had fisted together on the table in front of him. "I wanna protect this pack. I wanna be an enforcer."

I set my granola bar down and folded my own hands. "Why is that?"

He raised an unimpressed brow at me. "I've heard the rumors, Ellie. I know the Charlotte pack is going to attack us any day now."

I shook my head. "We really don't know that."

"We don't know when they'll strike, do we? It *could* be tomorrow, right?"

I tilted my head to the side and shrugged a shoulder. "I guess it could be. It's not very likely, though."

"Why do you say that?"

I blew out a big breath and sat forward in my chair. "Conrad has had more than a month to retaliate against us and he hasn't. I'm sure it's coming, but I don't think it's any time soon."

He leaned back in his chair and stared at me. "But it could be."

I sighed. "Yeah, it could be tomorrow. That's why we're doing everything we can to prepare now."

He nodded. "I wanna help," he said again. "Me and a couple other guys were talking about it and we wanna join the enforcers."

"Why now? Why not join them before?"

He sighed and reached up to scratch the side of his neck. "I'm not much of a *joiner*. I like to be by myself. To do my own thing." His features hardened as his eyes turned back to mine. "But this is my home and I wanna protect it. Let me do my part."

My chest filled with warmth as tears swam to my eyes.

What was wrong with me?

I took a deep breath and willed the moisture away before giving him a nod. "Okay, I can talk to Beatrice, but I don't think it'll be a problem. What about your duties as groundskeeper?"

He shrugged. "That's only a couple days a week. I can fit training in between that."

I picked up a pen and pulled my notepad toward me. "And who else was it that wanted to join the enforcers with you?"

"It's me, Marco, and Brad."

I wrote the names down before shooting him a look. "They've all got important jobs here on the pack lands."

Austin shrugged. "They said they'd work around their hours."

Well, I guess they had it all figured out, huh?

I shrugged and gave him a smile. "I'll talk to Beatrice and have her get in touch with you about training, okay?"

Austin's lips pulled up into the first smile I'd seen from him today. "Thanks, Ellie."

He rose from his seat and held out a hand for me to shake. I got up too and a wave of dizziness hit me, but I ignored it and took Austin's offering.

His smile widened, and he nodded. "I'll see you around."

"Bye, Austin." He was just pulling the door open when I realized I had more to say. "And thanks for this. It means a lot that you're willing to take on extra work to defend the pack."

He shrugged. "This is my home. I'll do whatever it takes to protect it."

Those damn tears swam to the surface again, and I was glad he hadn't waited for a response from me. I plopped back into my chair and choked down the rest of my granola bar. I really needed to get myself under control.

And I needed to go find Beatrice.

I checked the laptop I'd set up in the conference room and saw that, thankfully, Austin was my last appointment for the day. I quickly logged off and shut down the computer before leaving my makeshift office to go find Beatrice.

I didn't need to look long or far. She'd been out back running drills with the enforcers all day. Problem was, if I wanted to talk to her, I'd have to shift because she'd been in her wolf form since she got out there.

I walked through the back door and checked my surroundings before quickly disrobing and shifting right there on the balcony. It wasn't easy getting down the stairs on my four clumsy legs, but I managed.

I rounded the house at a trot, thankful to have the grass under my paws and the wind in my fur as I went searching for Bea and the other enforcers. They were in the grassy field we always used for practice, and it looked like they were sparring.

"Huxley, you just left yourself open for Mathias to attack your flank! If he didn't suck as much as you do, this fight would be over!"

I shook my head and did my best to stifle my chuckle. Beatrice could really be a tyrant when she wanted to be.

I trotted over and nudged her with my shoulder. She turned and gave me a wolfy smile.

"Hey, Ellie. You here to practice?"

I tilted my head. *"Yeah, I could go a few rounds after the morning I had."*

She chortled. *"That bad, huh?"*

I shook my head. *"Each one had a wilder story than the one before them."*

"That's what happens in a pack. It's like a giant game of telephone, and the farther down the line you go, the more wrong they are."

311

"*That pretty much sums up my morning. But my last appointment was what I'm here to talk to you about.*"

She was watching the two wolves fighting in front of us and shot me a look. "*One sec, Ellie.*" She turned back to the fight and yelled, "*Mathias? What the hell was that? Are you salsa dancing or fighting a werewolf?!*" She growled, and I was thankful I wasn't on the other end of her ire for a change. "*You know what? Why don't you all take five and work on removing your heads from your asses! Come back ready to actually fight and not just tap dance around your partner!*"

The rest of the enforcers trotted away grumbling just softly enough that we couldn't make out their words while I did my best not to laugh. When Beatrice finally turned to me, I could see the mirth in her eyes.

"*You have to speak their language, or you'll get nowhere with these idiots.*"

I finally let out the laugh I'd been holding in and she joined me.

Man, she was scary.

"*So, Austin Anderson came to see me today.*"

"*Oh, yeah. What'd he want?*"

"*He and a couple of his buddies wanna join your enforcers.*"

She raised a furry brow. "*Is that right?*"

I did my best to shrug. "*That's what he says.*"

She looked away and nodded slowly. "*Well, he's got the build for it. I don't see why we can't add him to some of these drills.*" When she looked back at me, her brow was raised again. "*Who else wants to join?*"

"*He said Marco and Brad were interested too.*"

She eyed me seriously for a moment before shrugging a shoulder. "*Sure. Why not? I'll get them on the schedule and have them start running patrols with the other guys.*"

"*I think he'll be happy to hear that.*"

"*Yeah, well, we can use all the help we can get.*"

I frowned. *"Abraham just sent over five guys today, didn't he?"*

"Yeah, but that still puts us at a disadvantage. And like Abey said, we can't expect every pack to send us that many enforcers. That would cripple most packs."

I didn't comment on the fact that Abraham said that to me on a phone conversation that was supposed to be private. I knew they'd been able to hear us, I just hadn't known she'd been listening. I suppose it made sense that she'd tuned into that part of the conversation since it technically involved her too.

And after a quick rundown of the rest of what we said, I thankfully realized there'd been no part of that conversation that would have been awkward for her to overhear. That time, at least.

There was something still bothering me though.

"How many enforcers do we have?"

She sighed and looked away. *"After we lost Calvin, that dropped our numbers to nine. Now that we have Austin, Marco, and Brad joining us, we're up to twelve, plus the Boone enforcers bring us to seventeen."*

My stomach sank as I did the math.

"That means we're still outnumbered by the Charlotte pack about two-to-one."

Beatrice nodded slowly. *"And don't forget, he may be finding allies of his own. He's been the alpha of that pack for almost fifteen years. He's made a lot of enemies in that time, but I'm sure he's also made at least a couple friends. We need to prepare for that possibility."*

Abraham's mission to find us more enforcers seemed more important than ever. According to Peyton, it wasn't *if* they attacked us, it was a matter of *when*. If he were to move on us today, we'd more than likely lose that fight.

I promised myself then and there that I would throw myself into the drills and practices too. The pack needed all the help it could get to defend what we had, and I wasn't going to sit aside and let everyone else defend us. This was my pack, and those were my people. I'd defend them as long as I was able to.

In the meantime, I had to hope Abraham could work that charm of his to get us the help we needed. It was more apparent than ever how important his trip was. As much as I couldn't wait until he got home, I also had to hope he'd be returning with some good news.

Chapter 36

"Ellie, I think I should get somebody."

I was hunched over the glittery trash bin in my office, my body heaving while I tried to get myself under control. All week I'd been feeling worse and worse, and now that we'd made it to Wednesday, I couldn't hold the nausea back any longer.

"I'm… fine…" I gasped as another wave hit me and I retched some more.

I heard Wyatt sigh and vaguely registered the click of the office door, but I was too busy vomiting to really care. I didn't know why my separation from Abraham was manifesting in that way this time, but now I had another reason to wish he'd get home faster.

My throat was burning, and my stomach was sore from expelling what little food I'd had in me so violently. For a split second, I wondered if I should go to the hospital, but I quickly threw that thought out. What would I say, anyway? My werewolf mate was out of town and I couldn't keep anything in my system for longer than thirty minutes? Yeah, that would go over well.

The door clicked again, and a soft voice reached me beyond my misery.

"Ellie?"

I glanced up to find Callie walking across the room with a concerned look in her pale blue eyes.

I opened my mouth to speak, but felt the bile rising and instead tucked my head back into the trash bin.

A soothing hand rubbed between my shoulder blades as my body dry heaved. There was nothing left in me to throw up at that point.

"Wyatt, go grab her a glass of water and a wet rag from the bathroom."

I didn't hear him answer, but the door clicked again, and I assumed he'd gone to do her bidding.

"I've never… heard you speak… so civilly to him… before," I gasped between retching.

Callie's hand on my back paused for a second before she was back to rubbing in circles. "I speak to him civilly."

I lifted my head far enough to shoot her an incredulous look. Unfortunately, it was probably not as effective as I'd have liked, because in the next instant, another dry heave wracked my body and I shoved my head back in the trash.

She sighed and smoothed the hair off my sticky forehead. "Still think he's not your fated mate?" she asked softly.

If I could have spoken, I'd probably have told her to shut up, but lucky for her, I was still gagging. A few minutes later, the door opened again, and a cool cloth was pressed against my forehead. I sighed in relief as my stomach seemed to stop gurgling for a moment.

I leaned back in my chair while Callie rubbed the wet paper towel around my face. I wanted to feel embarrassed at being taken care of like a sick toddler, but I couldn't find any shame in me. I was sick as hell and I could use all the help I could get.

My eyes were still closed when the rim of a glass was pressed against my mouth. I opened my lips and let whoever it was tip some water down my throat. It felt good and helped to settle my stomach even more.

When I felt a little more like a human–or a werewolf–I opened my eyes and looked around the room. Callie was still next to me, running the cloth over my face, and Wyatt was across the room, his gaze completely transfixed on Callie.

I wondered for the hundredth time what was up with those two. They acted like they couldn't stand each other, but I knew better. Intense feelings like that usually came from somewhere. Since, to the best of my knowledge, Wyatt had never actually done anything to Callie, there had to be more to the story. Some deeper secret they were both keeping.

My cell phone rang out in the quiet room and I turned to look at the lit screen. *Sexiest Man Alive* was scrawled across the top and a small smile tugged at my lips.

True to his word, Abraham had called me incessantly since he'd been gone. I probably talked to him more now than I ever had when he was home. It was nice, but it made me miss him even more.

I moved to sit up and grab my phone when another wave of nausea whipped through my body and I instead grabbed the trash.

"I'll get it," Callie said softly before picking up my phone. "Hey, Abey… yeah, she's right here… she's not feeling well, so I answered for her."

My mouth filled with saliva and I knew I was about to be sick again. I tugged the bin closer to my face and heaved into it, but all that came up was bile.

Callie's hand was back between my shoulders as I retched.

"Let me get her settled and I'll have her call you back when she's feeling better."

I didn't bother listening to what he had to say on the other end, and soon, there was the soft beep of the call ending.

This bout of nausea passed quicker than the last, and that time, it felt like it might really be over. I set the trash on the floor and sat back in my chair with my eyes closed.

"I think you should eat or drink something to calm your stomach," Callie said.

I shook my head. "Whatever I eat just comes right back up."

"What about some ginger ale? Ginger is supposed to be good for upset stomachs."

I shrugged. At that point, she could have probably poured arsenic down my throat and I wouldn't have cared.

"I'll go run to the deli." Wyatt's deep voice sounded from across the room.

Neither Callie nor I responded, and moments later, I heard the click of my office door again. Now we were alone, and I felt like I might be able to make it through a whole conversation without throwing up, I wanted some answers.

I opened my eyes and turned to her. "Callie, what's going on with you and Wyatt?"

She averted her gaze, but soon, it flickered toward the office door.

"It's nothing."

I pursed my lips and raised my brow. "Nothing? You practically had steam coming out of your ears when you found out he'd be coming to work with me every day."

She bit her lip and looked away again, but this time there was color creeping across her cheeks, and I knew I'd struck a nerve.

"I can keep a secret, Callie. I just want to know what's going on with you. Clearly, it's something big, or you wouldn't be reacting like this."

Her pale blue eyes flickered to me. "Promise you'll keep this between us?"

I nodded as I held her eyes. "I won't say a word to anyone. Not even Abraham."

She blew out a deep breath and looked away again. "It's a long story, and one I don't want to get into when he could be back any minute."

"Just give me the gist."

She sighed and tipped her head up to the ceiling. "He wants more than I'm willing to give."

I gasped, which almost brought on another round of sickness. "He likes you, doesn't he?"

She rolled her eyes. "We're not in middle school, Ellie."

I shook my head. "But he does, doesn't he? He likes you."

She shrugged a single shoulder but wouldn't meet my eyes again. "I guess you could say that."

"So, what's the problem? You don't like him back?"

She shot me an exasperated look. "Do you think we could talk about this like adults and not pre-teens?"

"Just answer the question."

She bit her lip again. "I don't know, Ellie. And I'm not willing to find out."

I frowned. "Why the heck not? Wyatt's a great guy."

"I never said he wasn't."

"Then what's holding you back?"

"It's complicated."

"I'm sure I can keep up."

She opened her mouth to speak again, and I just knew I was about to get some real information from her, when the sound of heavy footsteps stomping down the hall reached us. We both knew it was Wyatt and that meant our little sharing session was over.

I wouldn't forget it though.

There was something between them and Callie was holding back for some reason. I wanted to get to the bottom of it and hopefully help my friend.

Since things became serious with Abraham, I realized I'd been an idiot for pushing him away for so long. When someone was that devoted to you, when someone made you feel as much as Abraham made me feel, there was no reason to push back. No reason to fight what your heart knows is true. If I could help Callie see that, I'd do it.

The door opened, and Callie straightened her spine. I watched carefully, but her face was a mask of indifference and I knew I wouldn't get anything out of her. Stifling a sigh, I turned to the enforcer tasked with guarding me once again.

"Hey, Wyatt. Thanks for running to the store for me."

319

He shrugged and pulled a bottle of ginger ale out of a brown paper bag. He handed it to me, and I took a tentative sip, ready for the liquid to make a reappearance any second. When it seemed the soda agreed with my stomach, I took a bigger sip before setting it aside.

Now that I wasn't throwing up anymore, I felt ridiculous that so many people had to drop what they were doing to take care of me. Granted, Wyatt's only job was to watch over me, but that didn't mean nursing me, that just meant protecting me.

"Thanks, guys. I think I'll be all right for a while at least."

Callie eyed me seriously for a prolonged moment. "You sure? I can stay if you need me."

Even though she'd offered, I could see how uncomfortable she was in Wyatt's presence. I didn't know exactly what happened between the two of them, but it was clear she wanted to be anywhere but there.

I waved her off and took another sip of ginger ale. "I'm fine. I'm just going to get some research done while my stomach is behaving."

She picked up my cell and handed it to me. "Don't forget to call Abey back. You know he'll worry if you don't."

I took my phone and promised I'd call him. The problem was, I knew he was going to worry no matter what I did. I'd been trying to hide how sick I'd been, but I wasn't fooling him. He seemed to be under the weather, too, but nothing compared to me.

I wondered again why being away from him was hitting me so hard this time. What changed? Was it just because I lived with him and we were together more often?

I didn't plan to spend much time away from him in the future, but it had to be inevitable at some point, right? Would I only continue to get worse? Would it get so bad that I couldn't even leave my bed?

And speaking of beds, I hadn't had mine to myself since Abraham left. All the McCoy sisters had shared the king-sized mattress with me the first night, but every day since then, one of them had showed up. First, of course, was Evey, then Del and Bea, and finally last night was Callie's turn. I don't know how they chose that order or who'd be sharing the bed with me that night, but I couldn't deny I was grateful for their company.

It was funny, because up until a few months ago, I'd spent every night alone. Now it was almost unfathomable.

Callie left my office, and I watched Wyatt the whole time. His eyes would dart from her to anything but her over and over. I knew how that felt. To want to watch someone, but not be caught doing it. It was clear that he wanted more with her and I wondered why she was holding back from him.

Now that my head was clearing, something else Callie said was ringing through it.

Still think he's not your fated mate?

I'd been so convinced he wasn't. That because I couldn't explain it and because there was no record of this ever happening before that it had to be impossible. Somehow, I'd let myself forget how awful I always felt without him.

Well, there was no denying it this time.

Abraham was gone, and I'd never been sicker.

I guess I'd been foolish to think we weren't fated. Even though it didn't make any sense. Even though it should have been impossible. Having spent half my morning with my head in a trash can, it was hard to deny that fact now.

So, if we were fated, there really was no reason to prolong our ceremony, was there?

Even as the thought crossed my mind, my stomach clenched, and my palms began to sweat.

Okay, I could admit we were fated, but that still didn't mean we needed to rush into a ceremony. I was perfectly happy with the way things were and it seemed Abraham was okay with waiting, too. I'd give it another couple of months and see how I felt about it then. If we really were fated, neither of us was going anywhere, so there was no reason to jump into it.

I spent the rest of the day nibbling on crackers Callie brought me and sipping the ginger ale Wyatt kept me stocked with. It wasn't my most productive day, but I was just thankful I'd managed to get something done.

Matt continued to be a nuisance, though, and I had a feeling I'd have to deal with him soon.

"Hey, Ellie! Are you doing anything after work today?" he'd asked as I packed my things that evening.

I could hear Wyatt's soft growl from across the room and I shot him a look. He was there to protect me against werewolves, not overeager coworkers. His shoulders were still stiff, but he gave me a small nod and I knew he'd let me handle this.

"I'm not feeling well, Matt. I think I'm just going to head home."

He leaned against my desk and crossed his arms. It looked like he was making himself comfortable and I just barely held back a sigh. "Where's home for you?"

I shot a look at Wyatt who was resolutely looking the other way. Apparently, I was getting what I'd asked for and he was letting me handle it.

"Well, I was in Raleigh for years, but I moved out here to Asheville about a month ago."

A smile spread across his face. "So, you're new here! I bet you could use a tour guide! I know a lot of hidden gems around the city that I'd love to show you sometime."

I took a deep breath and pasted a smile on my face. "That's a nice offer, but I'm really pretty busy."

I shouldered my purse, and he straightened up, his arms falling to his sides. "What about this weekend?"

"I'm busy this weekend."

"What about next weekend?"

I shot him an exasperated look. "Matt, listen. I'm engaged. I don't think it's a good idea for us to spend time together outside of work."

His smile fell. "So, he doesn't let you have friends? That doesn't sound healthy."

Another growl sounded from the other side of the room and I knew I needed to wrap this up.

"My relationship with Abraham isn't a concern of yours. We're doing great, and we're getting married soon, and none of that has anything to do with you." I pushed past him and opened my office door. "I'm heading home for the night. I'll see you tomorrow, Matt."

His face fell even further, but there was a firm set to his mouth that made me think he wasn't going to drop this.

"Have a good night, Ellie," he said as he brushed past me just a tiny bit closer than necessary.

When he was gone, I shut the door behind him and slumped against it.

"You really have an issue with coworkers, don't you?"

I wanted to deny it but, how could I? He'd seen the situation with Ben Collins go from bad to worse back in Raleigh, and now I had Matt to deal with.

Honestly, my brain was too full of everything else to properly worry about Matt Miller. I pushed thoughts of him out of my head as Wyatt and I left my office for the night.

I hoped that Matt wouldn't prove to be a problem. That Abraham and Wyatt were overreacting, and he'd prove to be as harmless as I thought he was.

Chapter 37

"Hey, Wyatt. Do you think we could get an early start today?"

I'd come down to breakfast earlier than usual in the hopes I'd find him there. I'd woken up feeling less nauseated than the day before and thought I'd take advantage of the reprieve and get to the office before anyone else.

I'd fallen behind on my work and I needed to rectify that. I knew Callie understood that I'd been sick, but that didn't change the fact that they needed me, and I needed to pull my weight.

Wyatt shoveled the last few bites of scrambled eggs into his mouth. "I'm ready when you are."

I gave him my most grateful smile. Wyatt really was a great guy. He'd been tasked with babysitting me again, and instead of complaining like I knew some of the other enforcers would have, he just did the job. In fact, he usually went above and beyond expectations.

He stood from the long table and brought his dish over to Aubrey.

That was another issue that rested in the back of my mind.

The housekeeper still regarded me as nicely as you would a bug that had the audacity to die on your windshield. I didn't know what I'd be able to do to change her mind, and to be honest, I was running out of reasons to care. If she wanted to dislike me, she'd do it no matter what I did. I figured my best course of action would be to keep doing the best job I could at the alpha thing and hope she came around.

Wyatt sidled up next to me and gave me a look. "Aren't you going to eat something?"

I dug into my purse and unearthed a granola bar. "I've got breakfast right here."

He eyed my cereal bar with disdain. "That's all you're having?"

I patted him on the arm and headed toward the hall. "That's all I'll be able to keep down."

I heard his heavy footsteps and knew he was following me. I also knew I wouldn't be able to keep eating so little with how fast my metabolism was now I was a werewolf, but I figured I only had to hold out a little longer. Abraham said he'd probably be back by Friday and it was already Thursday. I could survive on bird food until then.

I reached my gray compact car and unlocked the doors for the both of us. Wyatt eyed my little vehicle like he did every morning, but this was something I wouldn't budge on. It was bad enough I had a babysitter again. I wouldn't let him cart me around, too. I needed to have at least a little independence, and that was my preferred method.

Wyatt folded himself into the car, making sure to grumble just loud enough for me to hear. I ignored him while I buckled my seatbelt and turned the key in the ignition. I started down the steep gravel drive, careful to drive slow enough that my little car didn't bottom out along the way.

"You seem a little better today," Wyatt commented as I merged onto the highway.

I shrugged. "Honestly, I still feel pretty crummy, but not as sick as yesterday. Maybe I had a stomach bug or something."

"Werewolves don't get stomach bugs."

I shot him a glance out of the corner of my eye. "Well, maybe humans turned werewolves *do*."

He grunted from the passenger seat but didn't comment further.

He was right though. I'd been told over and over that werewolves don't get sick. That their immune systems were far superior to humans'.

Why then, was I so ill? Was it really the distance between Abraham and me? If that was the case, I should have felt worse and not better. That was how it had always been in the past when I'd worked in Raleigh during the week and only saw him on the weekends. Each day, I'd felt crappier than the last until we were reunited.

I sighed as our exit loomed before us and flicked on my turn signal. There was no use worrying about it now. I felt better than I had yesterday, and I'd try to get as much work done as I could, just in case the sickness came back.

I hit the brake to slow down before the exit, but the pedal gave no resistance, and my foot pressed it almost to the floor. I pumped the brake again, but it did nothing.

I was already on the off-ramp, but I was going way too fast to take the turn.

"Ellie, you need to slow down."

I gripped the wheel tighter and tried pressing on the brake over and over again, but nothing was happening.

"I can't stop."

"What?"

"The brakes aren't working! I can't slow down."

The car continued to race toward the exit, only slowing slightly because I wasn't pressing the gas anymore.

"Ellie, you need to slow this car down. We can't take the exit going this fast."

"I know! I don't know what to do! The brakes aren't working!"

I continued to stomp on the pedal, but there was no change to the speed we were going.

That's when I remembered the emergency brake.

We were just approaching the bend in the off-ramp and I yanked on the lever between the two front seats. The car began to slow, and I was able to navigate the curve well enough to get us around it. Thankfully, right off the exit was a shoulder, and I pulled onto it, letting the car roll to a stop.

Other vehicles continued to drive past us, but all I could do was stare straight out my windshield.

I'd never had something like that happen to me before. Never even been in a fender-bender. The adrenaline was pumping through my system and my stomach was rolling. I just hoped it would hold until we got off that road.

"Are you okay?"

I was still gripping the steering wheel when I turned to Wyatt. I nodded slowly, not sure if I really was all right or not.

"I'm gonna call Brad and see if he can get us towed back to pack lands."

I nodded again and turned to stare out the windshield.

What happened? How had my brakes failed like that? I was no mechanic, but I had my car regularly serviced and I knew it wasn't time for me to have them replaced. Besides, even if they were old, it didn't make sense for them to just completely stop working like that, right?

Wyatt was talking on the phone but the ringing in my ears drowned out his conversation. I was still reeling from the accident we'd narrowly avoided.

"Ellie."

I turned to Wyatt again, my hands still white-knuckling the wheel.

"Can you pop the hood? Brad wants me to take a look."

I shook my head and reached underneath the dashboard to pull the lever. He slid out of the car and I watched as he walked around and lifted the hood.

With another shake of my head, I gave myself a little pep talk.

I was okay.

Wyatt was okay.

My car was okay.

Everything was okay.

I needed to get myself together and try to figure out what happened here.

I unbuckled my seatbelt and climbed out to join Wyatt.

"I don't know, man. It all looks the same to me."

I heard Brad's voice on the other line promise he'd be there with a tow truck within thirty minutes before they both hung up.

Wyatt turned to me and wrapped his big hands around the tops of my arms. When he ducked down to catch my gaze, there was only concern in his light brown eyes. "Are you sure you're okay?"

I took a deep breath and gave him a nod. "Yeah. I was just taken by surprise. I'm all right now."

He let me go and stood back up, placing his hands on his hips. "Yeah, I think we both had a shock this morning." He turned to me again. "Good thinking with the e-brake."

I nodded again. "Thanks."

We stood there with the hood open, both of us just staring at the mess of machinery beneath it.

"I thought you liked cars."

He shot me a look. "What?"

"Back in Raleigh, you were always reading hotrod magazines. Shouldn't you know something about this?" I asked, waving to the engine.

He chuckled. "Just because I like fast and pretty cars, doesn't mean I know shit about fixing them."

"I guess that's fair."

He nodded toward my car. "Come on. Let's get back in until Brad gets here. It's not safe standing out here so close to the highway."

Just as he said that, a car went whipping past us, probably driving even faster than I'd been going when my brakes stopped working. Wyatt glared at the offending vehicle as he ushered me back into my seat.

When he got in on the other side, he pulled his cell out and began pressing buttons. "I'm going to call Abraham while we wait."

I whipped around and put my hand over his phone. "Don't do that."

He frowned at me. "Why?"

"If you tell him about this, he'll come home."

He shrugged. "That's his right."

He tugged at his phone, but I wouldn't let go.

"Wyatt, you know how important it is that he keeps visiting other packs. He's only been able to send another twelve enforcers back to us. We need more than that if we're going to have a fighting chance against the Charlotte pack."

His frown deepened. "Ellie, I have to tell him about this."

I nodded. "Of course, but can't we wait? Let's find out what happened before we call him. Or we can just wait until he gets back tomorrow."

"He won't be happy we kept this from him."

"I'll take all the blame. I'll explain to him it was my idea, and I ordered you not to call him."

One of his blond brows rose. "Ordered me?"

I swallowed but shrugged. "If that's what it takes."

My voice could have been a little stronger, but it would have to do. Wyatt continued to eye me as I watched a battle play out across his features. Finally, he sighed, and his shoulders slumped. "He's not going to be happy about this."

I pulled my hand away from his phone now that it seemed like he wouldn't make the call. "And you know how important what he's doing is. If he found out, he'd just rush home and we need him to keep finding us new allies."

He pursed his lips but nodded. "Okay, Ellie. We can do this your way."

I let out a deep breath and leaned against the back of my seat. I wasn't sure if I was doing the right thing, but I knew Abraham. He'd be back in Asheville before nightfall if he thought I was in danger.

And until we knew one way or the other, there was no sense worrying him.

Brad showed up about twenty minutes later and we got out to greet him. He had a big smile for me, and it was nice to know some of my pack actually liked me.

"Hey, Ellie. You okay?"

I gave him the best smile I could manage. "I'm all right. Could have done without the brake failure this morning."

He nodded slowly. "I'm sure you could. Let's have a look."

He ducked his head and began fiddling with different things under the hood, none of which made any sense to me. Finally, after a few minutes, he straightened back up and sighed. He pulled a rag out of his back pocket and wiped his hands as he shook his head.

"There's nothing I can see from here. I need to get it back to my place and lifted before I can tell you more."

My spirits sank at that news. I was hoping he would be able to tell me this was nothing more than a system failure and we could all go about our day. But there was a deep, dark intuition inside of me warning that it wasn't that simple. That nothing ever was.

I watched as Brad got my little car hooked up to his tow truck. Wyatt walked up next to me with his phone in his hand.

"You want to go back to pack lands with him or head into work? We could probably walk to that store across the street and call an Uber from there."

I weighed my options and realized there was only one place I'd be of any use. "Let's head to the office. We'll only be in Brad's way."

We walked over to the new pack mechanic just as he finished getting my car all settled.

"Brad, we're heading into the office. Will you give one of us a call when you know something?"

He tipped the brim of his baseball cap and gave me a smile. "I've got Wyatt's number. I'll call him when I figure out what happened here."

"Thanks, Brad. Make sure you let me know what I owe you."

He shook his head. "Don't worry about this, Ellie." He nodded at Wyatt and then gave me another smile. "Try to have a good rest of your day."

We said our goodbyes and walked across the street to the little convenience store Wyatt pointed out. A few minutes later, a middle-aged man in a black suburban pulled up, and we hopped in.

When he dropped us off at The Asheville Initiative, Callie's car was already parked on the street and I realized all the time I thought I'd saved that morning had gone right out the window. On the bright side, my stomach was still feeling fine, so hopefully I'd be able to get a bunch of work done and make up for the past few days.

Unfortunately, my good luck ran out, and within a few hours, I was throwing up into my trash bin again. Wyatt paced the floor of my office while I was sick, asking over and over what he could do. Every time I waved him away, his pacing got more intense, and I almost had to send him out of the room because he was making me dizzy.

At a low point in my nausea, Wyatt's cell rang, and I lifted my head from the pail.

"It's Brad," he said before sliding his finger across the screen and raising the phone to his ear.

Another wave of sickness washed over me, and their conversation was drowned out by my retching. I lost track of time, but it couldn't have been more than a few minutes later when I heard Wyatt growl and promise to see Brad soon.

I wiped my mouth with some tissues and took a tentative sip of my room-temperature ginger ale before looking up at Wyatt.

"What's going on?" I croaked.

His jaw ticked, and I could hear his teeth grinding from across the room. "This morning wasn't an accident."

My stomach rolled again, but I swallowed and did my best to hold it down. "What does that mean?"

He pursed his lips into a thin white line as he squeezed his cell in his big hand. "It means someone cut your brake lines. This was intentional."

Chapter 38

"We need to get back to pack lands. Now."

My stomach was still gurgling, but it felt like it would hold for a little while at least. Knowing there was no use arguing with Wyatt when he was like this, I nodded and began to pack up my things.

He continued to pace the floor, his hand squeezing his cell phone.

"We need to call Abraham. He needs to know about this."

I sighed. "Yeah, I know. Let's go talk to Brad and get all the details before we call him, though."

Wyatt's shoulders slumped, but he nodded.

When I was done gathering my things Wyatt rushed to the door and opened it for me. With a hand on my back, he ushered me down the hall faster than I would have walked myself. We were almost to the lobby when Callie stepped out of her office and frowned at us.

"Hey. What's going on?"

Earlier, I'd explained that something had gone wrong with my car, but I hadn't gone into detail. I figured it didn't make much sense to worry her before we knew anything. Now seemed like the appropriate time to tell her, but Wyatt was on a mission to get me out of the building as quickly as possible.

Without pausing, Wyatt grunted, "The issue with her car is bigger than we thought. We're heading back to pack lands right now."

Callie spared him the smallest of glances before training her eyes on me. "I can give you guys a ride home if you want to wait a minute."

Wyatt shook his head. "Don't bother. Wes is almost here."

I turned and frowned at Wyatt. It wasn't what he said, but how he said it that was bothering me. Sure, Callie hadn't always been the friendliest toward him, but she didn't deserve for him to be that short with her.

I dug in my heels and Wyatt had no choice but to stop pushing me down the hall or knock me over. Thankfully for me, he chose the former.

"Thanks for the offer, Callie. You stay here and finish out your day. I brought a bunch of stuff home with me, so I can get more work done there."

She waved a hand. "Don't worry about that, Ellie. There are bigger issues you need to be focusing on than The Asheville Initiative right now." She shot another glance at Wyatt before turning back to me. "Have you told Abey yet?"

I winced, and her expression turned exasperated.

I held up both hands. "I didn't want to worry him when we didn't know if there was actually anything to worry about yet."

"Ellie, he's not going to be happy about that."

I sighed. "Yes, but his trip is more important than what's going on here."

She raised a brow. "Don't you think he should be the one to decide that?"

My shoulders slumped as I released a deep breath. "Probably. I thought I was doing the right thing by holding off. You know how important it is for him to find us more allies." I lowered my voice in case any of the humans in the office were listening. "The Charlotte pack could attack any day. We need all the help we can get if we're going to have a fighting chance. You know that."

She held my gaze for a long moment before she sighed. "Yeah, you're right. I just know he won't be happy about being kept in the dark."

I shot a glance at Wyatt who looked ready to throw me over his shoulder and march out of the office.

"Well, I'm going to take the blame for this one. I did what I thought was best at the time. Now that we know it was foul play, I'll call and fill him in."

Her pale blue eyes got wide. "Foul play?"

My smile was grim. "Apparently my brake lines were cut."

She gasped. "Oh, Ellie."

I shrugged. "Yeah, that was definitely not the news I was hoping for."

"What are you going to do?"

Wyatt stepped up next to me and grasped my bicep. "We're going to figure out who the hell is responsible and make them pay." He looked down at me, his expression hard. "We're leaving now, Ellie."

I narrowed my eyes at him before shooting Callie an apologetic look. "I'll talk to you when you get home."

The worried expression was still pinching her soft features. "Get there safe."

Wyatt grunted. "Thanks for the suggestion, Callista."

I shot him another annoyed look, but he wasn't paying attention. He was too busy dragging me down the hall and through the front door. When we were out on the sidewalk, I ripped my arm out of his grasp and turned on him.

"You didn't have to be so rude to Callie. She's just concerned."

He ran a rough hand down his face and looked away. "She's not always so nice to me, either."

I raised a brow at him. "And since when do two wrongs make a right?"

He sighed harshly and tipped his head back to stare at the bright blue summer sky. "Can we not talk about this right now? My only concern is getting you home safely. Everything else can wait."

I let out a deep breath and nodded. I knew the events of the morning were wearing on Wyatt. It was his job to keep me safe, and he almost hadn't been able to do that. Of course, it wasn't his fault someone cut my brake lines, and it was impossible for him to have known that in advance, but I knew none of that would matter to him. He had a job, and he needed to do it. It was as simple as that.

A dark red SUV pulled up to the curb and Wyatt let out a deep breath. "Thank fuck," he muttered as he ushered me toward the vehicle.

Wyatt's twin, Wesley, was behind the wheel and he shot me a small smile as I climbed into the backseat. I barely held back an eye roll as Wyatt insisted on watching me buckle up before getting in the front. I knew his protectiveness was in overdrive, but he was bordering on ridiculous.

The car remained mostly quiet as we drove back to pack lands. I had to assume Wyatt had already filled Wes in on the events of the morning. The rocking motion of the truck wasn't helping my weak stomach, but somehow, I held the sickness at bay.

When we arrived, Wyatt jumped out of the SUV before Wes even put it in park. He ripped my door open, almost pulling it from the hinges.

"Let's go."

I unbuckled my seatbelt and gathered my things as quickly as I could. He slid my briefcase and purse off my shoulder and handed them to Wes who'd just made it to our side.

"Make sure this stuff makes it up to their sitting room."

Wes nodded and accepted my bags before Wyatt placed another hand on my back and led me toward the pack houses. No words were exchanged while we walked, but my mind was a flurry of activity.

Who'd cut my brake lines?

Who hated me enough to sabotage my car?

With a soft snort, I realized that list was actually decent-sized. I'd made a few friends since I'd started acting like an alpha, but I'd also also accrued some enemies. I suppose it was inevitable, but it still didn't feel good.

We got to the tenth pack house and found Brad's garage open with my car lifted inside it. We walked up the driveway, and when we got closer, the mechanic popped his head into the open doorway.

"You guys got here fast," he commented.

"Explain what you found," Wyatt grunted without even a semblance of a hello.

I shot him another glare, but he ignored me. Man, he was moody today.

Brad sighed and nodded toward my car. "Come on over and I'll show you."

Wyatt did as he asked, but I hung back. To be honest, I didn't really want to see the evidence I knew would be there. But just because I didn't want to see it didn't mean I couldn't still hear what they were saying.

"If you look here, you'll see where the brake line was severed," Brad said.

Wyatt grunted again. "Is it possible this could have happened on its own?"

Brad sighed. "No, and I'll tell you why. Here, you can see there's a straight cut through most of the brake line, but not all the way. What that did was make it so the brakes would work the first few times you used them, but eventually they'd fail."

I didn't need to look to know Wyatt was grinding his teeth.

"So, they wanted her to already be well on her way to work."

I turned just in time to catch Brad shrug.

"And I bet they knew she'd be on the highway when they finally failed. They wanted to make sure she was going fast enough to do serious damage," Wyatt continued.

Brad shrugged again, the look on his face showing how uncomfortable he was. "It looks that way," he finally said.

Wyatt nodded, his hands fisting at his sides. "So, this was done by someone who knew what they were doing?"

Brad's eyes darted to me before he fixed them back on Wyatt. "That would be my guess. Your average Joe would probably have just cut

336

right through. Only someone who really knew about this stuff would sever them partially."

"Why do you think that?" I asked as I finally joined them in the garage.

Brad's chocolate colored eyes met mine. "If they cut the line completely, your brakes would have given out almost immediately. Then you would have known something was wrong and you wouldn't have kept driving." His eyes darted to Wyatt, almost as if he was afraid to keep talking. Finally, he sighed and met my gaze again. "But because they only partially severed them, you were able to use them a few times, giving you a false sense of security. If this person knew you'd be taking the highway to work, I can guess their intention was for your brakes to stop working then. When you were going the fastest and had the greatest chance of wrecking."

My stomach fell while Wyatt let out a menacing growl. "I bet it was that fuck, Craig," he grunted, his knuckles white with how tight he was squeezing his hands.

Brad looked uncomfortable as his eyes darted between Wyatt and me. He shrugged. "I guess it could have been Craig, but probably not."

"Why do you say that?" I asked.

I was grasping at straws. I knew Craig and I had our differences, but I didn't want to believe he'd try to kill me over them.

My stomach sank even farther as those words echoed through my head.

Someone tried to *kill* me today. That was the only reason someone would cut my brake lines in the hopes I'd be going too fast to stop.

Someone was trying to kill me.

Brad's voice broke me out of the dark turn my thoughts had taken.

"If it was Craig, he probably would have cut your e-brake line too."

"So, she would have had no way to stop," Wyatt spat between gritted teeth.

Brad looked scared as he nodded at Wyatt. "If I was trying to kill someone, that's what I'd do."

In the next instant, Wyatt had Brad pinned against the wall, his hand around his throat.

"Wyatt! What the hell are you doing?!" I screeched.

"Was it you?" Wyatt growled into Brad's face. "You seem to know an awful lot about this shit. Were you the one who tried to kill our alpha?"

Brad's face had turned completely white, his body shaking slightly. "No, man! Why would I kill Ellie?! She got me the job of my dreams! I'd never hurt her!"

I could hear the sincerity in his voice, and I hoped Wyatt could too. There was another tense couple of moments before Wyatt finally released Brad and took a step back. He ran a rough hand down his face and shook his head. "I'm sorry. I shouldn't have accused you like that."

Brad straightened back up. "It's okay, man. I get why you're upset. I'm pissed too."

Wyatt sighed, his shoulders so tense they almost reached his ears. He turned to me, the look in his eyes wild. "You're calling Abraham. Now."

I bristled at his tone but didn't comment. It was clear Wyatt was on the edge and I wouldn't be the one to push him over it. "Okay. I'll call him when we get back to the lodge."

Wyatt shook his head and stormed over, holding his phone out to me. "No. Now."

I narrowed my eyes at him and pulled my own cell from my pocket. "All right. Jeez."

Despite my cavalier attitude, my heart was racing with the coming confrontation. I knew Abraham was going to flip out, and I wasn't looking forward to it. I just hoped he was so mad about the brake failure that he didn't have time to be angry about the fact that I hadn't called him sooner.

I dialed his number and put the phone to my ear before I turned my back on the two men and walked down the driveway. I saw Maddy coming out of her house next door and I gave her a wave, hoping my smile didn't look as fake as it felt.

"Hey, baby. How's working goin'?" Abraham asked after answering on the second ring.

I took a deep breath. "Actually, I left early today."

"Still not feeling well? I'm starting to really worry, El. You've never been this sick before. Maybe you need to go see Doc Monroe and get checked out. There could be something else causing you to be this ill."

I shook my head even though I knew he couldn't see me. "That's not why I left. Something happened this morning, and we just found out some new information about it, so Wyatt and I left early and came back to pack lands."

He was quiet for a prolonged moment before his deep voice rumbled through the phone line. "What happened this morning and why am I just hearing about it now?"

I took another breath and launched into the story about what happened during my drive to work. I purposely avoided his question of why I hadn't told him earlier. Hopefully we could argue about it later, because a headache was forming behind my temples and I really wasn't in the mood to fight right then.

When I finished telling him everything Brad revealed to us, Abraham remained silent on the other end. So silent, in fact, that I pulled the phone away from my ear and checked the screen to make sure the call hadn't been dropped.

"Abraham?"

"I'm on my way home."

I sighed. "That's not necessary."

"It's not negotiable. I'm leaving now."

I let out another deep breath. "Where are you?"

"Outside Raleigh. I'll be home in a couple hours."

"Abraham, that's a four-hour drive."

"And with the way I'm feeling right now, I could probably run it in half that time."

I winced and looked down at my feet. "I know you're worried, but I'm fine. I'm here on pack lands and I'm sure Wyatt has no intention of leaving my side anytime soon."

There was a loud bang on the other end of the line, and I cringed. "I'm not fucking worried, El. I'm *murderous*."

Well, this was going worse than I thought.

I sighed again. "I know you're mad, but please drive safe. I don't need anything happening to you."

He laughed, but it was humorless. "It's clearly not me we have to worry about. I'll see you soon."

With that, he hung up and my stomach fell. I had a feeling there was a storm heading my way, and it was in the shape of a tall, dark, and handsome alpha werewolf.

Chapter 39

Wyatt waited with me in the kitchen while I paced the floor. It had only been a couple hours since I spoke with Abraham, but if he made good on his threat, he could be home any minute.

My stomach still felt sick, but thankfully, I hadn't thrown up since I was in the office. Which was good since I couldn't focus on anything but the coming confrontation with my fiancé.

The roar of a vehicle speeding up the drive reached us all the way in the kitchen, and I cringed. Apparently, Abraham was home.

My belly flipped as I made my way out to the lot. I was excited to see him because I'd missed him so much, but at the same time, I was worried about how he'd react to what happened that morning. It couldn't be good that he'd had hours alone to stew about this mess on his drive home.

The second his black pickup came to a screeching halt, he was out the door and storming over to me. I braced myself for the fight I knew was coming, but he surprised me by wrapping his arms around my shoulders and tugging me into his hard chest.

I let out a deep breath, letting his familiar scent wash over me as I wrapped my arms around his waist.

"I missed you," I mumbled against him.

The only answer I got was a grunt.

A few moments later, he pulled away and held me at arm's length. His dark blue eyes raked over every inch of my body before he nodded once. Seemingly satisfied with his inspection, he turned on his heel and stormed off.

I stood there confused for a moment before jogging after him. Heavy footsteps sounded behind me and I knew Wyatt was hot on my heels.

"Abraham! Where are you going?"

"Stay in the lodge, Elizabeth."

Ha. Fat chance.

I had to run to keep up with him as he raced toward the pack houses. He made a beeline to the fourth house and raised his fist to bang on the door. The second Craig answered, Abraham pulled him out of his house and wrapped his hand around his throat.

"Did you think I wouldn't know it was you?" Abraham growled inches away from his face.

Craig's dark eyes bulged out of his head as he turned red. "What are you talking about?" he wheezed.

Abraham pulled him back and slammed him against the side of his house. "You fucked with her car. You tried to *kill* my mate." He growled the last word so low I almost missed it.

I ran up to them and grabbed Abraham's bulging bicep. "It wasn't him, Abraham! Let him go!"

He tried to shake me off, his attention still riveted on Craig.

"You threatened her and then someone cuts her brake lines and you expect me to not believe it was you? Just admit it before I tear your throat out."

Craig's eyes were bloodshot as he clawed at Abraham's hand still wrapped around his neck. "I... didn't... do anything!" he gasped.

I tugged on his arm again. "Abraham, we don't think it was him! Just let him go!"

He finally turned to me and I almost wish he hadn't. His face had been transformed from the handsome features I was so used to seeing to this mask of fiery rage. I almost didn't recognize him.

"I know it was him, Elizabeth. You need to go back to the lodge and let me handle this."

He turned back to Craig and squeezed his throat tighter. The older man had to be close to passing out at this point and I knew I had to do something. I spun around to Wyatt who was looking on with wide eyes.

"Say something to him!" I yelled at Wyatt. "Tell him what Brad told us!"

Wyatt shook his head and stepped toward us. "She's right, Alpha. Brad doesn't believe it was Craig."

Abraham snarled and slammed Craig against the wall again. "Of course it was him! Who else could it be?"

I grabbed his arm again. "We're not sure yet, but it wasn't Craig. Let him go and we can talk about this."

Abraham turned his molten eyes toward me again and I held them as best I could. Finally, he growled and let go of Craig, who fell to the ground. He sputtered and coughed and wheezed, and I felt so bad, I knelt beside him.

"Are you okay?" I asked softly.

He looked up at me with wide eyes and nodded. "I'll be all right," he whispered. I figured his throat had to be sore and my insides twisted with guilt.

I should have filled Abraham in completely. I should have called him back after he hung up with me and made sure he had the whole story. Instead, he'd spent the hours-long drive home letting his rage build until he could unleash it on poor Craig.

I wrapped my arm around the ex-mechanic's shoulders and helped pull him to his feet. When we were both standing again, Abraham reached out and snatched me away from him. I shot a glare at my fiancé, but his gaze was trained on Craig.

"Explain to me why I'm not tearing this asshole apart right now."

I glanced at Wyatt, but he didn't seem too eager to speak up again. I took a deep breath and tugged on Abraham's arm until he was looking at me.

"Let's go talk to Brad. He'll tell you his theory."

Abraham's eyes darted back to Craig, and he nodded once. I let out a small breath of relief and hung on as Abraham stormed toward the new mechanic's house. I shot an apologetic look back toward Craig who was still rubbing his bright red neck. With a sigh, I realized he'd have even more reason to hate me now.

We made it to Brad's house and Abraham stomped up to his door and banged on it until he answered. The messy-haired werewolf's eyes widened as he took in the furious alpha werewolf and the rest of us struggling to keep up.

"Hey, guys. What's going on?"

Abraham took a menacing step forward. "I want to know everything you do about what happened today."

Brad nodded quickly. "Sure. Let's go take a look."

Abraham dragged me after him as he followed Brad to the garage. The mechanic immediately launched into the same story he'd told me and Wyatt earlier. The only indication that Abraham was listening was the ticking in his jaw. It would speed up or slow down depending on what Brad was saying at that particular time.

"If it was someone with any in-depth knowledge of cars and the desire to really kill her, they would have cut both the brake lines and the e-brake cable, leaving her with no way to slow down," Brad concluded.

Abraham snarled and let go of my arm so he could pace the length of the garage. "So, you don't think it was Craig."

He said it as more of a statement than a question, but Brad answered anyway.

"I think if Craig wanted to kill her, he would have done a better job of it."

Abraham halted his pacing and let loose a growl in Brad's direction. He stormed over to the skinny mechanic, his hands fisted at his sides. I figured he did that to stop himself from strangling another pack member.

"That is my *mate* you're talking about," he said, his voice deep and dangerous.

344

Brad held up both hands, his eyes wide. "I know, Alpha. I'm just telling you what I think. I don't want anything to happen to Ellie. I think she's the best thing that's ever happened to this pack."

My heart warmed at his sentiments, but I had little time to bask in his words. Abraham spun around and grabbed my arm again before tugging me back down the driveway. He didn't say a word as he hauled me back toward the lodge.

When we got to Craig's house, he was still outside, holding onto what had to be a pretty sore neck. Abraham stopped and turned to him, his voice low and deadly.

"If you so much as sneeze in her direction, I'll tear you apart piece by piece. You hear me?"

Craig held up his hands and nodded slowly. "I wouldn't hurt her, Alpha."

Abraham grunted and stormed off again, towing me behind him. I tried talking to him on our way back to the lodge, but nothing I said made any difference. With a sigh, I decided to keep quiet until he was ready to talk.

Clearly, what happened today was affecting him more than I thought it would. I knew he'd be mad, knew he'd be worried, but I hadn't prepared for this unadulterated rage.

We made it inside the lodge where most of the pack was convening for dinner. Abraham's head whipped around the room before he stomped toward the hall and up the stairs.

At that point, I was getting a little sick of him dragging me around, but I knew better than to say something when he was like that.

We made it to the third floor, and he turned down the sisters' wing before I could ask him what we were doing there. When we got to Callie's door, he pounded on it as viciously as he had at Craig and Brad's places.

When Callie opened her door, her eyes were wide as they looked between the two of us. "Abey, you're home."

He pulled me closer and shook me slightly. "She doesn't work for you anymore."

I whipped my head around to face him so quickly I almost gave myself whiplash. "What?!"

He ignored me.

Callie looked just as shocked as I felt. "Why? What happened?"

Abraham let loose a menacing snarl. "What happened? She almost died today on her way to *your* office and I won't let that happen again. She's done there."

Callie looked at me and shrugged before turning back to Abraham. "If that's what you think is best, Abey."

"Well, I don't think it's best," I said as I struggled to pull out of his hold.

He ignored me again and took off back down the hall. I figured he was heading toward our wing, but I'd had enough of being dragged around like a rag doll. I dug my heels into the carpet and wrenched my arm out of his grasp.

He turned to me with wild eyes and I almost balked. But then I remembered he was being irrational and unreasonable, and I wasn't going to take it anymore.

"I'm not quitting my job."

"You are. It's done."

"The hell it is, Abraham. You can't do that! I get a say in my life!"

He took a step toward me and I just barely held my ground. It was instinctual to back down, but I didn't. I tipped my chin and met his gaze head on.

"You are my mate and I'll tell you what you can and can't do."

An incredulous laugh shot out of my mouth. "That's not how it works."

"That's how *I* work."

"No, you don't because if you did, I wouldn't *be* your damn mate."

He took another step closer, and I fisted my hands at my sides to stop them from shaking.

"You say that like you have a choice," he rumbled.

I tipped my chin up higher. "Of course I have a choice. If I knew what an unbearable ass you would turn out to be, I'd have stayed in Raleigh!"

His eyes widened before he threw his hands in the air and paced away from me. "Someone tried to *kill* you today, Elizabeth! Don't you get that?!"

"I was there! Of course I get that!"

"Well, you're not acting like you do!"

"This is nothing new for me! Ever since I took that godforsaken trip out here, I've had someone trying to kill me! That doesn't mean I'm going to stop living my life!"

"If I don't find a way to protect you, you won't have a life to live!"

"Well, I'd rather die living my life the way I want than live under your thumb!"

His eyes widened further and his mouth fell open. "You don't mean that."

I narrowed my eyes at him and stood my ground. "Yes. I do. I won't be told what I can and can't do. You don't own me, Abraham. You never will."

His head fell back as he let out an exasperated growl. "I'm not trying to *own* you, I'm trying to keep you alive!"

"Then do it in a different way!" I yelled.

He took a deep breath, his hands opening and closing at his sides. Finally, he speared me with a look so full of anger, it almost knocked me back a step. "This conversation is over. You're not leaving pack lands again until the threat is eliminated. That's an order."

My spine stiffened without my permission as my eyes practically bugged out of my head. "An *order*? You're *ordering* me now?" I screeched.

He shrugged. "If that's what it takes."

My blood was boiling so violently, it felt like it would spew out of my orifices any second. I knew I needed to walk away or I'd do something I couldn't take back, like strangling my fiancé until he saw reason.

I stormed off, slamming into him with my shoulder on my way by.

"Where the hell are you going?" he called after me.

Instead of answering, I flipped him off over my shoulder. I knew it was immature, but I couldn't even form words at that moment.

Never in my life had I met a more frustrating person.

I knew he was concerned for my safety, but he was completely blowing this whole situation out of proportion. Like I'd said to him, this wasn't the first time someone had tried to kill me, and it seemed like it wouldn't be the last. My life had been in danger from the moment I'd stepped into Asheville months ago and not much had changed since then.

I stomped down the stairs and took off through the kitchen, ignoring every greeting I got. When I made it to the sliding glass door, I whipped it open and slammed it closed behind me. Out on the patio in the warm summer air, I took a deep breath and hoped it would ease some of my ire.

It didn't.

I jogged down the stairs and across the lawn, my anger pushing me to move faster. I felt out of control. Like I'd burst at the seams or explode into a million tiny pieces if I didn't get this feeling out of me.

I heard the back door open and close again before heavy footsteps sounded behind me. The wind carried a leather scent to my nose, and I knew it was Wyatt. Ignoring him, I made it to the tree line and let my body do what it had been craving since the moment Abraham told Callie I was quitting.

A large crack rang out in the quiet evening air, my clothes ripping and tearing at the seams until I was a wolf instead of a woman. I heard another series of cracks behind me and figured Wyatt shifted too.

I took off into the woods, running as fast as I could. I hoped if I moved fast enough, I could outrun the whole day. Like I could race back through time and stop that morning from happening all together.

"Ellie, where are you going?"

I wanted to ignore him. I wanted to tell him to fuck off. I wanted to tell him to go away, but I did none of that. I knew he was only doing his job and I would try to not make it harder for him.

"I don't have a destination. I just want to be alone."

I heard his steps fall back a few paces before he spoke in my head again. *"I'll give you as much space as I can, but just know I'm with you."*

My nose burned as tears swam to my eyes at his sweet words. I knew Wyatt was with me. He always was. I also knew Abraham was only acting so crazy out of love. But that didn't change how overbearing he was being and that didn't change the fact that he was trying to keep me caged there.

With those thoughts and more spinning through my head, I took off through the woods, hoping I could outpace every mistake I'd made that day.

Chapter 40

The sun had set a while ago, but I had no intention of going inside anytime soon.

I'd run through the woods for a long time and I'd almost been able to forget that I was being tailed. Almost.

When I'd made a huge loop around the pack lands, I'd circled back to the yard and come out to the lake. Now I was at the end of the dock, watching the placid water and hoping it would infuse me with some of its calm.

I was still angry.

No, *furious*.

I knew it was in Abraham's nature to be the boss of everyone around him, but he'd never gone that far with me before. I didn't even know he could go that far, but maybe that was my mistake. Maybe I'd underestimated him.

Maybe this wouldn't really work between us.

My heart clenched in my chest, and if I'd had hands at that moment, I'd have rubbed the sore spot.

Abraham was it for me. The only person I ever wanted to be with, but I would *not* be controlled. I would *not* be caged. I wouldn't let someone else control my life for me. That was all non-negotiable. And so, even though my heart ached with every beat, I sat out there and tried to imagine a future without all this.

Without Abraham.

Without my sisters.

Without my pack.

I'd have done anything to prevent that, but if Abraham didn't get some sense knocked into him soon, I didn't know if I'd have a choice.

I heard the sliding glass door open but ignored it. It was probably Wyatt. He'd been close by since I'd stormed out of the lodge, but I'd convinced him to let me come down to the lake by myself. The compromise we'd made was he'd sit on the patio where he could watch me. I felt his eyes on my back but did my best to ignore him.

As the sound of heavy steps thudded against the grass heading toward me, I figured my time was up and Wyatt was finally coming to get me. But, as they got closer, the scent of spearmint and soap hit my nose and my spine instantly straightened.

It wasn't Wyatt, it was Abraham.

I didn't know if I was ready to talk to him yet, but it didn't seem like I had a choice.

His heavy steps sounded against the planks of the wooden dock and I knew I had seconds before he reached me. I took a few steadying breaths, but kept my eyes focused straight ahead.

"I brought you some clothes," he said when he reached me.

I shot him a glance out of the corner of my eye before turning back around. There was a heavy sigh behind me before I felt the boards shift with his weight. He stepped up next to me and lowered his body to the dock.

"You missed dinner."

I ignored that, too.

I didn't want to talk about clothes or food or any of the other meaningless things he might have come out here to say. In fact, I wasn't really in the mood to talk to him at all. Thankfully, I was a wolf at the moment, and it wasn't possible for me to answer him.

He reached out to touch me, but I flinched away from him. The last thing I wanted right then was his touch. Because I knew if I let him put his hands on me, it would make me forget why I was mad in the first place. Abraham had a way of blocking out everything else and I couldn't lose focus like that.

We had a huge problem between us, and no amount of sweet words or touches would fix it.

He sighed again. "El, will you shift back so we can talk?" I ignored him again, but when he added, "Please," my resolve crumbled.

I looked around the yard, but there was no one I could see. Not even Wyatt. Abraham probably sent him away when he came out. He must have noticed my trepidation because he rose to his feet and set my clothes next to me.

"I'll block you if you want to shift back and get dressed."

I huffed out a breath as I considered my options. I couldn't avoid him forever, right? If I'd had it my way, I might have waited a couple more hours, but if he'd come to talk to me, that must have meant he had something to say.

I just hoped for his sake it was something along the lines of *I'm sorry*. If it was anything less, I was storming back into that lodge and sleeping in my old room.

I checked the clearing for stray pack members one more time before I willed myself back into a woman. Once I shifted, I tugged my clothes on as quickly as I could. It wasn't just because I didn't want anyone to catch me out there naked, it was also because I didn't want to feel vulnerable in front of Abraham.

Not when I was so mad at him.

When I was dressed, I took a seat at the end of the dock again and lowered my feet into the warm water. It was a nice reprieve from the sticky summer night, but it did little to cool my temper.

"Thanks for shifting back," he said as he took a seat next to me.

"What did you want to talk about?"

He sighed, and I caught him running a hand down his face out of the corner of my eye.

"El, I'm sorry." He took a deep breath and let it out slowly. "I'm really sorry."

Well, that was a start. The tension in my shoulders lessened by the smallest degree.

But sorry wasn't enough. That wasn't a complete apology and I wouldn't settle for anything less.

Without prompting, he spoke again. "Do you have any idea how scary it was hearing something almost happened to you today when I was so far away?"

My heart clenched without my permission as his words seeped into my brain. I hadn't really thought about that. Now that I did, I realized it must have been terrifying for him. He always felt like he needed to be on top of everything and protect everyone he was responsible for, and today, he couldn't.

I sighed. "Yeah, I'm sure that was scary for you. It was kinda scary for me too."

I saw his hand reach out for me again, but he fisted it and placed it back on his lap. "The whole drive here, all I could think about was something happening to you. Of losing you. Of not being there when you needed me most. It gutted me, El."

Another layer of ice melted from my heart, but I still didn't turn to him. "I don't blame you for feeling that way, Abraham."

He let out another deep breath. "It made me crazy. It felt like I couldn't even see straight. I was terrified, and instead of letting myself feel that fear, I let the anger take over instead."

I nodded slowly. He really had let his anger take over, and that wasn't a good look for an alpha.

"You probably owe Craig an apology."

"Yeah, I plan on that." He ran another rough hand down his face. "I was so sure it was him, but the more I think about it, the more I believe what Brad said. Besides, Craig is a more straightforward kind of guy. If he had a problem with someone, he wouldn't slink in the shadows and sabotage their car, he'd confront them to their faces."

I snorted. "Been there."

He chuckled once. "I guess you have, haven't you?"

I nodded again and waited for him to continue.

"Once it was clear I couldn't take my rage out on the person who did that to your car, I turned to the next closest thing. That was you."

My shoulders stiffened again at his honesty.

He sighed and turned his body until he was facing me. "I should have never spoken to you like that. Hell, I shouldn't have spoken to Callie like that either. I don't want to cage you here. I don't want to hold you back. All I want, the *only* thing I need is to make sure you're safe. As long as you're happy and healthy, I can deal with anything else that comes my way."

I sighed and finally turned to him. "That wasn't the tune you were singing earlier." The anger was still brimming in my system and a bit of it seeped out into my words. "You can't keep doing this, Abraham. You can't get scared and start ordering me around. I'm supposed to be your equal and I won't let you treat me like less. We're in this together or we're not in this at all."

His blue eyes darted away from me as his shoulders slumped. "I know. I was wrong. I handled this whole situation wrong. There are other ways to keep you safe and I should have been looking into them instead of ordering you to quit your job."

A humorless snort flew out of me. "Yeah, ordering me won't get you very far, McCoy."

He shot me a rueful smile. "That is something I'm fully aware of." He sighed and reached out for me again. This time, I let him take my hand and sandwich it between both of his. They were big and warm and rough and felt so much like home, tears swam to my eyes. "I'm so sorry, baby. Will you please forgive me? Will you let me make this up to you?"

I stared into his deep eyes and read every sincere word there for myself. That apology from him was more than I ever could have hoped for. More than I would have asked from him, and yet there he was, admitting his fears and laying his pride on the line. For me. How could I not forgive him?

I wanted this thing between us to work more than I'd ever wanted anything else in my entire life. If we were going to make it, I'd have to accept his apology, and we'd have to move past it. There just wasn't another option.

I sighed again and nodded. "I forgive you."

His smile was so wide and beautiful, I almost had to look away. Without warning, he tugged me onto his lap and wrapped his arms around me. Digging his face into the crook of my neck, he took a deep breath and let it out slowly, blowing strands of my hair across my face.

"I love you and I missed you so much. I'm sorry about today, but I promise to do better in the future. As long as you'll stick by my side, I'll do anything to keep you there."

Those tears that were previously being held at bay finally freed themselves and slid down my cheeks. He froze in place before pulling away from me. His expression fell as his hands cupped my face and wiped at the salty trails.

"Baby, why are you crying?"

I sniffed as I tried to get myself under control. "I don't know."

He chuckled and tugged me into his chest again, pressing kiss after kiss to the top of my head. "Please don't cry. You know it kills me when you do."

I took a deep breath and willed the moisture from my eyes. When I thought I had myself under control, I pulled away so I could look at him. "So, you're not going to try to make me quit my job?"

His eyes turned wary. "Not quit, no."

I raised a brow. "Why do I hear a *but* in there?"

He sighed and looked away before meeting my gaze again. "I was hoping you'd compromise with me."

I pursed my lips as I eyed him. "I suppose I'd be willing to compromise, but it depends on what you want."

His eyes darted back and forth between mine for a long time before he spoke again. "Will you let me take you to and from work from now on? That way I know you're getting there safely. It'll make me feel a lot better."

I thought that through carefully, knowing I only had one chance to get this right. Would it be such a big deal to let him drive me? I know I said I didn't want to be carted around by Wyatt, but things had changed that morning. If this would ease some of his fears and make him less crazy, would it be too much to agree to?

I took a deep breath and nodded. "I accept your terms."

His smile was wide before he kissed my mouth. When he finally pulled away, the wary look was back on his face. "Can I ask you for one favor, though?"

I tilted my head to the side. "What is it?"

"Will you work from home tomorrow? You can go back to the office on Monday like usual, but I'd just feel better if you spent tomorrow with me. Besides, I've missed you so much, I'd love to have a whole day with you."

I thought that one through, too, but it didn't take me long.

"Okay. I'll talk to Callie and let her know I'm working from home tomorrow. They shouldn't need me in the office, anyway."

He smiled again and tugged me against his chest. "Thank you, baby," he breathed into my hair.

Now that the worst was behind us, I let myself melt into his embrace. It felt like he'd been gone so much longer than he was, and I was just happy to be in his arms. When my stomach growled, I knew there'd be no hiding it from Abraham.

He pulled away from me. "You didn't eat dinner."

I shrugged. "Wasn't really hungry."

He grabbed my hips and lifted us both to our feet before taking my hand. "Well, you're hungry now. Let's go see what's left-over from dinner."

I let him lead me into the kitchen and, to our surprise, there was actually some food left. That was probably because the residents of the lodge had swelled, and the kitchen staff had to make so much more food. Thankfully, they overdid it, but that meant we'd get a good meal.

It had been a while since I'd eaten more than a few bites and I made up for it that night. After my second helping, I finally had to turn Ms. Elsie away. I swear, that woman would have fed me until I popped if I let her.

When we'd had our fill, the day caught up with me and I found I could barely keep my eyes open. I trudged up the stairs with Abraham's arm wrapped around my shoulders, but by the time we made it to the second landing, he'd had enough. He turned and scooped me into his arms and, for once, I was too tired to protest.

He carried me right to our bed and gently placed me under the covers before crawling in himself. I yawned so hard I almost unhinged my jaw, and Abraham laughed while he ran a hand down my cheek.

"I missed you so much," he whispered.

I turned to him with a soft smile and closed my eyes as he threaded his fingers through my hair. "I missed you too, Abraham." I yawned again. "Did you see all the packs you wanted to?"

I cracked an eye open and saw him shrug his big shoulders. "I visited as many as I needed to. From here on out, I'll contact other packs by phone and hope they'll be as sympathetic as the others." Another yawn wracked my body, and he chuckled before leaning over and pressing a kiss to my lips. "You're so tired, baby. Let's talk about this in the morning."

I meant to tell him *okay* or *sure* or *I love you*, but I was too tired to do anything more than sigh and let the blackness consume me. Tomorrow was a brand new day. One where I'd have my fiancé back. One where I wouldn't have to deal with the debilitating sickness anymore. There were infinite possibilities, and as it turned out, I wasn't prepared for any of them.

Chapter 41

I woke up the next morning, blissfully warm in my fiancé's arms. Unfortunately, the contentment lasted only a few minutes before the nausea rose in my system. Knowing I had only seconds, I jumped from the bed and raced to the bathroom, making it to the toilet just in time.

"El?" Abraham's voice called from the bedroom, but I was too busy being sick to answer him.

Moments later, I registered his presence in the bathroom with me before his hands were pulling my hair away from my face. I heaved and heaved as last night's dinner made a second appearance.

What felt like hours later, but was probably only minutes, my stomach felt like it would hold for a little while and I sat back against the wall. Abraham's dark blue eyes were worried as he crouched next to me.

"What's going on?" he asked as he passed me a wet rag.

I wiped my face as I fought to catch my breath. "I don't know. I've been like this for days. I thought it was from missing you, but you're back and I'm still sick."

As the words tumbled from my mouth, my stomach sank at the realization.

The whole time, I thought I'd been so sick because we really were fated. Now that he was back, and I was still ill, it looked like it had nothing to do with him.

That meant we weren't really fated.

Tears swam to my eyes as that sank in.

I'd gone back and forth for weeks, convincing myself it was one way and then being sure it was the other. Finally, I thought I had it right. I figured my sickness was irrefutable proof that we were fated, but now I knew that wasn't the truth.

We really weren't fated, and Abraham had been wrong all along.

Warm tears raced down my face as I struggled with the news. Abraham crawled closer and cupped his hands around my jaw. "Baby, why are you crying? What's going on?"

I'd kept this from him for so long, battling my fears in private, but I couldn't do it anymore. I couldn't hide how devastated I was.

"We're not fated!" I wailed, my voice hoarse with the tears still streaming down my face.

He rocked backward at my words before gripping me tighter. "What are you talking about? Of course we're fated."

"No, we're not! There's no way for a bitten wolf to be the fated mate of a born wolf. You know that, I know that, everyone knows that!" I cried.

He shook his head and sat on the cold tiles next to me before pulling my shaking body onto his lap. Wrapping his arms around me, he gently rocked us back and forth while his hands rubbed my back.

"Baby, I don't care if it's never happened before because it's happened now. I know you're my fated mate. I've known since the moment I met you. How can you think we're not?"

"Because it doesn't make sense! We've never made sense!"

He sighed and kissed the top of my head. "El, everything makes sense when I'm with you. The whole world aligns the moment I'm in your presence. I know we're fated. There's no other possibility."

I sniffed and hiccupped as I tried to get myself under control. "I had Callie do some research and she couldn't find anything."

He froze for a moment before resuming his rocking motion. "Why didn't you tell me that?"

I hiccupped again. "I didn't want to hurt you," I said softly.

He sighed again and squeezed me tighter. "Baby, if you'd told me you were having doubts, I could have helped. I could have made it better."

I pulled away, so I could look in his eyes. "How can you make this better?"

He cupped my face and smiled. "I could have reminded you of all the reasons why I know we're fated."

I sniffed and took a deep breath. "Like what?"

He pulled my head to his chest again so I could feel his words rumbling out of him. "Like how the moment you opened your beautiful brown eyes in the woods that night I found you, I knew right away. My heart yearned for you in that instant. Like it'd found its other half, and it was lying in a broken heap right in front of me." He ran his fingers through my hair and cupped the back of my head. "I could remind you of how sick we both get when we're apart–"

"But I'm *still* sick," I interrupted. "How could it have been the fated mates magic making me sick when I'm still throwing up even though you're here?"

"Well, what about me? I was so sick the whole time I was gone, I could barely get out of bed in the morning. But as soon as I got within a mile of the lodge, I started to feel like myself again. How do you explain that?"

I shrugged. "I don't know."

He sighed and pulled me away so he could look in my eyes again. "El, I know you can feel me." He placed his hand over my heart. "In here. Just like I can feel you. Do you think the average couple can do that?"

I looked away and shrugged again. "I don't know."

He chuckled and grasped my chin to turn my face back toward him. "They can't, but we can. That's because we're fated. We're meant to be together. I've always known this, and I know you know it too."

Tears flooded my eyes again and raced down my face before I could stop them. "Then why am I still sick even though you're here?"

His face fell and the lines around his eyes deepened. "I don't know, El, but it's worrying me. Maybe you should go see Doc Monroe today."

I took several deep breaths as I tried to get myself under control again. Abraham's words tugged at me in a way I hadn't expected. Everything he was saying was true. I did feel him deep inside of me. I did feel ill every time he was away.

But the question remained: why was I still sick?

I sighed and relaxed into his hold again. "I'll go see him after breakfast."

Abraham let out a deep breath and kissed the top of my head. "That would make me feel a lot better. I'll call and let him know to expect you."

I nodded but didn't answer him. I had too many thoughts racing around my head to settle on just one. Everything was a mess, and I needed some answers. I needed to know why I was still so sick and what I could do about it.

Finally, Abraham stood us both up and walked me back into our bedroom. "Do you want to get some more sleep?"

I shook my head. "Actually, I'm starving. Can we go down to breakfast?"

His eyes sparkled as he nodded. "Of course. Why don't you take a shower while I call the doc and I'll join you in a minute?"

As it turned out, a shower was exactly what I needed. The hot water seemed to wash away the events of the morning, and by the time we were dressed and ready to head down to breakfast, I felt like a new woman.

The kitchen was even more packed than usual with all the new enforcers we had living in the lodge. We greeted a frazzled looking Ms. Elsie before grabbing plates full of food and finding seats amidst the chaos.

I dug into my scrambled eggs like I hadn't eaten in weeks.

"I think we should hire some temporary staff to help Ms. Elsie," I said between mouthfuls.

Abraham took a long sip of his black coffee. "I think you're right. This is too much for just her and Aubrey to handle."

"Should we be expecting any more enforcers?"

He nodded. "Yeah. Three more from the Raleigh pack should be showing up today, and Bryson promised to put a call in with the Greenville pack."

I took a big bite of sausage, and instantly, my stomach rolled. Not wanting to embarrass myself, I finished chewing and swallowing before I took a big sip of tomato juice. Now, that tasted delicious.

"Sounds great. You did a good job, Abraham."

He smiled at me and my heart thumped harder.

When I'd finished everything on my plate except for the sausage that I figured had to be bad, Abraham grabbed both our dishes and carried them to Aubrey. He walked back over to me and took my hand to help me stand.

"Let's get down to Doc Monroe and find out what's going on with you."

I nodded and let him lead me to the back door. He'd just reached for the handle when his name was called from across the room. We both turned to find an irate looking Beatrice storming across the kitchen.

"Abey, we've got a problem."

He frowned. "What's going on?"

Her eyes darted to the many men surrounding us and she shook her head. "We should talk about this in private."

He sighed. "I was just taking El down to see Kyle."

Beatrice's head whipped in my direction. "Why? What's wrong?"

I shrugged. "I haven't been feeling well lately."

Her eyes narrowed. "Werewolves don't get sick."

My stomach twisted at the reminder. "So I've heard."

Abraham took a deep breath before pulling his phone out of his pocket. "El, if it's okay, I'll send Wyatt with you, so I can take care of whatever's going on with Bea."

I shrugged. "That's fine with me."

He shot me a grateful smile as he instructed Wyatt to meet me in the kitchen right away. Honestly, I felt bad for the guy. It couldn't be fun being at my beck and call.

Abraham leaned down and kissed my forehead. "Come and find me when you're back. I wanna know what he has to say."

I smiled up at him. "I will."

He followed a still angry Beatrice out of the kitchen, and moments later, Wyatt showed up.

"I'm sorry about this," I said as soon as he made it to my side.

He shrugged. "Doesn't bother me. Where are we going?"

I pulled the door open, and we both walked out onto the back patio. "I'm going to see Doc Monroe about why I've been so sick lately."

He shot me a look out of the corner of his eye. "You're still sick? Even with Abraham home?"

My stomach clenched at his words and I nodded. He too must have thought my illness was because I was separated from my fated mate. It seemed we'd all thought that, and we'd all been wrong.

We were quiet the rest of the walk to the pack houses as my mind spun with possibilities.

Maybe the shift hadn't been as successful as we'd thought. Maybe I wasn't a full werewolf. Maybe I had some weird werewolf disease no one had ever heard of before. Maybe I was contagious, and I'd infect the whole pack.

The possibilities were endless, and I was doing nothing but scaring myself by worrying about them all.

When we made it to the pack houses, I slowed to a stop as I realized I didn't know which one Doc Monroe's was. Wyatt must have realized my predicament because he pointed to the first house on our left. "That one is the doc's."

I gave him a grateful smile, and we both headed up his drive. However, the closer we got to his door, the more reluctant I was to go in there with Wyatt. When it'd been Abraham to accompany me, I hadn't minded, but I wasn't sure I wanted Wyatt to hear what was wrong with me. At least not until I had time to process it myself.

We reached the front door, and I turned to my personal bodyguard. "Could you wait out here?"

Wyatt looked a little shocked, but he covered it well. "Sure, Ellie. I'll be right here when you're done."

I gave him a grateful smile and knocked on the dark green door in front of me. Doc Monroe answered almost immediately, and he already had a warm smile on his face.

"Ellie! It's so nice to see you, although I wish it was under better circumstances. Come in and let's have a talk."

He led me into his homey living room, and I couldn't help but look around at the place. There were wall to wall bookshelves packed with books of all sizes, and comfy-looking overstuffed couches and chairs took up what little space was left.

"Is this a living room or a library?" I asked him with a smile.

He shrugged. "I guess it's a little bit of both. Come with me to my exam room and we can talk about what's going on with you."

He led me down a hall and to the last door on the right. When he opened it, I was shocked to see it looked like an actual room in a doctor's office. He motioned for me to sit on the exam table and I did cautiously.

When he was seated on a small rolling stool, he clasped his hands and gave me a reassuring smile. "So, Abraham told me a little bit, but I'd like to hear from you what's been going on."

I took a deep breath and launched into the story of how I'd been feeling for the past week. I explained that I initially thought it was because I was away from Abraham so long, but after I got sick with him right beside me, I knew it was something more.

He nodded slowly as he listened. When I was done, he spoke up, "Have you noticed any changes in your appetite? Things that used to taste good that don't anymore or vice versa?"

I nodded slowly. "Yeah, that's happened a couple of times lately."

He pursed his lips. "What about your emotions? Have they been a little wacky this week?"

My eyes widened. "Kinda, yeah. I feel like I'm always crying lately. Why? Do you think you know what's going on with me?"

He nodded and reached into one of the drawers behind him before handing me a plastic cup. "I have a hunch, but I won't know until I do a couple tests. Can you provide me with a urine sample?"

I shrugged and took the cup. "Yeah, sure. Where should I go?"

He stood up and helped me off the table. "There's a bathroom across the hall. When you're done, you can bring the cup back in here and then have a seat in the living room. I'll come get you when I'm ready."

I shrugged again and did as he asked. When I made it out to his library/living room, I found Doreen in there reading what looked like a textbook. She saw me, and her smile spread across her face.

"Hey, Ellie! What are you doing here?"

I took a seat next to her on the big cushy couch. "Haven't been feeling well lately."

She frowned and closed her book before setting it aside. "Oh? That's not typical for werewolves. What's going on?"

I told her what I'd explained to her mate but this time, I included the symptoms the doc had asked about, too. When I was done, there was a glint in her eyes and a small smile on her lips.

"Did Kyle have you give a urine sample?"

I frowned. "Yeah. He said he needed to run a test and for me to wait out here."

Her smile grew across her face as she stood up. "I'm going to go check in with him. I'll be right back."

She was gone from the room before I could protest. Now I was alone, I had a moment to try to understand what was happening. It was clear that both of the Monroes had a hunch as to what was going on with me, yet I was still in the dark.

I probably should have done some research of my own before I came down there. But what was I supposed to Google? Reasons a werewolf throws up? I snorted and shook my head. My life had become so much more complicated than it had ever been before.

I heard a door close softly down the hall before two sets of steps thumped toward the living room. When Kyle and Doreen came into view, they both had huge smiles spread across their faces.

"I have good news, Ellie," Doc Monroe said. "There's nothing wrong with you. In fact, I'd be willing to bet you're perfectly healthy."

I frowned at the glowing couple. "Okay," I said slowly, "but there has to be something wrong, right? I shouldn't be throwing up like this all the time."

The couple shot each other looks before Kyle crossed the room to sit next to me. He took one of my hands in his and the smile was so wide, I swore I could see every one of his teeth.

"The reason you've been so sick is you're pregnant. Congratulations!"

Chapter 42

"I'm *what*?!" I screeched.

There was a bang outside the front door before Wyatt yelled, "Ellie!" and came bursting inside. He ran into the middle of the living room, crouching low while his sharp eyes took in the scene.

I jumped from my seat and hurried over to him. "Wyatt, I'm fine!"

He slowly straightened out of his stance and narrowed his eyes at me. "You yelled."

A nervous laugh escaped my lips. "Sorry, I was just surprised. I'm fine, I promise. Can you please go wait outside again?"

He looked around the room once more, taking in the doctor and his wife before he nodded. "I'll be right on the other side of that door if you need me," he promised.

I gave him a grateful smile that I knew was paper thin. The moment the door was shut behind him, I turned on the Monroe's.

"I'm what?!" I asked again, my voice only slightly softer than before.

Their smiles had dimmed the smallest bit as they looked at each other and back at me. Doreen took a step forward. "The test was positive. You're definitely pregnant."

My eyes widened as I staggered toward the couch. Once the backs of my legs hit a cushion, I let my body sink. "This can't be possible," I mumbled as my mind raced at the speed of light.

Doreen walked over and took a seat next to me. "Do you remember when your last menstrual cycle started?"

I turned wide eyes to her as I wracked my brain. "I don't remember," I whispered. Clearing my throat, I spoke up again, "With the move and the new job, I wasn't even thinking about it." I jumped from my seat and paced the length of their living room. "This isn't possible. Your test has to be wrong."

"I did two tests, Ellie," Kyle said from across the room.

Another hysterical laugh escaped me. "But I have an IUD!" I yelled. "I can't *get* pregnant."

Doreen stood and held out a placating hand. "It's possible it could have dislodged."

"How could it do that? *Why* would it do that?"

Doreen shrugged. "Werewolves don't use IUDs. It's not practical because we shift into wolves every month. Yours probably moved during one of your shifts."

I let out a groan as I continued to wear a track in their carpet. "This can't be happening. I can't be pregnant," I muttered.

Doreen sighed and grabbed my arm when I got close enough. "Ellie, just take a deep breath and calm down. This isn't a bad thing."

I looked at her incredulously. "Not a bad thing?! How can you say that? I'm not ready to be a mom! I can't have a baby!"

Doreen winced and shook her head. "There's undoubtedly more than one in there."

I could feel all the blood drain from my face as I remembered that conversation I'd had with Ms. Elsie a while ago. She'd said werewolves came in pairs. In fact, she said since Abraham was one of five, there was no telling how many offspring he'd produce at once.

Holy shit.

I could be pregnant with a whole fucking litter.

I wrenched my arm from her grip and started pacing again.

"I can't do this. I'm not ready. I can't be a mom."

Doc Monroe sighed from across the room and spoke up, "Well, you do have options, Ellie. It's your body, and it's your choice."

I stopped dead in my tracks and turned to him. "Are you talking about abortion?"

He looked uneasy, but he shrugged. "If you really don't want this pregnancy, that's an option you could look into."

My stomach sank as this new information infiltrated my brain.

I could abort.

I could end this pregnancy.

I could pretend like this never happened.

I began pacing again, all these thoughts racing around my head like cars at the Indy 500.

"However," he continued, "I think that's something you should at least talk to Abraham about."

My heart nearly stopped.

Abraham.

Holy shit, Abraham.

What would he think? What would he do? What would he want *me* to do?

I reached up and pressed my palms to either side of my head. There was too much going on up there. I couldn't think straight. I didn't know up from down. I had no idea what I was doing.

Suddenly, I was exhausted. Like bone-deep tired. I shuffled back over to the couch and sat down with a huff. Bending over, I let my head fall between my knees as I took deep breaths.

"I see this was unexpected, but it doesn't have to be a bad thing, Ellie," Doc Monroe said. "Children are a gift. And for what it's worth, I think you'd be an excellent mother."

I laughed incredulously and speared him with a look. "What makes you say that? I can barely keep my cat alive. How am I going to raise a kid without killing it?"

"Kids," Doreen corrected softly from next to me.

I groaned and let my head fall between my knees again. "I can't do this," I repeated for what felt like the tenth time.

That was all I could think about, though. That I couldn't do this. That I wasn't prepared to be a mother. I didn't even know how to be a mom. My own was about as useless as a glass hammer. How could I think I'd be any better?

Doreen wrapped an arm around my shoulders and squeezed. "I don't know what you're going to do, but it's clear your IUD is ineffective and needs to be removed immediately. If you want, I can do that right now."

I looked up at her and nodded, my whole body so stiff, I wasn't sure if the gesture was apparent or not.

She smiled softly and stood up before grasping my hand and pulling me to my feet. Leading me back to the examination room, she instructed me to undress from the waist down and have a seat on the table with a blanket across my lap.

I did as she asked on autopilot. It was like my body was going through the motions while my mind sprinted in another direction.

I couldn't believe I was pregnant. It was actually inconceivable to me. I'd had an IUD put in, so I never had to worry about that possibility. I'd promised myself years ago that I'd never have kids because I didn't want anyone to have the kind of life I had. How could I subject someone else to that?

There was a knock on the door before Doreen popped her head through. "All set?"

I shrugged. "I guess."

She smiled softly and asked me to lie down and place my heels in the stirrups. It might have been awkward having a friend get up close and personal with my lady parts, but I was beyond that right then. My head was so clouded, I barely registered as she located my IUD and gently removed it.

"Just as I thought," she said from the foot of the bed. "It wasn't where it was supposed to be and was rendered useless."

I chuckled once humorlessly. "Clearly."

Her smile was thin as she finished up what she was doing. Finally, she stood and walked over to me. "I think while I have you here, we should do an ultrasound. It's probably too early to see much, but it should give us an indication of how far along you are."

My heart thundered in my chest as my palms began to sweat. This was too real. Too much. Too fast. But I knew she was right. I needed all the information I could get so I could make a decision.

Since I couldn't rely on my emotions or my foggy brain, I'd have to resort to cold, hard logic.

I nodded. "Okay, that's fine."

She smiled again and rolled a machine with a monitor over to me. "It's too early to do an external ultrasound, so we'll have to use this wand," she said, holding up something that looked like a thick drum stick.

I shrugged and looked away. "It doesn't matter. Let's just get it over with."

She talked me through the procedure and soon she began clicking buttons on the machine. A smile spread across her face as she turned the monitor to me.

It looked like an old black and white television that wasn't getting a signal.

"See there, there, and there," she said as she used the mouse to point out little black blobs on the screen.

"Yeah?"

"Those are gestational sacs. You've got three of them."

I swallowed harshly and closed my eyes. "What does that mean?" I asked, but I knew. Damn it, I already knew.

"You're pregnant with triplets," she said. It was as if she was giving me the weather report and not the single most significant fact I'd ever heard.

"Triplets?" I croaked.

"Yep. It's clear as day. We've even got three little fluttering heartbeats."

My head whipped toward the screen as I tried to see what she was seeing. "How can you tell?"

She used the mouse to point out little flickers in each gestational sac. "Those are heartbeats. It looks like you're measuring about seven weeks and three days."

"What does that mean?"

"Just that you're a little over halfway through your first trimester. It's the hardest as I'm sure you're aware of."

I leaned back on the table and stared up at the popcorn ceiling. "This is why I've been so sick? It's morning sickness?"

"Yep! That should clear up in a few weeks. We can get you some candies and stuff to help with the nausea, though, if you're interested."

"That would be nice," I whispered.

Triplets.

Not only was I pregnant, but there were three of them in there. Three lives that were now my responsibility.

Doreen finished up with the exam and left the room so I could get dressed again. A few minutes later, she knocked on the door with some pamphlets in her hands.

"I know you're not sure about what you want to do yet, but I thought you could use some reading material on the subject."

I took the papers from her and skimmed through them. Half were about pregnancy and half were about abortion. I swallowed harshly as my stomach sank.

I looked up at Doreen and she must have seen the terror on my face because she reached out and grabbed my hand.

"What would you do?" I asked her desperately.

She pursed her lips and shook her head. "I'm not you, Ellie. This isn't my decision. This is yours. No one can decide it but you." She paused and looked down at our clasped hands. "But, if you decide to terminate, you're going to have to make that decision fairly quickly."

Terminate.

Terminate.

Terminate.

The word blared through my head, getting louder each time.

It was so final. So abrupt. So decisive.

I met her soft brown eyes as I felt mine fill with tears. "I don't know what to do," I whispered.

She tsked and pulled me into her arms as the tears raced down my face. "It's okay, Ellie. Ssh, ssh, ssh. It's okay. You don't have to decide anything right now. You have some time."

I pulled away from her and wiped angrily at my eyes. "I don't think there'd ever be enough time for me to decide this. It's an impossible decision. Either I terminate my pregnancy, or I have three kids that I'm bound to mess up."

She frowned. "Why would you say that? I think you'd be a great mom."

I laughed, but it was cold and emotionless. "If you'd met my parents, you'd know why. They were awful people and let strangers raise me. How can I be a mom when I don't even know what one looks like?!" My voice was becoming shrill as the hysteria bubbled up inside me.

I felt the need to pace again and fisted my hands at my sides.

Doreen shook her head and grabbed one of my fists between both her hands. "Ellie, we aren't our parents. In fact, I believe we can be better than they were. We're able to see where they went wrong or where they went right, and do things differently when it's our turn. You know how terrible your parents were and I know you'd never be anything like them. Why can't you believe that, too?"

I pulled my hand from hers and wiped at my still-flowing tears. "I don't know the first thing about kids, let alone babies. I'm not prepared for this. I can't do this."

She smiled patiently. "All new mothers feel that way. Don't worry. Your instincts will guide you. Besides, you have a whole pack at your side. We wouldn't let you mess up too badly. We'll be there every step of the way no matter what you choose."

Those choices spun around my head while I tried to weigh them out. But it was impossible. I couldn't make that decision. I could never make that decision.

I stood up and wiped at my face again. "I think I need to go."

Doreen stood as well and folded her arms across her chest. "Are you going to talk to Abraham?"

I shook my head. "Not yet. I need to figure out what I'm going to do first."

She pursed her lips into a thin line. "I think Abraham would be a big help in figuring out your next step."

I took a deep breath and closed my eyes as I tried to imagine what his reaction would be.

Would he be happy?

Would he be mad?

Would he be scared like me?

I could guarantee one thing, and that was he'd be as surprised as I was. We'd been banging like bunnies for months when, for most of that time, I'd been completely without protection.

I cursed myself with every bad word I knew for not thinking of that sooner. Of course an IUD could come dislodged when my entire body shifted into a wolf and back into a human as often as it did. I was an idiot for thinking that would be a reliable method of birth control. This was all my fault.

Doreen walked me out to the living room where the doctor was waiting for us. His mate filled him in on everything that happened in the exam room while he listened intently. When they were done, they both turned to me expectantly.

"Listen," I said, but I couldn't meet either of their eyes, "can we please just keep this between us for now? I need to get my head around it before I tell anyone else."

They looked at each other before focusing on me. "Okay, Ellie. If that's what you want, we'll keep quiet." Doc Monroe paused and eyed me for a moment before continuing, "I do have to warn you though, your increased level of hormones will be noticeable very shortly."

Oh, what fresh hell was this?

I sighed. "What do you mean?"

"I mean you're going to start smelling like a pregnant woman very soon. It will be obvious to every single one of us and there'll be no hiding your condition."

Great.

So, my timetable just shortened considerably.

"How long do you think I have?"

He shrugged. "My best guess would be no more than a few days."

I nodded with a sigh. So, not only had my whole world just been tipped upside down, but now I had a fast approaching deadline to make the biggest decision of my life.

And just like that, knowing someone was out there trying to kill me became the least of my worries.

Chapter 43

I stepped out of the Monroes' house and almost walked right into the back of Wyatt. Honestly, with everything else I had going on, I'd almost forgotten he was there.

"You all set?" he asked.

I nodded and took off for the lodge. I knew I wouldn't be much of a conversationalist and figured, with Wyatt, that wouldn't be a problem. That man was taciturn on the best of days. Unfortunately for me, it turned out today he'd decided to be chatty.

"Everything go all right in there?" he asked.

I almost laughed, but I somehow held it in. Did everything go all right? Well, I wasn't the first werewolf to ever get sick. And I guess that meant Abraham and I were probably still fated mates, right? So, I guess all of that was good news.

On the other hand, I had to make the hardest decision of my life. Either I'd be a mom to triplets in eight months, or I'd terminate the little lives inside me. Little lives that were not only part me, but part Abraham. The most amazing person I'd ever known.

Could I go through with it?

Instinctively, my hand reached for my stomach and Wyatt's sharp eyes caught it.

"Are you still not feeling well?"

I ripped my hand away from my belly and fisted it at my side. "No, not really. I think I need to go lie down."

"Did the doc know what's wrong with you?"

376

I stumbled on my next step as my mind went blank. Damn it, I hadn't thought of a suitable excuse yet. My mind was so filled with thoughts of babies, I hadn't even considered what I'd tell Wyatt.

I almost tripped again as I remembered Abraham was also waiting to hear how the appointment went.

What the hell was I going to tell them?

"Um…" I said as I stalled for more time. "I don't really remember most of what he said, but he didn't seem worried."

Wyatt shot me a look as his blond brows furrowed. "You don't *remember?*"

I barely held back a wince. Now that he said it like that, I realized how dumb it sounded. I spent all that time in the doctor's house and I'd already forgotten what he'd said?

You've got to do better than that, Montgomery.

I took a deep breath and tried again. "Um, he said something about maybe my immune system is still part human since I've only been a werewolf for a little while." There. That sounded plausible, right? "He said sometimes the full shift from human to werewolf can take a while and I've just caught a regular old human stomach bug. I should be better in a few days."

Which was a lie. I wouldn't be better for another eight months.

But I was proud of myself. That lie didn't sound half bad. And lucky for me, bitten wolves were so rare, there weren't many people who knew any better.

Wyatt shrugged but remained quiet and I had to hope Abraham would swallow down my lies as easily as my bodyguard had.

When we made it back to the lodge, Wyatt followed me up the stairs to our floor, only letting me leave his sight when I'd stepped into Abraham's office. You really couldn't say that guy did his job half-way, could you?

"Hey, baby. How was Doc Monroe's?"

My smile was thin as I walked around his desk to take a seat on his lap. "It went all right."

377

I hoped he'd leave it there, but those hopes weren't particularly high. My fiancé wasn't the kind of man who would settle for half a story and today was no different.

"Did he figure out what's wrong with you?"

Boy, did he.

I cleared my throat and looked down at his desk, hoping that if I didn't meet his eyes, it would be easier to lie to him.

I launched into the same story I'd told Wyatt, hoping the words sounded more believable than they felt. When I was done, I left my eyes glued to his desktop while the words settled around us. Finally, he grasped my chin and turned my face toward his.

"So, you're just sick? It's nothing serious?"

Actually, it was the most serious thing that'd ever happened to me.

I pulled my lips into the closest thing I could get to a smile. "That's what he thinks. Apparently, I just need some rest and some fluids, and I should be better in a few days."

What I didn't say was the only way I'd be better in a few days would be if I terminated the pregnancy. My stomach clenched at the thought and I reached for my belly again. Abraham, who didn't miss much, caught the movement and frowned.

"Are you feeling sick now?"

I shrugged. "Kinda."

To be honest, I'd never felt more sick in my life, but it had nothing to do with my stomach and everything to do with my heart. There was a monumental decision ahead of me and I honestly didn't know what to do. Both options seemed impossible, and I felt like I was stuck in a tug of war between them.

Abraham stood us both up and scooped me into his arms.

"What are you doing?" I asked breathlessly as a wave of nausea hit me. Apparently, the babies didn't like being manhandled like that.

"I'm taking you to bed."

I smirked at him, feeling like myself for the first time in a long time. "That sounds like fun."

He grinned down at me but shook his head. "Not for that, El."

I pouted, and he laughed again before kissing my lips. "There'll be plenty of time for me to make up for the week we spent apart."

Butterflies took flight in my stomach at his promise, but I told them to settle down. It was clear that sex was not on the agenda just yet.

He walked us into our room and placed me under the sheets much like he had last night. When I was tucked in, I realized I actually was pretty tired. A yawn escaped my lips and Abraham looked at me knowingly.

"Why don't you take a nap and I'll bring you up some soup in a little while?"

I yawned again and wiggled into the soft mattress. "That sounds good. Thanks for taking care of me, baby."

He leaned over, caging me in with a thick arm on either side of me. His lips met mine in a gentle kiss that curled my toes. When he pulled back, his blue eyes full of so much devotion, it made my heart stop for a moment.

"I'll always take care of you, El. Every day for the rest of my life. You got that?"

I smiled softly. "Yeah. I got it."

He kissed the tip of my nose. "Good. Get some sleep."

I did as he asked and was out before he shut the door behind him.

I woke up a little while later feeling so much better than I had. Apparently, all I'd needed was a little nap. The bed dipped next to me and I frowned when I saw Abraham was lying there shirtless. When did he get here?

He cracked one of his beautiful eyes open and smiled softly. "You're finally up," he said, his voice deep and rough with sleep.

I frowned. "What do you mean?"

He yawned and stretched his arms above his head before wrapping them around my waist. "You slept through the night. I tried to get you up to eat some soup around dinner, but you were knocked out."

I froze in place. "I slept the whole day? So, it's tomorrow already?"

He nodded and placed a kiss on my cheek. "Don't worry, baby. It seems like you needed it."

I wracked my brain as I tried to figure out if there were any repercussions for me sleeping through a whole day. I was supposed to get more work done for The Asheville Initiative, but I could make that up this weekend. There hadn't been any appointments scheduled for me and I hadn't promised to do anything with anyone, so I guessed it wasn't a big deal. It kind of sucked, though.

I turned to Abraham and kissed his bare chest. "Sorry I slept all day."

He shook his head and pulled me closer. "Don't be sorry, baby. Are you feeling any better today?"

I shrugged. "So far, so good. Let's see what happens when I get some breakfast in me."

Speaking of breakfast, I suddenly realized I was famished. It felt like I hadn't eaten in weeks rather than a day. My stomach took that opportunity to rumble loudly and Abraham chuckled.

"Let's get you down to breakfast before we have a mutiny on our hands."

I smiled sheepishly. "That's probably a good idea."

We got dressed and walked hand in hand down to the busy kitchen. Abraham made us both plates overflowing with food and I didn't even bother to reprimand him. To be honest, I was pretty sure I'd be finishing all that food, anyway.

We found a set of seats and I wasted no time digging into my food. Abraham chuckled beside me, but I ignored him. I didn't know what Ms. Elsie had done with the eggs that morning but I'd never tasted anything more delicious. I could even eat the sausage and it almost melted in my mouth.

When my feeding frenzy slowed down slightly, Abraham spoke up next to me.

"Nana's coming over today."

I shot him a wide-eyed look. "Family dinner?"

He nodded, but his eyes were cautious. I knew he still felt immense guilt over the death of his cousin despite the fact that he'd turned out to be a psychotic serial killer. It didn't matter when it came to family, did it? You loved them no matter what, and I knew that would never fade for Abraham.

Not wanting to let him dwell on Calvin for any longer, I tried to change the subject slightly. "Are we going to pick her up this time?"

His eyes lit with fire for a moment before he shook his head. "That would not be a good idea."

I frowned as I shoveled another scoop of eggs into my mouth. "How come?"

He sighed as he pushed the home fries around his plate. "I doubt Conrad would allow me access to his lands in light of what happened with his son. It's best if we keep our distance for as long as possible."

I swallowed harshly as I heard what he was trying not to say. He'd avoid Conrad until it came time to face him head on. When that would be, we didn't know, but it could happen at any time. It was why Abraham was so adamant about getting us extra enforcers and why the lodge had tripled its occupancy in the past week.

I shook my head and pressed on. "So, who's going to get her?"

He sighed again. "She was trying to drive herself and I just barely talked her out of that. I don't like her making that trip back and forth all alone."

I smiled at my sweet fiancé. He was always thinking of others. Always trying to figure out how to take care of everyone around him.

"Evey and a handful of my enforcers are heading down there this afternoon."

I frowned as my stomach twisted uncomfortably. "Why Evey?"

I didn't want my friend and the smallest of the McCoys anywhere near that man and his pack. Who knew what he was capable of?

Abraham released a deep breath and speared me with a look. It was full of all the doubts that were circling my head. "She figured she was the least threatening of all of us."

I swallowed. "Isn't that a problem, though?"

He shrugged and looked away. "When she found out about my issue with getting Nana here, she insisted."

I looked back down at my plate as my stomach continued to clench uncomfortably. "How many enforcers are with her?"

"Three in the car with her and five more following them there and back. And they have orders to not cross into his territory. Nana is going to meet them at the gate."

My heart slowed its racing tempo slightly at that news. That didn't sound like a half-bad plan. I felt much more comfortable knowing Evey wouldn't be behind those gates with Conrad.

I let out a deep breath and rested my head on his shoulder. "I wish Nana would just stay here with us instead of going back there."

He leaned down and kissed the top of my head. "You'll have to tell her that. Maybe she'll listen to you since she won't listen to me."

That had about a snowball's chance in Hell of working, but I guess it couldn't hurt to try, right?

Abraham's phone rang in his pocket and he pulled it out and answered it right away. "Adam! Good to hear from you, man."

I could easily listen in on the other end of the conversation, but I worked to tune them out as I finished up my breakfast.

"You're kidding! That's great! Congratulations!"

I shot Abraham a look and found him smiling from ear to ear at whatever Adam was saying. I shrugged and turned back to my plate, scooping the last of the grits onto my spoon and shoveling them into my mouth. Truth be told, I could probably have eaten another plate just as full, but I figured I wouldn't push it. It was a miracle my stomach was agreeing with this amount of food. I'd just be happy if I could keep it down.

"We'll have to stop by sometime soon and meet your new additions! I'm really so happy for you, man. Let me know if there's anything I can do for the two of you."

There were a few more pleasantries before Abraham hung up and tossed his phone on the table. I looked at him expectantly and found his smile just as wide as before.

"That was Adam from the Greensboro pack. His mate, Maggie, just gave birth to two healthy boys."

My stomach curled as I tried to paste a smile on my face. "That's great."

He sighed and shook his head. "Isn't it? Adam's a lucky guy."

I gulped and looked back at my empty plate. "Why's that?"

He wrapped an arm around my shoulders and squeezed. "He gets to be a dad," he said simply.

My heart thundered in my chest as I turned to him. "You think he's lucky to be a dad?"

His brows furrowed, but his smile was still stretched across his face. "Of course he is! I can't wait until we have pups of our own."

My heart skipped a beat before pounding erratically again. "Really? I don't think I'd make such a great mom, Abraham. You might not want to have kids with me."

He laughed and waved a hand in my direction. "Don't be ridiculous, El. You'll be a great mom. Look at the way you love my sisters. Look at the way you love Charlie. Look at the way you love and take care of this pack. You're amazing and our kids are going to be so lucky to have you as a mom."

My nose burned as tears rushed to my eyes. I looked back down at my plate, hoping to hide them from him.

Abraham thought so highly of me, but was that just because he was in love with me? Or did he see something I was missing? Did I have the ability to be a good mom? Could I really do this?

Sitting next to this man who was so ecstatic over someone else's kid, I knew I'd be the luckiest woman in the world to have children with him. He'd be the most amazing dad. There was no doubt in my mind.

The only question that remained was, could I live up to that? Could I be as good of a mom as he thought I'd be? Was it possible for me to have the babies and actually do right by them? Or was I doomed to be as miserable of a parent as my own were?

Chapter 44

"Where are my babies?!"

Abraham rolled his eyes, but his smile was wide across his face. He stood up from the kitchen table we'd been waiting at and held out his hand for me.

"Looks like Nana's here," he said.

I let him lead me to the door where Nana was holding several trays of food, surrounded by her grandchildren. Abraham grumbled and dropped my hand before rushing over to his grandma.

"Nana, let me take those."

She handed over the aluminum trays, and once her hands were freed, she reached up and pinched his cheeks. "Such a good boy you are," she gushed.

I stood back while all the other McCoys greeted Nana. Even Clyde was there, although he looked like he didn't want to be.

I'd been seeing less and less of him and it worried me. I didn't think it was healthy for him to sequester himself away from everyone. He clearly had some deep issues he was dealing with and it's usually better to shine a light on them than let them fester in the dark.

Although, I wasn't one to really talk when it came to hiding things.

The last time we'd all been in the same room and everything that had been revealed about my past swam to the front of my mind. I'd thought that would be my first and last family dinner with the McCoys, but they'd surprised me.

Thankfully, they'd all seen through Peyton's attempts to turn them against me. They'd understood that the police report her brother Paul dug up hadn't been accurate and that I'd just been a kid when it happened. It was one of the few times I'd had someone look past what I'd done back then and see the real me underneath.

That was the night Beatrice decided to stop being antagonistic toward me. She claimed it bothered her when Peyton threw me under the bus. From that night on, we'd slowly but surely built our relationship into what it was today. We joked, we sparred, and we had a great time together. If you'd told me a couple of months ago that I'd be such good friends with Beatrice McCoy, I'd have laughed in your face, but we really were.

"Ellie! What are you doin' way over there? Come over here and give me some sugar!"

I was broken out of my thoughts by a very adamant Nana. I gave her a sheepish smile and did as she asked. When I was close enough, she pulled me into her arms and kissed both of my cheeks.

She pulled away until I was at arm's length and eyed me speculatively. "Did you get prettier or is that just my imagination?"

Instantly, my cheeks were on fire while I looked everywhere but at her. "I think it's your imagination, Nana," I mumbled.

I caught sight of Evey, who was seconds away from bursting out laughing, and I shot her a look. It only made her face turn redder as she tried to hold her laughter in.

A thick arm landed around my shoulders and I was bathed in Abraham's familiar scent. "No, you're right Nana. She gets more beautiful every day."

I rolled my eyes, but my smile couldn't be contained. Being complimented like that from the most handsome man I'd ever met will do that to a girl.

Nana shook her head, but her eyes were still trained on me. "Well, whatever it is you're doin', keep doin' it. Your skin is so beautiful, it's almost like you're glowing."

My stomach sank in that instant and I fought to keep the smile on my face. "I've been drinking a lot of water lately," I said lamely.

Nana raised a brow but shrugged. "I hear water is good for the skin. That must be it."

I did my best to hide my sigh of relief, but it looked like it hadn't escaped Abraham's eagle eye. Honestly, nothing ever did. That man was so attuned to me, he probably knew what I was feeling before I did.

But I had a secret I was keeping from him and I wasn't ready to share. I needed to do my best to hide it for as long as I could. I wanted to make up my own mind about what I was going to do before involving anyone else. I was afraid their opinion would sway my own, and I didn't want that.

This was my body, and it had to be my decision. I wouldn't be able to live with either outcome if it wasn't.

"I hope everyone's hungry because I brought extra food!" Nana hollered as she made her way down the hallway.

Abraham leaned in to whisper in my ear. "What did I tell you? She probably cooked enough to feed the whole pack." My stomach growled, and he chuckled. "Or maybe just you."

I elbowed him in the ribs, and he had the decency to wince.

It wasn't my fault I was eating for four.

As we followed Nana and the others down the hall, we came upon Will who looked lost in thought. I hadn't seen much of the original werewolf in recent weeks and I wondered why that was. He seemed like a loner and I wondered if that was by design or not.

Did he have trouble relating to people so much younger than him? Did he feel lost in this modern world? Did he not get along with the other werewolves or did he not even try?

There were so many questions surrounding his presence, I could have spent all day just thinking about them.

One of the biggest was: what was he still doing here?

It seemed like he was a wanderer, never staying in one place for very long. At least that was the way it'd seemed when he first got here. But it had been over a month and he was still hanging around the lodge. I wasn't sure what he did all day, but I barely saw him.

Suddenly, I felt immensely sad for him. He must have been so lonely, and I knew I hadn't made much of an effort to make him feel welcome. I figured it was time do something to change that.

"Hey, Will," I called out as we approached him.

He lifted his dark curly head and speared me with a gentle smile. "Elizabeth. How are you?"

I shrugged. "I'm doing all right. Are you heading somewhere important?"

He shrugged and looked over my shoulder. "I'd planned to go for a run in the woods."

"Could you postpone it? We're having a family dinner and I'd love for you to join us."

His eyes darted from me to Abraham before he reached up and rubbed the back of his neck. "I don't know that I'd be welcome."

I discreetly pinched Abraham's side, and he jerked in response before clearing his throat. "My grandma's made tons of food. You'd be doing us a favor by helping us eat it all."

Will's smile was wide and so genuine that I knew I'd done the right thing. Will needed to be included more. If he was planning on sticking around for a while, there was no reason for him to live on the outskirts of all of us. We needed to drag him right into the mayhem.

I pulled away from Abraham and linked my arm through Will's. "Come on. Let's go grab a seat. The food should be warmed up by now."

Will shrugged and let me lead him toward the dining room. When we arrived, the space was full of loud talking and boisterous laughter and Will hesitated in the doorway.

I felt for the guy.

My first couple of times with all the McCoys had been pretty jarring, too. After being used to solitude, their brand of crazy was a lot to handle. But I knew he'd grow to love it as much as I had if he let himself.

I dragged him farther into the room and found a set of three chairs on one side of the giant table. Nana was directing traffic and filling up plates while the sisters fluttered around her and Clyde sat quietly in a chair.

I wished there was something I could do for him, too, but I knew he wouldn't accept the help from me. Our relationship hadn't been the best before the mess with Calvin and I couldn't imagine it would be any better now. It was my fault his brother had gone off the deep end and wound up dead. That wasn't something you just forgave.

Once the plates were filled and everyone had drinks, we sat down to eat, Nana the center of every conversation. Soon, though, our mouths were too full of her delicious cooking and the room grew as quiet as it could with so many people in it.

"Would you pass the butter?" Will asked from my right.

I reached for the dish and set it next to his plate.

"Thank you, Granddaughter."

It wasn't the first time he'd called me that and it made me pause every time. I never had the courage to ask him what he meant by that, but apparently, Del didn't have the same issue.

"Why do you always call her that?" she spoke up from across the table.

Will raised his eyes to meet hers and frowned. "Pardon?"

Del swallowed the food in her mouth and reached for another roll in the center of the table. "I always hear you callin' Ellie granddaughter, but you call the rest of us daughter or son. How come she's different?"

He shrugged as he buttered his dinner roll. "That's because she *is* my granddaughter."

I almost spit out my drink. "I'm sorry, what? I'm not your granddaughter."

He shot me a curious look. "Of course you are. You're a descendant."

The whole room grew quiet. So quiet, I could hear every heart in the room thumping in time with mine.

What the hell was going on?

"What's a descendant?" Callie asked from the end of the table.

389

Will shrugged again. "She's related to one of my offspring. I call them my descendants."

Again, a hush fell over the room, and this time, I couldn't hear a single heartbeat because the ringing in my ears was too loud.

"What are you saying?" I asked. My voice sounded a little desperate, but it was coming from an honest place. I had no idea what he was talking about, and the more he said, the less I understood. "I thought your wife died. Did you have kids before then?"

His face fell the tiniest bit, and I felt awful for bringing it up. It was clear the death of his spouse was still a sore subject. But he was the one talking in riddles and I was just trying to understand what was going on.

He set down his roll and knife and met my eyes. "No. Unfortunately for me, Adela and I never had children of our own."

"Okay, then how am I a descendant of yours?"

His face turned the lightest shade of pink and I almost laughed. Was the original werewolf, the man who was thousands of years old, really blushing?

"She was not the only woman I've ever laid with," he explained softly.

My brain was working hard at putting the pieces together, but I felt like I was still missing a few.

"So, you've laid with other werewolves? Then shouldn't I have been born a werewolf? Shouldn't my parents be werewolves?"

The mere thought of Bill and Regina Montgomery being werewolves was laughable.

He shook his head, his cheeks darkening. "I've also been with human women before. There have been a few instances where, despite our best intentions, we procreated."

Another quiet fell over the room. This time Beatrice was the one to break it.

"So, you've just run around for centuries knocking up human women and taking off?"

He frowned at her, his shoulders stiff. "I did not run off. I stayed and raised the child as long as I was able."

"What the hell does that mean?"

"Is it not obvious?" He paused for only a moment but when no one spoke, he pressed on. "I don't age. There was only so long I could stay with any one person before they realized that, and I had to move on."

Beatrice scoffed and shoved her chair back, the legs screeching across the floor. "This is bullshit," she muttered before storming out of the room

I wanted to investigate her peculiar behavior, but I had bigger things to deal with at that moment.

"So, you think I'm related to one of the children you had with a human woman?"

His eyes were still fixed on the doorway Beatrice stalked through, but he nodded. "I don't think. I know. You're one of my descendants. I thought you knew."

A hysterical laugh bubbled out of me. "How the hell would I know that?"

He shook his head and finally met my eyes. "Because you're mated to a born werewolf of course."

Of course.

Of course.

Like it was so damn obvious I should have seen it before.

I really liked Will who, I guess, was my many times over great grandpa, but in that moment, I could have strangled the man.

"How would I know that? Why would I assume that?"

He frowned. "You came to me asking about bitten wolves being mated with born wolves. I thought you knew why that was possible for you."

"El?" Abraham asked softly from beside me.

I could tell by his tone that he was hurt I'd gone to Will with that issue, but I didn't have time for that right now. I had a million more questions for Will, and they were all spinning so quickly through my head, I didn't know which one to ask first.

Thankfully, Callie spoke up and asked one of the major ones.

"How do you know she's a descendant? Have you kept track of them over the years?" There was a hint of excitement in her voice, and if I had to guess, I'd bet it was at the thought of getting her hands on a document like that. She'd probably kill to study a family tree that old and complex.

Will shook his head. "That would be impossible since there's no way to accurately tell paternity. I suppose I could have followed the women of my line, and I have in the past, but after a few centuries, it becomes complicated and convoluted."

"Then how do you know I'm a descendant?" I asked.

He shrugged and picked up his dinner roll again. "I can just tell."

Another crazed laugh spilled from my lips. "What do you mean you can *just tell*? How?"

He shrugged again, and my hands itched to circle his neck and squeeze. "I've always been able to tell. I assume it has something to do with the magic in me responding to the magic in you."

"I have magic in me?"

"You *are* a werewolf," he countered.

I shook my head. "But what you're saying is I had magic in me before I was a werewolf. That I was born with some of your magic."

He nodded. "Yes, you were. I believe that was why you were able to be fated with a born werewolf."

His words echoed through my head as I tried to wrap my brain around them. There were so many, but a few swam to the forefront and I tried to focus on them.

I was a descendant of the original werewolf.

There was magic running through my veins before I ever became a werewolf.

But most importantly, I now had an explanation as to how I could be fated to be with Abraham. I had concrete proof that there was a cosmic force pulling us together. That I was born to love him and for him to love me. That we'd live our whole lives together and die the same way.

It seemed that family dinners around there always came with life-altering revelations.

Chapter 45

I was quiet the rest of dinner as my head spun with what I'd learned. Abraham was silent beside me, too, and I could only guess why.

He was probably upset at me. Probably hurt. And I felt awful about that. The reason I'd kept my doubts to myself was so I wouldn't hurt him, but it seemed like I had, anyway.

Thankfully, Nana and the sisters kept the conversation going, and we were left to our own thoughts. Beatrice never came back, and I had to wonder what her issue was. But that would have to wait for another day because right then, I had a million other thoughts in my head.

I was Will's descendant.

One of my parents was related to the original werewolf.

I'd had magic running through my veins my whole life and never knew it.

And most important of all, I finally had an explanation for what was between Abraham and me. I had proof we were meant to be together. My head could catch up with my heart and fall in line with what it always knew. That Abraham was the one person in the whole world meant for me.

That person, however, was not happy, and it hurt me that I'd hurt him.

As soon as our plates were clear, Abraham leaned close to speak in my ear. "Can we go to bed early tonight?"

I turned to him and nodded, my tongue tied in my mouth. His eyes were so sad that it broke my heart. Before my eyes, his face transformed, and he pasted on a smile, but I could still see the lines around his eyes and knew this was only skin deep.

"El hasn't been feeling well lately, so I think we'll go to bed early tonight," he said when there was a lull in the conversation.

Nana frowned at me. "What's going on with Ellie?"

Abraham gave her the lie I'd fed him, and my stomach clenched tighter with every word. Wasn't it amazing how a lie could grow and swell and travel from person to person until you felt trapped in the middle of it? I'd never understood the phrase web of lies until that moment and I wished I could have kept my ignorance.

Abraham stood and held out a hand for me. His was big and warm and rough as always and I hoped by the end of the night, everything else between us would be the same as well.

We walked over to give Nana hugs and kisses goodbye before we left.

"Nana, I think you should stay here tonight. If you want, one of us can take you home in the morning."

She waved a hand at Abraham. "I don't want to be a bother."

I took a step forward. "You could never be a bother, Nana. In fact, we'd all be ecstatic if you lived here full time."

She raised a brow, her eyes darting between me and Abraham. "Did my grandson put you up to this?"

I pursed my lips and shrugged. "He might have mentioned it, but I agree wholeheartedly. None of us like the idea of you living so far away. Your family is up here."

She sighed. "But my home is there. How can I leave everything I've worked for and built over the years?"

It was on the tip of my tongue to tell her she'd have a lot more to live for up here in about eight months, but I swallowed the words. There was no way I could tell Abraham like that. It would have been so unfair to him. Besides, I still wasn't entirely sure what I was going to do. However, the more time that passed, the more sure I became of one path in particular. I just knew I needed to talk to Abraham before I did anything.

I leaned over and gave Nana another big hug. "Well, stay the night and we can talk more about this in the morning, okay?"

She sighed and squeezed me back. When I pulled away, she shot a look at Abraham. "Your mate is convincing."

He smiled, but it was thin. "That's what makes her such a great lawyer."

Nana laughed, and the sound lightened the load on my heart by the smallest amount. We said goodnight to everyone else before Abraham took my hand and led me up to our room.

We were quiet the whole way, but my head was anything but. It was still racing with everything I'd found out and the repercussions of that information. I didn't know what was going through Abraham's mind, but he seemed as preoccupied as I was.

When we made it to the bedroom, he dropped my hand and spun to face me. "Why didn't you tell me?"

My heart dropped to the soles of my shoes. "Tell you what?" I whispered.

Holy shit.

Did Doc Monroe spill the beans before I could tell Abraham myself? Doreen maybe? They'd agreed to keep my secret, but maybe pack bonds ran deeper. Maybe they'd decided I was taking too long and took matters into their own hands.

Abraham sighed and paced away from me. "I knew you were having doubts about us. What I don't understand is why you couldn't come to me with them."

I let out the smallest sigh of relief. He wasn't talking about the pregnancy. He didn't know about the babies. That secret was still safe with me.

But I still had an unhappy fiancé to deal with.

I took a step toward him. "I didn't want to hurt you."

He scoffed and ran a hand down his face. "Well, I'm still hurt." He turned away and paced the floor in front of me. "I just don't understand you. Why are you so unwilling to believe we're meant to be together?" He stopped and turned to me, his face filled with so much pain, my heart clenched in my chest. "Do you not want to be with me?"

I staggered toward him on shaky legs. "No. Abraham, no. That's not it at all."

He sighed and spun around to pace again. "Then, what is it? After everything we've been though, why are you still doubting us?"

I sighed, and my shoulders fell. "Because it didn't make sense. *We* never made sense."

He shot a narrow-eyed look my way. "Nothing has ever made more sense in my life."

My heart twisted, and I tried again. "Abraham, I've let logic rule my life for so long and I can't just turn that off. I knew what my heart was telling me, but I didn't trust it. Not completely."

He took a step toward me. "And what was your heart telling you?"

I closed the distance between us and took both his hands in mine. "That I love you more than I could ever have imagined. That I never want to be anywhere but at your side. That you're it for me and nothing can change that."

He closed his eyes and took a deep breath before letting it out. "That's good to hear at least," he said softly.

"You know what my biggest fear was?"

He shook his head, but still wouldn't meet my eyes. "What?"

"What if we weren't fated and your real mate showed up one day? What if I poured my heart and soul into a relationship and then I lost you in the end? I couldn't go through that, Abraham. I wouldn't survive it."

He finally looked at me, his eyes as tortured as I felt.

"This never had anything to do with not wanting to be with you. In fact, it was the exact opposite. I wanted to be with you so bad, I went looking for reasons to believe we were fated."

"And what did you find?"

I sighed and looked away. "I didn't find anything. No one has ever heard of what's happened between us."

He pulled me closer. "And you still stayed? Even though you couldn't make sense of it?"

I looked deep into his dark blue eyes, making sure he felt every word I was about to say. "Of course I stayed. I'd never leave."

He closed his eyes again before tugging me into his chest. "I wish you'd told me you were having doubts, El. I deserved to know something like that," he said, his voice rumbling through his chest.

I sighed and nodded as I squeezed him back. "I know. I'm sorry. I just didn't want to hurt you." I pulled away so I could look at him again. "I thought if I could find proof on my own, I could put all my questions to rest and just be with you the way I always wanted to. With no regrets. With no doubts. With nothing but this crazy, limitless love I have for you."

His eyes softened before he dipped his head and pressed his lips against mine. "I love you too, baby," he whispered against my mouth.

I smiled before reaching up and deepening the kiss. When we were both out of breath, he pulled away and looked down at me. His eyes were wary, and I reached up to smooth the lines between his eyebrows.

"Does this mean you'll marry me now?"

My heart all but stopped at his words. I was so shocked by them, I couldn't even form thoughts for a moment.

"What?" was the only thing I was finally able to force past my numb lips.

He was silent, his Adam's apple bobbing before he finally spoke. "I know you wanted to put off our ceremony because you doubted what we were. Now that you know, now that it's clear we're fated and meant to be together, what's stopping us?"

What *was* stopping us?

What was stopping *me*?

My hang ups had all been based on human expectations. In the world I grew up in, you didn't marry a man after only having known him a few months. Not unless you were irresponsible or drunk.

But that wasn't my world anymore. This was. This world of myths, and legends, and werewolves, and magic. This was where I belonged now, and it came with a whole new set of rules.

This new world also came with a new set of expectations.

Fated mates didn't wait to get married. Hell, Abraham's parents got hitched after only knowing each other for a week. If that was the norm, Abraham, and I had practically been together for years by now.

Could I do this?

Could I set aside my human reservations and give him what he wanted?

For that matter, what did *I* want?

Did I want to be married? Did I want to have this mating ceremony with him? Did I want to make what we had official?

The questions were numerous, but the answer to all of them was the same.

Yes.

I wanted to be with Abraham for the rest of my life.

When you find that one person in the whole world that was made just for you, why would you wait to make your union official? What could possibly stop me now?

But then I remembered the three little secrets I'd been hiding and knew what I had to do.

"Abraham, there's something I need to tell you."

He frowned. "Okay," he said, dragging out the word.

I sighed and looked away. "Well, I think I need to apologize first."

I could almost hear his brain churning from where I stood. He looked at me, confusion clouding his blue eyes. "What could you possibly have to apologize for?"

I sighed again and fisted my hands at my sides. "I lied to you. When I told you what Doc Monroe said about why I've been sick, it was a lie."

His frown deepened, and in the next instant, and he pulled me into his arms. "What does that mean? What's wrong with you then? Are you okay?"

I placed my hands on his chest and felt his heart hammering inside his ribcage. I smoothed a wrinkle in his shirt and kept my eyes trained there. "I'm okay. There's nothing wrong with me. It's something else."

He grasped my chin between his fingers and tilted my face to his. "What is it, El? Please. I can't take this. I need to know what's going on with you."

I sighed and let my eyes fall closed.

I didn't know how he was going to react to this news.

I didn't know if he was going to be happy or upset. He'd said he couldn't wait to be a dad, but I didn't think he ever expected that to happen so soon. What if he wasn't really ready? What if he didn't want the babies like I did?

Because I wanted them. So badly. With every fiber of my being, I wanted them. I wanted to meet them and love them and do everything I could to give them the life I never had.

Now, all I needed to do was make sure their dad was on board.

But I didn't know how to tell him. I didn't think it was something you could just blurt out, but I also knew he wasn't the type of man who appreciated when you beat around the bush. I decided to start at the beginning and hope I did it right.

I took a step away from him and crossed my arms over my chest, hoping it would protect me from what was coming next.

"So, you know how I've been throwing up a lot lately?" He nodded, and I pressed on. "Well, I've also not really had much of an appetite. All of a sudden, things I used to love smelled and tasted awful. At first, I thought it was because you were gone. When I lived in Raleigh and had to spend the week without you, it was always like that."

He nodded, his eyes still wary. "It's the same for me."

I nodded. "Right. But the problem was that when you came back, I was still getting sick. I was still throwing up and foods still tasted all wrong. On top of that, I've been so over emotional, I'm almost sick of myself at this point. Every little thing brings tears to my eyes and I'm not normally like that."

He shook his head. "No, you're not."

I took a deep breath and let my hands fall to my sides. "Well, it turns out my IUD moved out of place. Doreen thinks it must have happened during one of my shifts. She said IUDs aren't a method that werewolves use for birth control because our whole anatomy moves around, and they can come dislodged. And, well, mine did."

His frown deepened. "So, you've been sick because of your IUD?"

I shook my head. "No. But the IUD had a lot to do with it."

He sighed and crossed the distance between us to grasp my arms. "El, just tell me. Please. I'm dying here."

I took another deep breath and let it out slowly. This was Abraham. The most amazing man I'd ever known. I could tell him this. I could trust him.

I looked up and smiled. "Well, I guess the IUD hasn't been working properly for a while now and the thing we were trying to prevent happened."

His eyes widened, mouth falling open the smallest bit. "El. What are you saying?"

I looked away and took another fortifying breath before meeting his gaze head on. "I'm saying that I'm pregnant."

Chapter 46

"What?" he whispered so softly I almost missed it.

I kept my eyes glued to his, waiting to see what his reaction would be. "I found out yesterday that I'm pregnant. That's what's been going on with me. I'm not sick, I'm just pregnant."

"Just pregnant?" he deadpanned.

I shrugged. "You know what I mean."

He shook his head, his hands gripping my arms hard enough to almost be painful. Finally, he met my gaze again. "Are you sure?"

I nodded, my lips twitching with a smile. "I got to see their heartbeats yesterday."

His eyes widened again before he released me and took a step back. Shock was painted across his features and I imagined he looked a lot like I did when I got the news. He ran a rough hand through his dark hair before he looked at me again. "You're really pregnant?"

I shrugged and held my arms at my sides. "I'm really pregnant."

His Adam's apple bobbed as his eyes traveled from my face to my stomach. With halting steps, he crossed the distance between us. When he reached me, he dropped to his knees and reached up with shaking hands to cup my still-flat tummy. He looked at me, his eyes filled with tears which signaled my own to start watering.

"You're having my babies?" he asked softly.

I laughed as my nose burned and tears cascaded down my face. "Yeah, I am."

He shook his head and looked at my stomach again, almost as if he could see through the tissue and muscle to the babies beneath. His thumbs rubbed circles across my jeans and my heart pounded with the tender way he held me.

Finally, he shook his head and jumped to his feet. Grabbing my hand, he began dragging me toward the door. "Let's go."

I struggled to keep up with his long stride. "Where are we going?"

He raced through the sitting room and out into the hall. "We're going to see Doc Monroe. Right now."

"Why? Abraham, it's eight at night. Can't this wait until morning?"

He shook his head and pulled me down the stairs after him. "No. I need to see my babies tonight."

My heart filled with so much love as the tears welled in my eyes again. However, he was about to pull my arm from the socket with his eagerness to get to the doctor's house. Finally, I dug my heels into the carpet and pulled my arm out of his grip.

He turned to me with wide eyes. "What's going on? Why are we stopping?"

I rotated my shoulder and winced. "You were pulling on my arm, Abraham. Just slow down. We'll get there."

His eyes filled with remorse as he walked back to my side. He wrapped a hand around my strained shoulder. "I'm so sorry, baby. I don't know what I was thinking. I won't let it happen again."

I shrugged. "It's fine. I'm all right."

He shook his head and ran a hand through his hair. "I'm sorry," he repeated. "Maybe I should just carry you down there."

I laughed and slapped his chest. "I can walk, Abraham, you just don't need to drag me."

He gave me a sheepish smile as he wrapped an arm around my shoulders and led me down the hall at a much more reasonable pace. "Did you really get to see their heartbeats?"

I smiled up at him. "Yeah, I did."

He sighed and shook his head. "Lucky."

I laughed as he led me out the back door and across the field to the road that led to the pack houses. When we got to the first one, Abraham left my side to race ahead and pound on their door. Kyle Monroe answered with a confused look on his face until he saw me walking up his front path. Then his eyes darted between me and Abraham as his lips curled into a smile.

"I'm guessing you told him."

I shrugged. "Yeah, it was time."

He turned back to Abraham and wrapped him in a tight hug, both men slapping each other on the back. "Congratulations, Abraham. I couldn't be happier for the two of you."

Abraham grabbed my hand when I was close enough and kissed it. "I was hoping I could see the babies tonight."

Doc Monroe nodded and waved us inside. "Of course. Let me get Doreen."

We stood in their living room while the couple prepared the room for us. Abraham squeezed my hand again, and I looked up at him.

"Isn't it so lucky we have an obstetric nurse practitioner in our pack?" he asked. "She'll be able to monitor you during the whole pregnancy. Not all werewolf mothers are as lucky. We can't go to regular hospitals, and if there are no members of their pack or friendly neighboring packs that can take care of them, they have to do it on their own."

I nodded slowly. "That's why you offered Adam and Maggie to have Doreen look at her."

"It was the first checkup she'd received. Thankfully, werewolves are healthy and don't normally have complications with pregnancies, but there's always a chance. I'll feel so much better knowing you'll be taken care of the whole time."

That made two of us.

I couldn't imagine how hard it would have been if I couldn't receive medical care during my pregnancy. How did those women do it?

"Ellie?" Doreen called from the opening of the hallway, and we both turned to her. "We're ready. Come on back."

I led Abraham down the hall to the exam room I'd been in last time. She instructed me to get naked again, and I almost had to kick Abraham out of the room. It took me twice as long because he couldn't keep his hands to himself. When I was finally ready for them, Abraham opened the door and called for Doreen.

She came in with a huge smile on her face. "I'm so glad to see you two back here. Kyle says you want to see the babies again?"

I nodded my head toward Abraham. "I don't think he'll really believe me until he can see them for himself."

He scoffed and grabbed my hand. "I believe you. I just want to see my babies."

My heart melted at his words. He kept calling them *his* babies. How had I ever gotten so lucky? Why had I questioned for even a minute how he would react to this news? I should have known he'd be ecstatic. Over the moon. Absolutely crazy about hearing we were going to be parents.

Doreen got the machine running and held up the same wand as last time. "You remember the drill?" she asked.

I nodded. "Go ahead."

She talked me through her movements until we had an image on the monitor. Abraham practically climbed on top of me to get closer to the screen.

"If you can see that, there are three gestational sacs in there."

Abraham's eyes grew wide. "Does that mean there are three babies?"

Doreen nodded as she clicked around some more. "That's right. And it looks like all their heartbeats are well over one-forty which is great. I don't know if Elizabeth told you this or not, but she's about seven and a half weeks pregnant by now."

Abraham's eyes were still glued to the screen as he shook his head. "No, she didn't tell me. What does that mean?"

Doreen printed out a couple pictures before removing the wand and setting it aside. She handed the black and white images to Abraham who took them with shaking hands.

"It just means she's about halfway through her first trimester. It's the hardest, so she's going to need the most support right now."

Abraham looked from me to Doreen before taking the free chair in the room. "I want to know everything."

I laughed, but I could tell he was serious. He really did want to know everything he could about what was going on with me. If I wasn't already crazy in love with this man, I would have been by then.

Doreen spent the next half hour going over more information than I ever imagined. She covered everything from what I could and couldn't eat, to the medications I was allowed to take, to the symptoms I could expect in the coming weeks. I'd already experienced most of them, so that wasn't news to me, but the rest was eye-opening.

"Also," she continued, her gaze wary as it landed on me. "We recommend you shift as little as possible from here on out. Of course, you'll have to shift at every full moon, but you should try to limit it to then only."

I frowned. "Why?"

"It's not like there have been studies on pregnant werewolves or anything, but we like to advise against shifting as often as possible. It puts a lot of strain on your body that is already working really hard to grow these little lives. If you can abstain, we recommend that you do so."

My spirits sank as my mind ran though the repercussions.

That meant no more training with Bea.

That meant no more runs through the woods.

That meant no more feeling the freedom of my wolf except at the full moon.

I sighed and accepted my fate. The lives of the babies were more important than my love of being a wolf. I could go for eight months with only shifting at the full moon. I'd just have to take advantage of those nights every month.

I nodded. "Okay, I got it. No more shifting unless absolutely necessary."

Doreen smiled and patted my leg. "Other than that, try to eat as healthy as you can and stay hydrated. I know it's difficult while you're getting sick so often, so don't be too hard on yourself. You can only do your best and your babies are going to be just fine."

After that, she left me to get dressed as Abraham continued to study the pictures she'd printed out for him.

"What do you think they'll be?" Abraham muttered.

"Huh?" I said as I yanked my jeans up my legs.

He looked up and met my eye. "Boys? Girls? What do you think?"

I shrugged. "Hopefully we get some of each, right?"

He smiled wide and dipped his head to study the picture again. "Yeah, that would be perfect."

I stared at him as he studied the ultrasound picture. "You're really okay with all of this?"

He looked up with a frown. "With what?"

I motioned around the room. "With me being pregnant. I'm sure you would have preferred to wait. I know I would have. But I guess we don't always get to make those decisions."

He stood up and crossed the room until he could pull me into his arms. "El, the only time I've ever been happier in my life was the night you agreed to be my mate. I don't care that we weren't expecting it. I don't care that we weren't ready, because we'll get ready now. We have eight months to prepare for our children and a whole pack to help. This is going to be the greatest thing to ever happen to us."

My eyes filled with tears again and I tried to sniff them back, but it was no use. They raced down my face and dripped off my chin before I could stop them.

Abraham set down the ultrasound picture and cupped my face. "Baby, what's wrong?"

I shook my head. "I was just worried about how you'd react. I'm so happy you're happy."

He shot me an incredulous look. "Why would you be worried? I get to have little replicas of my favorite person running around. You think I wouldn't love that?" He pulled me closer and wiped at the trails of tears. "Baby, I didn't think I could love anyone, or anything more than I love you, but I already love those babies so much I feel like I'm going to burst. You've made me a father. I couldn't be happier."

He probably thought his sweet words would stem my tears, but they had the opposite effect. Sobs wracked my body as I gripped tight to him. He ran soothing hands down my back as I tried to get myself under control.

"El, what's going on? What's the matter?"

"I'm just so happy," I wailed.

He laughed softly and pulled me closer. "If you're happy, then why are you crying?"

I sniffed and pulled back to look at him. "I told you, it's the hormones. I cry all the time now," I explained through stuttering breaths.

He chuckled again and wiped my face. "I still don't like to see you cry."

I took a deep breath and let it out slowly. "I'm sorry."

He shook his head and kissed my lips. "No, baby. Don't be sorry. This is the second greatest day of my life. Nothing can change that."

I smiled up at him, but soon than grin was broken by a big yawn. Abraham frowned at me.

"You're tired. I should get you home."

I shrugged. "I get tired easier these days."

He nodded. "That's common in your first trimester."

I rolled my eyes, but the smile was spread across my face. "Yes, I was here for Doreen's lecture too, you know."

He shot me a cheeky grin and led me out of the examination room. When we made it to the living room, we found both of the Monroes with huge smiles on their faces.

"We're so happy for the two of you," Kyle said.

We accepted hugs and kisses from him and his wife before we prepared to leave. When we made it to the door, Doreen called out to me.

"Ellie, I think you should know that, even though you're a werewolf, having triplets isn't an easy pregnancy. I'm going to want to monitor you closely throughout, okay? Let's have you back here in two weeks for another ultrasound. I want to make sure everyone is growing like they're supposed to be."

I opened my mouth to answer, but Abraham beat me to it. "She'll be here."

I rolled my eyes and elbowed him. "Yes, I'll be here," I told her.

He shook his head as we turned to the door. "That's what I said."

"Yes, but you should have let me say it."

He huffed with exasperation, but I didn't think anything could have pried the smile off his face.

We took our time walking back to the lodge, both of us enjoying the warm summer night. Even though I was tired, I didn't want the moment to end. Nothing mattered but us and the family we were creating together.

I didn't care about the issues I'd had with our pack members, I didn't care about the coming conflict with the Charlotte pack, I didn't even care that there was someone out to hurt me again. I had this bone-deep intuition that everything would work out. That we were on the exact path we were supposed to be on. That no matter what happened, we'd find our way through it.

"You know, you never answered my question," Abraham said softly.

I turned to look at him, having no trouble seeing his handsome face despite how dark it was. "What question?"

His eyes were wary as he brought us to a stop. "I asked if you'd marry me now."

Oh, that question.

Despite my reservations in the past, there was no more hesitation for me. Maybe it was finding out that there was a plausible reason for us being fated. Maybe it was because I was pregnant with his babies. I didn't know what was clearing my mind of all doubts, but I didn't question it. I just gave him the answer he wanted to hear.

"Yeah. Let's get married."

His eyes widened as his lips pulled into a huge grin. "Seriously? We don't have to wait anymore?"

I shrugged. "No more waiting. I've never been more sure where my path is supposed to lead and every road ends with you."

He laughed and wrapped his arms around me until my feet left the ground. He spun us in so many circles I began to get dizzy, but I couldn't stop laughing.

I was in love.

I was pregnant with his babies.

And we were going to be together forever.

Nothing else could compare to those truths.

Chapter 47

"… you'll grow up in the mountains, but we'll take you to the beach as often as you want. We'll make sure you see cities and deserts and oceans and forests..."

I was barely awake, but Abraham's rumbling voice was pulling me out of the deep sleep I was in. I cracked an eye open and found him hunched over me, his mouth just inches from my exposed belly. Propping myself up on my elbows, I frowned down at him. "Baby, what are you doing?"

He looked up at me with a smile. "Just talkin' to the babies."

It's too early to cry.

It's too early to cry.

It's too early to cry.

Despite my sound logic, my eyes began to water. "What are you saying to them?" I asked softly.

His smile widened as he looked back down at my stomach. "First, I told them how much we love them and that we're so excited to meet them."

At that, a tear broke loose and ran down my face. "What else?" I whispered.

"Just now I was telling them about all the fun stuff we're gonna do together." He sighed and met my eyes. "My parents always promised we'd get to go to the beach, but with a large pack to run, we never got around to it. They thought they'd have time for the fun stuff later on, but they never got the chance."

411

It was too damn early for a full-on hysterical cry, so I sniffed the tears back and reached out to run my fingers through his hair.

"I'm so sorry."

He took a deep breath, his shoulders rising and falling with the motion before he met my eyes again. "It's okay, baby. We'll just have to do better with our family."

Our family.

Until then, that had just included his sisters and grandmother, but now we were making one of our own. I'd been adopted into his, but now this one would belong to me. That thought brought so much warmth to my chest, it felt like it would burst.

Smiling through the tears that still clouded my eyes, I asked, "Did you tell them anything else?"

"Well, I was just about to tell them about all their aunts, but you woke up."

I sighed as I continued to thread my fingers through his thick hair. "I suppose we should tell them all today, huh?"

He nodded. "Doreen said everyone will be able to tell really soon. In fact, I think you already smell a little different. They might not be able to tell yet, but they will soon. I think it would hurt their feelings if we didn't break the news to them ourselves."

I sighed again. "Yeah, you're right. Let's tell them after breakfast."

He nodded. "We'll call a family meeting, so we can tell Nana and Clyde too."

Nana, I agreed with, but Clyde was a different story. I wasn't sure he was going to care that I was pregnant, but he was Abraham's family and I'd go along with it for his sake. Besides, it wasn't like it could hurt. The worst-case scenario would be him showing no interest. That was about all we'd gotten out of him for months anyway, so that would be nothing new.

We got dressed and began our day like always, walking hand in hand to breakfast. Today, though, seemed different. The sun seemed a little brighter and the lodge a little homier.

It was like I was seeing everything in a new light.

This would be the hallway my children would run down some day. This was the kitchen I'd feed them in. That was the backyard they'd play in for hours when they got old enough. Every sight and sound came with a brand new perspective.

We found all of his sisters along with Nana at one end of a table and we joined them with our overflowing plates. They were already deep in conversation, so we tucked into our breakfasts, our hands interlocked beneath the table.

When there was a lull in the conversation, Abraham spoke up. "Can you all meet us in the conference room after you're done here? I have some things I need to go over with you."

Their quizzical expressions were so funny, I had to hide my smile behind a glass of tomato juice. They each asked their own variation of what Abraham needed to talk to them about, but he turned each one down with a tight-lipped smile. When he squeezed my hand under the table and shot me a wink, I almost spit out my juice.

They all finished before us and Abraham asked them to wait in the conference room while we ate. They shot us a few more questioning looks but did as he asked. When they were gone, he blew out a deep breath and turned to me.

"Holy crap, how did you keep this secret for a whole day? I felt like I was going to pop just now."

I laughed and shook my head. "I was terrified. That's how."

His brows furrowed as he pulled my hand onto his lap. "I don't know why you were so worried, baby. Don't you know me better by now? How did you not know I'd be out of my mind excited about this?"

I looked away and shrugged. "I guess since I was so scared, I thought you would be too."

He grasped my chin and turned my face toward him. "I *am* scared."

"You are?"

He nodded. "This is a big deal. A huge responsibility. I'd be an idiot if I wasn't a little scared." He leaned close, so he could whisper in my

413

ear. "But knowing I get to be a parent with the most incredible woman I've ever known makes it easy for the excitement to outweigh the fear."

I turned my head and pressed my lips to his. He was frozen in shock for the briefest moment before he gripped the back of my neck and deepened the kiss.

"Would you two get a room? I'm eating here."

We broke apart and sent glares in Huxley's direction.

"Then don't look," I said.

He scoffed. "I didn't need to look. I could hear you two sucking face from over here."

My cheeks heated but Abraham just chuckled. "You're just jealous you've only got your hand to keep you company at night."

Huxley shook his head, but his lips twitched with a smile. "At least my hand doesn't snore."

"I don't snore!"

He shot me an unimpressed look. "Sure you don't."

I opened my mouth to fire back another insult when Abraham leaned close. "Come on, baby. The girls are waiting for us."

I shot Huxley a narrow-eyed look that he just smirked at. As soon as the babies were out, I was challenging that over-bearing pain in my ass to a sparring session. We'd see how smug he was when I had my teeth wrapped around his throat.

Abraham leaned close again. "El, you're cutting off the circulation to my fingers."

I looked down to see my hand almost completely white with how hard I was gripping Abraham's. I let go and gave him a sheepish smile that he just laughed at. "Don't let Huxley get to you. It's exactly what he wants."

I shook my head. "Don't worry. He'll get what's coming for him," I said loud enough for the enforcer in question to hear.

Huxley rolled his eyes at me as he shoved a whole sausage in his mouth. There was so much food in there he couldn't even close his lips. I shot him a disgusted look and stood up with my plate.

"Neanderthal," I muttered under my breath.

He laughed loudly, the chewed food in his mouth almost falling out of the gaping hole. I shot him another nasty look and left him to his breakfast. He had eight more months to talk all the shit he wanted until I got my revenge. I could barely wait.

We handed out plates to a typically silent Aubrey before Abraham grabbed my hand and led me to the conference room. When we got there, five sets of eyes were trained on us, each with a varying degree of confusion.

Abraham walked me over to a chair before reaching in his pocket for his phone. I heard the other line ring until Clyde's voicemail picked up and Abraham ended the call with a sigh.

"We'll have to fill him in later," he muttered to me.

"Fill who in on what?" Evey called from the other end of the table.

Abraham sat down and shot me a wide smile before turning back to his sisters and grandmother. He watched them for a minute before looking back at me. "How do you want to do this?"

"Do what?! Would y'all just spit it out!" Evey hollered.

I rolled my eyes and turned to my fiancé. "Maybe we should have come up with a game plan."

"Now you're startin' to irritate me, too. Would you just tell us what's goin' on?" Del said from next to me.

Finally, an idea struck me.

I sat up straighter in my chair and turned to the youngest McCoy sibling. "Hey, Evey. Do you still have those wedding binders and stuff?"

She nodded slowly. "Yes," she said, dragging out the word.

I looked at Abraham and then back at her. "Well, I guess we're going to need them pretty soon."

Evey's face lit up, but it was Bea who spoke next.

"So, you two brought us in here to tell us you're having a mating ceremony? Didn't we already know that?"

I shrugged. "Sure, but you didn't know that we're going to have it in a month."

"A month?!" Evey cried.

I shrugged. "I'd rather not be showing in my wedding pictures."

"Showin' what?" Del asked, the irritation clear in her voice.

I shrugged again and cupped my belly as every set of eyes widened and fixed on my hand.

"What?" Callie whispered.

"Don't you dare play with my emotions," Evey said.

But as always, it was blunt Delilah who cut to the chase. "Abey, you knocked her up already?"

He narrowed his eyes at his sister, but a smile tugged at his lips. Abraham shrugged. "I guess so."

The room erupted in sound as every woman jumped up and hustled over to me. I was pulled into embrace after embrace as everyone kissed me and rubbed my belly. Tears were filling my eyes again, but I held them back.

"That's why you were so sick," Callie said softly from next to me. "I should have known."

Del scoffed. "You don't know everything, Callista."

"But I know most things, Delilah."

Del opened her mouth to retort when Nana yelled, "Girls!" and they both pressed their lips together.

Abraham's grandmother was the last one to pull me into her arms and I went willingly. When she backed away, she pinched both my cheeks. "I knew you were glowin'."

I gave her a smile. "You almost spilled the beans that day."

416

Nana laughed as Evey weaseled her way between me and Abraham. "Do you know how many you're havin' yet?"

"It's triplets," Abraham answered with the proudest smile I'd ever seen on him.

Evey's head turned to her brother before whipping back to me. "Triplets?" she whispered. I nodded, and she pulled me into another hug. "Oh my God. I get three nieces and nephews! This is the greatest day of my life."

I laughed at my dramatic future sister-in-law but couldn't remember ever feeling happier or more loved. This was what it meant to be a part of a family. This was what I'd been missing my whole life.

I pulled away from Evey. "So, can you do it? Can you plan the ceremony in a month?"

She raised an eyebrow at me and placed a hand on her narrow hip. "Well, I'd like a little more time, but I think I can make it work. I have half the thing planned already."

Of course she did.

I wrapped my arms around her shoulders and squeezed. "Thanks, Evey. You're the best!"

She hugged me back. "Yeah, yeah. Just take care of my nieces and nephews and we'll call it even."

When I pulled away, Abraham wrapped an arm around my shoulders. "I plan to make sure of that," he said, his tone leaving no room for argument. He shot his eldest sister a look. "Bea, that means no more training with El. She's not allowed to shift except on the full moon."

Beatrice's eyes widened almost comically as she looked from him to me and back again. "You're kidding."

I shrugged. "That's what the doctor said. Apparently shifting is hard on the body and I need to take it easy. I guess we'll just have to wait until the babies get here."

She shook her head sadly. "That's gonna suck for you."

Nana slapped her on the arm. "None of that out of you. A pregnancy is a gift and you'll treat it as such."

417

Beatrice looked properly chastised, and I had to hold back a laugh. I didn't think I'd ever seen someone put her in her place like that. That would have been even better to see back when we were enemies but was still funny as hell.

"Nana, I was hoping this might convince you to move up here permanently," Abraham said, his hand squeezing my shoulder.

Nana looked between us and shrugged. "Oh, what do you two need with an old woman like me?"

"Nana, you know we all love you and want you around more. Now that you'll have great-grandbabies that need you, how can you say no?"

I had to bite my lip to hide my smile. Abraham was laying it on a little thick, but if it worked, it worked, right?

Nana pursed her lips. "I don't know, Abey. What help can I be?"

"Well, you know we'll need your help on the full moon. We have Ms. Elsie, but three babies will be a lot for her to handle on her own."

I frowned up at my fiancé. "Why do we need help on the full moon?"

He smiled and shook his head. "El, what happens when we have to shift, and the babies are left alone?"

The ramifications raced through my head as I gasped. "Holy shit! What are we going to do with the babies when we all have to shift?!"

Of course, we could stand watch in their room, but what if one had to eat? What if they needed a diaper change? What if they were sick and up all night? What if they didn't want to go to bed before the moon rose? What if–

"El, calm down. That's why we have pack elders."

I frowned at him again. "What do you mean?"

Nana stepped in to explain. "When you get as old as me, you don't have to shift every full moon."

My frown deepened. "I thought every wolf had to shift no matter what."

Everyone in the room shook their heads. "What would happen to all the children of the pack then?" Callie asked.

I threw my hands in the air. "That's why I'm freaking out!"

Abraham chuckled and pulled me closer. "Don't worry, baby. It's the elders' job to take care of all those too young to shift whenever there's a full moon."

"But why don't old people—"

Nana cleared her throat loudly, and I shot her an apologetic smile.

"But why don't elder werewolves need to shift?"

Callie spoke up again, "It isn't feasible for elder werewolves to shift every full moon. Like Doc Monroe said, it's stressful on your body. Now imagine how frail an older werewolf might get. It makes sense that the urge to shift lessens with age."

"Callista, I'm gonna let that one slide, but I don't wanna hear you usin' the word *frail* to describe me again," Nana said with a raised brow in her direction.

Callie's face reddened, and she immediately backtracked. "I didn't mean *you*, Nana. We all know you'll be shifting for years to come. I meant wolves that are much older than you."

"Uh huh," Nana said, her blue eyes still fixed on the middle McCoy.

"So, what do you think, Nana?" Abraham interrupted. "Will you move up here with us? We'll really need your help in a few months."

Nana pursed her lips and met every eager eye in the room. Finally, she sighed. "I guess I can't expect Ms. Elsie to be the only one watchin' after the pups. Besides, if I'm up here, I can make sure Ellie's eatin' right."

Abraham's big smile spread across his face. "So, you'll move here?"

Nana's grin matched her grandson's. "I'll start packin' as soon as I get home."

Chapter 48

The next week flew by.

Between my duties as alpha, my work with The Asheville Initiative, and how tired the babies were making me, I was lucky to make it to eight p.m. before I was dead on my feet.

Abraham, though, was a saint. He took care of me in every way imaginable and some I would never have thought of. Every night I got a foot rub, and every morning I woke to him talking to the babies through my stomach.

The first Monday back to work after he found out I was pregnant was difficult, though. He wanted me to stay home where he could watch over me and make sure I wasn't overworking myself. Both Callie and I had to talk him down and eventually he agreed, although reluctantly. I had to promise to check in with him often and leave work if I got too sick.

It would have felt overbearing if I didn't know it came from such a genuine, loving place.

"Are you ready for breakfast, baby?" he asked from behind me.

I was in our large bathroom, smoothing my hair into a simple ponytail. I might have done something more elaborate at my old job, but not only was that not expected of me here, I couldn't be bothered.

Although I was only about eight weeks, the babies were kicking my butt.

I was so tired all the time, and yet I found myself waking every few hours throughout the night. The morning sickness, or *all damn day sickness* as I called it, was still as strong as ever.

Katie tried to eat a tuna fish sandwich in her office down the hall earlier in the week and I threw up for an hour. After that, we had to ban smelly sandwiches from the office. I would have felt bad if I hadn't almost turned my organs inside out with how sick I got that day.

I smiled at my fiancé. "Yeah, I'm ready. I'm starving."

He chuckled and wrapped an arm around my shoulders. "You're always starving."

I just shrugged. He wasn't wrong.

Before I became a werewolf, I barely thought about food. It was something I did whenever I had time and, occasionally, I'd spring for a favorite takeout option.

As soon as I was bitten, my hunger had increased, but it was nothing compared to now. I needed to eat about every three hours, or not only would I get nauseous, I'd also get dizzy. I made sure to walk around with granola bars in my pockets just in case hunger struck when I wasn't able to sit down for a full meal.

We arrived in the kitchen to a mostly empty room. I'd been getting Abraham to take me to work earlier than usual lately. I liked getting there before everyone else because, often, the morning sickness was worse late in the afternoon and I had to leave early. For whatever reason, I felt best in the morning and tried to be the most productive then.

We greeted Ms. Elsie who heaped an extra serving of eggs onto my plate before shooting me a wink. I smiled back at her, not complaining about the extra food. I knew I'd eat it all.

We'd told the pack about my pregnancy shortly after telling the McCoys. I hadn't expected the great outpouring of love and affection, but I'd received it in spades. Since that day, I hadn't been able to go a whole twenty-four hours without a pack member or two checking up on me. I didn't mind in the least. It felt good to have that many people care for me after being alone for so many years of my life.

I wondered how much of their excitement stemmed from my pregnancy alone, and how much from their own ability to have children now.

Since I'd found out I was pregnant, a conversation I'd had with Abraham at the first pack barbecue kept spiraling through my mind.

He'd said no member of a pack would have children before their alpha. I'd asked if it was some weird wolfy rule of theirs and he'd explained it all had to do with stability. A pack is only as stable as their alpha, and if the alpha isn't having children, it sends a message to everyone else. Once the alphas felt safe enough to reproduce, that meant the rest of the pack would too.

I wondered how many other couples would turn up pregnant in the coming months.

Predictably, the news of my pregnancy hadn't been received well by everyone. The one person I noticed looking less than thrilled was Paul, Peyton's brother, and his mate, Annalise.

I didn't fully trust him, and I knew I never would. He was Peyton's twin brother, and I'd had a hand in getting her kicked out of the pack. No matter what he told Abraham, I was sure he held a grudge against me. Knowing that, I kept an extra watchful eye on him whenever I could.

There were a few surprises that came with our announcement as well. Most noticeably was Craig. After almost everyone had hugged me, kissed me, and rubbed my belly, the old pack mechanic had sought me out. I'd been wary initially, but that faded with the first words that fell from his lips.

"I wanna thank you," he'd said.

When all I'd been able to do was frown at him quizzically, he'd chuckled and shook his head.

"I know that probably sounds weird comin' from me, but I wanted to let you know I appreciate you steppin' in with Abraham the other day. He probably would've just killed me if you hadn't."

I'd opened my mouth to tell him he was wrong but shut it just as quickly. With the way Abraham had been acting that day, I wouldn't have put murder past him.

Craig reached up and stroked his frizzy gray beard. "I know we got off to a rocky start, but I wanna let you know there are no hard feelings on my part. I wasn't doin' right by this pack and you called me on my shit. I didn't want to listen, but you were right."

My jaw practically hit the ground, and he chuckled again.

"Yeah, I know. You probably never expected me to apologize and that would make two of us, but you deserve it, and I'm sorry for everything I said to you. I hope we can have a clean slate goin' forward."

Tears welled in my eyes and I'd tried to will them away. Now was not the time to turn into a blubbering mess. I'd walked forward and wrapped my arms around Craig, taking the old man by surprise. He'd huffed out a surprised breath before squeezing me back. When I'd pulled away, there was a huge smile on his face.

"We can absolutely start fresh," I'd told him.

His smile grew even wider. "That's real good to hear. And I'm happy for you and Abraham. You two are gonna make great parents and we're all gonna be here to help you."

This time, there was no taming the tears as one raced down my face. Craig's expression turned horrified and I couldn't help laughing, although it was a bit watery.

I'd wiped at my eyes and shook my head. "Don't worry about these." I'd waved at my teary eyes. "This happens all the time now. Can't seem to turn the damn things off."

I'd hoped my joke would lighten the mood some, but he still looked incredibly uncomfortable. Deciding to let him off easy, I'd patted him on the shoulder and said, "I better go find Abraham before he sends a search party for me."

Craig's face filled with relief and I'd had to hide a giggle. It seemed all men were the same. Big and tough until they saw a tear and then they ran scared.

"Something wrong with your eggs, baby?"

I snapped back to reality and turned to look at Abraham. Concern was clouding his beautiful blue eyes, and I shook my head.

"No. Sorry. I was just lost in thought."

He grunted and pointed at my plate. "Then get to eating. You need at least an extra thousand calories a day."

I just barely stopped myself from rolling my eyes. Someone had been set loose in the bookstore and almost bought out the entire pregnancy section. He probably knew more about motherhood than me.

I did as he asked though, because I really was hungry, and I wanted us to get on the road soon. The rest of breakfast passed quickly, and I finished everything on my plate which satisfied my fiancé.

We handed off our dishes and Abraham led me out to his truck. Abraham's phone went off and I let my mind drift as he talked to whoever was on the other line. When he hung up, he squeezed my hand to get my attention.

"Wyatt got held up with his mom this morning so he's going to meet us there in a little while."

I shrugged. "I'll be fine."

He frowned and shook his head. "I'll be waiting with you until he arrives."

I shrugged and let it go. I knew my safety wasn't something he would compromise on and it honestly wasn't worth the argument. When we got to his truck, he opened the passenger door for me.

I turned to get in the massive vehicle when his hands landed on my hips. His hard chest pressed against my back and my insides instantly heated.

"I was thinking of stopping by for lunch today," he whispered in my ear before kissing the side of my neck.

I shivered in his embrace. "I love when you come for lunch," I said, my voice breathy.

Abraham pressed even closer to me, his erection hard and straining against my back. "It's *you* who's going to be coming for lunch."

A smile tugged at my lips as liquid heat pooled between my legs. I wasn't sure if it was the pregnancy hormones running wild in my system, but it felt like I could never get enough of him. Don't get me wrong, my need for Abraham was strong as hell before, but now it was almost ridiculous. I could barely go a few hours without thoughts of when we'd get to be together again crowding my head.

It was the best kind of distraction.

I spun in his arms and trailed my hands up his chest. "I can't wait."

He growled softly and leaned down to nip the tender skin of my neck. "We need to stop now or I'm going to fuck you in this truck."

I shrugged again. "That doesn't sound like a threat to me."

He surged forward again and gripped the back of my neck, tilting my head toward him. "If you'll behave long enough for me to get you in this truck, I can race us to your office and make you come twice before anyone else arrives."

My stomach flipped deep inside me as I nodded quickly. "I like that plan."

He smirked down at me before capturing my lips in a searing kiss. When we finally pulled away, we were both breathless, and I was needier than ever. I spun around and hopped onto the seat before he could say another word.

When I turned and found him still standing there, I snapped my fingers in front of his dazed eyes. "Chop chop, McCoy. Let's get this show on the road."

He shook his head and shot me a devastating smile. "Yes ma'am," he said before shutting my door and walking around the truck to his side. I divided my time between fastening my seat belt and watching the way he moved. He was so powerful, so sure of himself. It made the ache between my legs even stronger.

When he got into the truck, I was practically panting. "How fast can you get us there?"

He shot me a wink and fired up the engine. "I'll hurry, but I'm not willing to risk you or our babies' safety." I groaned, but he picked up my hand and kissed the back of it. "I promise to make it worth it."

I grunted. "You better."

He laughed and threw the truck into drive.

The trip to my office felt longer than usual and I knew he could smell my arousal from across the cab. His jaw ticked with the strain and his knuckles were white where they gripped the steering wheel.

Thankfully, he found a spot right outside my building. He slammed the truck into park, and I unbuckled myself as quickly as I could. I slid off the leather seat and he was already there to catch me.

425

His hands were tight on my hips as he pulled me hard against his chest, but it would never be hard enough. Close enough.

I knew I'd always want this man as desperately as I wanted him right then.

He gripped my hand and began tugging me toward the door.

"What about my things?" I asked breathlessly.

He didn't even pause. "I'll get them later."

I shrugged and picked up the pace. He wouldn't hear a complaint out of me.

When we got to my building, I handed him my keys, and he unlocked it before holding the door open for me.

"Ladies first."

I shot him a smile and preceded him into the office.

And that was when all hell broke loose.

Something hard tackled me from the side, sending me across the lobby like a rag doll.

"Elizabeth!" Abraham roared.

I crashed into a wall, my head taking the brunt of the impact. Confusion swamped me as I tried to figure out what was happening and why.

Whatever hit me was still on top of me and I struggled beneath the heavy weight.

"Just sit still, bitch."

I froze for a fraction of a second before I started bucking wildly. I still didn't know what was going on or what was happening, but I knew I needed to get out from underneath whoever was on top of me.

Their big hands reached up to circle my throat, and I thrashed harder.

My body itched to shift, but I held back. I knew I wasn't supposed to, but in human form, I was useless. I decided to try to fight back a little longer before I gave into my wolf's desire to be set free.

"Just… stay… still," the person panted above me.

There was something in my eyes and I couldn't see who my attacker was, but it sounded like a man and he felt a lot bigger than me. I scratched at his hands and kicked at every fleshy part I could reach.

I didn't know where Abraham was, but I could hear the sounds of another fight going on nearby and I hoped he got to me soon. I was doing everything I could not to shift, but in a few more moments, I wouldn't have a choice.

The room felt like it was spinning as my blurry vision began to narrow. A ringing static sound was blaring in my ears and I knew I only had moments of consciousness left.

Suddenly, the weight on top of me disappeared, and I struggled to take in a deep enough breath. There were screams and snarls and tearing and snapping sounds coming from every corner of the room, but I was paralyzed where I was.

Finally, everything went dark as I lost the battle to stay awake.

Chapter 49

"Beatrice! I need you to get to The Asheville Initiative with Doc Monroe and whoever else you can round up. Now."

I blinked my eyes open as the room spun. I still couldn't see clearly, and I reached up to wipe at whatever was clouding them. I squinted down at my hand and saw it was covered in crimson blood. The sight made me queasy, and I squeezed my eyes shut so I wouldn't lose my breakfast.

Abraham was still yelling into his phone, but I tuned him out. I needed to figure out what happened and why as soon as possible. With great effort, I heaved my top half into a sitting position before big, gentle hands pressed me back down. My first instinct was to fight against them until his voice reached me.

"El, it's okay. It's just me. I want you to stay down until the doctor gets here."

I blinked up at Abraham, my vision still fuzzy. "What happened?"

I didn't need perfect vision to see his jaw tense and his lips purse. "There were three humans that attacked us when we came through the door." He shook his head before looking back down at me, his expression torn. "I'm sorry I didn't get to you sooner." He looked away, his jaw ticking with the strain. "I shouldn't have let you walk in first. This is all my fault."

I reached up to cup his face. "Hey. This is not your fault. Don't say that."

He leaned into my hand but shook his head. "I should have walked in first. I should have made sure it was safe for you."

It was my turn to shake my head. "You couldn't have known this would happen. Please, stop blaming yourself. You saved me."

He sighed. "Your life shouldn't have been in danger again." He pulled away from me and began pacing the lobby. "It's always you and it's bullshit." He spun to face me, his hands fisted at his sides. "I won't let something like this happen to you again."

I tried to sit up, but he was at my side almost immediately.

"I know you won't, Abraham. It's okay. I'm okay."

I said the words, but I didn't really know if they were true or not. Honestly, I would have said anything in that moment to get the haunted look off his face. I tried to assess my injuries, but my head was pounding, and I could barely think straight. I was glad Kyle was on his way. I knew neither Abraham nor I would relax until we knew the babies were okay.

"Holy shit. What happened here?"

Abraham spun around, his body crouched over me in a protective stance. I stretched my neck to look around his big form and found Matt standing in the doorway, his eyes wide as they assessed the room.

"Get the hell out of here," Abraham snarled.

Matt apparently didn't have the best survival instincts, because he walked farther into the office as his head whipped back and forth. "What happened?" he repeated.

Abraham growled, and I reached out to place a hand on his back. Matt wasn't a real threat, and he needed to tone it down.

"We were attacked," I said simply. "We're waiting for the authorities to show up. You should probably leave," I suggested, hoping he'd take a hint and get lost.

His bright green eyes widened even further when he caught sight of me. He took a couple steps forward, but something in Abraham's gaze must have changed his mind because he stopped short in the middle of the lobby.

"Ellie, what happened to you?"

"She was attacked, Miller. Didn't you hear her the first time? Now, get the hell out of here."

Matt shook his head and wrung his hands together. "I hope this doesn't have anything to do with your cousin."

Abraham's shoulders tensed further as I struggled to see around him.

"I don't have a cousin," I said.

Matt's eyes widened further. "She said she was your cousin. Why would she lie?"

I had a bad feeling about this.

"What was her name?" Abraham grunted.

"I don't remember! We only talked for a couple minutes and then she was gone."

Abraham took a menacing step forward, and I was seriously starting to worry about Matt's future wellbeing.

"What did she look like?" I asked.

Matt shook his head and met my eyes. "Pale, dark hair, dark eyes. She had a really high-pitched voice too."

I closed my eyes as the blood in my veins began to simmer. "Peyton," I growled softly so only Abraham would hear. "That wasn't my cousin," I said loud enough to include Matt.

"This is all my fault," he muttered. Too bad for him, he was in a room with two werewolves that would have heard him even if he'd whispered.

Abraham took another step forward. "What do you mean this is your fault? What did you do?" he spat.

Matt's eyes darted from Abraham to me and back again. Finally, they settled on me. "She stopped me outside the office last week when I was heading to my car. She said she and your uncle wanted to talk to you about your wedding, but you weren't answering their calls. She said you were making a huge mistake, and she needed to talk to you before you went through with it."

Abraham's whole body froze as my breath got caught in my lungs.

Oh, shit.

"And what? You thought you'd help them keep her from me?" Abraham snapped. "What was in this for you, Miller? Thought you'd be there to pick up the pieces when I was gone?"

Matt shrugged, and I squeezed my eyes closed. If that man got out of here in one piece, it would be a miracle.

Abraham growled and took another step toward Matt. I knew I needed to wrap this up and get him out of the office before Abraham tore him apart like he had the other three humans who'd dared to cross him today.

"Matt, what did you tell her?" I asked.

Matt's eyes met mine again, their green depths swimming with remorse. "She asked when the best time would be to get you alone, so she could talk to you, and I told her you'd been coming into work early lately."

"Did you let her in, too?" Abraham snarled.

Matt shook his head fast. "Of course not."

"Of course not," Abraham mocked him. "It was enough that you told her just when Elizabeth would be alone and most vulnerable." He fisted his hands so tight I could hear his knuckles grinding. "What if I hadn't been here with her, Miller? They would have killed her and that would have been on *you*. I suggest you get out of my sight before you end up like the other men in this room."

Matt's wide green eyes looked around at the carnage again and his Adam's apple bobbed. "Are they d-dead?"

Abraham snarled. "Well, they're not napping."

"Matt, you should go. You don't need to get caught up with the police."

His eyes met mine again. "You've already called the police?"

I nodded, although I knew that was a lie. I wasn't sure what Abraham was going to do about the situation, but I knew he'd be talking to his enforcers before he did anything.

"Please," I said. "Just go."

"Yeah, you've done enough," Abraham spat.

Matt swallowed harshly again before nodding, and without another word, he left the office, closing the door behind him. It was only shut for a moment though before Beatrice, Wyatt, Wes, and Doc Monroe came spilling through.

Beatrice's icy blue eyes assessed the room carefully before landing on me. She winced and grabbed Kyle's arm, pointing in my direction. The doctor raced across the room, and soon I had him on one side of me and Abraham on the other.

"What happened here?" Kyle asked.

I opened my mouth to answer, but Abraham beat me to it.

"One of them tackled her into the wall. She hit her head, but I don't know what else happened because I was busy with the other guy." His remorseful eyes met mine, and I gave him a soft smile.

I knew there would be no way to keep him from blaming himself, but that wouldn't stop me from trying.

"I hit my head and then he tried to strangle me, but he didn't get too far before Abraham pulled him off."

My fiancé squeezed my hand almost hard enough to hurt. "Why didn't you shift, El? You know you're more powerful as a wolf."

I shrugged, the action pulling at my sore throat muscles. "I was trying to hold off for the babies."

Abraham swallowed harshly and shook his head. He picked up my hand and pressed his lips to the back of it. "But, El, you could have died."

I shrugged. "I would have shifted eventually," I said, but even as the words fell from my lips, I knew they weren't entirely truthful. My vision had darkened, and I knew I was seconds from losing consciousness and I still hadn't shifted. Apparently, my desire to protect my unborn children was stronger than my self-preservation.

"Abraham, give me some space. I promise I'll give you a full update as soon as I have more information," Kyle said.

He looked like he was going to argue with the doctor, but he finally nodded and got up to join the other werewolves.

With more room to work, Kyle got started examining me. He shone a light in my eyes and poked and prodded as I worked to remain calm. Finally, I couldn't wait anymore, and I asked him the only question that mattered.

"Are the babies going to be okay?"

Kyle pursed his lips as he continued his examination. "You aren't experiencing any cramping, are you?"

I shook my head quickly.

"Well, it looks like your head took the brunt of the impact, but I won't know more until we get you back and do another ultrasound. I'm positive you have a concussion though, so regardless, you're going to have to take it easy for a day or two."

I shook my head. "I don't care. The only thing that matters is the babies. I need to make sure they're okay."

Kyle sighed and nodded. "I suspected you'd say that. It should be safe to move you, so let's get you back to my house and find out, okay?" I moved to get up, but he placed a hand on my shoulder. "Slowly, Ellie."

I nodded and did as he asked, using his support to crawl to my feet. When I was upright, I got my first good look at the lobby and winced. Poor Callie would have to close the office for the day again, so they could get the place cleaned up.

Abraham must have seen me get to my feet because he broke away from the other enforcers and hurried to my side. "What's going on? Is she okay?"

Doc Monroe placed a hand on Abraham's shoulder. "She has a bad concussion, but I'm pretty sure everything else is okay. We're taking her back to my place, so we can do an ultrasound to check on the babies."

Abraham nodded once and wrapped an arm around my waist. "I'll drive. Let's go."

He called out a few commands to the other werewolves as he walked me slowly out the door and to his truck. It amazed me how different our attitudes had been when he'd parked his truck to now as we got back into it. Was it only thirty minutes ago that I was looking forward to a quickie with my fiancé? Now, I was fisting my hands and hoping like hell my babies were all okay.

Abraham drove even faster back to pack lands than he had to get to the office. He passed the lodge, heading straight to Doc Monroe's house before hopping out of the truck and racing around to my side. He wrenched my door open, and I'd just gotten my belt unbuckled when he scooped me into his arms and carried me up their drive.

"I can walk," I told him.

He shook his head. "Don't fight me on this right now," he grumbled.

Sensing how close to the edge he was, I let this one go. Doc Monroe raced ahead and opened the door for us, and Abraham whisked me inside and directly to the examination room.

Abraham helped me undress and, soon, Doreen was there, a worried look on her face. I tried to remind myself that she was just as anxious as I was to find out if the babies were okay. That her expression didn't mean she already knew to expect bad news.

Despite the reassurances I kept repeating to myself over and over, I gripped Abraham's hand hard as Doreen fired up the machine.

When the overlapping thumping sounds of multiple heartbeats rang out in the room, my nose immediately burned with tears.

"I'm still seeing three heartbeats here," Doreen said.

My body deflated onto the exam table as the worry I'd tried to keep at bay fled my system. My babies' hearts were still beating. They were okay.

"Does everything else look good?" Abraham asked, his hand still gripping mine.

Doreen nodded as she moved the wand around inside me. "I don't see any issues at all. There are still three healthy babies in there. You two have nothing to worry about."

The tears I'd been trying to hold back now raced down my face. Abraham tried to catch them with his rough fingers, but there were too many for him. I met his anxious blue gaze and smiled.

"They're okay," I whispered.

A big breath gusted out of him before he pressed his forehead to mine. "I know, baby. You're all going to be okay."

After that, Doc Monroe came in to clean up the cut on my head before sending me off with strict instructions to stay in bed at least until tomorrow. I had no doubt I'd be following his instructions no matter what. Abraham wouldn't hear of anything less.

He drove us back to the lodge and insisted on carrying me up to our room where he gently placed me on the bed. He then turned to our dressers and pulled out a comfy t-shirt and shorts for me. With slow gentle hands, he undressed and redressed me with all the care in the world.

When I was dressed and beneath the covers, he leaned over and placed a soft kiss on my lips. "I'm so sorry, baby," he murmured against my mouth.

I pulled away and frowned at him. "For what?"

He sighed and turned his head. "I never should have let you go in first. I don't know what I was thinking."

"You were being a gentleman, Abraham. There's nothing wrong with that."

He shook his head, his jaw tensing. "It should have been me they got to first. I should have been the one on the front line. I shouldn't have ever let you walk into somewhere before me."

I reached up and cupped his jaw with my hand. "Please, don't blame yourself for this. It wasn't your fault."

He nodded, but I knew my words weren't penetrating. He felt like he'd failed me and I knew nothing I could say would change that idea in his head. I just had to hope that time would eventually erase those thoughts.

"I don't want you going back there," he said.

I rolled my eyes. "Abraham, we're not doing this again."

He shook his head again and pulled away from me. "Bad things only happen to you when you leave pack lands. How can you expect me to be okay with you going back there?"

I pulled myself into a sitting position and had to close my eyes for a moment while the room spun. When everything was still again, I opened them and speared him with a look. "You promised not to do this. I'm not giving up my job, Abraham. That isn't an option that's on the table right now."

He ran his fingers through his hair and tugged on the ends as he paced away from the bed. When he spun back around, the expression on his face was so lost, my heart ached. "What can I do then? How can I keep you safe?" His voice was as broken as the look in his eyes and my hands itched to hold him.

"We'll come up with a compromise. That's how this works, remember?"

He watched me silently for a moment before nodding. "A compromise. What kind of compromise?"

I yawned and shrugged. "I'm sure you'll come up with something."

He sighed and crossed the room to the bed where he pulled the covers up to my chin. "Get some sleep, baby. I'll wake you up in a couple hours and we can talk more then."

I nodded as another yawn escaped my lips. "As long as we're clear I'm not quitting my job."

He sighed. "Yes, we're clear."

I smiled as he kissed my lips again and left the room. I knew it wasn't easy for him to rein himself in like that. Knew it about killed him to know I'd be leaving pack lands again as soon as I was cleared by the doctor, but he was trying and that was all I could ask for.

Chapter 50

I didn't know how long I'd been asleep, but when my phone rang from somewhere in the room, I crawled out of the bed to find it. Abraham must have brought my things up while I'd been passed out because my purse and briefcase were on the couch along the wall. Before I was able to pull out my phone, it rang again, but this time with a text message.

I pulled out my cell and clicked on the message.

Evey: Hey, can you talk for a sec? I have some ceremony questions for you.

I stifled a yawn as I tapped out a response.

Me: I'm in my room. Just come in.

I crossed the room to climb back in the massive bed when my phone went off again.

Evey: What are you doing home???

I nestled into my pillows and began to draft a response when someone came through the outer door and wasted no time whipping open the interior one. Evey stood there, phone in her hand and a worried expression on her face.

"What the hell, Ellie? Are you okay?"

I shrugged and put my phone on the nightstand. "I've been better."

She crossed the room to sit at the end of the bed. "What happened? Are the babies okay?"

I knew this wouldn't go over well, but it was better she heard it from me than someone else. So, I launched into the story of my awful morning, purposely keeping the parts about me and Abraham vague. I knew werewolves were pretty open about sexuality, but that didn't mean his sister needed to know the details.

By the time I was done explaining, Evey had crawled up next to me on the bed, her hand gripping mine.

"Why doesn't anyone tell me this stuff?" she complained. I could hear the tears in her voice, though, and knew she'd rather focus on something small than the repercussions of the bigger picture.

I squeezed her hand and shot her a lopsided smile. "I thought there were no secrets in a pack."

She snorted and then sniffed, looking away from me. "That's what I thought, too." She took a deep breath before meeting my eyes again. "So, you think it was Peyton and Conrad behind the attack?"

I shrugged. "That's how it seems. I don't know why they're going after me, though. I mean, I get why Peyton would be holding a grudge, but what did I do to Conrad? He has no reason to want me dead."

Evey shook her head, her eyes sad. "He's tryin' to get to Abraham by hurtin' you."

I frowned and shifted in bed so I could see her better. "That's what Abraham said about the first incident we had at The Asheville Initiative. I didn't think he'd go this far, though. I didn't think he'd try to kill me."

Evey sighed and squeezed my hand harder. "If his end goal is to take Abraham out, it makes sense that he'd try to do it by gettin' to you."

The repercussions spun through my head as we lay there quietly. I hadn't really understood what kind of threat we were up against until then. I didn't know this game we were playing with the Charlotte pack could have such deadly consequences.

"You're really okay, though? And the babies? They're good too?" she asked softly from beside me.

I turned to give her a reassuring smile. "The babies are fine. We heard their heartbeats and everything. And don't worry about me. I've got a headache, but I'll be fine."

Evey shook her head. "I'll always worry about you just as much as my nieces and nephews. You're just as important to me and I'm just as unwillin' to lose you. Never forget that."

My nose burned with tears that I desperately tried to sniff back. I knew how Evey felt about me because it was the same way I felt about her, but there was something about hearing it said out loud that messed with my insides. Or maybe it was the pregnancy hormones. Honestly, it was probably a mixture of the two.

I sighed and squeezed her hand. "We're all okay, so there's no need to worry."

She didn't look convinced, but she let it go.

"What did you want to talk to me about, anyway?" I asked.

She shook her head. "It's really not important. After everythin' you went through today, the ceremony guest list is the last thing you need to be worryin' about."

I frowned. "What about the guest list?"

She sighed again and looked away. "Well, I know this is a werewolf ceremony, but we could keep it more human-like if you wanted to invite people from your old life."

It only took me a moment to answer her. "There's no one in my old life I'd want to come to my wedding."

She arched a brow. "Not even your parents?"

My stomach sank as the thought of them entered my head. I hadn't talked to them in months, which wasn't unusual, but I knew they'd eventually reach out. Or a member of their staff would. They always did, even if it was only once a year.

I sighed. "I don't want them there, either. They've never cared about me and they have no place in my new life."

Evey shook her head, her eyes sad. "Why don't you think about it for a little while? This isn't somethin' you can take back."

I shrugged and relaxed back onto my pillow. I'd do what she asked and think about it, but I didn't see that my answer would change anytime soon.

My parents hadn't been a part of any aspect of my life for so long. From the moment they kicked me out of their house and shipped me off to boarding school, I'd been on my own. They usually remembered to call me on my birthday, but not always. I'd called them on theirs for years before I realized it made no difference to them. I was little more than a responsibility they were happy to have off their hands. I didn't see that changing, either.

We lay there quietly, hand in hand, for a long time as the sun rose high on the other side of the sheer blinds. I didn't know how long it'd been before we heard heavy footsteps in the hall that led right to the bedroom door.

When Abraham poked his head into the room, the lines around his eyes lessened as soon as he saw me awake on the bed. "Hey, baby. I was just coming to wake you up."

I nodded. "Yeah, I've been awake for a while."

He frowned at his youngest sister. "I hope you weren't the one to wake her up."

Technically, it was her call that had done the trick, but he didn't need to know that.

"I texted her to come in here," I told him.

He didn't look entirely convinced, but he dropped it. "Evey, do you think you could give me a couple minutes alone with my mate?"

She wrapped an arm around my waist and gave me a gentle squeeze before sliding off the bed. "Sure thing, Abey." I thought she was going to leave the room, but when she got closer to her brother, she stopped short and placed a hand on her hip. "Next time my sister-in-law is hurt like this, I better find out sooner."

He sighed. "Sorry, Evey. It's been a long day."

She was quiet for a moment before she launched herself into his arms. He caught her with an *oomf* as the smallest McCoy wrapped him in what I was sure was a surprisingly tight embrace.

"I'm worried about you, too," she murmured into his chest. "I want you to keep yourself, my sister-in-law, and my nieces and nephews safe, you hear me?"

She leaned back to spear him with a look, and he smiled down at her. "I will. I promise."

She released him and nodded once. "That's what I like to hear."

With that, she flitted from the room, closing both doors behind her.

Abraham turned to me with a crooked smile on his face. "I always forget how strong she is."

I chuckled. "The littlest ones are often the mightiest."

He shook his head, a smile still ghosting across his lips. He covered the distance between us and sat next to me on the bed. "How are you feeling?"

I shrugged. "My head hurts, but I'm fine."

His lips thinned as his eyes scanned my face. "You're sure? I can have Kyle back up here in minutes."

I reached out for his hand. "I promise. I'm fine. If you could grab me some Tylenol, I'll be even better."

I'd barely finished my sentence before he hopped up from the bed and raced to the bathroom. He came back in with a bottle of pills and a glass of water. I sat up with his assistance and swallowed a couple tablets before relaxing back onto the bed.

"Is there anything else I can get you?"

"Not right now. I just wanna know what happened at The Asheville Initiative after we left."

He sighed and placed the glass of water on the nightstand. "What do you want to know?"

"Everything."

He shot me a small smile and shook his head. "Typical," he muttered. He leaned back on the bed and turned his head toward the windows. "Wes, Wyatt, and Bea took the humans out to the woods. The plan was to make it look like an animal attack and leave them for the authorities to find."

I swallowed harshly as the repercussions of this morning sped through my head.

What if the authorities found evidence that led to the pack?

What if they found something that linked Abraham to their murders?

"I can hear your mind whirling from here," he said.

I looked up and met his denim blue gaze. "Is that enough? Will they be able to track their deaths to you?"

He shrugged, but I could see the worry he was trying to hide in the lines around his eyes. "We should be good. Those humans smelled of heavy amounts of drugs. That coupled with the animal bites they'll be found with and the authorities should think they'd gone on a binge that ended badly. I don't want you to worry about this."

I shot him a look. "Of course I'm going to worry. Maybe you should have called the police right then. It was self-defense, right?"

He shook his head. "And how would I explain killing three men by myself? And what kind of motive would they find? It's not like we could tell them we're in the middle of a dispute between two werewolf packs."

He was right. I knew he was right. But that didn't stop me from worrying.

"How will we know if they bought the story?"

He sighed and looked down at his lap. "In the past, we'd have Paul keep an eye out for us."

"But you don't trust him anymore either, do you?"

He looked up at me and I could see the answer clear in his eyes. "No. I don't. Not with this. I don't have any proof he's not loyal to this pack anymore, but I'm not willing to risk it. We'll just have to wait and see."

I let out a deep breath and relaxed back onto the pillows. "I guess there's nothing else we can do, is there?"

He picked up my hand and brought it to his mouth. "Please don't worry about this, baby. It's handled. You just concentrate on yourself and our babies and I'll take care of everything else."

I turned my hand to cup his face, his stubble rough beneath my fingertips. My love for him filled my whole body from top to bottom as I looked in his eyes. I knew he'd do anything it took to protect us and that he always would. His devotion was something I never needed to question.

"What did Evey want, anyway?" he asked.

And just like that, the warm feelings that had been coursing through my system fled just as quickly.

I sighed. "She was asking about the wedding guest list."

"What about it?"

"More specifically, who I wanted to invite."

He frowned. "Like friends and family?"

I shrugged. "I guess."

"What did you tell her?"

"That there's no one from my old life I want to be there."

His frown deepened. "Not even your parents?"

"Especially not my parents."

He was quiet for a moment before speaking up again. "Are you sure, baby? We won't get another mating ceremony. This is your only chance to include them in our lives."

I laughed humorlessly. "That's pretty much what Evey said."

"Because family is important to us."

I shook my head. "Family was never important to me until I met yours."

His features turned sad, and I wished I could take the words back, but they were already out there.

He squeezed my hand again. "Maybe you should talk to them. Give them one more chance to be in your life. That way you can say you tried."

I pursed my lips as I thought over his request.

Was he right? Would I regret not including my parents in my wedding?

What about the babies? Was I ready to include them in that?

Didn't I want my children to grow up with grandparents? Because Abraham's parents were gone. We had Nana, of course, but that was it. Did my children deserve the chance to meet their only living grandparents?

I sighed and grabbed my phone from the nightstand before scrolling through my contacts.

"What are you doing?" he asked.

I sighed again. "I'm going to call them."

"Really?" I didn't have to look up to know his smile was spread across his face.

I just barely held back a third sigh. "Yes, really. But I'm only doing this for the babies. And I don't think it'll work. My parents have never cared about anything having to do with me unless it negatively impacted them. I don't expect that to be any different now."

"It doesn't hurt to try, baby."

"Famous last words," I muttered as I hit dial and held the phone against my ear.

It rang and rang and just when I thought it was going to go to voicemail, my mother answered.

"Yes?"

"Hello, Mother. It's Elizabeth."

"I know. I have caller ID."

I took a deep breath and squeezed my eyes closed. I could do this. I could give this one more try for my babies. That was all I had to do. Just one more try.

"I was hoping we could all get together sometime soon. Maybe have dinner."

"Why?"

Abraham jerked backward, and I shot him a look. He wasn't used to the callousness my parents dished out, but I was. This barely fazed me.

"It's been a while since we've seen each other, and a lot has happened in my life. I wanted to share some of that with you."

She was silent for so long that I pulled the phone away from my ear to check the call was still connected. Finally, she released a deep breath that rustled through the phone line like a gale force wind.

"I suppose that could be arranged. When were you thinking of coming?"

Of course, I'd have to come to them. It was out of the question that they'd go out of their way for me.

I squeezed my eyes closed again and took a deep breath. "How about this weekend? We can be there on Saturday around five?"

"Who is we?"

I opened my eyes and shot Abraham a look. I hadn't cleared this with him first, but if I had to deal with them, he was going to be right there with me.

"My boyfriend, Abraham, will be coming with me."

She sighed again, and I heard the clacking of her heels on the other end. "Fine. I suppose that's all right. We'll see you at five. Don't be late."

With that, she hung up. No goodbye. No see you soon. And of course, no I love you. I don't remember ever hearing those words come from either of my parents' mouths.

I tossed the phone aside and looked up at Abraham. "Happy?"

His lips were pressed into a thin white line. "Why did you call me your boyfriend and not your fiancé?"

I let out a deep breath and crawled out of the bed. "Because I didn't feel like getting into that with her on the phone. We'll tell them at dinner that we're getting married." I turned around and muttered, "Which should be *so* much fun."

I threw on a sweatshirt and headed for the door.

"Where are you going?" he called.

"Downstairs to eat. I'm starving."

He chuckled as he caught up to me and grabbed my hand. "Of course you are."

Chapter 51

"Baby, stop fidgeting."

I sighed and pulled my fingers away from the hem of my dress. I'd been smoothing it out for so long that it was practically wrinkling beneath my hands. I looked down at myself and cringed. I was about two and a half months pregnant, and even though that was still pretty early, there were three babies in me, and they were beginning to show. I'd picked the dress that covered me the most, but I had a feeling it wouldn't matter.

"Sorry," I muttered.

He reached over and picked up my hand before bringing it to his lips. "Don't be. What are you so nervous about, anyway?"

I sighed again. "I don't know. We have a lot to tell them and I'm worried about their reactions. They're not like normal parents, Abraham."

He shrugged and put my hand in his lap before grasping the wheel again to make a turn. "You've gone this far in your life without them, so it's clear you don't need them. You're being the bigger person by giving them one more chance to be a part of our future. If it doesn't work out, then you're not really losing anything, are you?"

When he put it like that, it made so much sense.

I had lived so long without them and done just fine. More than fine. And besides, I had the McCoys now, and they were more family than anyone could ever ask for. I didn't need my parents, but deep down inside, I knew I wanted them. I wanted what Abraham had when he was growing up. A loving mom and dad who did anything they could to support their children.

Maybe my parents would see how much they'd missed in my life and want to be a part of it.

Maybe the idea of being grandparents would snap them out of their uncaring daze.

Maybe they'd hear I was getting married and want to be involved.

Or maybe I was delusional, and this would be a disaster.

"You're fidgeting again."

I looked down at my hands and found them tugging at my dress once more, so I folded them in my lap. Hopefully, if I clasped them tight enough, they'd stop betraying my anxiety and stay still.

While I'd had almost a week to worry about this dinner, thankfully it had been uneventful. There'd been no more attacks, and we hadn't heard from or seen Peyton, Conrad, or any of the Charlotte pack.

I'd been surprised by Abraham, though. After we'd been attacked, and he'd suggested I quit my job, I thought I'd get more of an argument from him. But, true to his word, he found a compromise we could both live with.

Abraham had a state-of-the-art security system installed in The Asheville Initiative practically overnight. That building was locked up tighter than Fort Knox. He'd also insisted on not only driving me and Wyatt to work every day, but one of them always entered the building first and checked every nook and cranny before I was allowed inside.

Honestly, after what happened, I wasn't complaining. In the past, I might have griped about Abraham being overprotective, but those days were gone. It was clear I had a target on my back, and I was in danger. And it wasn't just me now. I had three little lives to think about too, and I took that very seriously.

So, I sat back and waited patiently while Abraham performed his security checks every morning, thankful I had a fiancé and father of my children who cared so much about our safety. Thankful that he wouldn't let anything bad happen to us.

"Turn down this street," I instructed as the butterflies in my stomach took flight.

We were on my parents block now and there was no stemming my anxiety. I tried taking deep breaths, knowing that stress wasn't good for the babies, but it was no use. I wouldn't be able to relax until we were back in the truck and heading home.

"It's this one," I said, my voice weaker than I'd intended. I cleared my throat and tried again. "Just park on the street. They wouldn't like you parking in their driveway."

He frowned but did as I asked. "How come?"

I sighed. "They think that any vehicle that isn't luxury is bound to leak oil on their custom cobblestone driveway."

Abraham laughed. "You're kidding, right?"

"I wish."

His laughter died as he shook his head. "Tonight is going to suck, isn't it?"

I shrugged. "It'll be a lot better with you there."

His smile was soft when he turned to me again. "All right, baby. Let's get this over with."

He slid from his seat and hurried to my side to help me out. I hoped my parents were watching this display of chivalry because I knew Abraham would need all the brownie points he could get.

He laced his fingers with mine as we slowly made our way to the front door of the massive home. Its size rivaled the lodge. The difference was, the lodge housed a dozen or more people, and this monstrosity was for only two and a small handful of employees.

When we reached the door, I took a deep breath and rang the doorbell. We didn't have to wait long before it swung open and I was greeted by one of my favorite people.

"Ms. Elizabeth?"

"Hi, Tracy. It's so good to see you."

The elderly housekeeper shot a look over both shoulders before she wrapped her arms around me. I dropped Abraham's hand, so I could properly greet one of the women who'd raised me. Her hugs were some of the only ones I'd had growing up, but she was always careful to not do it in front of my mother.

Regina Montgomery didn't believe in displays of affection and would have been horrified to find the help with their arms wrapped around her daughter.

When I pulled away, Tracy's eyes were wet, but her smile was wide. I turned to Abraham and pulled him up next to me.

"Tracy, this is my fiancé, Abraham. Abraham, this is one of the women who raised me, Tracy."

Abraham held out a hand, his smile bright. "It's a pleasure to meet you."

Tracy shook his hand, her eyes widening. "You've been holding out on us, Ms. Elizabeth."

My cheeks heated, but the corner of my lips twitched with a smile. "You know why I haven't been by."

Tracy's smile fell as she shot another look over her shoulder. When she turned back, her expression was serious. "Can't say I blame you, dear."

"Tracy!"

The shrill sound of my mother's voice cut through the air like a knife. The poor housekeeper straightened up immediately, her expression transforming back into the cool professionalism she wore around my parents.

"Yes, ma'am."

"Has Elizabeth arrived yet? She's late."

I rolled my eyes and pulled Abraham through the door. "I'm right here."

My mother's clacking heels preceded her into the foyer. The rest of her was as impeccably dressed as always and I just barely resisted the urge to tug at my dress again.

"There you are. You're late."

I sighed and glanced at the ornate golden clock hanging on the wall. "Mother, it's five-oh-one."

She nodded. "Exactly. You're late."

I just barely repressed another sigh and decided to drop it. It wasn't like it would change anything if I kept arguing. That was a lesson I wished I'd learned in my teenage years. It would have made living in this house much more bearable.

"Tracy, go inform Mr. Montgomery that we're convening in the formal dining room."

The housekeeper nodded and took off through the house.

Now that we were left alone with my mother, the urge to fidget was stronger than ever.

"Are you going to introduce me to your... friend?" she asked.

I winced at her description of him, but let it go. We'd only just gotten through the door. I wasn't trying to start anything so soon.

I tugged on Abraham's hand until he was standing next to me. "Mother, this is Abraham. Abraham, this is my mother, Regina Montgomery."

He stepped forward and held out a hand to my mother. "It's a pleasure to meet you, Mrs. Montgomery."

My mother eyed his hand like she would a plague-infested rat. Finally, she let out a deep breath and placed her dainty hand in his for the briefest moment. When she pulled it back, she wiped her palm on her skirt and my blood instantly began to boil.

"Abraham, do you have a last name?"

"It's McCoy, ma'am."

She narrowed her eyes at him, her gaze traveling from his plain black button-down shirt, to the dark jeans he had on, and finally to his feet which were, as always, in his work boots. When her gaze landed on his footwear, I knew the first of the night's embarrassments was upon us.

"I hope you don't intend to track dirt across my marble floors. I just had them waxed."

"Mother!"

She turned wide, brown eyes my way. "Do you know how expensive it is to wax all these floors?"

I shook my head, my hands already trembling with my emotions. I needed to lock it down because shifting in front of my uptight parents was something I'd never be able to take back. They'd probably have me locked up, or shot, daughter or not.

"Abraham isn't going to track dirt across your precious floors. Can we please just go to the dining room?"

She gave him one more scathing look before she turned her attention to me. Her dark brows furrowed as her gaze traveled up and down my body. "Have you gained weight?"

No preamble. No attempt to deliver the question with tact or civility. Just a crude comment meant to wound.

I tipped my chin up. I knew I'd gained a bit of weight with the pregnancy and I refused to be ashamed of that. "A little."

She tsked and shook her head. "Have you been exercising?"

My chin dipped a fraction of an inch. "Well, no. Not lately."

She shook her head again. "You were always such a lazy girl. More content to read a book than to work on your figure. It's no wonder you're gaining weight."

The words, although I'd heard them a hundred times before, still had the power to sting. Not as much as they once did, but enough to feel them burrow under my skin.

Abraham stepped up next to me and wrapped an arm around my waist. "She's perfect the way she is," he said.

I wanted to thank him for his support, but feared he'd just turned her attention and negativity back onto himself.

She eyed him critically for another moment before pursing her lips. "Yes, well, I wouldn't say she's *perfect* by any stretch of the imagination." She turned back to me. "Just don't let your weight get out of control. You know you don't wear extra pounds well."

I grit my teeth and just barely stopped my eyes from rolling. Abraham's arm tightened around me and I knew he was seconds from

452

speaking up again when she spun around and started across the foyer. She didn't say anything else. She didn't invite us to follow, it was just expected.

I grabbed Abraham's hand again and whispered, "I'm sorry."

He looked down at me with a soft smile and shrugged. "Don't worry, she doesn't scare me. But I'm not going to let her talk about you like that again."

"I'm fine. This isn't anything I haven't heard before," I muttered as I dragged him across the foyer toward the dining room. I knew he wasn't happy with that, but I hoped he'd let it go.

Fighting with the Montgomerys wouldn't get him anywhere. Those people were stuck up and set in their ways. That was why I hadn't wanted to come. I knew what they were like and I knew nothing I could do would change that. Somehow, the McCoys had convinced me that all family was important. It was becoming more and more clear that they weren't right. Only some family was important. And some family was better left in your past.

When we made it to the dining room, I was first struck by how different it was from the one we sometimes ate in at the lodge. Instead of a homey feeling, filled with boisterous laughter and loud talking, the room was quiet and austere. It wasn't a place where a family gathered to eat, it was simply another show of their wealth. A room meant only to impress.

There were two place settings on one side of the table that I assumed were for Abraham and me, so I dragged him over and we took our seats. He made sure to hold my chair out for me like he always did, but I was sure his good manners were wasted on my parents. I didn't think they cared one way or the other about how I was treated as long as it didn't make them look bad. Appearances mattered over everything else to Bill and Regina Montgomery.

My mother was already seated across from us, and a few moments later, my father walked in the room. I stood to greet him as he walked around the table.

"Hello, Father."

He turned bleary brown eyes my way. "Elizabeth. How are you?"

I shrugged. "I'm doing well, thanks. How are you?"

This stilted conversation was typical between us. We were nothing more than strangers who shared DNA.

He took his seat at the head of the table and leaned back in the chair, his belly just a bit bigger than I remembered it. "The firm is doing well. We just got a new high-profile case that's set to make us a lot of money."

I hadn't asked how his business was doing, but it was clear what was important to him. It had been the same when I was growing up. The few times a week I actually saw him, all he would talk about was his work.

He surprised me this time, though, by asking about mine.

"How are things going over at Hildebrandt & Moore?"

I pursed my lips as I sat and placed my linen napkin on my lap. "I've actually left that firm."

He turned his red face toward me, his bushy eyebrows furrowing. "Oh? Got a better offer somewhere? You know I could always find you a spot at my firm."

That was one instance where my father had actually cared enough to help. Ever since I enrolled in law school, he'd been offering me a position with his firm. I'd resolutely declined back then, knowing I needed to get as far away from my parents as possible and never regretted the decision.

"Actually, I'm already working with a new company out in Asheville."

Both my parents frowned in my direction.

"Asheville?" my mother asked, the disdain clear in her voice. "Why would you want to work all the way out in the mountains?"

I shrugged a shoulder. "Well, I moved out there a couple months ago and found a position with a great new company."

The silence in the room was deafening.

"You moved to *Asheville*?" my mother asked, her voice as icy as her gaze.

"Yep."

454

I knew it would annoy them that I didn't speak properly, but I was already past caring.

"Why would you move to Asheville?" my father chimed in.

I glanced at Abraham who looked interested in what I had to say, too.

"Well, that's where Abraham and his family live. I moved in with him."

Their gazes jumped from me to him and back again and I clasped my hands under the table to stop from fidgeting.

"You moved out to the country for a man? What were you thinking?" my mother asked, her voice dripping with icicles.

Here it was.

It was time to dole out one of the things I'd come to tell them. I'd hoped we'd be able to have a course or two of dinner before I had to drop a bomb on them, but things don't always work out the way you think they will.

I cleared my throat. "Well, we're getting married, so it only makes sense that I'd move out there to be with him."

The silence was so deafening, it was like someone hit the mute button.

As my parents digested the information I'd handed them, I turned to Abraham. He had a twinkle in his eyes, and if I wasn't mistaken, it seemed like he was enjoying their discomfort. I shot him a small smile and turned back toward my parents. This was just the first of the revelations, and by the time we were done, I knew their heads would be spinning.

I couldn't wait.

Chapter 52

"You're getting *married*? To *him*?" my mother snapped.

I grit my teeth and pulled my lips into something resembling a smile. "Sure am."

"But why?" she asked as if she truly couldn't fathom a reason for our courtship.

I rolled my eyes and grabbed a fancy dinner roll from the center of the table. It had been a while since my last meal and my stomach was growling for me to fill it. Despite the tense conversation at the table, I was going to sneak a few bites while I could.

"Well, Mother, we're in love."

She scoffed and picked up her glass of red wine. "You're in love? How long have you even known this man?"

I shrugged as I slathered a bit of butter on the warm roll. This was an instance where I could lie, and they wouldn't know any better. If I wanted, I could make this news a little easier for them to swallow and tell them we'd been dating for a while.

But I was past caring about their opinions, so I told the truth.

I turned to Abraham. "What's it been? About four months?"

His lips twitched with a smile but somehow, he held back. "About that."

I turned back to my mother. "About four months."

Her mouth opened and closed over and over like a gasping fish left to die on land. "You are getting married to a man after only knowing him for four months? What are you thinking?"

I shrugged again and took a bite of my roll before answering her. "I'm thinking I'm in love and I want to get married. Especially before the babies come."

My newest revelation was met with another silence so thick I felt it trickle along my skin.

I really hadn't expected to give them the news that way. I thought I could ease them into the information gently. Give it to them piece by piece and hopefully lessen the shock of it all.

But I'd changed my mind.

Maybe it happened when my mother insulted my fiancé by assuming he'd track dirt across her fancy marble floors.

Maybe it was when she so graciously pointed out that I'd gained weight.

Maybe it was just years and years of this crap that had built up in my system until I finally couldn't take it any longer.

Whatever it was, the outcome remained the same.

I'd just told my parents I was pregnant and getting married within five minutes of sitting down to dinner. That must have been a record of some sort.

"You're *pregnant*?" my mother hissed.

I looked at Abraham and smiled wide. He returned the gesture before I turned back to her. "Yep."

My mother's mouth opened again as if she had something to say before she snapped it closed. Her eyes darted around the room as if she thought more unexpected news might ooze out of the walls to surprise her. She picked up her wine glass with a shaking hand and took a long sip. When she set the glass back down, she turned to my father. "Bill, what do you have to say about all this?"

My red-faced father was probably a good five scotches into his typical night of drinking and I wasn't sure he even heard what I'd said. But then he surprised me by shaking his head and sighing. "I can't believe she left Hildebrandt & Moore to work at some country bumpkin firm. What were you thinking, Elizabeth?"

My eyes rolled to the ceiling without my permission.

Then another thought came to me. If I was already giving my mother heart palpitations, why not bother my father just as much?

"Actually, I'm not working for a firm in Asheville. I signed on with an environmental agency and I'm doing legal work for them."

His bloodshot eyes widened. "You're practicing *environmental* law?"

My smile widened as I hammered the final nail into the coffin. "Yep. At a non-profit, too."

Abraham snickered from beside me, but I knew I would be the only one able to hear him. I was glad he was enjoying dinner as much as I was. Which was a whole hell of a lot.

"A *non-profit*? Elizabeth, have you lost your mind? What about all I've taught you? What about that expensive law degree we paid for from Duke? You're just throwing that all away?"

I shook my head. "No, Dad. I'm using that degree to make a positive difference in the world. I'm using it for something greater than helping criminals get away with crimes they should be held accountable for. I'm doing something worthwhile with my degree and my life for once."

He opened his mouth to argue again, his face getting redder and redder by the minute, but my mother interrupted.

"Oh, Bill, shut up about the job. Who the hell cares where she's working? Our only daughter is knocked up by some hillbilly blue-collar worker from the sticks and all you can think about is what kind of law she's practicing?!"

I didn't realize my hands were shaking until the butter knife between my fingers started rattling against the fine china plate in front of me.

"Don't talk about him that way," I warned her.

She rolled her dark brown eyes. "Elizabeth, how do you think this will look for us? We groomed you to marry someone worthy of a Montgomery. Someone with a family of importance. Someone that will further our reputation in the community. Instead, you ran off and jumped in bed with the first average Joe who knocked on your door? This is ridiculous!"

My hands were shaking harder than ever, so I set the knife down before I did something stupid. Abraham's warm palm landed on my back and I drew strength from his presence.

I took a deep breath and leveled my mother with a look. "He is who I want, and he is who I'm marrying. Deal with it."

Her eyes widened in her pinched face. "How dare you speak to me like that!"

"How dare you speak about *him* like that!"

She laughed once, hard and loud. "You don't even know this man."

"I know him well enough to know he's what I want."

My mother rolled her eyes. "You've only known him a few months! What could you possibly know about the man?"

I narrowed my eyes at her. "I know he's the best man I've ever known. I know there's nothing he wouldn't do to make sure I was happy and safe. I know he loves me and always will. And I know all that is a hell of a lot more than I can say for either of *you*."

"Elizabeth, don't talk to your mother that way," my father piped up from next to me.

We both ignored him.

"If you marry that man, you'll be making the biggest mistake of your life. If you have his children, you'll be stuck with him forever. You can't be that far along. There's still time to take care of this problem."

My mother had just suggested I call off my wedding and abort my children all in one breath.

With that, I knew I'd had enough. There was nothing here for me and I was an idiot to think I could change their minds. My parents were who they were and nothing I said or did would make a difference to them.

I rose to my feet and Abraham stood up next to me. Calmly, I placed my napkin on my still-empty ornate plate and leveled both my parents with a look.

"The only mistake I've made was coming here. You're both awful people who deserve each other and this cold, miserable house. I thought I would give you both one last chance to be in my life, to be in my children's lives, but I see now that was a mistake. I wouldn't want you within a hundred feet of my children. You're both toxic and I'm done with letting you poison me."

I grabbed Abraham's hand and spun around, ready to leave my parents and this terrible place behind me. It held nothing but bad memories and regrets, and I didn't need any of it.

"If you go through with this, you won't be welcome here anymore. If you walk out that door, we'll both be done with you," my mother warned from behind me.

I looked over my shoulder and gave her a smile. "Sounds like a plan."

With that, I calmly walked through the house I grew up in for the last time, really seeing it for what it was.

A gilded prison.

And I'd just broken out for good.

Tracy was waiting by the door, her face somber and her shoulders hunched. I stopped and pulled her into my arms. "The only thing I'll miss about this place is you," I whispered against her salt and pepper hair.

I heard her sniff and a tiny piece of my heart broke in my chest. When I pulled away, Abraham was there next to me, holding out a business card to Tracy.

"My cell number is on there. Please, feel free to reach out to us anytime. We'd love to keep in touch."

My eyes watered as I looked up at the wonderful man I was about to marry. I knew choosing him would always be the right decision.

Tracy took the card he offered and slipped it into her pocket. She nodded at both of us and we turned to leave just as my mother screeched her name. Not wanting to linger any longer than necessary, I hurried toward the massive doors and tugged them open.

Stepping out of that house for the last time was freeing. It felt like I was shedding an old skin, relinquishing a part of me I'd held onto for all that time. A part of my past I thought I needed to take with me into my future. Now, I knew I didn't. Everything I could possibly need was right beside me.

Abraham held my hand tight as he led me down the cobblestone drive to his black truck. We'd only been in my parents' house for about a half an hour, but it seemed everything had changed in that time.

He helped me into his truck before finding his own seat and firing up the engine. He made a wide U-turn in the middle of the road and headed back toward the highway. We were all the way out in Raleigh, so we had a long trip ahead of us.

The first half of our drive was spent in mostly silence. I think we were both lost in thought over what happened. A million emotions were swirling inside me, but the one that kept swimming to the surface was embarrassment.

It wasn't that I had trouble believing my mother would think those things about Abraham, it was more shock over the fact she'd actually said them out loud. She usually had better manners than that, but she might have been hitting that red wine earlier than I'd thought.

"El, I'm sorry."

I turned wide eyes in his direction. "What do *you* have to be sorry about?"

He sighed and tightened his grip on the steering wheel. "It was my fault you subjected yourself to those people. You told me how awful they were, and I guess I didn't believe you. I should have just stayed out of it."

I reached across the seat and grabbed one of his hands, sandwiching it between my own. "It's me who needs to apologize. I'm so sorry for the things my mother said about you. None of them were true."

He squeezed my hand. "So, you don't think I'm some hillbilly blue-collar worker from the sticks?"

My stomach dropped to the soles of my feet until I saw he was smiling.

"I'm just kidding, baby. Don't worry about it."

I sighed and turned to look out my window. "No, I don't think those things about you. I know what you do and how successful you are at it. But it wouldn't matter to me if you weren't successful. I love you for who you are, not what you do or how much money you make. None of that matters to me."

He squeezed my hand again. "I know, baby. I love you too."

My insides warmed the smallest amount at his words. But the guilt was still sticking to me like a film I couldn't wash off.

"I really am sorry about what she said. She's usually more discreet with her opinions than that."

"You mean she thinks those things, but doesn't say them out loud?"

I chuckled. "Exactly."

He shook his head, a smile still on his face. "Really, don't worry about it. What she says doesn't matter. All I care about is how you think of me."

"I think you're the most amazing man I've ever known. I think I'm lucky to have ever met you, let alone get the opportunity to fall in love with you. I think the fact that I've earned the love of a man like you is one of the greatest accomplishments of my life."

He slowly turned his head toward me, his eyes wide and his lips parted. He watched me for a long moment before he turned his eyes back to the road and shook his head. "I don't know what I ever did to deserve you, El, but I'm gonna spend the rest of my life earning it."

We lapsed into a comfortable silence after that, his hand still clutched between mine. It seemed we'd said all that needed saying for the moment.

Although I was happy things were good between Abraham and me, my insides still churned with everything that happened with my parents. I felt restless and wished more than anything to shift into my wolf and go for a run. Because that wasn't an option, I had to settle for something else.

When we pulled up to the lodge and Abraham helped me out of the truck, I looked up at him and spoke for the first time in a while. "You head in. I want to go sit by the lake for a little while."

He pursed his lips and eyed me warily. "I'll send Wyatt to watch from the patio, okay?"

I wanted to sigh, but I held it in. At least I'd have some semblance of privacy. "Okay," I said softly.

He pulled me close and pressed his lips against mine before letting me go.

I made my way across the field behind the lodge and down the wooden dock. When I got to the edge, I kicked my shoes off and dipped my feet into the warm water. Even though it was dark, I had no trouble seeing the lake and the surrounding forest as well as I could during the day.

I willed it to quiet, but my mind continued to whirl. It pinged between anger at my parents, and longing for a mother and father who cared. What hurt most was how easily they'd dismissed my children. They weren't here yet, but I loved them fiercely and would protect them with my life. The fact that my mother had so callously suggested I abort them, simply so I wouldn't be tied to Abraham, stung in ways I hadn't anticipated.

Despite my best efforts, tears formed in my eyes and soon slid down my cheeks.

My children wouldn't grow up with grandparents. The ones that would have loved them were dead and the ones that were still alive didn't care about them. What kind of situation was I bringing them into? Would our love be enough?

The dock creaked behind me and I barely held back a sigh.

"I'm fine, Abraham. I'll be in soon."

Light footsteps continued down the dock and, this time, the sigh broke loose.

"Honestly, I'm okay," I said as I turned to face him.

But instead of my fiancé, I found the original werewolf, Will.

I hurried to wipe the moisture from my face, but I had a feeling I wasn't hiding anything from him.

"Granddaughter, what's wrong?"

I sniffed and shook my head. "Nothing, Will. Just had a long day."

He nodded, and although I was pretty sure he was old enough to take a hint, he continued down the dock and took a seat next to me. "I could smell your tears from across the field," he said softly.

I sniffed again, hoping to stem their flow, but they still leaked out of my eyes.

"Will you tell me what's wrong?" he asked.

I'd spent much less time with Will than I should have. Especially since I found out that I was his descendant. I really should have made more of an effort to get to know him. However, with the attack at The Asheville Initiative and the pregnancy, I just hadn't found time.

Here he was, though, caring enough to ask me what was wrong when it wasn't his responsibility to do anything about it. And despite my desire to keep it all locked inside me, something about the gentleness in his eyes made me want to confide in him.

I took a deep breath and looked back out toward the lake. "I met with my parents today and told them about my upcoming wedding and the babies, and they took it about as well as I thought they would."

"They weren't happy?"

I chuckled once, but it lacked humor. "No. They were pretty pissed, actually."

He hummed softly next to me but didn't say anything else.

"Maybe it was stupid, but I guess I thought maybe they'd want to be a part of this. That maybe they'd stop for a minute and see how happy I am. For the first time in as long as I can remember, I'm truly happy and content with my life. I thought there was a chance they'd be happy for me, but I was wrong."

"And that's what's making you so upset? The fact that they don't approve of your choices?"

I shrugged one shoulder. "I guess." Then I thought about it and shook my head. "Actually, no. That's not really what's upsetting me. I knew they wouldn't be happy. I knew they'd denounce all my choices just as easily as they always had. I think the hardest pill to swallow is that was the only family I had left. And that my children will have to grow up without grandparents now." The tears welled up in my eyes again and a few raced down my face. "I feel like I failed my babies already. Like my first role as a mother was to provide my children with a happy family that will love and support them, and I have nothing to show for that. No contribution from my side at all."

Will was silent for a while before he leaned over and nudged me with his shoulder. "*I'm* your family."

I froze in place. I think my heart even stopped beating for a second. I turned slowly toward Will to see him wearing a soft smile.

"What are you saying?" I asked.

He shrugged. "I'm saying you still have me, and I'll be happy to welcome your children into the world with you."

The tears were back and stronger than ever. "You want to be my babies' grandfather?" I asked, my voice barely above a whisper.

His smile widened. "I already am, aren't I?"

A small chuckle fell from my lips as I shook my head. "I guess you are, huh?"

He nodded. "I am." He said it with so much decisiveness, there was no room for argument.

Not that I wanted to.

"There haven't been many instances in my life when I've been able to stick around and be a part of my descendants' lives, and I'd like to change that with you. I'd like to be as much a part of your and your children's lives as you'll allow. You're my family and I'm yours if you'll let me."

The tears were falling so fast now, I could barely see Will's face anymore, but I knew if I could, it would be just as gentle as it always was. And he'd be just as real and offering just as much to me in this dark hour.

I didn't need to think about it. Didn't need to debate or run through my options. I knew my family and I would be lucky to have him. I also knew I'd wasted enough of my time with him, and that from here on out, I'd work harder to get to know him better.

Without thinking, I launched myself into his arms, squeezing him tight. He laughed and returned my embrace, his hold just as strong.

"I'd love that," I whispered.

Chapter 53

"Morning, baby."

I snuggled closer to Abraham's large, warm body and smiled against his skin. If I woke up every day to hear *morning, baby* in his gravelly, sleepy voice, I'd be able to die a happy woman.

"Morning," I murmured, my voice considerably less sexy than his, but he didn't seem to mind.

His hands curled around my bare shoulders, pulling me even closer to him. In that instant, I knew I'd made the right choice in putting my foot down and insisting we spend the night together.

Apparently, Evey had been researching human wedding traditions and found out that the bride and groom weren't supposed to spend the night before their wedding together. She'd spent at least thirty minutes lecturing me on bad luck and dark omens before she'd finally given up.

My defense was simple and hard to refute. Abraham and I were infinitely better together than we ever were apart, so why change that now?

She'd finally relented, but she'd grumbled the whole way down the hall. We only smiled at her antics and let her complain. She'd get over it soon enough. Besides, that was only a human custom, and I wasn't a human anymore.

Despite my status change to werewolf, Evey was doing her best to provide us a ceremony that blended the two cultures together. She wouldn't give me many details, but I knew she'd been working hard and steadily over the past couple of weeks to give us the best possible day. I had no doubt that the party planner extraordinaire would put together something better than I could ever have imagined.

"Are you ready for today?" Abraham asked softly, his voice breaking me out of my thoughts.

I looked up at him and smiled. "So ready."

A few months ago, the idea of having a mating ceremony with Abraham might have sent me running, but those days were behind me. Far, far behind me. I knew I was making the best decision of my life and nothing could stop me now.

Except of course, the threat that constantly dangled over our heads.

I squeezed Abraham tighter and voiced my concerns. "You don't think the Charlotte pack will try anything today, do you?"

He sighed and pulled me closer until I was draped across his chest. His thick fingers threaded through my hair and gently rubbed my scalp. "I don't know, baby. I hope not. I've done everything I can to prevent them from ruining this day for us. All the enforcers we have are running patrols, and we even got a few new ones from some of the coastal packs. No one will get within ten miles of us without someone knowing."

I swallowed his words and hoped they'd be enough to calm the nagging feeling in my gut. Something told me that Conrad was just waiting to take a piece of our happiness. And something even louder was telling me that Peyton would be the driving force behind it.

I had no doubt that she knew we were having a ceremony, and I was sure she even knew it was today. If there was a chance she could ruin it, I knew she would. That was why the feeling in the pit of my stomach wouldn't go away. I had a feeling it would stick around until the threat from the Charlotte pack was eliminated. Whenever that would be.

"Are you all packed?" Abraham asked.

I knew it was a thinly veiled attempt to change the subject, but I let him. It was our wedding day, and I didn't want to spoil it with what-ifs. We'd done enough worrying, and like Abraham said, we were as covered as we could be. I needed to do my best to relax and enjoy the day.

I looked up at him and quirked a brow. "Yes," I said, dragging out the word. "I'd still like to know where we're going, though."

He shook his head, his smile widening. "I told you it wasn't far, right?"

I rolled my eyes. "Yes, but that leaves pretty much all of the Blue Ridge Mountains." His smile widened, and I huffed out an exasperated breath. "That's really all I'm getting?"

He leaned down and kissed my forehead. "You'll find out tonight after the ceremony. Have some patience, baby."

I made a face and snuggled back into his chest. Patience was not one of my virtues and he was well aware of that fact.

He'd been hinting at the honeymoon he'd planned for weeks. He insisted it was his wedding gift to me and wanted to have full control over what we did and where we went. Since it seemed like such a big deal to him, I'd gone along with it. Now, though, I was anxiously anticipating finding out exactly where we were going.

"I got you something else, too," he murmured against my hair.

I turned to look at him again. "Oh?"

He shrugged. "It's kind of a hybrid gift. But, yeah, it's ready whenever you want to see it."

I crawled out of the bed as quickly as I could. "I'm ready now."

He chuckled and climbed off the mattress too. "How did I know you were gonna say that?"

I shrugged. "You know me well, McCoy."

He shook his head, the smile still spread across his face. "Get dressed and we can go see it."

I hurried over to the dresser and threw on the first clothes my hands landed on. When I was done, I spun around to find him still naked, his tanned skin so smooth my fingers itched to touch him.

"If you keep looking at me like that we aren't going anywhere," he muttered as he crossed the room to the dresser.

I bit my lip and turned away. Honestly, it was impossible to not look at him like that. The best I could do was not look at all.

A few minutes later, he grasped my hand and spun me around. "Come on, baby. Let's go see your present."

I smiled up at my fiancé and let him lead me through the sitting room and out into the hallway. I didn't know where we were going, but when he stopped at the door that used to be my bedroom when I visited Asheville, I frowned up at him.

"It's in here?"

He shrugged. "Go on in and see."

I turned back to the door and swung it wide open, eager to see what this mysterious gift was. But it wasn't just one thing, it was a whole room.

I stepped in cautiously as the tears gathered in my eyes.

Abraham had talked about making this room into an office for me, but I guess with the news of my pregnancy, he'd made other plans.

He'd turned my old bedroom into a nursery for our babies.

The walls were painted a soft gray, and lining them were three beautiful wooden cribs.

"Did you make those?" I asked, my voice soft and shaky with the tears I was trying to hold back.

He walked up behind me and wrapped his arms around my waist. "I did."

And that was all it took. The first of the tears went cascading down my face, and I didn't even bother to wipe them away. My head rotated back and forth as I took in the changing tables, baby swings, toys, and rocking chairs that he'd lovingly placed around the room.

It was all so perfect, my heart filled to capacity and overflowed as I tried to take it all in. Finally, when the tears were so plentiful that I couldn't see properly anymore, I spun in his arms and squeezed him as tight as I could.

"Do you like it?" he murmured in my ear.

I pulled away with a laugh. "I love it."

He smiled wide and reached up with both hands to wipe the tears from my face. "I'm glad, baby. All I want is for you to be happy."

If I thought my heart felt full before, it was nothing compared to now.

"I am, Abraham. I'm so happy."

His smile softened as he pulled me against his chest and gently rocked me back and forth.

"I feel like my gifts are pretty lame compared to yours," I muttered against his hard chest.

He pulled away and frowned down at me. "Don't say that. I'm sure they're great."

I shrugged. "I can give you one now and one later if you want."

A brilliant smile spread across his face as he nodded. "Sounds perfect."

I sniffed back my tears and took his hand. "Come on. It's upstairs."

He let me lead him up to the rooftop where I'd stashed his gift. I'd had to employ his sisters to help me take care of it for the past couple of weeks because I wasn't always able to get out from under Abraham's ever-present gaze.

I sat him down on one of the couches and clasped my hands together. "Close your eyes, and I'll go get it."

He did as I asked, and I scurried away to fetch his present. When I got back over to him, I set it on the coffee table and took a seat beside him.

I took a deep breath. "Okay, you can open them."

He blinked his beautiful blue eyes open and his gaze landed on the little potted tree I'd set before him. Turning to me with a quizzical smile he asked, "You got me a plant?"

I shrugged. "It's a tree, actually. A weeping willow to be exact."

He looked back at the pathetic looking twig with its half-dozen leaves and then back at me. "Thanks?"

I laughed, although it sounded more strained than I would have liked. "Let me explain," I said, and he turned back toward me. "This tree is about five months old, just like our relationship. I thought it would be a

471

nice idea for us to plant this guy next to the lake next spring and it can grow with us. Kind of a like a physical manifestation of our life together."

He blinked slowly and then turned back to the tree. When he'd been quiet for so long that my skin began to itch, I raced on. "It's not that big of a deal and if you hate it, I can bring it back. I just figured getting you something like a watch or a pair of cuff links would be kind of lame and that this had more symbolism to it. I can take it back, though," I repeated with a wince.

Finally, he turned toward me, his eyes wide with what looked like wonder. He scanned my face over and over before pulling me onto his lap.

"I love it," he said, his voice deep and rough with emotion.

I pulled back so I could see his face clearly. "Really?"

He shook his head. "It's perfect, baby, and so thoughtful. I'm just imagining sitting beneath it with our children someday, or hanging a swing from its branches when it's bigger." He looked down at me and cupped my face in his big hand. "I love this, and I love you so much for thinking of it. It's perfect."

I blew out a deep breath as my muscles relaxed. I hadn't realized how worried I'd been to give him his gift, but seeing how much he liked it, I felt so much better. He got it just like he got me, and I'd always be endlessly grateful for that.

"I had the same thoughts," I said softly. "I imagined our kids playing beneath it, or us reading to them in the shade. I think the idea of a swing is perfect."

His smile widened as he pulled me closer and rested his forehead against mine. "I'm so lucky to have you," he murmured.

The tears sprang up again, but I willed them away. "I love you," I said.

He squeezed me tighter. "I love you too, El."

We sat like that for a long time, his arms wrapped tightly around my body and my heart. I knew there was no way he was letting go of either for a long time.

But like it was prone to, my hungry stomach gurgled its displeasure at being left empty for so long and Abraham released me with a chuckle.

"Let's go take care of that."

I gave him a sheepish smile as he took my hand and led me to the stairs. "That's probably a good idea."

When we made it back to our floor, I made a pit stop in our room to throw on a bra. In my haste to see his present, I'd neglected to put one on, but I wasn't walking down to a crowded kitchen without one. Especially because my boobs had already grown what felt like a cup size since I got pregnant.

I was just shrugging my t-shirt back on when there was a knock on the sitting room door.

"Ellie! I need you out here!"

It was Evey, and I knew that meant her day filled with wedding preparations was about to begin.

We must not have answered quickly enough because she hollered through the doors again. "Don't make me come in there Birdbox-style, 'cause I will!"

I turned to Abraham, and we both laughed. "Your sister is crazy, isn't she?"

He shrugged. "If you didn't know that by now, you weren't paying very close attention."

"I heard that!" she yelled, and we laughed harder.

Abraham grabbed my hand and led me through the sitting room and out into the hallway. Evey was there, already dressed impeccably, although I knew she'd be changing before the ceremony.

Although she hadn't let me see my dress, I'd been allowed to see the bridesmaids' dresses already and knew they were stunning. If she did half as good a job at picking out my dress, I knew I had nothing to worry about.

Not that I was all that concerned, anyway. I was so ready to marry Abraham that I'd have done it in a burlap sack if I had to.

Evey grabbed my arm and went to drag me down the hallway. "Let's go," she said without preamble.

Abraham grabbed my other arm and halted her march. Thankfully, I was a werewolf, otherwise the tug of war between the siblings might have been painful.

"She's eating breakfast first, Evey."

My soon-to-be sister-in-law pursed her lips and looked me up and down. "I suppose that's all right."

Abraham scoffed and pulled on my arm until Evey let go. "Her health is more important than whatever you have planned, Evelyn."

Evey rolled her eyes. "I have a jam-packed day for her, and *you* aren't gonna mess that up." Abraham opened his mouth to argue with her some more when she went on, her voice louder and drowning his out, "Thankfully, I've allotted some extra time, so she's got thirty minutes for breakfast." She turned to me. "Think that'll be enough?"

I shrugged. "Should be."

Evey smiled in satisfaction. "Sounds good. Come up to my room as soon as you're done, and we can get started."

With that, she stormed off down the hall, her presence like a category five twister, except instead of leaving behind a wake of destruction, she left a path of preparation, order, and schedules behind her.

"What did I get myself into?" I muttered softly to Abraham.

Evey had just reached the stairs when she yelled back, "I heard that, too!"

Chapter 54

When I'd sufficiently stuffed myself with breakfast, Abraham offered to escort me to Evey's room where I was sure I'd be stuck for hours. We walked hand in hand like always, a comforting silence between us.

When we got to his youngest sister's door, he pulled me into his chest and dipped his nose to the crook of my neck. "I'm going to miss you."

I shook my head, but there was no stopping the smile from spreading across my lips. "You'll see me in just a few hours."

He sighed and pulled back far enough that I could see the brilliant blue of his eyes. "I know. I just feel like I've been waiting for this my whole life. I can't wait to officially make you mine."

Somehow, my smile widened further as my heart thumped hard in my chest. "I'm already yours, baby."

His eyes softened before he dipped back down to press a kiss on my lips. "I know. This is just a formality, but it's important to me."

"It's important to me, too, Abraham. I want to be bonded to you in every possible way."

His smile grew before he dipped his head again and pressed his lips against mine. The kiss was just starting to get heavy when Evey yelled from the other side of the door.

"Quit suckin' face out there and let Ellie come in here! Y'all will have plenty of time to roast the broomstick later!"

We pulled away with a laugh and a mutual shake of our heads.

"She's relentless," he whispered.

"What does *roast the broomstick* even mean?"

His eyebrows wiggled suggestively as he pulled me close again. "Want me to show you?"

I had to cover my mouth to suppress my laugh.

"Ellie get in here, you're already late!" Evey hollered through the door again.

Abraham sighed. "I'll see you in a few hours," he murmured against my lips.

I smiled. "I'll be the one racing down the aisle toward you."

He smiled against my mouth. "And I'll be the one standing there with a stupid smile on my face wondering how I talked the most amazing woman I've ever met into being my mate."

I pulled away so I could look into his handsome face when the door behind us whipped open.

"If you make her cry and get her face all red, I'll kill you myself, Abraham," Evey warned, her hands on her hips and her face leaving no room for argument.

My fiancé chuckled and pressed one more kiss to my forehead. "Yes, ma'am. I'm leaving now. No tears were shed."

Evey nodded once with satisfaction and stormed back into her room. I held onto Abraham's hand as long as I could as he walked away from me. It didn't feel right spending time away from him on our special day and I vowed that would be the last time I saw his back again any time soon.

With a sigh, I turned and trudged into Evey's room, ready to face whatever she had in store for me. To my surprise, there was a pair of middle-aged women in there I'd never met before. My first instinct was to be wary because I didn't know if they were werewolves or if we had to keep our true natures hidden while they were here.

Evey must have sensed my hesitation because she waved me over. "This is Linda and Lucy. They're here to give you your manicure, pedicure, and facial." When I still looked cautious, she added, "They're on loan from the Boone pack."

My shoulders dropped with relief as I hurried over to the women and held out my hand. "It's nice to meet you, ladies. Thanks for being here today."

They each shook my hand enthusiastically. "We're happy to be here, Ms. Ellie. If you'll just have a seat, we can get started."

And thus began my transformation.

I was scrubbed and scraped and polished and plucked until it felt like they'd revealed a new layer of skin. Just when I thought it was done, they'd bring out a new oil or ointment to rub into my skin. I'd never felt more pampered or fussed with in my life.

I could have done without half of that stuff, but I kept my complaints to myself. Evey was trying her hardest to give me the best possible wedding day, and I was going to be nothing but appreciative. On the outside, at least.

When the Boone werewolves finally finished with me, my chair was spun toward an eager-looking Evey.

"Now, it's my turn," she said, her words sounding ominous and the clink of the lash curler in her hand seemingly a warning of what was to come.

She dove into working on my make-up, her hands sure and swift as she puffed and powdered and shellacked all kinds of products onto my face. I'd thought I'd received the Evelyn McCoy treatment before, but it was nothing compared to what was happening today.

At some point, Del slipped into the room and got working on my hair. She brandished a curling iron like a sword, her quick fingers curling and draping strands of my blonde hair across my shoulders.

As usual, my gurgling stomach interrupted us, and I smiled sheepishly up at Evey. She just shook her head and continued to powder my cheeks. "We don't have time for that, Ellie."

Del tsked from behind me. "She's pregnant, Evelyn. She needs to eat."

Evey sighed and straightened up to shoot a glare at her older sister. "And she also needs to be dressed and downstairs in less than an hour."

Del huffed and picked up another lock of my hair to curl around her wand. "You're bein' a bit tyrant-y today, sister."

"Tyrant-y isn't a word, Delilah."

"Tyrant-y is the perfect word to describe *you* right now, Evelyn."

"It's my job to make sure–"

"Ladies!" I interrupted.

They both shut their mouths with a snap. "It's okay, I'll be fine until after the ceremony." My mouth said one thing, but my growling stomach said another.

Evey took a step back and shook her head. "No. Del's right. I can't starve a pregnant woman. I'll get someone to bring you up somethin'. That way, I can still work on the rest of you while you're eatin'."

I smiled up at my future sister-in-law. "Sounds perfect."

I knew this day was stressing her out, but none of it was affecting me. All I could feel was the raw anticipation swirling through my veins. I didn't care if my make-up wasn't spot-on, or my hair wasn't in the perfect up-do. All I cared about was promising myself to Abraham and spending the rest of the night on his arm.

Evey grabbed her phone from the vanity behind her and pressed a button before holding it to her ear. "Callie, I need you to get Ellie some food. Make sure she can eat it with a fork, got it? Thanks," she said and hung up. "She'll be up in a minute."

I reached out and grabbed Evey's free hand before she could begin to paint my face again. "Thanks, Evey. For everything. I know you put a lot of work into today and I know it's going to be amazing."

Her blue eyes, so much like her brother's, softened. "You're welcome, Ellie. I'm glad to do it."

We lapsed back into silence while both women worked on different sides of my head. Callie wandered in shortly after with a plate of pasta and a bottle of water. I thanked her and dug into the food like I hadn't just eaten a few hours ago. When I was done, Evey put the final touches on my face, including painting my lips before taking a step back to evaluate her work.

"I think you look perfect," she declared.

Callie and Del walked around to see me from Evey's position and both of their eyes widened. "You look stunning, Ellie," Callie said softly.

I felt my cheeks heat and was thankful Evey had smeared so much makeup on them.

"Thanks, ladies." I turned to Evey. "Do I get to see my dress now?"

Her eyes lit up before she tossed the make-up brush she'd been using onto her vanity and scurried away. She walked back over a few moments later with a big white garment bag. She had Del hold the top while she unzipped it and pulled the dress out for me to see.

My heart thundered as I looked upon the dress I'd be wearing as I married the man of my dreams.

It was a soft pink color with lacy straps at the top, and a twisted ruched bodice that would end right below my breasts and flow to the floor. I knew my little baby bump would pop out of the curtain of fabric and loved it even more.

"It's perfect," I whispered.

Evey's smile widened as she looked at the dress she'd picked out for me. "I know it's customary for the bride to wear white in human weddings, but at a werewolf ceremony, all the guests wear white and the bride wears somethin' colorful. I thought this was a nice mix of both."

"It's perfect," I said again, because really, there were no other words. I couldn't have picked a better dress if you'd given me a week in a bridal shop.

Evey nodded once and held out a hand to help me stand. "Let's get you in this so the rest of us can finish gettin' ready. We're due downstairs in thirty minutes."

The next half hour flew by as we all rushed around Evey's room putting on finishing touches and getting into our dresses. Beatrice showed up at one point, already dressed in her white bridesmaid's dress with her make-up and hair perfectly styled for the event. She helped the rest of us as we hurried to finish on time.

When we were done, we lined up single-file for our inspection. Evey walked past each of us, inspecting everything from our shoes to our hair before giving her nod of approval. "We're ready."

With that, we all grabbed our bouquets that Beatrice had brought in earlier and hustled down the stairs to the kitchen. I'd expected to find it empty, but there was one lone man standing there, his back to us.

"Will?"

The original werewolf turned around and gave me a soft smile. His eyes widened as he took me in. "Elizabeth, you're a vision."

I smiled back at the man who looked my age but who was technically my many times over great grandfather.

"What are you doing here? Why aren't you seated with the other guests?"

He shot a questioning look over my shoulder before fixing his brown eyes on me again. "Isn't it customary for the bride to be walked down the aisle?"

My eyes instantly watered, and I blinked to hold them back. If I ruined all the work Evey had put into my face, she'd kill me.

My future sister-in-law leaned in close and whispered, "Don't worry, everythin' is waterproof."

A watery chuckle fell from my lips as I crossed the room to stand at Will's side.

"Is this okay?" he asked, his dark eyes darting down to me. "I thought you knew."

I shook my head and willed the tears from my eyes. I didn't want to miss a second of this day. "No, I had no idea, but I'm so happy you're walking me down the aisle, Will. Thank you."

He shook his head and held out his bent arm for me. "The pleasure is mine, Granddaughter."

I wrapped my hand around his elbow as Evey hustled to the front of the room. "All right, everyone. It's showtime. Bea, you're up first, followed by Callie, Del, me, and then Will and Ellie. We're gonna take our time walkin' down the stairs and through the guests until we get to the altar. We'll line up in the order we walked in with Ellie right across from Abey. Anyone have any questions?"

When we all remained silent, she nodded once and turned to slide open the glass doors. "All right, Bea. Go on."

My first bridesmaid gracefully stepped through the door and we all watched silently as she made her way down the stairs. When she was at the bottom, Evey motioned for Callie and then Del. When it was Evey's turn, she looked back at me with a wide smile.

"See you down there, Ellie."

She turned to leave, and that left just me and Will there. We stepped up to the glass doors, and I got my first good look at the transformed backyard. If I'd thought there'd been a lot of foliage at the solstice celebration, I'd been sadly mistaken.

Flowers of all shapes and sizes in colors ranging from white to the palest pink hung from every structure while multiple vases stood around the clearing reaching well above the guests' heads. The aisle was strewn with pink and white rose petals that looked beautiful and whimsical, but my eyes sought only one thing.

Abraham stood at the end of the aisle in a khaki-colored suit that fit him like a glove. His dark hair was styled for a change, and even from where I stood, I could see the smile stretching across his tan face.

"Are you ready?" Will asked softly.

I nodded. "Absolutely."

Music began to play and the first few notes were lost to me until I caught on. It was an instrumental version of The Beatles song *I Want To Hold Your Hand*. That was the first song Abraham ever sang to me, and the memories of that night flooded my mind as tears flooded my eyes.

Will led us through the sliding glass doors and down the stairs. I lost sight of Abraham behind the swell of guests and willed my feet to not speed up so I could see him again. The whole pack was here, including wolves I recognized from the solstice celebration. There would be time to greet them later, though, after I got to my fiancé.

481

The man who I could soon call husband.

Or mate.

Depending on who you were.

Will glided me down the aisle and it felt like I floated instead of walked. When Abraham's large frame came back into view, he was sporting the smile he'd promised, and I was sure mine looked similar.

When we'd finally made it to the end, Will kissed me on the cheek and passed me over to Abraham who took my hand eagerly. After that, the original werewolf turned and took his place in front of us. It surprised me that it seemed he'd be officiating our ceremony, but it shouldn't have. Who else was more qualified for the job?

I looked into Abraham's ocean blue eyes and in them, I found my place. Where I'd always belong, where I'd always be wanted, and where I'd always be loved. It was right there beside him, and I swore then and there to never stray far.

Chapter 55

"Now, we've come to the portion of the ceremony where you'll each recite the promises you've written for each other. As you do, I'll be tying a ribbon around your clasped hands. This signifies the bond between you both and this ceremony that is binding you together."

Will grasped my hand as I looked up into my future husband's eyes.

"Abraham so much has changed in the little time we've known each other. I've moved, I've switched career paths, I've gotten pregnant, and last but not least, I turn into a giant werewolf every full moon."

There was a soft round of chuckles and I waited until they died down before I continued.

"But the one thing that's remained the same, the one constant in my life has been you. Your devotion, your loyalty, and even before I could put a name to it, your love has always been there with me. I know that tomorrow, none of that will have changed. Next week will be the same, and next year will be, too. Your love is the one constant thing I've had to fall back on in these past few months and it's what's gotten me through. I didn't know what I was looking for. Hell, I didn't even know I was looking for anything until I found you. When that happened, everything became crystal clear. I was made to love you and I want to spend every day of the rest of my life doing that. Now that I've found you, I'm never letting you go. I love you today, I'll love you tomorrow, and I'll love you until the day I die."

His dark blue eyes filled with tears as I looked up at him. He mouthed *I love you* and my heart soared. With a deep breath, he recited his promises to me.

"El, I've loved you from the moment I laid eyes on you. It was compulsory. The mating bond was so strong in that instant, there wasn't anything that could have kept me from you. I watched my parents and the fated mates magic between them and always knew how strong it could be. How life-changing. How all encompassing. I thought I knew what I was getting into, but nothing could have prepared me for you."

There was another round of quiet laughter that died down just as quickly. Abraham squeezed my hand and pressed on.

"What I never expected, though, was how much I'd grow to like you or how much I'd grow to respect you. I didn't imagine that when I found my fated mate that I'd also be finding my best friend. But that's what you are to me, El. You're the love of my life, my soul mate, the mother of my children, and the best friend I've ever had. I couldn't have imagined being fated to a woman more perfect for me than you. I'm so lucky I found you and I promise to treasure every second of our lives together. Today, we start our forever."

How he'd held back his tears I didn't know, because mine flowed freely down my face. I sent out a quick mental thank you to Evey for painting my face in waterproof make-up because I was really putting it to the test.

Abraham's eyes held mine in their tight hold as every word he'd said to me flashed in their depths. I knew every syllable came from the deepest places of his soul and he meant every bit of it. He'd said he was lucky, but in that instance, I knew I was luckier.

Will cleared his throat softly, but my eyes were still riveted to Abraham's.

"You two may now seal your union with a kiss."

Thank goodness.

I reached up and wrapped my free arm around Abraham's neck, pulling him down to my lips as fast as I could. He chuckled softly against my mouth before our kiss intensified and all humor was lost.

I ran my fingers through his silky hair as he held me tightly against his body. I could have stayed there like that for the rest of the night, but Abraham dug up some self-control from somewhere and eventually pulled us apart.

When he noticed the disgruntled look on my face, he laughed and kissed my lips once more before whispering in my ear. "There'll be more time for that later, Mrs. McCoy."

The sound of my new name sent a thrill through my veins.

This was a new start for me with my new family. I didn't have to carry around the burden of being a Montgomery anymore. There were no more expectations for me to live up to, no more rules I had to abide by. I was finally free of my family, and at the same time, thrust into a new and wonderful one. A family that accepted me and loved me for who I was, not what I did or how well I did it.

The feeling of release wasn't something I expected, but I reveled in it as I was inundated with hugs and kisses from my new family. When we'd made it through them all, and with our hands still bound, Abraham and I walked back up the aisle, our smiles the widest they'd ever been.

I wasn't sure where we were going because we hadn't practiced what happened after the ceremony, but apparently Abraham had a clue, so I followed him. He led us back up the stairs to the sliding glass doors and into the kitchen where he finally came to a stop.

With slow, gentle movements, he untied our hands and pocketed the ribbon.

"I don't need a piece of string to know how deeply we're bound," he said, his voice rough with emotion. When he looked back up at me, his eyes were the bluest I'd ever seen them. "You're in my bones, El. In my soul."

My heart thundered in my chest so violently, it felt like it would burst through my ribcage. I stepped into his space and wrapped my arms around his neck. His lips hovered over mine, the anticipation building between us until it was almost a tangible thing.

"You look so beautiful, baby. I've never seen anything so stunning," he murmured against my mouth.

I smiled and pressed my lips against his for a moment before pulling back. "When I saw you standing at the end of that aisle, you took my breath away," I admitted.

His hands tightened around my hips before he pulled me harder against his chest and claimed my mouth. Although we'd kissed hundreds of times before, there was something different about this one. It felt deeper, truer, more real than any other. It dug deep inside me until it felt like we were just two halves of the same piece. Like we'd never be whole without the other.

When we finally pulled away, we were both breathless, but smiling. I couldn't ever remember being so happy in my life. The threats we faced, and the uncertainty of tomorrow, were pushed aside as the joy of finally being married to Abraham engulfed my system.

"We should probably get back out there before Evey comes looking for us," Abraham said as he tucked a stray lock of hair behind my ear.

I pressed my face into his hand until his rough palm cupped my cheek. "If we must." I sighed.

He chuckled and reached up to curve his other hand around my face. "We have this whole weekend to be alone, baby. Just you and me."

I smiled up at him. "That sounds perfect."

He kissed me once more, but this one was quick before he grasped my hand and led me back out onto the patio.

"There you are! Get down here, we're takin' pictures!" Evey yelled from below.

Abraham squeezed my hand and leaned down to whisper in my ear. "Just a few more hours."

I took a deep breath and nodded. I could get through a few more hours of this. Knowing having Abraham all to myself was the prize at the end of this night was enough motivation for me.

The next couple of hours flew by as we took pictures and greeted our guests one by one. Every werewolf had well wishes for us and our future children and I felt my heart fill more and more with each person we spoke to. When it seemed like we'd greeted hundreds of people, Evey came and found us.

"It's almost time for your first dance. Head on over to the big tent."

She was the boss for the day, so we did what she said. As soon as we were both on the dance floor, the rest of the guests cleared the space for us, and the music began to play. I recognized the opening notes as that Ed Sheeran song Abraham sang for me at the solstice party and I looked up at him with a smile.

"I love this song."

486

The words were barely out of my mouth before I realized something else. It wasn't Ed Sheeran's voice I was hearing, it was my husband's.

I whipped my head back in his direction and frowned up at him. "Is this you?"

He shrugged, his lips tipping into a smile.

I shook my head as I listened to Abraham's deep, powerful voice play through the speakers. He picked up my hand and drew me closer to his body. I looked back up at him in wonder.

"When did you do this?"

He shrugged as he wrapped a hand around my waist and started swaying our bodies to the beat. "Del set up some studio time for me a couple weeks ago. I thought it would be a nice surprise for you. Do you like it?"

I shook my head, the smile still plastered to my face. "I love it."

His smile widened as he pulled me closer and I lost myself in the song and movement of our synchronized bodies. When he dipped his head down to whisper in my ear, I had to fight off a shiver.

"Do you remember the first time we danced together?" he asked.

My smile grew again as I nodded. "I do. That's when you asked me out on our first date."

He nodded against the side of my face. "I was so nervous that night."

I pulled back slightly. "Why would you be nervous?"

He quirked a brow and pulled me closer again. "You weren't exactly an easy nut to crack, baby. I knew we were meant to be together, I just had to convince you. Something deep inside told me that if I took baby steps with you that we'd finally get there. That you needed to come to the conclusion on your own and that I couldn't force the issue. So, little by little, I worked my way into your heart and look where we are now."

My head fell back with a laugh as I gazed up at him. "So, this was a part of your plan all along, McCoy?"

He shook his head, his smile crooked. "I couldn't ever have planned for you, El. I just trusted my instincts and every one of them led to you," he said with a shrug.

My eyes watered as I pulled him close again. We finished our dance in silence, the only sound the thumping of our hearts as they beat in time with each other. When the song finished, the crowd erupted in applause for us and I felt my cheeks heat.

But then came the inescapable rumbling of my stomach.

Abraham laughed and led me off the dance floor. "Have you eaten since breakfast?"

I nodded. "Callie brought me up some food while Evey was doing my makeup."

He nodded with approval as he led me toward the tables full of food. "Good. Now it's time to eat again."

I pulled on his hand, but there was no slowing him down. "Shouldn't I be mingling with our guests?"

He shook his head and tugged me along. "They can come find you while you eat."

I knew this was something he wasn't willing to budge on, so I let it go. It was very important to him that I get enough food for me and the babies and I couldn't be anything but grateful that he cared so much. He piled a mound of food on my plate before he found us a set of chairs at a random table.

Nana found us a little while later and, thankfully, I'd finished most of my food by then. "Oh, I'm so happy for you two!" she gushed as she pulled us both into fierce hugs. "I think you'll be happy to know that I brought most of my things with me this visit. I plan to stay from here on out if you have a place for me." The uncertainty in her eyes just about undid me.

I hopped up from the table and clasped her hands in mine. "Of course we have a place for you. Abraham's been working on your room since you agreed to move in. It's in the same hallway as the girls."

Nana's eyes lit up as she turned to her grandson. "You did that for me?"

He shook his head and stood to pull his grandma into a hug. "Of course, Nana. We're so excited for you to come and live with us, we'd do just about anything to get you out here."

Her pale blue eyes filled with tears as she looked back and forth between us. "I feel like this is the start of a new chapter for all of us. We got new lives brewin' in here," she said as she patted my belly, "and y'all have got a new roommate!"

We laughed with her as she embraced both of us again. We chatted for a while before we were pulled away by some of our other guests. The next couple of hours were a flurry of hugs, and kisses, and laughter, and dancing. By the end of it, I was exhausted. I wasn't sure if it was the babies making me so tired, or what, but the party was still in full swing when I finally sat down and propped up my legs.

Abraham, who was never far from my side, lifted my feet, and sat beneath them, setting them on his lap.

"You tired, baby?"

I nodded. "So tired."

"You wanna get going?"

"Are we allowed to leave our own ceremony?"

He shrugged. "I don't see why not. We've greeted everyone here already. We've danced, and eaten, and taken pictures. I think it's a perfectly reasonable time to head out."

I pulled my feet off his lap and stood up. "You don't have to tell me twice."

He chuckled as he rose to join me and grasped my hand. "Let's let Evey know we're leaving and then we can sneak out."

I squeezed his hand tightly. "Sounds like a plan."

Chapter 56

The familiar notes of a popular song pierced the night air, and I was sure Del was behind it.

"This pack is really obsessed with Taylor Swift, aren't they?"

Abraham nodded. "I wasn't kidding when I told you we were all Swifties."

I chuckled as he led me with an arm around my shoulders toward his black pickup truck. "What did Evey say when you told her we were leaving?"

He shrugged. "I blamed it on the pregnancy. Told her you were overtired, and I needed to get you to bed."

I patted my stomach. "No complaints there."

He leaned down to kiss the top of my head before opening the passenger door and helping me inside. Once he'd climbed into the driver's seat, I asked, "So, where is this place?"

He shook his head with a smile as he adjusted his rearview mirror. "You're going to have to wait and find out when we get there."

I huffed and crossed my arms over my chest. "That's annoying."

He laughed but didn't respond. I leaned back against the dark leather seat and let out a deep breath. I really was tired, and although the day had been amazing, I was glad it was over. Glad that we were married and bound in every way we could be.

The rocking of the vehicle was so soothing, and it wasn't long before I'd lost the battle with my eyelids and closed them. The next thing I knew, my door was open, and Abraham was unbuckling my seatbelt.

"We're here?" I asked, my voice raspy with sleep.

He leaned over and kissed my cheek. "Yes, baby, we're here, but you can go back to sleep."

I shook my head and sat up straighter. "No, I'm good. I just needed a nap," I said around a yawn.

He didn't look convinced, but he stepped back and helped me climb out of the truck. We were in a dark clearing, but when I turned, I found where we'd be staying lit up bright.

I turned to Abraham. "Is this...?"

He nodded and shrugged. "I thought you should get that peaceful weekend in the mountains you always wanted."

I turned back to the cottage that began this whole journey. It was the same one I'd rented when I'd first come out to Asheville and gotten attacked by Calvin in the woods. You'd have thought the place would hold bad memories for me, but it didn't. To be honest, I hadn't spent much time in there at all. Apparently, Abraham was trying to change that.

I turned to look at him again, my eyes wide and starting to water.

"Is this okay?" he asked, his gaze wary. "We can get a hotel in town if you want."

I shook my head. "This is perfect."

He released a big breath, and I realized then that he'd been nervous about his choice of our honeymoon destination. Silly man.

I wrapped my hand around his arm and tugged him toward the cottage. "What made you think of this?"

He shrugged. "I always felt bad that you had your weekend interrupted. Besides, this is close enough to pack lands that I was able to widen the patrols to include this cottage. We'll be protected and close enough to home that I can be there quickly if anything happens." He reached up to scratch the back of his head. "I wish I could take you to some exotic location, but I didn't think it was a good idea to be too far from pack lands right now. Maybe when things die down, we can–"

I reached up and placed a finger against his lips. He smiled and kissed my finger.

"This is perfect. A weekend alone with you at the foot of the Blue Ridge Mountains is the best kind of honeymoon I can think of. Thank you for this."

His eyes got soft as he looked down at me. "Anything for you, baby."

My heart thumped harder as our eyes connected in the darkness. I'd forever wonder how I'd gotten so lucky to find a man like Abraham.

His expression changed suddenly, his eyes glinting with mischief before he bent down and scooped me into his arms.

"What are you doing?" I asked breathlessly.

He repositioned me in his arms and started toward the door again. "Aren't I supposed to carry my bride across the threshold?"

I rolled my eyes, but my smile was wide. "You watch too many movies."

He shrugged. "Maybe. But I'm going to do this husband thing right from the start."

I reached up to cup his face. "You could never do it wrong, Abraham."

He smiled down at me as he fished a key out of his pocket and unlocked the door. His expression instantly changed again as he lifted his nose in the air and took a deep breath. He slowly lowered me to my feet and pressed me against the closed front door.

"I had someone check this place a little while ago, but I'm going to do another sweep before you come in. Stay here."

I nodded, and he was off, running through the small cottage to the bathroom and then up the stairs to the loft where we'd be sleeping. It didn't take him long, thankfully, and soon he was back down the stairs and heading in my direction.

He jerked his head toward the living room. "If you want to get comfortable, I'll go grab our bags."

I stifled a yawn as I nodded. "Okay. I'll head upstairs. I really want to get out of this dress."

His eyes heated as they raked down my body. "Couldn't agree more."

I chuckled as he shot me a wink and disappeared through the door. When he was gone, I turned and headed deeper into the cottage. Although I hadn't spent much time in here, the memories still surfaced and swept me up in them.

Funnily enough, most of my memories had to do with Abraham. He'd brought me here as soon as I was well enough to travel after I'd been bitten. We'd stopped along the way at the places I'd been attacked, and I'd tried to give him as many details as I could. Even though I knew the man who'd hurt me was dead, a shiver still raced down my spine.

As I climbed the stairs, I remembered when I'd been too injured to make that journey myself. Abraham had carried me to the second floor and left me there to change into some of my own clothes. He'd agreed to stay downstairs, but when I'd hit my injured leg and started crying, he'd gone against my wishes and come up to check on me, anyway.

Now my memories clashed with things Abraham has told me as well.

Apparently, that was the day he knew he loved me.

My heart swelled with those thoughts as I looked around the small loft. The bed was still puffy and inviting, the space still only big enough for one or two people max, but it took on a new meaning as I stood there.

This was where our love story really began. Not in the woods when I'd been broken and bleeding, but here, where I'd let someone in for the first time. Where my husband fell in love with me and I began to see him as something more than just my savior.

"Baby?"

I'd been so lost in my thoughts, I hadn't heard Abraham coming up the stairs behind me. That was concerning, but something to worry about another day.

I spun to face him, my eyes already filled with tears.

He dropped our bags and rushed over to me. "El, what's wrong? Are you okay?"

"I'm fine. I was just remembering the day you took me here right after my attack."

His eyes still searched mine as he nodded slowly. "I remember."

I sniffed. "And later you said that was when you first realized you loved me."

His eyes softened as he gathered the moisture that had leaked from one of my eyes. "I know."

I took a deep breath and closed my eyes as he cradled my face. "This is the perfect place to spend our honeymoon."

He pulled me closer and kissed my lips softly. "I'm glad you think so, baby. I just want you to be happy."

I sighed in his arms as he gently rocked me back and forth. When another yawn escaped me, he pulled away and frowned. "We should get you to bed."

I shook my head. "Not yet."

"What do you want to do then?"

I twisted my lips to the side as a hundred thoughts of what I wanted to do with my husband flashed through my mind. But then, another idea struck me.

"Do you want your other wedding gift?"

His eyes widened in surprise and if I had to guess, I'd say he'd had those dirty thoughts swirling around his head too. "Of course."

I smiled and grabbed his hand, leading him to the bed. "Sit here, close your eyes, and I'll get it."

He did as I asked, and I scurried over to my suitcase to unearth the box I'd stored his gift in. I'd been excited to give it to him, but now the time had arrived, I was worried it was kind of lame.

"Uh, Abraham?"

"Yes?"

"This gift isn't a big deal, okay?"

494

He frowned, eyes still closed. "Of course it's a big deal. It's from you."

I sighed and shook my head as I walked back over to him. "I just mean it's nothing big. Just something I thought you'd enjoy, but now I'm second guessing myself."

His frown deepened. "Baby, I'm sure I'll love it."

I sighed again and placed the box in his hand. "Fine. You can open them now."

His denim blue eyes blinked at me and he smiled before looking down at the box in his hands. When he looked back up at me questioningly, I just shrugged.

"Go ahead. Let's get this over with."

He rolled his eyes with a smile before pulling the lid off the box. He reached in and picked up the three pieces of wood connected to one keyring. His brows furrowed as he looked at the dangling keychains and then at me.

I took a seat next to him and grasped one of the pieces of wood, flipping it over. "See what's etched into the wood?"

He nodded, his finger tracing the lines.

"That's one of our babies' heartbeats."

His hand froze, his wide blue eyes meeting mine before he picked up the next keychain, and then the next.

"I got the sound wave of each of their heartbeats etched into a piece of wood for you. I thought you might like to have their heartbeats with you wherever you go. It's kind of dumb, though, so if you don't like them, you don't have to use them. I was just out of ideas for what to get you."

He was still staring down at the little pieces of wood, so I rambled on some more.

"I got the wood from a tree near our lake, too. I thought it would be more meaningful than just some random piece of wood." When he still didn't speak, I word vomited again. "I had Wyatt sneak me over there one day when you were out at a job site." He still wasn't speaking, and I was

495

losing my mind. "If you really don't like them, we can just get rid of them, it's no big deal."

He finally raised his head to look at me, his eyes so blue and watery my heart clenched in my chest. "I love this, El." His voice was so deep and full of emotion that I felt the tears swimming to my eyes, too.

"Really?"

He nodded slowly, his eyes twitching back toward the keychains. "I can't think of a better gift. Thank you so much. I'll treasure this."

I released a deep breath, my shoulders deflating. He reached out and wrapped an arm around my waist, dragging me closer until he could press a kiss to the top of my head.

"Baby, why were you so worried? This is the best gift I've ever gotten. I get to take my babies' heartbeats with me every day. What could be better than that?"

I shrugged. "But it's a keychain. That's kind of a lame wedding present."

He shook his head as he clasped them tightly in his hand and looked down at me. "Not lame at all. Incredibly thoughtful and sweet." He sighed. "I love you so much."

A small smile twitched on my lips. "I love you too."

He returned my smile before reaching into his pocket and pulling out his truck keys. He pulled his arm from around me so he could attach his new keychain. When he was done, he took one more look before pocketing them again.

I tried to hide it, but another yawn fell from my lips and Abraham shook his head. "We need to get you to bed."

But I wasn't ready to go to bed. I wanted to spend as much time with my new husband as I could. I knew arguing with him wouldn't get me very far, but I had another idea up my sleeve.

I stood up and turned my back toward him, "Okay. Will you help me out of my dress?"

I could hear him swallow harshly behind me and I tried to hide my smile. He stood up, and with gentle fingers, slid my zipper down to the base of my spine. I shrugged out of the lace straps and let the soft fabric fall to my feet.

Stepping out of the puddle of dress, I turned to find his eyes heated as they traveled up and down my body. His hands, fisted at his sides, were trembling slightly and I knew he was holding himself back from touching me.

"You've had that on underneath your dress all day?" he rumbled.

I looked down at the sheer white strapless bra I had on with lace that crept toward my baby bump. The matching panties were not much more than a scrap of lace barely protecting me from his eyes. Not that I wanted to be protected in that moment.

I nodded. "Yes."

He took a shaky step forward before halting, his jaw ticking with tension. "You need to sleep," he rasped.

I shook my head. "I need you more."

He closed his eyes tightly as his hands fisted over and over again. Knowing he'd talk himself out of it if I let him, I took a step closer and wrapped my arms around his neck. Reaching up, I was just able to reach his ear to whisper in it.

"Please, make love to me. Don't make me wait any longer."

He groaned softly before his big hands wrapped around my hips. They stroked my sides up and down as he took deep breaths that bumped his chest against mine. "Are you sure you're not too tired?"

I pressed against him harder. "I'm never too tired for you."

He groaned again as his hands gripped my waist. When his eyes opened, I could see he'd made his decision. And that I'd won that round.

His mouth crashed against mine in a kiss so ferocious it took my breath away. I held onto his neck as his hands wandered my body, touching every available inch of skin he could reach. When he finally tore his lips away from mine, he took a step back and dropped to his knees.

It wasn't the first time he'd knelt before me, but it never failed to cut me to the core. Knowing that a man as powerful and respected as Abraham would kneel at my feet was a powerful thing.

His hands rose to cup the small swell between my hips. He reached forward and placed three kisses beneath my belly button as he slid my panties off. Next, he slipped his rough fingers beneath the lace around my breasts and pulled that off me too. When I was standing before him naked, he took his time watching me, savoring me, almost seeming to memorize every inch of my body.

"You're so beautiful," he whispered.

And I felt it. Beautiful, and powerful, and desired, and loved. It all wrapped tightly around me to form an impenetrable barrier. His devotion was like armor. Something that protected and fortified me when I needed it the most.

He rose to his feet and quickly stripped out of his clothes. When we were both naked, he pulled me into his arms and kissed me again. This time, it was slow and sensual, every lick and nip purposeful. He turned me around and walked me back toward the bed, laying me down on the soft blankets and covering me with his body.

When he slipped inside me, I knew every decision I'd made up until that point had been the right one. Even when they'd felt wrong, they couldn't have been because they'd led me here. To this place. With my husband above me, and my babies inside of me, and the perfection of our love swirling around us.

Our words were few as we made love in the loft of that cottage. In the same place he'd fallen in love with me. In the same place I'd learned I could lean on him. Where our love story began in earnest. The most perfect of nights followed the most perfect day, and I fell asleep in his arms knowing I'd never leave them.

Chapter 57

"Can I get you more tea, baby?"

I looked up from my book to find Abraham leaning over his chair, staring at my empty mug. I gave him a smile and handed over my cup.

"That would be great. Thank you."

He shot me a wink before hopping up and heading into the cottage. I took a deep breath and released it slowly, letting the scents of the forest fill my senses.

Abraham was right.

I needed this peaceful weekend in the mountains.

We needed it.

Time to just be us. To be a newly married couple with no responsibilities other than making our partner happy. We didn't have to worry about work, or the pack, or tensions with Charlotte. We just existed.

We took walks in the woods during the days and spent long nights making love in the loft. It was a perfect honeymoon, and I was sad that it was our last day here.

The screen door creaked open and Abraham handed me a mug full of steaming hot liquid. I shot him a grateful smile and took a tentative sip.

"Ready to get back to pack lands tomorrow?"

I made a face, and he laughed. "That's what I was just thinking about," I said.

He leaned back in his chair, his long legs extending in front of him and crossing at the ankles. "It was nice to get away, but you know we have jobs to do."

"I know, and I accept that. To be honest, as nice as the alone time has been, being away this long has kind of made me anxious. I'll be happy to get back to the lodge."

He nodded slowly. "I know what you mean. I've checked in with Bea every day, but she has nothing new to report. Everything is running smoothly and there hasn't been any sign of the Charlotte pack."

I set my mug aside and pulled my knees up to my chest. "Does that worry you?"

He turned his head to look at me. "That we haven't heard from them yet?"

I nodded, and he sighed.

"A little," he admitted. "I'd rather face an enemy head-on. This waiting game is brutal."

I pursed my lips and looked out into the woods as I let my thoughts settle. "I bet that's part of his strategy. To make us anxious while he waits to strike."

Abraham sighed again. "I'm sure you're right."

It was quiet between us for a few moments while I gathered the courage to ask my next question. Finally, I took a deep breath and spoke up.

"How do you think this is all gonna end?" I hadn't intended for my voice to be that quiet or small, but I couldn't help it. Thoughts of the coming confrontation and what it would mean for both packs were constant worries in my head. I'd held them off for as long as I could, but they couldn't be ignored any longer.

Abraham let out a deep breath but didn't respond right away. When he did, his voice was rough and full of emotion. "I'm sure it will end with a fight between me and my uncle. I don't see any other way to end this."

I turned to look at him, fear clogging my throat. "Are our people going to die?"

His jaw ticked as he ground his teeth. Finally, he nodded once. "It's possible."

My stomach plummeted as the faces of all our enforcers flashed through my mind. And worse, if our enforcers couldn't hold back the Charlotte pack, what would happen to the rest of our people? Maddy, and Sophie, and Fran, and Kyle, and Doreen, and Ms. Elsie, and the dozens of other people I considered family.

"I don't think anyone should die for this. What can we do?" I whispered.

Abraham took a deep breath, and I watched as his face seemed to age before my eyes. "I'm going to have to kill Conrad before his pack can inflict too much damage on ours."

I reached out to grasp his hand, knowing he needed me in that moment. It was bad enough when he'd had to kill his cousin. The thought that my sweet, sensitive husband would have to kill another one of his family members gutted me.

"Is that really the only way?" I asked.

His eyes met mine, and in them, I saw resignation. "Conrad won't stop. I know that for sure. We either stop him or he kills us and I'm not willing to risk a single person in my pack. If the choice is between defending them and killing my uncle, I'll choose them every time."

His words settled around us, each syllable like another nail in Conrad's coffin.

I squeezed Abraham's hand. "Maybe it won't come to that. He's probably not expecting us to have amassed a force as big as what we have now. Maybe he'll back down when he sees he isn't outnumbering us."

Abraham squeezed my fingers back and sighed. "I hope so, baby. But if not, I'll do what I have to."

I watched my poor husband as the heaviness of this reality settled on his shoulders. And I knew, no matter what I did, this was a load he'd bear on his own. No amount of support from me could change what he had to face.

"I know you will, Abraham. You always do."

Just as the silence settled around us again, a loud howl broke the stillness like a gunshot. We both sat up straight before glancing at one another.

"Was that one of ours?" I asked.

Abraham's eyes were shrewd as they glanced around the forest. "Yes. I need you to go inside."

I shook my head and stood. "I want to know what's happening. I'm staying with you."

He marched over and lifted me off my feet. "You'll be able to hear from inside." He walked me through the cottage's front door and set me down in the living room. My protests meant nothing to him. "Stay in here," he said before he stormed back out and slammed the door behind him.

There was no way I was going to miss what was happening out there. I'd stay inside, but he hadn't said anything about opening a window and watching through it, had he?

I raced to one of the front windows and pulled back the curtains before wrenching it open. From my vantage point, I could see Abraham standing at the foot of the porch steps, his shoulders rigid and his hands clenched as he waited for whoever had howled in the distance.

A few moments later, a large wolf went careening through the trees and skidded to a stop in front of Abraham. I didn't recognize the wolf and I couldn't smell them from where I was, but a few loud cracks later and a naked Wes was standing there, panting.

"Alpha."

"What is it?"

Wes took a deep breath as two other wolves raced into the clearing. "They're coming from the North. It looks like he's sent every one of his enforcers."

Abraham's shoulders inched toward his ears. "Are our men in position already?"

Wes took a deep breath as the other two wolves shifted into humans. It was Wyatt and Mathias and they were just as out of breath. It took a lot for a werewolf to get winded and I had to wonder from how far away they'd run.

"Yes. Beatrice has them stationed along their path ready to strike when they get close enough."

"I want a group of men stationed closer to home to defend the rest of the pack in case any wolves break through our defenses."

Wes nodded. "I'll shift and tell her now."

"Tell her I'm on my way, too."

"No," I whispered, even though I knew he had to. Even though I knew he'd never let his enforcers fight without him.

I ran to the front door and flung it open, careful to stay inside the cottage like he'd asked. "Abraham, I'm coming with you."

He spun around and stomped back over to me. "No. You're staying here with Wyatt."

I shook my head. "I can fight, Abraham. You know I can. I want to help. I want to defend our people. I want to be by your side where I belong."

He took a deep breath and reached out to grasp my shoulders. "Elizabeth, I can't have you out there with me. I wouldn't be able to focus knowing you were in danger. I need you to stay here and stay safe while I go protect our people. Please. Do this for me."

I shook my head as tears swam to my eyes. "Don't ask me to sit back and let you run off into danger, Abraham. I can't do that. I won't."

He took a deep breath and pulled me closer, one of his hands slipping off my shoulder to cup my stomach. "El, you have to think about our children. You're their only protector. You can't put yourself in danger because something could happen to them. Please, keep yourself and our babies safe and stay here."

I closed my eyes as a tear escaped and raced down my face. "I can't believe you're asking me to sit this out," I whispered.

He pulled me close and squeezed me hard. "I'll be back. I promise."

I opened my eyes and speared him with a hard glare. "You better be."

He grasped my chin and tilted my face toward his. "My life is entwined with yours, El, and I would never do anything to endanger you. That means I'm going to make it through this and come home to you. You have my word."

The tears were flowing unchecked now as I resigned myself to the fact that I was being left behind. That I'd be stuck here wondering and worrying about my people and my husband while they fought a force that might be greater than ours.

I reached up and pressed my lips to Abraham's hard before pulling away and wiping my face with the back of my hand. "Go," I said. "Go end this and come back to me."

He nodded once before stepping forward and pressing a kiss to my forehead. "I will. I promise." He pulled away and looked into my eyes. "I love you. I'll be back soon."

I firmed my chin and tipped it toward him. "I love you too."

He gave me one last lingering glance before he turned around and raced down the porch steps. A few feet later, and his body was shifting mid-leap. Wes and Mathias shifted back into wolves as well and the three of them raced away without another word.

Wyatt was left standing naked in the clearing.

"Come on in, Wyatt. I'll find something of Abraham's you can borrow."

He shook his head. "I should shift back. We'll need to keep up communication with the rest of the pack and I can defend you better that way."

I shrugged as I did my best to keep my eyes above his chest. "Before you shift, can you tell me anything more about what's happening? Did you see them? Were there a lot of them? Where's North of the pack lands? Was Conrad with them?"

He shook his head, his lips twitching with a grin. "Maybe you should at least grab me a pair of shorts so I can answer your questions without making you uncomfortable."

I shot him a small, grateful smile. "That's a good idea. I'll be right back."

I raced inside and up the stairs to the loft. Rifling through Abraham's things, I quickly located a pair of black basketball shorts and ran back down the stairs with them. I tossed them toward Wyatt and turned around as he clothed himself.

He chuckled behind me. "You always gonna be this shy?"

"Probably."

He laughed again before he said, "All good. You can turn around."

When I did, I found him walking up the porch steps toward me. I motioned toward the chairs Abraham and I had been sitting in and he took one while I took the other.

For a moment, I thought about how, just thirty minutes ago, we'd been enjoying a peaceful morning. I'd been reading and drinking tea while he played games on his phone and chugged black coffee. It was so blissfully boring and average and now everything had been turned upside down.

My stomach knotted with anxiety as all the possibilities raced through my head.

What was happening?

What was being done?

Who was out there?

Would everyone make it through this?

If not, which one of my friends would I lose?

Or would it be one of my family members?

Could it be my husband?

"You had some questions?" Wyatt asked, breaking me out of my dark thoughts.

I turned to him and found the lines around his eyes had deepened, and I knew he was as worried as I was. His brother was out there on the front lines. His family was in danger while he had to stay behind and watch over me. That couldn't be easy for him, and in that moment, I felt more kinship with him than I ever had before.

"What can you tell me about what's going on?"

He took a deep breath and looked out into the forest, much like Abraham had when I'd asked him a question he didn't want to answer.

"There seems to be a lot of them. If our estimates are correct, there are about forty."

I gasped. "That's more than we have."

He nodded, his eyes wary. "I know. Our hope is they're not all enforcers. We were sure Conrad had closer to thirty last we knew, and Nana confirmed that for us. He could have borrowed from other packs, but the more likely scenario is he made some of his pack members join the enforcers. If that's the case, that's lucky for us because they won't be trained in battle and won't put up much of a fight."

Suddenly, this was all too real for me. Men and women were laying down their lives for this conflict. Because one alpha had a problem with another one. It all seemed so petty. So ridiculous that lives might be lost because of a dispute between two men.

"Not everyone is going to make it through this, are they?" I asked, my voice soft.

Wyatt sighed before reaching over and grasping my hand. "We're well prepared, Ellie. We've been training for this for a long time and the enforcers we've borrowed are just as skilled."

I shook my head. "I don't want anyone from the Charlotte pack to die either. No one should have to lose their lives because Conrad has an issue with Abraham. That's not fair to anyone."

Wyatt sighed and pulled his hand away to run it through his sandy blond hair. "That's why we're hoping to locate Conrad soon so Abraham can confront him directly. If he can defeat his uncle, the rest of the pack will stop fighting as they'll be under Abraham's command. That's the best way to end this for good."

I bit my lip as I looked out at the forest, wondering where my husband was and how close to the conflict he'd managed to get. "Has anyone spotted Conrad yet?"

Wyatt shook his head. "Not last time I checked in."

I stood up and nodded toward the woods. "Then you should shift back. We need as much information as we can get."

Wyatt stood as well. "Okay. You go back inside, and I'll run the perimeter. If I hear something, I'll shift back and come tell you."

I nodded. "Okay, that sounds like a plan. Thanks, Wyatt."

He shrugged. "Of course, Ellie."

He turned to walk down the porch steps and I headed back inside to give him some privacy. I heard the loud cracks that signified he'd shifted and closed the door behind me. I also made sure to turn the lock, just in case.

Now that I was inside, I didn't know what to do with myself. I knew that book I'd been reading earlier wouldn't hold an ounce of my attention now I had Abraham and the rest of my pack to worry about.

With nothing left to do, I started to pace. I needed to get the pent-up energy out of my system, or it felt like I'd blow apart at the seams. The minutes ticked by as I listened to Wyatt's thumping feet race around the cottage. I didn't know how long it'd been, but he hadn't come to me with any new information and I had to assume that meant he knew nothing new.

That didn't sit well with me.

The cottage was set on a desolate side road that saw very little action, so when I heard a car approach, it only barely registered in my head. I assumed it would drive right past the driveway, but when I heard the crunching of gravel coming closer, I stopped in the middle of the room to listen.

The tires kept approaching, their speed faster than I would have driven down a gravel drive. I heard Wyatt's heavy paws thundering toward the moving vehicle before a series of loud pops rang through the quiet forest.

My heart fell to the soles of my feet as I listened carefully to what was happening outside. I couldn't hear Wyatt anymore and I wasn't sure what the loud bangs had been, but my gut told me it was nothing good.

Two car doors opened, and I turned around to face the front door.

Who could it possibly be?

Who knew we were here?

And where the hell was Wyatt?

I heard footsteps climbing up the porch steps before there was a knock on the front door. My heart raced out of control as I slowly crossed the room. I didn't know if I should answer the door, but I also didn't know if I had a choice. I tried to use my nose to see if I could tell who was on the other side but couldn't pick anything up.

Where was Wyatt?

There were only two possibilities.

One was, he knew who this was, and he was allowing them to get this far.

The other was, he was hurt and couldn't protect me anymore.

If that was the case, I was on my own now and delaying the inevitable wouldn't change the outcome. With that in mind, I straightened my spine, tipped my chin up and reached for the lock.

I flung the thick wooden door open to find the last person I wanted to see at that moment. And that was when I knew the kind of trouble I was really in.

"Hello, Elizabeth," Peyton said.

Chapter 58

Abraham

I raced through the woods faster than I ever had in my life. Leaping over roots and crashing through brush, the trees whipped past me in a blur.

"Bea, I need a status update."

Although we were still miles apart, thankfully, there was no limit to our mental communication.

"They're almost within reach of our first group of enforcers. We'll attack and hold as many of them back as we can while the next group readies for whoever gets through us."

My sister was on the front lines.

That thought played on repeat in my head as I dug my feet harder into the soft earth and propelled my body even faster.

She shouldn't have been out there without me. I should have been in the first group. I should have been spearheading the fight against our enemies.

"Abey, stop worrying about me. You know I can handle myself."

I shook my head and pushed my limbs harder. Faster. Testing my limits like never before.

"I don't like the thought of you out there without me. I should be there within minutes. Did you send a group to protect the pack?"

"I have five men stationed on the edge of our property. If anyone gets past the enforcers I have stationed along their path, they'll be there to protect the rest of them."

"Maybe we should evacuate just in case. Or at least get them all to the lodge. We can defend them easier if they're all in one place."

"I'll tell them that now."

I could feel the mental communication between us severed as she turned her attention toward whoever she had stationed closer to pack lands. Technically, she could have talked to both of us at the same time, but it didn't matter to me. I knew I could trust Bea to handle my orders with swift precision. She was the best beta any alpha could ask for.

"They're moving the rest of the pack into the basement of the lodge as we speak."

I nodded, although I knew she couldn't see me. *"Remind the enforcers with you that we aren't going for kill shots. Break their spines and leave them. I want as little blood shed as possible today."*

Bea hesitated before she spoke up in my head again. *"Abraham, is that wise? The Charlotte pack won't hesitate to kill any one of us. Shouldn't we fight them with the same kind of force?"*

I shook my head, my mind made up long ago. *"This is a quarrel between Conrad and me. I won't have my enforcers responsible for taking innocent lives."*

"If that's what you think is best."

I did.

I had full confidence in that order, and the conversation I'd had with El just before our honeymoon was cut short solidified that decision. My goal was to end the confrontation with as few lives lost as possible.

The only one who needed to die today was Conrad.

Even thinking the words left a bad taste in my mouth.

If there was any other way. If there was anything I could have said or done that could have swayed Conrad, I'd have done it, but I needed to be realistic. He was here to kill me, and I knew he wouldn't stop.

I couldn't help the next question that swam to the surface of my mind.

Was this really all about Calvin's death?

Was this really all about retaliation for killing his son? A son he had barely spoken to in over a decade. A son who was murdering women for months. A son who was clearly deranged and needed to be stopped.

I didn't know the answers to any of those questions, but something deep in my gut told me there was more to this. That Conrad wouldn't go to so much trouble just to avenge his son.

The truth of the matter was, he didn't care that much. It was cold, but true. The only things Conrad cared about were himself and power. Everything else had always taken a backseat, and I couldn't imagine that had changed.

"We can see them. They'll be here within seconds," Bea said in my head, breaking me out of my thoughts.

I willed my legs to run faster, knowing that I was only minutes away, but that was still too far.

"Be careful, Beatrice."

She snorted. *"Please, Abey. This will be fun."*

Sometimes I wondered if there was something seriously unhinged about my sister, but now was not the time to worry about it.

But if I wasn't worrying about Beatrice or the rest of my enforcers, my mind instantly traveled back to my mate and unborn children. The worry for them was constant, but I'd done my best to block it out.

I'd left Wyatt with her and knew he'd lay down his life to protect his alpha, but would that be enough? I also knew El could handle herself. It'd been hard to admit, the most bitter pill to swallow, but she didn't really need me to protect her. She was a fierce, intimidating wolf all on her own. I had no doubt that between the two of them, she'd be all right.

So why did I have a feeling deep in the pit of my stomach that something was wrong?

"Wyatt, how are things there?"

He answered right away, and that uneasy feeling lessened the smallest bit.

"Running a small perimeter now. Ellie's in the cottage and there's no one around for miles."

I let out a deep breath and let the worry for my mate slither from my veins. She was safe. She was as protected as she could be. She'd be fine, and I'd see her soon.

"Let me know if anything changes," I said, and he quickly confirmed that he would.

"Abey, we've stopped about ten of the Charlotte pack with our first attack, but another thirty or so are still on their way through."

Damn it!

I needed to be there. I needed to help. The sidelines were no place for an alpha to be when his people's lives were in danger.

I reined it in, though, and asked the most important question. The only thing that really mattered.

"Have you spotted Conrad yet?"

"He was at the back of the pack. Fucking coward."

My sister was never one to mince words, and this was no exception.

Couldn't say I blamed her, though.

The back of the pack was not where an alpha should have been, but it didn't surprise me. Conrad was well-known for sending others to do his dirty work. I'd known this would be no different.

"Have you alerted the next group?" I asked.

It took her a minute to respond, and that whole time, every terrible scenario flashed through my mind. Finally, her voice rang through my head, breathless but seemingly uninjured.

"They know and we've eliminated this group. No deaths, just broken spines like you asked."

I let out a deep breath of relief and powered my body forward.

"Good. I'll meet up with the second group and hopefully catch Conrad there. This needs to end now."

Moments later, I could hear the conflict ahead and I pushed my body even faster than before. Seconds later, I burst through the trees to find the fight in full swing. I whipped my head back and forth, searching for my uncle, but couldn't find him.

The first unlucky wolf sprang toward me and I dispatched him with ease. Like I'd instructed Beatrice and the rest of the pack to do, I grabbed him by the back of his neck, and with a vicious twist, snapped his spine. It would hurt like a bitch and take a while to recover from, but he'd live.

I raced through the flurry of bodies, dodging my people and snapping the necks of any Charlotte wolves I could. I saw there were a few that escaped and were making a beeline toward pack lands, but we'd halved their numbers in this battle.

"Beatrice, alert the next group. They'll have wolves incoming shortly."

She responded affirmatively, but I barely registered her voice in my head. I'd finally spotted my uncle and knew it was time to end this.

I sprinted through the melee, my sights set on Conrad and no one else. Before I could get close enough to confront him, one of the wolves running on either side of him broke away and lunged for me. He was a better fighter than the last wolf I'd come across, but still no match for me.

I was larger, stronger, and angrier than anyone else here. There was nothing that could have stopped me from confronting Conrad.

Seeing that I was taking down the first line of defense, the other wolf that had been flanking him broke away and came charging at me, too. This wolf was bigger, and I could tell he was an even better fighter than the last.

He darted toward one side and then attacked on my other with quick precision. I prepared to launch myself at him when another smaller wolf appeared out of nowhere, taking that larger wolf down easily.

"Get Conrad!" Beatrice yelled as she danced away from the larger wolf.

Despite the protective instincts inside me, I knew Beatrice had this. She was a better fighter than even I was.

Now that my uncle was without his bodyguards, there was nothing to stop me from taking him down. I stalked toward the older wolf, recognizing the fear in his eyes before he quickly smothered it with cocky arrogance.

"Hello, Son," he said inside my head.

I snarled and snapped my teeth in his direction. *"I'm not your son."*

Conrad's genial disposition morphed in that second and I could truly see the crazy that lay underneath his façade.

"No. You killed *my son."*

"He was a psychopathic killer, Conrad. If I hadn't taken him down, someone else would have."

"But it was you, *wasn't it? You* took my son from me, and now I'm going to take something precious from you."

My blood ran cold at his proclamation.

What could he mean?

This fight?

My pack?

My lands?

"Haven't figured it out yet?" he taunted. *"Let me make this perfectly clear for you. Your precious mate will be dead within minutes and then I'll be able to take you down. Your pack, your lands, and that gem mine will all be mine. Your minutes are numbered."*

My heart plummeted as the blood pumped furiously through my veins.

How was he going to get to Elizabeth when he didn't know where she was? Only my pack did, and they'd never betray me like that. They'd never betray her like that. He was bluffing. He had to be.

514

"Still don't believe me?" Conrad asked when I failed to respond to him. *"It won't matter in a few minutes. You'll be able to feel her loss soon and you'll know I always mean what I say."*

I took a menacing step forward. *"You're lying."*

Conrad's laugh in my head was loud and out of place in the clearing where bodies littered the ground.

"I'm not. But you'll see soon enough. I'll take you out like I took out your foolish parents and I'll have one more pack under my belt."

My blood turned to ice in my veins as I staggered back a step.

"My parents?" I whispered. Shaking my head, I spoke more forcefully. *"You didn't kill my parents, you deranged old man. My mother died in a car accident."*

Conrad laughed again, the sound grating, making me want to rip out his throat just so I wouldn't have to hear it again.

"If anyone had bothered to investigate, they'd have found her brake lines were cut, just like your mate's were. Only, when I did the job, I made sure to also cut the emergency brake line. That idiot Paul could have saved me a lot of time if he'd just done it right the first time."

The hits just kept on coming. I felt like I had mental whiplash from everything he was revealing to me.

"Paul? He was a part of this, too?"

"Of course he was, you imbecile! You think he's going to allow you to banish his sister from your pack with no repercussions?" He laughed again and I grit my teeth, willing my body to hold its ground. *"He's been working with me all along. You're just too soft in the head to have caught on. He's the reason I knew exactly where your pretty little mate was. He and his sister are taking care of her right now."*

I slammed the door on the mental communication with my uncle and mentally shouted to my enforcer. *"Wyatt! What's going on there?"*

When there was no answer, my heart stopped all together before picking up the pace in double time.

"Bea!"

"I'm already gone," she assured me.

My heart was thumping harder and faster than it ever had before as thoughts of what was happening to El flashed through my mind.

I never should have left her. I never should have taken my eyes off her for a second. I'd promised to protect her, and I'd failed. Again. What kind of mate did that make me?

As the despair settled in, one small thought kept my hopes alive. One small flame in the darkness of my mind kept my sanity intact.

"She's not alone," I told my uncle.

He tilted his head to the side as if he didn't have a care in the world. *"And Paul is armed. I'm sure he'll be able to dispatch any little guard dog you have assigned to your mate. Her time will be up soon, and that means so will yours. I'll have your pack, I'll have your lands, I'll have your gem mine, and I'll have vengeance for my son. Not a bad Sunday in my opinion."*

That was the second time he'd mentioned this damn gem mine. Was that what this was really about? A couple of goddamned stones?

"You didn't do this all for Calvin, did you? This has nothing to do with your son and everything to do with your greed."

Conrad tipped his head to the side once more, his expression flat and almost bored. *"Yes, well, when Paul informed me they'd found that large mine on your property, I just knew I had to have it for myself. I've watched what you've done up here in the sticks of North Carolina and bided my time in Charlotte. I knew one day I'd take what you'd built here for myself, like I'd taken what your father created in Charlotte. As soon as I found out about the money you stood to make off that mine, I knew it was time to make my move. This was a long time coming, Son. Something you can't stop. Something you should just resign yourself to. Your pack and your lands are mine."*

My mind raced as I tried to think my way through this. If he was right, I only had minutes of strength left before El died and my heart began to fail. Even now, knowing her death was near, I could feel the power leaching from my body, leaving me slow and impotent.

I'd completely underestimated my uncle. I hadn't accounted for how evil he was. How greedy he was.

I hadn't realized he'd stoop so low as to kill his own kin for power.

What could I do at that point?

What was left?

I knew El was strong, but could she face two wolves? One of which had a gun? Did she have any shot at making it through this?

Did I?

Conrad's laugh rang through my head again and something inside me snapped. I whipped my head toward my uncle and began my advance.

I might not have had long to live, I might have been losing my mate and my unborn children, but I wasn't going down without a fight. Even if this was the last act of a dying man, I'd take Conrad with me.

See, although I'd underestimated him, he'd underestimated both El and me.

While he was fighting for power, we were fighting for love.

And family.

That made us infinitely stronger than he could ever have hoped to be.

If I only had minutes left on this Earth, I'd spend them tearing my uncle apart and making sure he couldn't ever hurt someone else again.

Conrad was still laughing when I launched myself across the distance separating us, my teeth aimed right at his jugular.

Chapter 59

Elizabeth

"Peyton, what the hell are you doing here?"

The black-haired woman tilted her head to the side, a small smile tugging at her lips. "I'm here to kill you."

My heart stopped for a second before picking up speed and galloping out of control.

I guessed the time for pretenses were gone, huh?

I glanced over her shoulder wondering where Wyatt was or what happened to him when Peyton giggled, the sound as high-pitched and annoying as ever.

"Your little guard dog won't be coming to your rescue. Paul and his Glock took care of him."

My heart clenched as her words sank in. That was what those popping sounds had been. Paul shot Wyatt.

Where was he?

Was he still alive?

I looked over Peyton's shoulder again to try to get a glimpse of Wyatt, but she moved to block me.

"I wouldn't be worried about him right now. You have bigger things on your plate."

She was right.

I had a homicidal werewolf right in front of me that was all too happy to take me out. And, apparently, her brother was somewhere out there with a gun, ready to kill me if she didn't succeed.

Fucking Paul.

I knew he couldn't be trusted. Abraham should have gotten rid of him as soon as he threw Peyton out of the pack. Of course blood is thicker than water. He should have known that better than anyone else.

But that was another worry for another day.

I had to figure out how to get out of this situation and my options were severely limited.

"Peyton, maybe we can talk about this. Do you want back in the pack? Is that what this is about? I can talk to Abraham about it."

She laughed again, the sound even more high-pitched and grating. "No. Fuck this pack. I wouldn't rejoin it if you paid me."

I crossed my arms over my chest and sighed. "Then what is it? Why are you here?"

The smile slid from her face as she took a menacing step forward. "I told you. I'm here to kill you."

"Sending people to attack me in my office wasn't enough?"

She shook her head, a small smile on her pinched face. "That was just an appetizer. Just something to make you realize you aren't safe anywhere. That I can get to you wherever you are."

My hands fisted, but I kept them tucked against my chest. "Why, though? What did I do to you?"

She tipped her head back and laughed again, the sound eerie and off somehow. "What did you do? *What did you do*?! You took everything from me. My mate, my position, my pack. And now, I'm going to take it all back."

I took a deep breath and willed myself to calm down. I needed to find a way out of this situation that didn't involve fighting her. I had no doubt I could win against her, but at what cost? Would I hurt the babies in the process? It wasn't a risk I was willing to take. Not yet.

"Peyton, I didn't take anything from you. You lost those things yourself."

"Bullshit!" she screeched. "I had Abraham right where I wanted him before you waltzed your pathetic ass into his life. How a stupid human caught his eye I'll never know. At first, I thought he just felt bad for you, but eventually, I realized it was *you* that was the problem. You manipulated and played him to get what you wanted and I'm here to end that."

I shook my head slowly, her words tumbling through my head.

She'd completely lost her mind.

"Peyton, none of that is true. If Abraham wanted you, he could have had you years ago, but he didn't. Why do you think that is?"

Her nostrils flared as her hands fisted at her sides. "He just needed a little more time. He would have come around."

I shook my head again. "You know that's not true. You were hoping for something that wasn't going to happen. I didn't take anything from you."

"You did! You took him and you took my position as alpha of this pack, and when you weren't satisfied with that, you took my home from me."

Nothing I said was penetrating. She wasn't hearing me. Maybe she couldn't hear me. Maybe after months of repeating those lies, she'd come to believe them. I still couldn't give up yet, though. I had to keep trying to get through to her.

"Peyton, Abraham told you multiple times to stay out of our relationship. You couldn't do that, and that's why you were excommunicated. If you'd left us alone, you'd still be a member of the Asheville pack."

She sneered at me as she took a step closer. "That is until you found another reason to get him to throw me out. I know how people like you work, Elizabeth. You didn't want the competition around, so you needed to get rid of me. Admit it."

I shook my head. When had her delusions become a reality? When had she flown so far off course? At one point, she'd been a close family friend of the McCoys. Surely she hadn't always been so crazy because they'd have seen it sooner. You couldn't hide that kind of lunacy.

"Peyton, it's over. You need to move on. Even without me in the picture Abraham wouldn't want you."

She pressed her lips into a thin white line, her nostrils flaring again. "I don't want Abraham. I'm over him. Besides, he doesn't have much longer to live, either."

My heart stopped again as I tried to process her words. "What are you talking about?" I asked, my voice not as firm or confident as I'd have liked.

Her thin lips twisted into a smile. "As soon as Abraham finds out you're dead, he'll be so distraught that Conrad will be able to fight him and kill him. You'll both be dead before the sun sets."

I took a step back, my whole body shaking. "Conrad would never be able to beat Abraham in a fight."

Peyton shrugged. "If you really believe you're his fated mate, then you also believe that your death will weaken and eventually kill him." She shrugged again. "Either way, you're both dying today. There's no doubt about that."

My limbs were trembling, and I wasn't sure if it was from fear of what was happening with Abraham or the need to shift, but I held back. I wasn't done trying to talk my way out of this. I needed to do everything I could to avoid a physical confrontation with Peyton.

Abraham made me promise I'd protect our children, and I'd do anything to keep that oath.

"Peyton, please don't do this."

She smiled, the expression on her face the furthest thing from happiness. "And why shouldn't I? Why shouldn't I get revenge on the one woman who stole my life and future from me?"

My mind raced as I tried to think of what to say. Finally, it came to me, but I didn't know if it would help or hurt my cause. Either way, it was the last card I had to play, and I had to give it a try.

"Peyton, please don't do this. I'm pregnant."

Her black eyes widened as they fluttered from my face to the small swell of my stomach. She tipped her nose into the air and took a deep breath before leveling me with a glare.

"Paul!" she screamed, her eyes never leaving me.

Her brother ambled out of nowhere, his hand still wrapped around his shiny black gun.

"You fucking lied to me," she said to him, her eyes still darting from my eyes to my stomach.

I glanced at Paul to see an uncomfortable look pasted across his face. My body trembled more as I added his betrayal to the list of shit that was pissing me off in that moment.

"You didn't need to know," he finally said.

She spun to face him, her body rigid with anger. "Of course I needed to know, you idiot!"

Paul dropped his gaze to the ground and shrugged. It was clear who the dominant sibling was in that situation. However, he was the one with the gun, so I wasn't counting him out anytime soon.

Peyton turned back around to face me, her complexion tinged pink. "I don't give a fuck that you're pregnant. All the more reason to kill you. When Abraham finds out that not only did his precious mate die, but with his unborn children, it'll be all the leverage Conrad needs to get rid of him."

I took a step back, one of my hands going to my stomach without my permission. There was a bone-deep need to protect my children at all costs. To shield them as best I could.

"Why are you doing this all for Conrad? What's in it for you?"

Peyton smiled at me and a shiver ran up my spine. "He promised to make me alpha of the pack and split the money he makes off the gem mine."

I frowned. "Gem mine?"

She rolled her black eyes and pointed at my chest. "Where do you think that ridiculous stone in that tacky ring came from, genius?"

I reached for the engagement ring that always rested on a chain around my neck. I was so used to it that I often forgot it was there. My fingers grasped the cool metal as I thought through what she was saying.

When Abraham gave me this ring, he'd said it came from his property. I hadn't known what he was talking about at the time, but a couple weeks later, he actually took me to the gem mine they'd found on his lands. I thought it was beautiful and amazing but hadn't thought much more about it.

Was it really worth that much money?

Enough that Conrad would go through all of this?

Enough to kill Abraham and me over it?

"Are you caught up yet?" Peyton snarked.

I jerked my head in her direction, catching the gleam in her eyes. She was enjoying this. The thought sent another shiver down my spine.

"I'm not going to fight you, Peyton."

She crossed her arms over her chest and jutted out one of her slim hips. "Why? Afraid you'll break a nail, princess?"

I fisted my hands and took a deep breath. "I'm not going to fight you because I don't want to hurt you. We can end this without a physical altercation."

"Why don't you just let me shoot her, P?" Paul piped up from next to us.

Peyton whipped her head toward him and snarled, "Go wait in the truck while I finish this."

Paul shrugged and walked off, his gait perfectly normal, like he wasn't walking away from a potential murder scene.

I knew then that my time was limited. Peyton wasn't going to just let this go, and I'd run out of options. I needed to shift and fight her if I had any hope of surviving.

And I *was* going to survive.

Abraham's life as well as the three little lives inside me depended on that fact and I wasn't going to let any of them down.

I released a deep breath and let the magic of my wolf run through my veins. She'd been held prisoner for so long, I was worried she wouldn't respond to my call, but she was right there. As ready as ever to protect what was hers.

My body trembled harder than ever as I held onto the last shred of my humanity.

"Last chance, Peyton. We can settle this without a fight. You can go and we'll leave you alone. You live your life, we'll live ours, and we'll never cross paths again."

Peyton snorted and shook her head. "I'm well past that."

I shrugged and let the magic zip through my veins, shifting my bones and tissue to that of a wolf. Seconds later, I stood on four feet, watching while Peyton's body shifted as well. Hers was a slower transition and I could have taken advantage of that fact, but I was determined to win with my skill alone.

I leapt over her shifting form and onto the gravel at the base of the porch steps where we'd have more room.

When Peyton was done shifting, she turned around and stalked down the stairs. As she approached, I went over every maneuver Bea had ever taught me. Every move, every technique, every piece of advice. I knew I was ready for this battle. I just hoped I put her down before she hurt my babies.

Do not show weakness.

The voice was back in my head, and like always, I listened and obeyed.

Without warning, Peyton leapt toward me, and I easily sidestepped her advance. She went sailing past me, but not before I raked my claws down the side of her body. She howled in pain and landed in a graceless lump before springing to her feet again.

"You're gonna regret that, bitch."

I sighed. Always with the bitch comments. You'd have thought someone would have some originality.

524

She charged me again, and I moved out of the way at the last second but countered with my own attack as well. When she was close enough, I barreled into her side, knocking the wind out of her and throwing her to the ground.

She crawled to her feet and shook her head. Not bothering with anymore pleasantries, she lunged toward me again. This time, she feinted one way and then struck the other, but I'd been trained in this as well. I anticipated her move and one of my paws struck her as she flew past me, my claws scratching down her face.

The gouges were over one of her eyes and she was bleeding pretty profusely, so I had to assume she wasn't seeing well from that eye anymore which gave me even more of an advantage.

She was injured. She was clearly not as good of a fighter as me, and I wanted this over with. I needed to take Peyton out and then somehow incapacitate Paul before I could locate Wyatt and figure out if he was okay.

Werewolves were sturdy creatures, but a bullet was a bullet.

As Peyton pawed at her face, I took that opportunity to advance on her. I ran toward her at top speed, taking advantage of the fact that she couldn't see me well. Leaping, I landed on top of her, my teeth sinking into her back leg.

She yelped, and I dug my teeth in further until the bone snapped in my mouth. She shook me off then and I danced backward out of range of her claws.

"Peyton, give this up. I don't want to kill you."

She crawled to her three good feet and shook her big head. *"The only way this is ending is with one of us dead."*

She limped toward me as fast as she could but still not very quickly at all. It was nothing to dodge her attack and let her pass right by me with another set of my claw marks in her hide. She howled in pain again and turned to face me, murder in her dark eyes.

I knew I needed to end this. I needed to get out of this situation before something happened to me.

Not waiting for another one of her attacks, I feinted one way, and then the other, before striking on the first side. My teeth dug into the back

525

of her neck and I whipped my head side to side as she dangled from my jaw. Finally, I heard something snap before I jerked her one way and then tossed her the other, making sure her body slammed into the thick trunk of a pine tree.

She slid to the base, her body nothing more than a lump of fur. I could tell she was still breathing, though, so I knew I hadn't killed her, which had been my intention.

I stood there, barely out of breath as I watched her still form for any sign of movement. When it seemed she was down for good, I turned my back on her. I needed to find Paul and then Wyatt and finish this before I went looking for my husband.

Chapter 60

The driveway was on the side of the house and we were in front of it, so I figured I had a couple minutes before Paul came looking for his sister. In that time, I needed to find Wyatt and make sure he was okay.

I lifted my nose in the air, hoping I could smell him, but couldn't pick up any scents besides Peyton's and the forest. With one last look at her still form, I darted into the woods, hoping they'd provide enough cover for me to see what was going on with Paul and, hopefully, find Wyatt.

I crept though the foliage, careful to make as little noise as possible. Finally, a dark green Jeep came into view that I had to assume belonged to Paul. I held perfectly still while I watched, but there was no movement in the Jeep.

Finally, a low moan cut through the silence and I froze in place. If it was Paul, that meant something happened to him. If it was Wyatt, that meant I needed to get to him because he was hurt but still alive.

Did I take the risk and expose myself in the hopes it was Wyatt and not Paul?

What if Paul still had his gun? Werewolves were tough and could bounce back from most injuries, but I couldn't afford to be shot. If the bullet hit my stomach, it could reach the babies, and that wasn't a risk I was willing to take.

There was another moan, this one louder, and I made up my mind. I'd be careful, but I needed to figure out who that was and what I was up against.

Moving as quietly as possible, I inched out from between the trees and scanned the clearing. Seeing nothing, I walked around the other side of the Jeep and came across two bodies. One was deathly still, and the other was barely moving.

Taking my time, I inched closer until I could identify who was who.

Paul lay in a puddle of blood, his throat ripped out and his gun lying useless next to his still body.

And next to him was my guard.

Wyatt was sweating and moaning, his face deathly pale and his hands clutching his stomach. I hurried over and nudged him with my nose, and his brown eyes opened. It took him a moment, but he finally focused on me.

"Ellie?"

I nodded and the corners of his lips tipped into a grin. "You made it."

I nudged him again and quickly scanned him for injuries. He looked mostly unhurt, but his hands were covering a portion of his stomach and I was almost too afraid to see what was underneath. Knowing I needed to get the full picture, I gently bumped the tip of my nose against his hands, and with a hiss, he slowly removed one of them to reveal a small, bloody hole in his abdomen.

I reared back and looked up at his face, but his eyes were closed again.

"Don't worry, Ellie. It's not as bad as it looks."

I highly doubted that.

He'd been shot in the stomach. There was no telling what the bullet could have hit or where it ended up. There were numerous important organs all floating around in that general region and any one of them could have been ruptured. We needed to get him to Doc Monroe as soon as possible.

But with no way of knowing what was happening back on pack lands, I didn't know if that was possible. I also didn't think it was a good idea for me to shift back until I knew we were safe. I could only protect us in wolf form.

Thundering footsteps sounded behind me and I turned to see who it was when someone shouted in my head.

"Ellie!"

I whipped around just in time to find a small gray wolf leaping from between the trees to attack another wolf that had crept up on me.

My heart sank as I tried to think, but my brain was frozen. All I could do was watch the two wolves grapple, but that didn't last long.

Both of the wolves were similar in size, but one clearly had an advantage over the other. That one pinned down the other and dug their sharp teeth into the other one's neck. With a gurgling sound I'd never forget, the wolf on top jerked their head backward, tearing the throat out of the one underneath.

The bottom wolf twitched for a couple seconds before they became perfectly still. Slowly, their limbs shifted and grew as they turned back into a human. Soon, the lifeless body of Peyton was lying where the dead wolf had been.

I looked up at the other wolf and finally recognized them.

"Bea?"

She turned to me, her muzzle bloody and her eyes wary. *"She was going to kill you."*

My heart stuttered in my chest as I stumbled toward my sister-in-law. The ramifications of what she'd just done slowly sank into my brain as I moved closer to her.

Bea looked back down at her dead friend before she tilted her head back and let loose a long, mournful howl. It seemed to go on and on. I felt her pain as acutely as if it was my own.

When I reached Bea, I let the magic recede from my body until I was a human again on my hands and knees. I inched closer until I could touch her, and as soon as I did, she collapsed in my arms. Her body trembled slightly as I soothed a hand down her back.

"Thank you, Bea. Thank you so much," I murmured against her fur.

I couldn't imagine what it must have taken for her to do what she just did. She and Peyton had been friends for years, and although that friendship had ended, no one expected this outcome. I was still trying to wrap my head around it all when Bea shifted in my arms.

When she was a human again, she looked up at me, tears streaming from her icy blue eyes.

"I couldn't let her hurt you, Ellie. I couldn't let her hurt the babies," she whimpered.

I wrapped my arms around her shoulders and pulled her closer, my hand smoothing the hair away from her face.

"I know, Bea. I know you did what you had to. Thank you so much," I whispered in her ear.

She continued to sob into my shoulder as her best friend's body turned cold.

I'd never seen Beatrice like that before and I assumed most never had. She was one of the strongest women I'd ever known, but in that moment, she was broken. She'd done what she thought was necessary, but that wasn't going to make it any easier for her. I knew nothing but time would ease the pain she felt.

My own heart ached knowing she only felt that way because of me. If I'd been strong enough to kill Peyton on my own, Bea never would have had to. If I'd just ended it when I'd had the chance, we could have avoided this.

My heart broke along with Bea's as I rocked her back and forth, her cries lessening and finally subsiding all together. Even then, she held me as tightly as I held her.

Finally, another set of pounding footsteps reached us, and we pulled far enough apart that we could see each other's faces.

"Friend or foe?" I whispered.

She shook her head, her eyes wary. Finally, she pulled away completely and whispered, "I'm going to shift back just in case." She wiped the back of her hand against her face before steeling her features and shifting into a wolf.

I sat there, completely naked and exposed as Bea took up position in front of me. Soon, though, her posture changed, and she trotted toward the sound of the footsteps.

A large wolf came barreling into the clearing that I immediately recognized as Abraham. I might not have been able to tell most of the wolves apart, but I'd have known him anywhere, in any form. I climbed to my feet, doing my best to cover as much of me as possible.

"I'm fine," I told him, knowing that would be his first question. "But Wyatt was shot, and we need to get him to Doc Monroe as soon as possible."

Abraham swung his head toward his sister, and I had to imagine they were communicating. Thankfully, they must have realized it was rude to talk to each other while I couldn't hear them, because in the next instant, there were a series of loud snaps and they both rose to two feet.

Abraham wasted no time crossing the distance between us and pulling me into his arms. He held me close, his head dipping to the crook of my neck where he inhaled deeply.

"I never should have left you," he whispered against my skin.

I shook my head and pulled back far enough to look in his remorseful eyes. "You did what you had to. Your pack needed you."

He shook his head, but instead of arguing, he pulled me back into his arms. I went willingly, basking in the knowledge that he was okay, and I was okay, and so were our babies. But that wasn't the end of my list of worries. Not by a long shot.

I pulled back again. "Conrad?"

Abraham's jaw tensed before he spat one word. "Dead."

I released a deep breath, relaxing muscles I hadn't realized I'd been tensing. "And the rest of the pack? Are they still fighting the Charlotte wolves?"

Abraham shook his head. "Just like I thought, as soon as Conrad was dead, that ended the conflict. None of them wanted to fight us. They were all under Conrad's orders."

I nodded slowly, millions of other questions swirling in my head. Abraham must have realized I had a slew of concerns because he leaned forward and kissed my head.

"We can talk more later. Go inside and get dressed. Grab something for me and Wyatt and meet us back out here. We need to get him into my truck and back to pack lands now."

I nodded once and spun around to do as he asked. I ran past Peyton, not giving her body a second glance.

As far as I was concerned, she got what she deserved. She was a nasty, vindictive person who would have stopped at nothing to tear me from Abraham. When she realized she couldn't do that, she settled for trying to kill me instead.

I just wished Beatrice hadn't had to be the one to pull the metaphorical trigger. My sister-in-law's pain still pulsed through my system, but I shoved it down. There would be time for mourning and healing later. First, I had to make sure my friend got the help he needed.

I raced up the stairs to the loft and threw on the first set of clothes I found. Next, I grabbed a couple pairs of shorts and sprinted back downstairs. As I was running through the living room, an ear-piercing screech shocked me to my core.

"Wyatt!"

The scream stopped me in my tracks for a moment, but I shook myself and darted out of the cottage. When I got back to the driveway, I found Callie, naked and crouching on the ground beside Wyatt. Her hands shook as they fluttered above his pale body.

I'd never seen her so distraught before and it tugged at my already bruised heart.

"Callie?" I called as I walked up to the gathering of people surrounding Wyatt.

She looked up at me, tears streaking down her pretty face, her pale blue eyes bloodshot. "What happened, Ellie?"

I kneeled down and placed a hand on her shoulder. "Paul shot him when he tried to defend me. We need to get him back to pack lands so Kyle can take a look at him."

Her shoulders were quaking with her sobs. She leaned down close to Wyatt's ear, and I did my best to give her some privacy. When she lifted her head again, she cupped his face and placed a gentle kiss on his lips.

After the day I'd had, you'd have thought there wouldn't be anything that could have shocked me, but Callie kissing Wyatt did the job.

She turned to me, not an ounce of shame on her face. "Can you find me a shirt or something? I'm coming with you guys."

I shook myself out of my stupor and nodded. "Um. Sure. Yeah. Here," I said, handing a pair of shorts to her for Wyatt. "See if you can get these on him." I turned to find Abraham not far away, a look of confusion on his face, too. I handed him the other pair of shorts before darting inside to find something for Callie to wear.

When I came back outside with an oversized shirt for Callie, Wyatt had already been loaded into the back of Abraham's pickup. Bea was back in her wolf form and Abraham was behind the wheel waiting for all of us. I handed Callie the shirt, and she shrugged it on before climbing into the back of the truck with Wyatt.

As soon as I was in the passenger seat, Abraham gunned the engine, racing down the gravel road and back toward pack lands. It was a quiet trip that only took about ten minutes, but felt at least five times longer. When we made it up the steep gravel drive, Abraham passed the lodge and drove straight to the first pack house.

Kyle and Doreen must have heard the roaring of Abraham's engine because they ran out of their house, twin looks of confusion on their faces.

Abraham hopped out and called over his shoulder, "Wyatt's been shot in the stomach. We need help now."

Doreen ran back inside while Kyle hustled over to help Abraham get him out of the truck. Callie was hot on their heels as we all raced inside the pack doctor's house. Kyle took Wyatt into the back and, although they tried, there was no keeping Callie out of that room.

Abraham walked back out a few minutes later, his face weary and his shoulders slumped. He took a seat next to me and picked up my hand to hold between both of his. We sat there quietly for a long time, the only sound the ticking of a wall clock in their living room.

There were a million things we needed to say to each other, and yet, we both held our tongues. It was enough to know that he was alive and by my side. It was enough to know that my family had made it through this.

There were a hundred other questions, but they could all wait. My friend's life hung in the balance and nothing else was more important than that.

So, we sat and waited to hear if we'd be helping our friend limp out of here or planning his funeral.

Chapter 61

"Their wisteria is a menace! You have to do something about it before my poor bleeding-heart plants are overrun!"

I stifled a sigh and jotted down a couple notes. "And which house are you in again, Nicole?"

She sat up straighter. "I'm in nine and those damn plants are coming from seven."

This time I had to stifle a roll of my eyes as I wrote down the house numbers and clicked my pen closed. "Okay. I'll reach out to them as soon as possible."

She looked suspicious but nodded slowly. "And what if they refuse to do something about it?"

I stretched out in my chair, my lower back aching from sitting still for so long. This was the sixth appointment I'd had to sit through today, and thankfully, my last. I'd had enough of hearing about creeping vines and who borrowed what and didn't return it.

Although, I shouldn't have complained. In a way, it was nice hearing about mundane problems when we'd had such big ones to deal with lately.

It had been about two weeks since the conflict with the Charlotte pack and things had finally returned to mostly normal. The lodge had emptied of the borrowed enforcers and the injured Charlotte wolves had all recovered and gone back home.

Unfortunately, our side hadn't been as lucky.

Nicole continued to drone on about her plants while my stomach clenched uncomfortably like it always did when I thought about what we lost that day.

Although our men had been instructed to hurt and not kill, the Charlotte pack had been given no such order. We'd lost two men that day and their deaths weighed heavily on everyone, most of all me and Abraham.

One of the enforcers had been ours, a man named Jonah. I hadn't known him well, but saw him at most meals and every pack barbecue. His presence and loud laugh were missed every day in the lodge. His funeral service had been held shortly after the battle with Charlotte and I knew the feeling of his loss would continue to ripple through the community for a long time.

The other enforcer had been on loan from the Greensboro pack. I only met him once, but his sacrifice didn't go unnoticed or unappreciated. I was with Abraham when he'd had to make the call to that alpha, Adam, and I hoped to never see that look on my husband's face again.

Despite the losses we'd suffered, we'd pulled together and pushed through our grief. We celebrated the fallen and remembered them often. Their sacrifices were heavy on our hearts, but we got up each new day and did our best to keep living our lives as a testament to theirs.

"So, what if they won't tame their vines? What happens then?" Nicole asked, breaking me out of my thoughts.

I shook my head and set down my pen. "If they won't comply, I'll send our gardeners to do it for them. I promise, one way or another, those vines won't be a problem for you for much longer, okay?"

Nicole's lips twitched with a smile and she nodded. "Okay, Ellie. Thanks."

I rose to my feet, hoping she'd follow my lead. A headache was brewing behind my eyes and I needed to hunt down some Tylenol before it worsened.

"It's no problem, Nicole. Please, don't hesitate to come to me with any other problems you have."

The dark-haired woman reached out a hand that I gratefully shook. I led her to the door of the conference room and watched as she made her way through the lodge.

Releasing a deep breath, I gathered my notes from that afternoon and turned off the lights. I was done with appointments until next week and so thankful for that. I loved being an alpha alongside Abraham, but there was only so much whining I could handle in a day before I was over it. And I'd just reached my limit.

I walked into the kitchen, hoping to grab some pain pills and a snack. I'd been bringing Charlie downstairs a lot more often lately, and usually, when I entered the kitchen, he'd come running toward me, but not that day. I looked around but didn't see anything or anyone except a small group of enforcers playing cards at one of the tables.

I found the pills and washed them down with some water before I went searching for my cat. So far, his transition into life in the pack house had been pretty seamless, but it was still early. Maybe something happened to him, or maybe someone accidentally let him outside.

Remembering that sometimes my nose was stronger than my eyes, I lifted it in the air and gave a sniff. I could smell him, so I followed his scent over to the group of enforcers. It took me a minute, but I finally located him. Square on the lap of the person I least expected.

I waltzed over with a raised brow until I was standing beside Huxley's chair.

"What's going on here?"

Huxley jumped slightly in his seat and turned wide eyes toward me. When he noticed I was looking at the lump of fur in his lap, he glanced at it quickly before throwing up both hands.

"Hey, *he* jumped on *my* lap."

Mathias snorted from across the table. "Don't lie. You picked him up and put him there."

There was a loud thud under the table and Mathias jumped before shooting a glare at Huxley.

I pursed my lips and leaned a hip against an empty chair.

"Is this coming from the man who insinuated my cat would get eaten by one of the werewolves in this house?" I asked.

Huxley shrugged. "It's still a possibility."

I shook my head and pressed my lips together to smother my smile. "Admit it, Huxley. You're a big fat softie for that little kitty."

The big man snorted so loudly I was worried for his sinuses. "Not even a little bit."

"You've been snuggling that cat for the past half hour, man," Mathias spoke up again, scooting his chair away from the table so he wouldn't get kicked again.

Huxley glared at his fellow enforcer and shrugged. "Whatever. The cat wanted to sit on my lap. Who wouldn't, honestly?"

I rolled my eyes so hard a sharp pain shot through my head. "You keep believing that, Hux." I turned to leave before calling over my shoulder, "Just don't eat my cat."

"I'm not making any promises!" he yelled back.

I shot him the middle finger over my shoulder but ignored him. His secret was out. Underneath that bravado and macho behavior was a big, fluffy, teddy bear, and I wasn't going to forget that anytime soon.

I made my way to the other end of the kitchen, hoping to scrounge up a snack. Aubrey was there doing dishes as usual, but also like usual, I ignored her. Her attitude had continued to be frosty toward me, but I'd trained myself to stop caring. There was only so much you could do to change someone's opinion. If they weren't willing to give you another chance, there wasn't much you could do.

"Hey, Ellie?"

I froze in place at the sound of her voice. Slowly, so as not to spook her, I turned around to find Aubrey drying her hands on a dish towel.

"Are you talking to me?" I asked stupidly.

She nodded. "Do you have a minute?"

I could feel how wide my eyes were in my head and I worked to make them look a little more normal. I cleared my throat and nodded. "Sure. Do we need privacy?"

She shrugged. "I can say what I need to right here." She looked down at the floor for a moment before taking a deep breath and meeting my eyes. "I want to apologize to you."

My eyes were doing that creepy wide thing again, and I struggled to control my reaction. "Apologize?" I squeaked.

She nodded. "I wasn't fair to you. I'd listened to Peyton and let her color my view before I even really knew you." She took another deep breath before speaking again. "I heard what happened the day we were attacked, and it made me realize she'd always had her own agenda. She wasn't a good person and I never should have believed her. If you can, I'd like you to give me another chance. We see each other so often and it doesn't make sense for us to not be friendly." She paused before adding, "If that's what you want…"

It took me a moment to process everything she'd said before I could respond. I'd never expected this from Aubrey, and I was stunned silent for a prolonged moment. Unfortunately, it seemed like I took too long because the housekeeper's shoulders hunched, and the corners of her mouth curled into a frown.

"I guess it's too late, huh? The damage is already done."

I took a step forward, shaking my head. "No, no. Not at all, Aubrey. Thank you so much for this. It's not too late, and I'd really like the chance to start over with you, too."

Her smile was wide as she nodded. "That would be great! Thanks, Ellie."

I didn't know if it was the pregnancy hormones or what, but this little scene was making me more emotional than it should have. Not wanting to respond for fear I'd cry instead, I closed the distance between us and pulled her into my arms. She froze for the smallest fraction of a second before returning my embrace.

When we pulled apart, we both had smiles on our faces.

"I need to get back to work, but thanks for hearing me out. I'll see you around," she said.

I swallowed the tears I could feel swimming to the surface and nodded. "Okay, yeah. I'll see you around. Thanks, Aubrey."

She smiled again and turned back toward the sink to finish what she'd been working on. It took me a little longer to recover from that conversation, but I finally spun around, grabbed a granola bar from the pantry and left the kitchen.

My mind was still spinning so I didn't see the original werewolf until I almost ran head first into him. He stopped me with two gentle hands on my shoulders and a smile on his face.

"Granddaughter. How are you?"

I smiled up at him and shrugged. "Doing pretty good, actually."

He nodded at my ever-growing belly. "And my grandchildren? How are they?"

My heart swelled in my chest at his question. I never imagined I'd be able to provide my children with loving grandparents until Will stepped up to the plate. He'd been more present than usual and closely following my pregnancy's progress. He was the family I'd always wished for and now was so lucky to have.

I cupped my belly as my smile grew. "They're doing great. We get to find out what we're having in a few weeks."

His eyes lit up. "That's great news! May I accompany you to that appointment?"

My eyes did that weird widening thing as the shocks just kept hitting my system. "S-sure, Will. That would be great!"

He nodded, his smile bright, but for the first time, I saw the dark bags under his eyes and noticed how much paler he seemed to be. I reached out and grasped his arm.

"Are you doing okay, Will? You don't look so great."

His smile turned forced as he shrugged. "Fine, Granddaughter. Don't worry about me. Just keep those babies healthy."

I nodded and let it drop, but I wouldn't forget it. There was something going on with Will and I wanted to know what.

Now that I thought about it, he'd been acting strange since the conflict with the Charlotte pack. Was it the fact that he'd had to witness the fight between wolves he considered his children? Was it the losses we'd suffered that were bothering him so much? Or was it something else?

Initially, Will had declined to fight alongside our enforcers. He'd claimed it would be too hard for him to choose a side when we were all his children. However, I'd learned later on that once everyone had been

540

evacuated to the lodge, he'd volunteered to stand watch with the other enforcers stationed on pack lands. I didn't know what changed his mind, but I was grateful he was there to help us after all. I was even more grateful that, in the end, there hadn't been a need for him to fight.

I continued through the lodge, my mind drifting toward Beatrice like it often did since that day.

Something changed in her the day of the conflict and she hadn't been the same since. She put on a brave face and did her best to pretend, but all of us closest to her could see a difference. There was a tightness around her eyes that she never used to have. A slump to her shoulders that didn't used to be there. Having to kill her best friend was weighing on my sister-in-law and it was eating me up inside.

Unfortunately, there wasn't much I could do about it from here. Shortly after the battle, Abraham had dispatched Bea to Charlotte to take over that pack until a new alpha could be assigned. Technically, since Abraham killed the last leader of the Charlotte pack, he was their new alpha, but he didn't want the position. Unlike Conrad, my husband had no desire for the power that came with running two packs.

It had been hard to adjust to life in the lodge without Bea, but hopefully Abraham would figure out a permanent solution for the Charlotte pack and she could come back home. What condition she'd be in, I wasn't sure, but I couldn't help her if we weren't even in the same city.

I reached the stairs and began climbing them to the third floor. Abraham wanted me to check in after my last appointment and he was in his office as usual. I figured *check in* really meant *lunch date* which actually meant *sex*, but I wasn't going to complain. Again, I didn't know if it was the pregnancy hormones or what, but I couldn't get enough of him. Thankfully, the feeling was mutual.

"Callista, I can walk."

"Barely."

There was a deep masculine sigh before I heard a hiss and a low curse.

"See? Just stop being a pain in my butt and let me help you."

I turned the corner and Wyatt and Callie came into view. It had been a couple weeks already, but my heart still filled every time I saw Wyatt up and walking around.

It had been touch and go for a little while. The bullet Paul had fired at Wyatt struck his spleen and ruptured it. He'd been bleeding internally when we got him to Doc Monroe, and according to him, we'd almost been too late.

Kyle was forced to operate on Wyatt immediately to remove his spleen and patch up everywhere else the bullet had struck. We were all lucky he'd made it out of that alive.

I'd learned later on that, despite the fact he'd been shot, as soon as he could, Wyatt had attacked Paul, killing him and eliminating the threat against me. That had used up the last of his energy and that was why I'd found him on the ground so close to Paul's body. I tried not to think about it too often, but if Wyatt hadn't taken Paul down, I might not be here today.

I'd always be grateful to my protector, but he would barely listen to my thanks. He insisted he was just doing his job, and if he'd done it better, he wouldn't have gotten shot. The fact that he could still be that exasperating even after recovering from major surgery assured me he'd be just fine.

"Hey, Callie. Hey, Wyatt. How are you feeling?"

The former shot me a smile and the latter only grimaced. "Fine, Ellie. Don't worry about me."

I shook my head. "Not gonna happen, pal."

He rolled his brown eyes as he struggled down the stairs. Whether he liked it or not, Callie had been practically glued to his side since he'd gotten injured. Even though he complained, I had a hunch he liked it. A lot.

"Where are you two heading?" I asked.

Wyatt was grumbling in pain, so Callie answered for him. "He has a check-up with Doc Monroe. We're heading there now."

I frowned. "Everything's okay, right?"

Callie opened her mouth to answer, but Wyatt beat her to it. "I'm perfectly fine. I just want everyone to quit fussing over me."

I walked past and patted him on the shoulder. "Again, not gonna happen, pal."

Callie laughed while Wyatt continued to grumble all the way down the stairs.

I made it to our floor and hurried to Abraham's office. When I knocked, he called for me to come in. Without needing to communicate, he pushed his chair back as I rounded his desk and took a seat on his lap. He pulled me close and kissed the top of my head.

"How were your meetings, baby?"

I sighed and snuggled into his big chest. "Long. Nothing I can't handle, though."

He kissed me again. "I'm well aware. You've done nothing but handle every change in your life with grace and I knew this would be no different. You've become an amazing alpha and I'm proud to have you by my side."

I pulled away so I could look in his eyes, mine filling with tears. "You always have so much confidence in me, even when I didn't deserve it."

He shook his head, his expression serious. "I've always seen how amazing you are, El. I was just waiting for you to catch up."

A tear escaped one of my eyes before I buried my head in his chest and breathed in his familiar scent.

The past few months had been a rollercoaster for me, but I wouldn't have changed one second of what we'd been through. It took being bitten and turned into a werewolf to find my spot in the world, and I wouldn't have given it up for anything. Sitting there in my husband's arms, I knew we'd face whatever came at us next together and get through it just like we always had. I had him, I had my family, I had my pack, and that was all I needed.

Epilogue

Abraham

The room was quiet for the first time in a long time.

Too long.

My poor mate had struggled through sixteen hours of hard labor before we'd been gifted our first child. A boy.

My son.

After that, the other two made their grand entrances quickly and my family had been complete. Of course, that didn't slow down the pace of the frantic energy in the room.

The babies needed to be evaluated, El needed to be checked out, and everyone needed to be monitored for a while before both Kyle and Doreen were satisfied. I was thankful for their dedication to my family's well-being, but I was also glad to have them gone.

Now, in the dim, quiet room, I held my daughters while El nursed our son.

I looked down at their perfect faces, still a little pink, but so perfect my heart ached in my chest. When I could finally tear my eyes from them, they sought El. My mate. The mother of my children and the most amazing woman I'd ever known.

As if she could feel my gaze, she turned to me, her beautiful brown eyes filled with tears.

"I'm so happy," she whispered.

A single tear streaked down her face and I itched to catch it, but nothing could make me move from my spot. I'd been snuggling with my girls for the past half hour and I couldn't ever remember being so happy.

Except, of course, when El agreed to marry me.

Or the day she told me she was pregnant with these little miracles.

Or even the day we'd finally had our ceremony.

Okay, so I was a pretty happy guy. It seemed like every day I had a new reason to count my blessings and it all started with the woman lying on our bed, nursing our son.

He'd been the first to come out and the last to drift off to sleep, but I could tell he was almost there. He'd been nursing for the past few minutes and his little body had finally had enough. It was tough work being born, and he'd done all he needed to do today.

I looked back at my mate and smiled. "I am too, baby. I'm so proud of you."

Another tear traced down her face and my heart twisted in my chest. I yearned to hold her, to make sure no other tears escaped her eyes, but I knew they weren't out of sadness. I knew she was just as blissfully happy as I was.

I could feel it.

Just like I'd felt every ounce of labor pain she'd endured. Although the pain wasn't as intense for me, I'd felt each contraction twist my gut, knowing I couldn't help her. That this was something she needed to do herself and I couldn't shield her from it.

She'd handled the drawn-out process with the grace she met every obstacle with. Even red-faced and sweaty from exertion, she'd been the most beautiful woman I'd ever seen.

We stared into each other's eyes for a long time, speaking things that didn't need to be said and basking in the soft glow of our happiness. Today was the beginning of the rest of our lives and I couldn't wait to live it with her.

Footsteps thundered through the sitting room outside our door and I barely suppressed a groan. How they'd managed to wait so long was a mystery, but I knew it was time. Our tiny bubble of peace and solitude was about to be popped in a very real way.

El smiled and shook her head. "What took them so long?"

I shrugged as there was a light knock on the door and it swung open to reveal the most tenacious of my sisters.

"Can we come in now?" Evey whispered.

I nodded, and she spilled into the room, followed by Callie, Bea, Del, Will, Nana, and even Clyde. Our whole family had come to greet the new additions to the McCoy clan, and I felt my heart swell inside my chest.

Half of them crowded around El while the other half circled me. Their eyes filled with tears as they each reached out shaking hands to touch our children. I watched as my family met my babies and knew I'd never felt love like that before.

"What are their names?" Evey asked.

I looked to El, giving her the opportunity to explain. It had been her idea after all.

She gave me a smile and cleared her throat. "Well, I know repeating the first letter is popular with werewolves, but I liked the direction your parents were going in. Since your parents named you all Abraham, Beatrice, Callista, Delilah, and Evelyn, we thought we'd pick up where they left off."

Evey sniffed, and I met her eyes over the rest of our guests. She was remembering our parents as acutely as I was, and we shared in a moment of commiseration for our loss.

That idea had stuck with me through all nine months of El's pregnancy. How I'd wished our parents could have still been around. How happy they would have been to be grandparents. How unfair it was that they were ripped from us so young.

My temper rose as I remembered what Conrad had revealed right before I'd ripped his throat out. He'd admitted to being the one who'd killed our mother, and subsequently, our father.

One of the babies in my arms grunted, and I worked to calm myself back down. Now was not the time to think about such dark things. I needed to remember what I had and not what I'd lost.

I looked up to find El watching me from where she lay. I knew she'd felt what I was feeling, and I worked even harder to calm myself. I shot her a tense grin that she returned before she continued.

"So, anyway, we had names picked out for girls and boys from each letter because we didn't know who'd get here first."

"And?" Del asked as she took a seat at the end of our bed. "Who was it and what're their names? I'm dyin' here."

We both chuckled as El held up our son. "This little guy came rushing out first and his name is Franklin."

There was a round of oohs and ahs as El placed him into my youngest sister's arms. Evey sniffed again and reached out to trace a finger down his cheek.

"Welcome to our family, Franklin," she whispered.

El looked over at me and the rest of the room followed suit. I cleared my throat and nodded to the baby in my right arm.

"Next came Gracelynn." I jerked my chin to the baby on the left. "And then Hadley finally made it out last."

Nana clapped her hands together softly. "Franklin, Gracelynn, and Hadley," she whispered. "They're perfect."

I smiled at my mate again before I focused on my grandmother. "Would you like to hold Gracelynn?"

Nana rushed over to my side and carefully scooped the baby from my arms. I found Will toward the back of the group and nodded at him. "Will, would you like to hold Hadley?"

His eyes widened before he crossed the space and held out his hands. I gently placed my youngest baby in his arms and watched as the original werewolf looked at her with eyes full of wonder. He turned toward El and shook his head.

"I'm very happy everyone is safe and sound, Granddaughter. And I'm glad you've allowed me to be a part of this."

I reached out to grasp Will's shoulder. "You're family, Will. And our family always sticks together."

I felt those words to the depth of my soul and knew they were some of the truest I'd ever spoken.

Our family had been though a lot. Everything from our parents' death, to the betrayal of my cousin Calvin, to the conflict with my uncle Conrad had brought us to this place. I'd like to say that all family deserved an equal part of our lives, but we'd learned the hard way that wasn't true.

However, every person in that room had proven over and over that they were the good kind. The forever kind. They'd been with us through our ups and downs and never strayed far from our sides. That was the kind of family you held onto. That was the kind of family you laid your life down for.

As I watched my relatives pass around my children, I sat down next to my mate and pulled her hand into mine. There was so much love in the room that I felt it in every breath I took.

Our babies had been born into a great family and I'd be sure to teach them how lucky they were. As they grew, they'd learn what it meant to love not only each other, but every extended relative they had. Our children would grow up with the love and attention that had been missing from my poor mate's life. They'd know what it meant to be loved and cherished every day of their lives. I couldn't think of a better way to end one story and begin another.

Dear Reader

Whew! It's been a long journey and for those of you who've been with me from the beginning, I want to thank you from the bottom of my heart. For those of you who are new, I want to thank you for taking a chance on me and my Southern Werewolves. I hope you've all enjoyed Elizabeth and Abraham's story because I loved writing it.

Looking for more from the Southern Werewolves Series? Wondering what was going through Abraham's head when he found out El was pregnant? Sign up for my newsletter by going to my website www.heathermackinnonauthor.wordpress.com and I'll send you a bonus scene from Rise and you'll get all your questions answered!

I'm not done with this world or these characters yet, so keep your eyes peeled for more!

Acknowledgements

No book is a one-man job. Rise was no exception and I have a few people to thank for helping to get me to this point.

First, as always, I need to thank my husband, Ryan. You're my number one supporter and the strongest backbone I could have ever asked for. You're always there to remind me why I love doing this on my darkest days, and to keep me grounded on my best days. You're my best friend and the reason I can do what I do. I love you and I'm thankful for you every day.

Next, I need to thank Brianna, my ride or die beta. You deserve extra thanks this time for taking on extra work for me. When I was feeling a little lost, you stepped up to the plate and filled a role that you didn't have to. Thank you for reading Rise as I wrote it. You helped to shape this story in a way I never would have been able to on my own. It wouldn't be what it is without you and I'll never forget that.

The next person I need to thank is my other beta Jade. As always, your insightful feedback was invaluable. I know your time is coveted and I'm lucky you still carve some out for me. Please, never leave me!

Lastly, I need to thank all my readers who've devoured this series. You've made my dreams come true and given me opportunities I'd only ever dreamed about. I hope I've done this series justice and I hope you stick around for future projects of mine. Thanks for your time, thanks for your dedication, and thanks for loving my werewolves.

What's Next?

If you're already missing the Southern Werewolves, I'm here to help! Even though Abraham and Elizabeth's story has concluded, that still leaves a lot of characters who have stories of their own to tell. If you loved the McCoy sisters, then you'll want to stick around for my next series that features all of them! First up is Callie McCoy and the blurb for her book is below!

Can she deny her destiny and ignore the pull of her soul mate?
Callista McCoy is a strong, well-educated werewolf with no desire for a mate. Sure, she's seen how great love has worked out for her brother, but she's not in any rush. Her work as an environmental scientist and activist is enough to keep her busy and her love life is the least of her worries. But when one of the new wolves in her pack starts to make her feel things she thought she'd successfully suppressed, her only hope is to ignore him. And avoid eye contact at all costs.
Wyatt Carter's only concerns are taking care of his sick mother and proving his worth to his new pack. But the moment he gets a look at his new alpha's sister, all bets are off. There's something irresistible about Callie that draws him in. Something that makes him want to get close to her. So, why is she so determined to push him away? And how hard is he willing to push back?
With the pack expecting an attack any day, will Callie keep pushing Wyatt away, or will she finally give in to what she's fought against for so long?

More from Heather MacKinnon

Southern Werewolves Series
Shift
Howl
Rise

Love in Providence Series
Send Sunshine
Beyond Beautiful (Coming spring 2019)

Standalones
Changed
Trying

About the Author

Heather MacKinnon is a romance author living in North Carolina with her husband and two troublemaking dogs. She grew up on Long Island and spent her young adult years in various states in New England. This led to her subsequent addiction to Dunkin' Donuts lattes and her gratuitous use of the word "wicked". After a lifetime of enjoying other people's words, she decided to write down some of her own. You can get up-to-date information about Heather MacKinnon's books at www.heathermackinnonauthor.wordpress.com.

She loves hearing from her readers! Find her on social media here:

Facebook.com/HeatherMacKinnonAuthor

Twitter.com/HMackAuthor

Instagram.com/HeatherMacKinnonAuthor

25914987R00314

Printed in Great Britain
by Amazon